DEAD NORTH

The Exile Book of Anthology Series, Number Eight
CANADIAN ZOMBIE FICTION

Edited by Silvia Moreno-Garcia

CANADIAN TALES
OF CLIMATE CHANGE

THE EXILE BOOK OF ANTHOLOGY SERIES, NUMBER FOURTEEN

EDITED BY
BRUCE MEYER

The Exile Book of Anthology Series
Number Eleven

The playground of LOST toys

Edited by Colleen Anderson and Ursula Pflug

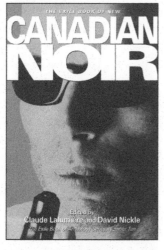

THE EXILE BOOK OF NEW

CANADIAN NOIR

Edited by
Claude Lalumière and David Nickle
The Exile Book of Anthology Series, Number Ten

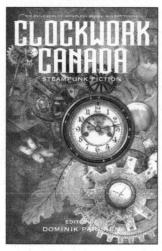

CLOCKWORK CANADA

STEAMPUNK FICTION

THE EXILE BOOK OF ANTHOLOGY SERIES, NUMBER TWELVE

EDITED BY
DOMINIK PARISIEN

THOSE WHO
CANADIAN CREATURE, MYTH, AND MONSTER STORIES
MAKE US

THE EXILE BOOK OF ANTHOLOGY SERIES, NUMBER THIRTEEN

EDITED BY
KELSI MORRIS AND KAITLIN TREMBLAY

FRACTURED

TALES OF THE CANADIAN POST-APOCALYPSE

The Exile Book of Anthology Series
Number Nine

Edited by Silvia Moreno-Garcia

EXILE editions
Fiction, Poetry, Translation, Drama and Nonfiction

Library and Archives Canada Cataloguing in Publication

Fractured : tales of the Canadian post-apocalypse /
edited by Silvia Moreno-Garcia.

(Exile book of anthology series ; number 9)
ISBN 978-1-55096-409-7 (pbk.)--ISBN 978-1-55096-412-7 (pdf).--
ISBN 978-1-55096-410-3 (epub).--ISBN 978-1-55096-411-0 (mobi)

1. End of the world--Fiction. 2. Science fiction, Canadian (English).
3. Short stories, Canadian (English). 4. Canadian fiction (English)--21st century.
I. Moreno-Garcia, Silvia, editor

PS8323.S3F73 2014   C813'.087620806   C2014-902982-9
                                                     C2014-902983-7

THIRD PRINTING (POD to 1,000 copies)
Copyrights to the stories rest with the authors © 2018
Design and Composition by Mishi Uroboros / Cover Photograph by Stokkete
Typeset in Fairfield and Trajan fonts at Moons of Jupiter Studios
Printed and bound in the USA

Published by Exile Editions Limitd ~ www.ExileEditions.com
144483 Southgate Road 14 – GD, Holstein, Ontario, N0G 2A0, Canada

We gratefully acknowledge the Canada Council for the Arts,
the Government of Canada, the Ontario Arts Council,
and the Ontario Media Development Corporation
for their support toward our publishing activities

Canadian sales representation:
The Canadian Manda Group, 664 Annette Street,
Toronto ON M6S 2C8   www.mandagroup.com   416 516 0911

North American and international distribution, and U.S. Sales:
Independent Publishers Group, 814 North Franklin Street,
Chicago IL 60610   www.ipgbook.com   toll free: 1 800 888 4741

For my mother

CONTENTS

INTRODUCTION

One of the more interesting apocalyptic movements I've read about is the one spearheaded by a farmer from upstate New York by the name of William Miller. Not because apocalyptic beliefs are anything new – remember Y2K or the supposed Mayan prophecies? – but because the Millerites seemed to gain so much traction back in 1843. When the apocalypse didn't take place the movement fragmented, an episode that is called the Great Disappointment.

That's what makes me smile. The Great Disappointment, a title that seems to imply a desire for an eschatological outcome. Certainly, something in our hearts makes us covet this dark path, for it reappears in fiction over and over again. Admit it. Didn't the punk fashions of *Mad Max* tickle your fancy? Katniss lives in a post-apocalyptic (and dystopian) society, but in a burst of irony the books and movies have inspired *Hunger Games* tie-in makeup. Much of the enjoyment of a zombie video game is not in the fear of the undead, but our trigger-happy fingers that allow us to blow everyone to pieces. *The Road* isn't exactly my idea of a party and *Oryx and Crake* paints a rather depressing picture, but even when you are dealing with murder, mutants, cannibalism or disease, the post-apocalypse is something we eagerly consume because we like to think about our survival.

By that I don't mean that we are all hoarding cans of food and ammunition in our homes. But we do like to imagine we can survive a great disaster. There is something hopeful about the post-apocalypse precisely because it is *post*.

The post-apocalypse caters to our more selfish fantasies. Wouldn't the world be more fun if we didn't have to go to work tomorrow and became vampire hunters instead? Small matters, like our commute, would dissolve into nothing. This volume explores the Canadian post-apocalypse. What is it we in Canada fear, desire, worry and fantasize about? Ecological disasters, for one. This was a constant issue in the submissions I read and several of the stories I accepted consider the depletion of natural resources and global warming. Another common concern was the maintenance of Canada as a nation-state, a topic that seemed to be rather odd compared to American post-apocalyptic fiction: it doesn't seem such a big issue to our southern neighbours. A number of characters in *Fractured* are marginalized individuals who did not fit comfortably in the pre-apocalypse. Because of this, even though it is the end of Canada as they know it... they feel fine.

Canada is touted as a polite, even dull, nation. But *Fractured* is not about our good manners. It is about the cracks and the fragments of a shattered future, and what rises from the rubble. In these tales the Canadian post-apocalypse is frightening, exciting; sometimes it's even beautiful.

Silvia Moreno-Garcia
April 2014

NO MAN IS A PROMONTORY

H.N. Janzen

Kelowna has changed in the last five years. Back then, this was City Park. When Pennyweight and I snuck in under the protective shroud of darkness this morning, though, the dead trees and bare earth made it hard to think of this place as anything other than what it is now – a graveyard. Heaps of brown earth hastily scraped over the bodies of the fallen fill the void where the grass used to be, and charred bits of bone and teeth litter what used to be a kid's water park before it was repurposed for disposing of those killed by the fallout. Apart from Pennyweight, I haven't seen a kid in years. The bio-weapons killed almost all the plants above water, and some people will eat anything. Not Pennyweight and I. We're the last people in this city, and we have food for two.

There's a promontory on the beach, a little rock toe stretched cautiously into the lake. On top of it is a raft made of barrels that some keen individual roped together in an attempt to cross the lake after the bridge went out. Beneath the rusty barrels, huddled together for warmth, Pennyweight and I are scoping the lake. Pennyweight is wearing a man's medium corduroy suit jacket, the closest we could find to camouflage for a 12-year-old. He looks like a bundle of sticks in fancy dress. I'm wearing my old army uniform; with my gaunt frame and my face paint made from water milfoil, I look like a photograph in *National Geographic,* something with a title like *Woman Soldier at the End of Days.* Sometimes it amuses me that we're both Indian, but different kinds, with Pennyweight coming from across the lake and my mother having come here from across the ocean.

Despite our clothes, the seeping moisture always finds its way in, and what heat it can't take, the cold rocks leach away. The frigid air deadens my sense of smell, but I know that when we are warm in our beds tonight, the scents trapped in our clothes of plant rot and the last glacial run-off before winter will make the room smell like a camping trip. As it stands, all I can smell is Pennyweight's salty breath.

It wasn't always like this. I used to be in the Canadian Armed Forces infantry. I got back from my first tour overseas right before all this began. When I was selected for advanced training, my mother insisted that I come back to Kelowna so that she could throw a party for me. No matter how old I got, I was still a little girl in her eyes. Sometimes, when I have a hard time falling asleep, I wonder if, as I cradled her in my arms that last time, she had finally gazed up at me and seen a woman instead. I doubt it. Even as I stared down at the weak, ephemeral husk she had been at the end, I still felt as though I were looking up at her.

Across the lake is a dilapidated building on the hill, along with a gigantic wooden "L." I think it used to be part of a series of signs that said THE BLUFF, but I never really paid attention to it when I had the chance to. I linger on the "L," combing over the flecks of white paint. Pennyweight is trying hard not to shiver against my arm, but I can feel his shoulder jiggling against my ribs. Rather than pushing him away, my hands clench, steadying the scope.

I wouldn't describe myself as a soft-hearted person – I've stolen food from a woman giving birth – but Pennyweight had managed to find his way in anyway. Three years ago, I was passing by the Starbucks on the edge of Glenmore, trying to ignore the sweat dripping down the middle of my ribcage, when I came across a scene I'd seen many times before. Two winters had passed since the mass deaths and, by that summer, children had become desirable because they couldn't fight back. I watched from behind a house with melted siding as a man in his thirties slammed a bat with nails in it into a spindly goblin with skin too small for his bones. The child was beyond wailing tears, but every time the bat came down he made a sharp sigh like air being pumped through bellows. Seeing that the man was occupied, I bent down and picked up a rock, took aim at the man with my gun, then threw the rock at an overturned plastic tub on his other side. The man's head whipped toward the noise, and my finger twitched. He was dead before he hit the ground.

I was totally indifferent to the child. All I cared about was reducing my competition for the remaining food, and I'd seen wild children before. They had judged that it was better to starve than to be raped, eaten, or forced to crawl into collapsed buildings in search of food, which, more often than not, seemed to result in a stuck child starving to death. I couldn't say that I blamed them. As I approached, he folded into himself like a paper airplane but I went to the dead man instead, stripping him of his clothes and belongings. He had brought a snack, a little box of Sun-Maid raisins, which I opened and dumped in my mouth.

There are always two or three that stick to the bottom, so I lowered the box to scrape them out. Before I had even gotten the box to digging level, the child had sprung up and snatched it from my hands. I went for my gun, then thought better of wasting ammo, and by the time I had taken 10 steps in his direction, he had disappeared. Was it worth following him into his territory and risking injury over two raisins he had probably already eaten? I tied the dead man's possessions in his jacket, made a bindle with his bat, and started back to the tree house I was living in at the time.

None of my traps went off that night, or the next. It was on the third day that I heard a squeal. The boy was standing as still as possible, one of his feet stuck through rotted plywood, the other on the dirt. If he tried to pull his foot free, then there was a very good chance that he would lose his balance and fall forward. There was nothing he could do but watch as I approached, gun at the ready.

"You're lucky that you're so light," I said. "Otherwise, you would have fallen into a pit full of nails and broken glass."

He stared at me, taking in the massive knot of scar tissue that I called my left cheek, and my broken nose. I returned his gaze. He seemed to have cleaned up somehow, and whatever swelling his face might have suffered, it had gone down enough for me to tell that he would once have been considered an indigenous person. As I paused to assess him, his cracked lips broke into a tenuous smile, and he pulled something out of the garbage bag he was wearing, then held it out to me. It was a bullet from my gun. He held his other hand out as well, palm outstretched and empty, and after a moment I took the bullet from his hand. His smile widened.

"I'll let you out, but don't come around here again," I told him, and once I freed him, he ran off.

As I covered the hole in the board with Gyprock, I considered what had happened. Perhaps he had felt that he had to pay me back. I doubted that he had felt any qualms about retrieving my bullet after what the body it was buried in had done to him. Well, hopefully, he would have enough sense not to test my traps again.

A week passed, and I forgot about the child. During the second week, though, I came across a cache of ammo and food stowed away in the Rutland Salvation Army, and waited in sight of the entrance for its owner to return. I was there for almost a full day before I heard shrieking not far off. Stalking quietly but slowly, I located the source of the noise one street over. The child was standing beside the body of a woman with a broken, rusty knife stuck in her skull. She had managed to graze his ribs with a bullet before he had finished her off, and she had tiny, bloody handprints on her corpse where he had touched her in order to remove her clothes. Now, his slight, elfin frame was dressed in cargo shorts, and he was struggling with her leather jacket. When he saw me he paused, and then, setting the jacket down, he gathered everything else she had on her.

"For you," he said.

I am snapped out of my reminiscence when I feel a tap from Pennyweight on my forearm, followed by two lines down and one to the left – his left. As I swing my scope down, I feel him tap me three more times, and a glandload of adrenaline trills through my veins. He saw someone.

Sure enough, as I focus on the old docks near the remains of the bridge, two people are emerging from the shack, both male and in hunting garb. Apart from their years, they look identical. The older one has grey hair streaked brown and a braided beard, while the younger one, around my age, only has a goatee and keeps his hair under a black toque. The young one aims a shotgun at the scenery while his elder approaches the houseboat attached to the dock. Stroking his beard as he goes, he walks up and down the mildew-slicked boards, and when he sees that the boat has no leaks, his coarse face splits into a grin. Tonight, I am sure he is thinking, they will cross the lake. Tonight, they will eat again.

He turns around to give the younger man the news. When he does, I can see the M21 on his back. Though their clothes are filthy, their guns are clean. I wonder if the older man taught the younger one how to clean a gun. I feel Pennyweight quivering beside me, and then I wonder if the older man ever brought the younger one to the beach. As the older man brings up his rifle to scope out my side of Lake Okanagan, I wonder if, five years ago, they might not have been here before. Maybe they took pictures in front of the sails and got goat cheese scones at the Bean Scene before the younger one went off to play volleyball and the older one read Dean Koontz on a towel with nothing on but shorts and a driftwood necklace. Maybe they dangled their feet in the lake and fed the ducks and maybe, just maybe, the younger one went through the water park.

But that was a long time ago. The Bean Scene's been torn up for firewood, the beach is a graveyard, any ducks that made it to winter that first year did not come back the next, and Pennyweight's parents burned up in that first wave of dead set alight in the old water park.

Pennyweight buries his face in my shoulder.

By the time the older man catches the glint off Pennyweight's scope, I've already fired the first shot, and he crumples like a paper doll left out in the rain. As I reload, the younger man falls to his knees and hunches over the body of the older man, pulling it onto his lap and rocking it. His shoulders, wide as a bookcase, shake as he buries his face in the corpse's chest. He knows I'm out there, but maybe he knows he'll never get the M21 up in time, or maybe he doesn't care. I fire the second shot, and he collapses over the older man.

We don't know when the plants will come back. Maybe next spring. Maybe next decade. We can last that long provided we adhere to a single rule.

We have food for two.

PERSISTENCE OF VISION

Orrin Grey

I want you to act like this is all a movie. That'll make it easier.

If it was a movie, it would open with darkness. No credits, no titles, just a black screen that you stare into waiting for something to appear, waiting for the darkness to resolve into a picture. Instead, there's a voice reciting familiar words: "911, what is your emergency?"

Then another voice; a woman, crying, terrified: "There's a man in my house. He's in my bedroom."

"Are you in a safe place?"

"Now he's in the living room. He's in whatever room I go into. He's standing in the corner, pointing at me. He's talking, but I can't hear what he's saying."

At this point, you'd get the titles.

◄ ►

It wasn't the first 911 call. No one knows what the first one was. There's no way to separate it out from the others, even if anyone had wanted to. There's no way to draw the line and say, "This is the first real one. All the ones before this were just hoaxes, crazy people, misunderstandings." And then there's the question, of course, about how many of the ones before *were* crazy people, hoaxes? How long had it been going on, before we even knew?

And once it started, it took everyone so long to figure it out, because how do you figure something like that out? What do you do with that call, the one that played there in the dark, when the police and the EMTs arrive and find the woman crammed under her couch somehow, huddled up there like a frightened cat, dead from shock, the phone still gripped to her ear, the house otherwise deserted? What do you do with the call from a college kid who says that his fiancée went into the closet and never came out? When you look in the closet and find that it's maybe two feet square, just enough room for some clothes and the vacuum cleaner and no place for a person to go? You dismiss them at first, of course. You take the kid into custody, notify the woman's next of kin. But after a while, there are too many. After a while, people are no longer calling 911. After a while, the phones don't work anymore, and when you pick them up all you hear is voices, hundreds of them piled atop one another, all whispering your name.

◄ ►

If this was a movie, we'd have to have some kind of song playing over the opening credits, right? Something at once unexpected and appropriate. Not Johnny Cash, because Zach Snyder's *Dawn of the Dead* remake beat us to that punch, and besides, "The Man Comes Around" isn't quite right. So let's go just one step to the side, and get Nick Cave and company singing Dylan's "Death Is Not the End."

And while the music plays, there'd be snippets of footage in the background. Stuff from security cameras, blurry cell phone videos, clips of news shows. You'd see hands coming out of a shadow where a light was just shining, showing an empty corner. You'd see a window filling with bloody hand-prints. You'd see a girl, being pulled into what looks like a solid wall, sliding up it, into the ceiling. Someone is running, hold-ing the camera. The door is just a few feet away, and they look behind themselves, turning the camera with their gaze, and there's nothing behind them to be afraid of, but as they turn back the door is gone, bricked up in those few half-sec-onds, and then you hear a scream, and the camera goes to static.

Yeah, that's the opening credits.

◀ ▶

The trick, when you're trying to compress any story into a cou-ple of hours, is how to handle the exposition so it's not so clumsy. We'd want to avoid a text crawl or an opening narra-tor, because those are old-fashioned; reserved, nowadays, for more epic films, or things that purport to be "based on a true story." And while we want verisimilitude here, we also want to distance you from what's happening. That's kind of the point. Hence the song, right?

If this was an indie film, or something from overseas, we'd probably not give you any exposition at all right away. You'd just get dropped into the middle of the action, and you wouldn't have any idea what was going on. Just like in real life. Nobody knew what was happening. Most people died without ever knowing, they explained it whatever way they had to, or no way at all. There were street-corner preachers and politicians alike saying that it was God's judgment, there were cults that sprang up in the last days. There were people who were trying to give it some kind of scientific explanation – hallucinogens and black holes – even as the walls were bleeding and doorknobs were disappearing under the sweaty grasps of desperate hands. Outside my window, someone had spray-painted across the side of an office building, "Now 'tis the very witching hour of night, when churchyards yawn and hell itself breathes out contagion." It seemed as good an explanation as any, at the time.

The studios wouldn't stand for that, though, so your protagonist would be someone who worked at the facility. Or maybe someone who was married to someone who worked at the facility. Someone like me.

(I'm lying to myself, of course. If Hollywood had the purse strings, we wouldn't be married, we'd be dating. And 15 years younger. And our genders would be flipped, so that I was the one working at the facility and she was the one at home, tapping out movie reviews on her laptop in the kitchen window. We probably also wouldn't be in Montreal, but hey, maybe. They're filming more and more movies in Toronto these days, or they were, back when they were still filming movies.)

Maybe she'd tell me about the project in the evenings, over plates of spaghetti, like she really did. Or maybe she'd keep it all secret from me, but I'd read some notes or something, after the whole thing started. One way or the other, I'd discover how they found the machine in a bricked-up basement underneath an abandoned insane asylum. (The studios would love that!) They thought it was some kind of computer, maybe one of the first computers ever built. Not really a computer at all as we know them today, but something more like a difference engine, like the ones Turing worked on. All brass and levers and numbered keys, like a cross between some kind of ancient cash register and a pipe organ. All the project was ever supposed to do was to see what this thing did, what it was. This was going to be a big break in the history of computing, but, instead, it was the end of the history of anything.

They knew that something was wrong the minute they started the machine. There wasn't some slow build-up, it all happened at once. When they turned it on, there was a wave of poltergeist activity that swept out from the machine throughout the entire lab, across the river, and through all of Montreal. Every table and chair in the lab was shoved against the wall farthest from the machine. In the lunchroom a few floors up, chairs and tables overturned, plates slid off shelves to smash on the floor. Silverware magnetized. Every electronic device in the building shut down, and the entire city suffered a massive power failure.

In our apartment, all the doors slammed shut simultaneously, and the handful of VHS tapes that I still had in a box under the entertainment centre all melted.

Things went to shit from there.

Following on the heels of the poltergeist activity, so close behind it that no one in the lab had even reacted, the ectoplasm began to materialize out of the valves of the machine, flowing down the sides, forming a sort of barrier around it, something that shimmered and moved almost like water. Nobody in the lab had any idea what it was then, of course, but the first one who touched it died instantly. His hair turned white, he fell to the floor choking and slapping at his chest. By the time anyone else got to him, he'd ossified, and there were hundreds of spiders crawling out of his mouth and nose.

◀ ▶

In the movie version, the machine would have been the heart of everything. Its destruction would have been the end of the film, the salvation of mankind. That makes for a better ending, sends the folks in Peoria home happy. In real life, though, the machine was just the key that turned the lock. Once the door was open, there was no closing it.

They did manage to destroy the machine, eventually, and when they did, they found a corpse in the middle of it. The mummified body, hooked to thousands of copper wires, of a woman named Katrina Something, the rest of the name illegible, a powerful physical medium, born 1899, died 1916. We only know any of that because there was a plaque on the inside of her abstract coffin that told us.

By then, the handful of people who were left from the facility had figured out sort of what the machine did. Or, at least, what it *had* done. By then, almost everyone had kind of figured it out. Everyone knew, at least, what was happening, even if a lot of them didn't give it a name. Some did, though. The Internet, when it still worked, came to our rescue, prepared to turn anything, even the end of the world, into a kind of meme. They called it the Ghost Apocalypse.

It's funny, in a way, because we had all been culturally preparing for the dead to come kill us for years by then. We just expected it to be their bodies, not their restless spirits. We had zombie apocalypse survival guides, and over on the U.S. side of things the CDC supposedly had a disaster plan for a zombie outbreak. Nobody had a plan for ghosts, and they proved a lot harder to deal with than zombies because, frankly, nobody knew how they worked. You couldn't lay them to rest or settle their unfinished business, destroy the fetters that bound them to this mortal plane. They were pouring through now, this was their world. And you certainly couldn't just shoot them in the head. Sometimes they already didn't have a head. Sometimes they were just a voice, or a shape, or a cold draft, or the elevator door suddenly closing on you no matter what you did, and then the rest of the elevator dropping 27 stories to the underground parking garage, killing everyone on board.

We only had one movie that predicted this. Well, two if you count the remake. It was *Kairo* in Japan in 2001, *Pulse* in the U.S. in 2006, during the height of the J-horror boom, starring that girl from *Veronica Mars* and that guy from *Lost*. Well-known prognosticators of the end of the world.

(Did *Ghostbusters* and *Ghostbusters 2* predict a kind of ghost apocalypse, albeit one staved off, twice-over, by a more Hollywood-friendly happy ending? Maybe a little bit.)

It was from *Pulse* that we got the idea that saved those few of us who got saved long enough to see what a world was like populated mainly by the dead. Some kid figured it out, disseminated it on Reddit and everywhere else. After most of the power went down, people started spreading the news with hand-lettered flyers written on red paper.

It wasn't just red tape, like in the movie, though that was a great touch, guys. It was red *anything*. Something about the colour red kept them out. Some people speculated it was a spectrum thing, that ghosts were some kind of light or energy themselves, and that the red spectrum disrupted them somehow. Others thought that red was the colour of life, of blood and the heart and human passion. That maybe it reminded ghosts of mortality, or that it protected those who still pulsed with living blood and heat. People brave enough to do research in the big, abandoned, spooky libraries full of books that floated off the shelves or opened themselves up to thematically relevant passages turned up records of Victorian-era "ghost traps" that were just red-painted rooms, or even containers with red interiors, designed to cage spooks.

Whatever the proof of it, it seemed to work, and so those of us who survived did so by painting the insides of everything red. Red walls, red floors, red ceilings. Painting over windows. When paint wasn't at hand, we used red paper, red markers, even red ballpoint pens, though those didn't work so well, it turned out.

From inside our red rooms we sent out parties dressed in red clothes to try to bring back food, fresh water, more paint. Most of them didn't return.

That's not a very good Hollywood ending, is it? All of us sitting in our red rooms, waiting to get picked off one by one and join the ranks of our oppressors? What they don't tell you about surviving the apocalypse is that it's really not worth it. Everyone you care about is probably dead, there's nothing fun left to do, and not a whole lot to live for. With the zombie apocalypse or whatever, at least you'd have some hope, however naïve. You could imagine a cure being found, or the zombies eventually all just rotting, if only you could outlast them. What are you supposed to do when the dead really do come back, though, and not just their carcasses? What's the endgame on *that*? They're not going to rot, get bored, go away. They're not going to sleep, or die again. There's nothing left to do, except delay the point at which they get you, a line of hopeless desperation that stretches out forever into the horizon, like a hallway in a Kubrick film.

◄ ►

I'm not going to tell you how Georgiana died. That was her name, though everyone just called her Georgie, me included. If this was a movie, you'd see it. If this was a movie, and I was the protagonist, *I* would have seen it. It would have been dramatic, would have happened at some climactic moment. I would have been there, inches away from saving her, clutching at her hand as her fingers were pulled from mine, one by one. But this isn't a movie, and that's not how it happened.

I'm not going to tell you how she died, because I don't know. I wasn't there. Am I even sure that she's dead? Well, I'm pretty sure. One of her co-workers told me she was gone. Those were his words, "Georgie's gone," just before he himself was gone, pulled around a corner and just *gone*, the hallway empty for 100 feet in both directions.

I didn't give up on her, even then. I went out looking, after the first of the red rooms got put up. In my red clothes, red hood pulled up, I went searching like I was on my way to grandmother's house. And maybe I finally found her, or she found me. I don't really know, not for sure, not anymore.

I won't tell you how she died, but I will tell you this. One last bit, and maybe it'll make for a better ending. I still go outside to smoke. How crazy is that, right? But I don't see any reason to quit anymore, and sometimes it's worth maybe being dragged down into a storm drain, or disappearing into the street, or just suddenly turning white and weeping blood.

Sometimes I just want to be outside again, and there's no death horrible enough to make staying in that goddamned closed-up red room worth it for even one more minute.

On nights like that, I go out behind the building where we've been staying – it used to be a hospital, we painted up an entire wing – and I smoke a cigarette while I look out over the river. And lately, every time, I see Georgie there, standing on the edge of the water. I know that it's her, even though I can't really see her face. I'd know her in a crowd, by now, from the way she stands, the way her hair falls. I've seen her against the back of my eyelids every day since she was gone, and I'd know her backward, blindfolded. I know that it's her, and I know what she wants. Not to drag me away, not like the others, not yet. Give her time, maybe. For now, though, she just wants me to follow her. To go willingly into that good night. To grind out my cigarette and walk down into the freezing water of the St. Lawrence. And I know, as surely as I know any of this, that one night soon, I will.

Roll credits.

ST. MACAIRE'S DOME

Jean-Louis Trudel

Before entering the port of Quebec, the *Express de Rouen* skirted shallows, the pilot identifying each one aloud for the handful of passengers on deck.

"The old harbour."

Straight lines intersecting at right angles beneath a stretch of calmer water.

"The former train station, to starboard."

Darker waters, choppier waves, and a squat angular shape coming into focus as if rising out of the inky depths.

"When the tide goes out, the pinnacle pokes out."

Above the reef, a madly bobbing buoy warned away incoming ships.

"And over there is where the ruins are closest to the surface. And where the fisherfolk set their traps for lobster."

Darrick gazed in the direction indicated. Beyond the shallows, a broad bay extended westward between St. Macaire's heights and the foothills of the Laurentides. To his left, in the distance, the phallic dome of St. Macaire's Basilica towered above the middle parts of the island of Quebec. To his immediate left, the morning sun lent the ruins of the *château* Frontenac a golden hue. To his right, windmills on the heights of Lorette and Charlesbourg duelled with the sea breeze.

"Can you sail around the island that way?"

"No sea captain would risk his ship in those narrows," a fellow passenger asserted. "At least, not under sail. There's no room to manoeuvre."

The tone of his voice held more confidence than usual. The other man had told Darrick that he was originally from Quebec. He was coming home and the relief showed.

"Not through the Cap-Rouge channel," the pilot confirmed. "There are ruins everywhere."

"No doubt," Darrick sighed.

"Not that it's really impassable, my lord ironbearers," the pilot added. "The fisherfolk of Sillery and St. Foy manage just fine without wrecking their fishing dories. And the lads from Cap-Rouge know every rock and ruin of the narrows." The pilot was no less skilful, still talking as he guided the three-master toward the entrance to the harbour. Buoys outlined the channel, but Darrick admired the pilot's sure-handedness. He tried to convince himself he was seeing the city for the first time, the better to play his part.

"Your city was lucky," he observed. "In France, most major ports ended up underwater. At best, we were left with suburbs originally standing on higher ground. But here…"

"Here the suburbs were flooded instead, yeah," the pilot agreed. "But we still remember the neighbourhoods beneath the waves. I could name them if you asked… My grandpa told me stories that were told to him by his own grandfather, who was in charge of a major library over there. Care to try to spot it?"

The pilot waved vaguely. Darrick made it look like he was trying to find the ruined building, even though he was perfectly familiar with the stories about Quebec's lost library. A cable length from the old train station, sandbanks stretched lazily in the sun, pounded by the surf and trampled by seabirds. Gulls and terns flew away as the shadow of the *Express de Rouen* swept by.

Darrick pondered.

"Down there too?"

"Yeah, like the rest. Most of the ancient buildings collapsed. Their remnants became the foundations of today's reefs."

"Any sunken treasures?"

"Back then, the sea just kept inching higher, year after year. The Ancients had plenty of time to move out and take what they wanted to bring. They didn't leave anything useful or valuable, at least by their standards. Sure, they overlooked stuff we could use today. But when the saltwater leached the metal inside the concrete and the shells collapsed, it was too late to go back."

"Has anybody ever tried mining the rubble?"

"Not sure it would be worth it. The interesting stuff rusted away years ago."

For a short moment, the prospect of a profitable enterprise entranced Darrick. An ironbearer such as himself was not supposed to dirty his hands with buying and selling. However, working a mine was not considered to be as sordid an occupation.

But he couldn't forget. Ever since he'd first seen the battered ramparts of the Château Frontenac rise above the horizon, he'd felt like killing someone. Painful memories were surfacing like ruins exposed by the departing sea. Anger was an old friend of his, and it too had made the trip across the ocean.

"Haul up all sails!" the ship's captain shouted from the bridge.

The sailors swarmed up the rigging to wait for the order to furl the sails. The pilot kept a light touch on the tiller and the ship slowed.

Beneath the feet of the passengers, the light buzzing of the electric motor changed pitch as the ship's propellers awakened. The three-master rounded the watchtower erected at the end of the jetty and came to a stop inside Gabrielle Harbour. The ship hadn't been this close to land in weeks.

They were almost there. Darrick nodded to his neighbour, the ironbearer Somptueux de Lauzon, who had never suspected he was sharing his cabin with a fellow Québécois.

"And there's the shallop of the port police."

Startled, Darrick turned around to greet the ship's captain who had joined the ironbearers. She managed to look unassuming, aware that some of her passengers were nervous around uniforms. Instead of an ironbearer's rapier, she carried a cutlass in a sheath tied to her thigh. If Darrick could believe the first mate's tales, the captain had used the weapon to repel a dozen attempted boardings by pirates.

Darrick felt the weight of the commander's gaze on him and he did not ask for details. He'd endured two weeks of pretending, but he was tired of dissembling. Enough.

As the ship's captain watched, the ironbearer Darrick d'Épernon leaned on the railing, as if to observe the men straining to row the shallop.

And then he jumped overboard.

◄ ►

The Phénix-France compound sprawled along the edge of the island, just beyond the historic Parc des Braves. A four-metre-high wall surrounded the grounds, hiding the buildings inside. A few chimneys loomed over the company's facilities, spewing coal-black smoke. And the sulfurous stink that went along with it.

When Darrick presented himself at the compound door, a squad of heavily armed guards stopped him from entering.

"Apologies, my lord. May we know your identity and that of your companions?"

"Karim de Neuilly, company shareholder. My secretary, Cavalin Rufiange. And my bodyguard."

"You walked here?"

"I landed today. I needed to stretch my legs."

The port was near enough for the story to be plausible. Darrick soon got to meet the director's assistant, who checked his papers and introduced him into the director's office.

The new factory manager was a middle-aged man, though his few blond curls were outnumbered by the white ones. His long, strong face might have seemed open and friendly when young flesh softened its outlines, but it was now a mere bony mask, whittled down by age and its pains.

"Jéconiah Jutras."

They shook hands and kissed in the French manner. Darrick was on the lookout for any hint of distrust, but the director was treating him exactly as he should treat a visitor from France who was a major shareholder of the CPF.

The ironbearer expected nothing less. For years, he'd waited for the appointment of a manager who wouldn't recognize him. Jutras was from Montreal, where the hydroelectric dams built across the Ottawa and St. Lawrence supplied a few factories and universities with enough electricity to function. But Quebec was best situated to trade with the French, and Montreal had dwindled into relative insignificance.

From the first words they exchanged, the ironbearer sensed that Jutras wasn't merely loyal to the Compagnie Phénix-France, but genuinely in love with French culture. Darrick won him over with a gift of an excellent olive oil from Normandy.

"You didn't waste any time," Jutras said approvingly.

"Why do you say that?"

"I saw a ship come into the port earlier."

"Yes, I was aboard. She's leaving again in three or four days, and I expect to sail with her."

"So soon? You're not staying to visit then."

"My business interests in France require my presence. I cannot stay away too long."

"Of course. I understand. And how are things in France?"

Darrick tried to gauge his counterpart's intentions. On the North American side of the Atlantic the question could be considered subversive. Quebec's governor was adamant that the Laurentian Valley sheltered a civilization on par with the remaining technological societies found elsewhere on the planet.

"Nothing like here. The whole country doesn't lack for electricity and there's enough for everybody. Industry, transportation, city lights…"

"At home too? Is it true that you still have televisions and computers, like in the old days?"

"The age of miracles is over. There's enough wattage to run such devices, but we no longer know how to manufacture them. You'd need rare earths that are only found in recycling centres in France. And microchips so complex that giant factories were once needed to produce enough to justify the initial investment. France alone can't justify building a factory large enough to supply half a continent. So, yes, there are televisions, but they're built with tubes. And the only computers belong to the government. Not that they're telling anyone whether or not they still work."

"What about the other European countries?"

"More like what you have here. Lots of wind turbines, a few hydroelectric dams, biofuels for vital transportation needs. France retains its nuclear advantage over the rest."

"But what would it do without our uranium?"

The director smiled smugly, without realizing how offensive his smirk looked.

"Speaking of which, what *is* the current state of Canadian reserves?"

The man waxed optimistic. Canadian uranium came in part from old Saskatchewan mines, but it was also recovered from the ruins of Ontario's nuclear power plants. And the company's envoys were still negotiating with the Algonquin farmers of the Far North to open new thorium and uranium mines.

Farther east, the company had set a pilot project to strain out the uranium in seawater, using the electricity produced by wind farms around Rimouski.

"We could do as much in France," Darrick commented. "What about the taxes?"

"What about them?"

"Did the governor increase them since last year?"

"Granger de Limoilou is smarter than that. He's got a new family to provide for – his fifth – and the new relatives are grabbing all the plushy jobs. My sister studied medicine for 10 years, but she was passed over for a young niece of the governor's new wife. She had to take a position out West. Last I heard, she'd set up shop out of a fort in the middle of the Rockies."

"I'm sorry to hear that," Darrick said in a voice that implied quite the contrary. Jutras snapped to as he realized his rashness. He inquired instead as to the reason for the ironbearer's visit.

"I've come to pick up the new fuel rods."

"Today? I wasn't expecting it. Nothing is ready."

"No, not today. Tomorrow morning will do. My men will show up to pick up the first load at eight sharp. The captain of the *Express de Rouen* promised me to clear out the needed space in the holds of her ship, and I trust her to keep her word."

Jutras called in his assistant and gave him his instructions. When they were alone once more, the director got up to see his visitor out.

"You know I'm in your debt. Thanks to the new capital you raised, we've doubled the size of our facilities. Just to set up the new centrifuge chains, we had to build and hire more people than the city of Quebec had seen anybody do in over a century. And then there were the new vessels to produce uranium oxide, the vats for mixing the zirconium alloy of the cladding, the—"

"I expected no less. I just hope the final product is up to snuff."

"The enrichment is above the minimum you requested," Jutras asserted, visibly irked. "We took advantage of the existing enrichment of the metal recovered in Ontario to go faster, but the centrifuges still had to spin all winter to process the Saskatchewan ores. I can guarantee you that we followed your specifications for the moulds to the nearest tenth of a millimetre. Each tube contains the required number of pellets. Yes, the quality is what you asked for, and you can have my word for it… I hope it won't be the last order of the kind."

"Labour is less expensive here than in France," Darrick said, repeating the lie he had already used on the shareholders in Paris. "As long as we get the same price for our electricity, our profit margins will fatten like ducks before the slaughter."

Jutras nodded, mollified.

"Don't you wish to see our facilities?"

"That won't be necessary. Sea air has left me with quite an appetite. I'm heading back to my inn for a real meal. The rods will be…"

"In custom-made trunks lined with lead. The radioactivity is essentially undetectable from the outside."

"That's great. I wouldn't want to worry the captain of the *Express de Rouen*. She's a fine woman, but there are still people who are scared of anything nuclear."

They laughed, in complete agreement at last.

◀ ▶

Twenty years later, Darrick still remembered the large house abutting the enclosure of the wind farm on the Plains of Abraham. It was a link to his childhood. Other places he had known in his youth still stood, no doubt, but the old house was the only one he associated with happy memories.

He was in such a hurry to see it again that he only stopped once on his way, by the foot of a streetlight set up by the Ancients. A black and stinking rain was falling. The drops darkening the pavement near the base stoked his hate anew, but he managed to stifle it again before he reached the house. While memory might be more powerful than time itself, time was mightier than flesh and houses. The three-storey stone building, roofed with slate from Montmorency, bore its share of new scars. And though the ground floor was still occupied by a bicycle rental shop, the faces of the people in charge were unfamiliar. The colour of the shutters was different, too. The steps of the staircase running up the outside of the house sagged a bit more than he remembered, as well.

The passage of time had been even harsher on Réjean Lacombe. The former chancellor of the Court of St. Macaire's Dome still boasted a full head of hair: he'd been famous for his lion's mane, but it had gone white. His sunken cheeks and deep wrinkles testified to the years gone by. For a second, Darrick was embarrassed by his still-youthful frame, its powerful muscles and as yet unblemished skin... For a second. Only the weak believed strength was shameful. Exile had taught that lesson to Darrick.

The old man seemed surprised to see his former pupil. "You've returned!"

Lacombe didn't rise to greet him, but Darrick expected it. In his youth, Lacombe had been captured by a tribe of Newfs when he had ventured west of Lake Superior. The tribals had crossed the Saskatchewan steppes to sell him to the highest bidder in the slave markets of Kananaskis.

And to make sure he wouldn't get away, they had cut open the soles of his feet and forced him to walk on tiptoe across the grasslands, hands tied to the back of a horse-drawn cart. Walking had kept either cross-shaped gash from closing and the open wounds would have prevented him from getting very far if he had tried to escape.

He had been ransomed by the Quebec consul in Kananaskis, but Lacombe had been lamed for life. He could still walk if he needed to, but he avoided it whenever he had the chance. As chancellor, he had rarely been required to stand for anyone. Darrick glowered, unhappy with his old friend's tone.

"You sound like you regret it."

"You didn't tell me you were coming."

"I let as few people know as possible. Just Carolin and Naoufal."

Darrick pointed to the young men with him. One was standing guard in the vestibule visible through the door. The other was in the living room with them, keeping a lookout by the window.

"Why them?"

"They've been my main contacts here in Quebec, and I needed them to get things ready for my return. If they had stopped receiving my messages, they would have been worried for me."

"Wasn't there a radio aboard the ship you sailed on? Couldn't you have called?"

"Access to the radio was strictly controlled. And bringing all the apparatus of a short-wave radio set onboard the *Express de Rouen* would have looked suspicious. Ironbearers aren't known as radio fans…"

"Since you are here, I assume you evaded our gallant border police."

"Fortunately for me, an outboard is much faster than a shallop. By now, my description is no doubt being typed up for every police unit on the island. Too late."

"What are your intentions?"

"Rebuilding. Quebec has grown rich by exporting thorium and uranium to France, but what has it done with its riches? Nothing. The city is sitting on a pile of gold. The poor aren't getting anything out of it and the rich are living behind walls, whining about taxes."

"So, you want to bring back the glory days of the Dark Age."

"No! Enough grovelling before the Ancients. We've indulged in too much of it. Let's tell the truth: our ancestors built things halfway and half-assed, and they paid too much. They accumulated so much debt that we're still paying the interest owed to the biosphere. If Quebec is an island, if the West is a desert, if we're short of metal because we don't have the energy it would take to produce more, it's because the Ancients burned everything they could, turned the world into their private garbage pit, and willed us their leftovers."

"I remember a young man saying the same kind of thing. But a grown man should know enough to leave naïve dreams to youth."

"Unless he's learned how to turn his dreams into realities."

Lacombe shrugged wearily. Darrick stared, unable to find in his mentor's eyes excitement to match his own. His first impression had been the right one. The former chancellor was a man as worn down by the years as the staircase outside. The ironbearer suddenly felt absolutely certain that not one hopeful word, not a single animating ideal would shake the inertia weighing down his friend. He turned to Naoufal.

"I was wrong. I shouldn't have come. Let's go."

Naoufal left the window. Darrick had reached the door when Lacombe hailed him. "Tell me, Darrick, were you happy in France? Do you have a wife and children? Did you start a new life?"

"I'm an ironbearer," the traveller answered coldly. "I did not demean myself. I never begged, if that's what you want to know."

"You should have stayed over there."

"Until recently, I fully intended to."

"So what happened?"

"I discovered the reason why my father's Court is next to St. Macaire's Dome."

The man nodded slowly, as if against his will. "What do you hope to achieve? Make a great public fuss?"

"Much more than that, old friend. My father's reign of terror must end. Even in exile, I've managed to follow what's happening here. Letters from my friends countered every happy radio bulletin broadcast from St. Macaire. My father no longer tolerates any check on his power. I was crazy enough to hope that my exile would at least allay some of his fears. But no! Don't deny it. His rule has become a reign of terror. I've seen with my own eyes the cages hanging at the crossroads, dripping with the rotting flesh of his victims or rattling with their bones. And what about the crosses drawn on the walls where his thugs beat or killed innocent bystanders? I knew what they meant before landing, thanks to the letters of Naoufal, but they still gave me the shivers. Isn't it past time to put an end to it all?"

Lacombe refused to be moved.

"Those so-called 'victims' of your father were criminals and troublemakers. You have to keep a strong grip on the rabble to have law and order."

"That's not what you taught me once upon a time! What about the consent of the governed? And the respect of basic rights?"

Lacombe shrugged.

"I got old."

"Me too," Darrick replied. "And I saw in France that it was possible to do things differently. We just need to wake up and give change a chance. It's not because we live on an island that we must cut ourselves off from the rest of the world."

"Depends what the rest of the world is like. France isn't surrounded by semi-barbarians and lands ruled by sheer savagery."

Despite himself, Darrick glanced at the shrivelled legs of the old chancellor. He could hardly reject Lacombe's point. In North America, the collapse had been shattering when cheap oil had run out. The cost of coal and gas had climbed to dizzying heights. States supplied with electricity from hydroelectric dams, nuclear power plants or wind farms had gone off the grid, bringing down electric lines and pylons to hoard the power they would no longer sell to their neighbours. Retaliatory raids led by hotheads had wrecked more than a few surviving reactors and wind turbines.

The electricity wars had complicated coal mining, already made tougher by the shortage of gasoline for trucks and excavators. In the larger cities, lack of heating during the winter had killed thousands. As gasoline ran out for farm machinery and natural gas for the synthesis of nitrogen-based fertilizers, crop yields dropped and prices rocketed. Since North

American transportation depended on fossil fuels, famine had struck by the end of the second winter and visited time and again until the population's dieback had matched the reduced food supply.

The powers that be, blamed for their improvidence, had withered away while cities took over essential tasks. The oldest ones retained denser neighbourhoods better suited to the new era than their younger, sprawling counterparts.

In some areas, economic migrants had tried to return home without the help of planes or cars, giving rise to wandering tribes who ended up choosing a nomadic lifestyle. The Trucker Tribe. The Newfs. The Hicanos from Mexico.

"I'm making you think?" Lacombe asked.

"Yes. And I still say that we must reject barbarism. If we do not wish to see Quebec fall as low as Toronto, we must take action. Blow up the old power structures and start over again."

The chancellor's shoulders slumped.

"You talk about it as if it would be easy. Building is harder than destroying. Rebuilding after blowing things up would be even more so."

"You would be wrong to underestimate my anger."

"I fear it will only make things worse."

"We'll speak again after I've offered Quebec a new start. And I hope you will help me build the city that my father refused to restore."

◀ ▶

Cap-Rouge never changed. Every day, the fisherfolk went out with the tide and they returned to the village with the tide, bringing back enough fish to feed their families, and a few more to sell to any taker waiting on the beach.

Visitors made their way by boat from villages farther west to buy their catch. Sometimes, they stayed after roasting their purchases on a driftwood-fed fire. When night fell, they found shelter in the inns and taverns standing on the tip of the island.

Through the gloom and noise of the common room slinked less savoury visitors. Strangers whose clothes smelled of the forest. Who carried blunderbusses and single-shot pistols. Who wandered in with bows and arrows. Who didn't answer many questions, but paid their fare with good copper coins, occasionally with slivers of silver or gold.

Darrick was drinking alone at a table in a corner of the biggest inn on the strand. He was sitting so as to display clearly the sword by his side. Nobody would bother an iron-bearer.

Except the man he was waiting for. Who only showed up after nightfall, ordering a beer at the counter before turning around to scan discreetly the rest of the room. The man's disguise was good. The newcomer looked like an Algonquin farmer from the Upper Laurentides, one of those who earned the equivalent of a year's income by joining a brigade of western Voyageurs from time to time. Yet, the venison bag slung over his shoulder sported a bit of tartan that could pass as a mere patch but wasn't, of course.

Darrick called him over, pointing to the empty chair in front of him. The man circled in.

"Ségole Portelance."

"Philippe Taillefer," Darrick answered.

Passwords exchanged, they hugged like old friends meeting again after a long separation, though somewhat awkwardly, each one wondering if the other was going to stab him in the back.

"You've come a long way?"

"You said it, ironbearer! A Voyageur isn't afraid to voyage, and I've paddled all the rivers between here and Saskatchewan."

"I didn't think there were any left."

"No, they still flow in the spring when the snow melts. Nothing better to ship boatloads all the way to Lake Superior or Hudson Bay. But I've also escorted my share of caravans crossing the steppes in high summer."

Escorted or attacked? Darrick reminded himself to keep in mind who he was dealing with.

"But you're retired now, right?"

"Soon enough, I hope," the man said without smiling.

His black hair was streaked with grey, but there was no sign in the man's face of Lacombe's beaten-down weariness. Darrick nodded, as if he were contemplating old age and its pastimes.

"Some men, when they stop working, they no longer know what to do with themselves."

"Speak for yourself, ironbearer! Me, I think I'll take up fishing."

"It's pleasant enough, if the sea is kind and the fish plentiful."

"You just need to know the good spots, that's all. What do you think? Any likely ones around here?"

"I'd advise trying the waters near Port-Sillery. Tomorrow, you'll be completely alone."

"If you say so… Maybe I'll go bother the fish with some friends of mine. What do you think I could get for my catch?"

"Whatever you want."

"Nothing less."

His reply snapped like a whip-crack, setting Darrick's teeth on edge. The ironbearer held the man's stare. If the man didn't trust him, his whole plan would come to naught. The murderous light in the Voyageur's eyes met Darrick's self-confident gaze until the older man yielded.

The deal was done. They revived the conversation by broaching less perilous topics, but the man called Ségole grew uneasy when a group of the governor's guards took over a nearby table. Darrick too had strained to appear unconcerned, telling himself the guards did not seem to be on the lookout for anything but an evening meal, even assuming that they'd been provided with a reliable description of their quarry.

When the Voyageur took his leave, Darrick found himself alone. He was giving in to the pleasant stupor induced by a good meal, a couple of pints, and his exertions atop a stolen bicycle from one end of the island to another. Had he run himself ragged just to elude pursuers?

Or had he run so hard because he was afraid of enjoying his return too well? He could still give up. The fate of Quebec's population did not seem so harsh. He was free to head back to France, or to move to Montreal if he wished to live out his days in more familiar surroundings. He would still dream of building a better world, and that world would retain the unsullied perfection of dreams never put to the test of reality.

At the other table, the governor's guards were picking over the scraps of their meals when the serving girl stopped by to ask them to pay up. The commanding officer snickered.

"What's wrong with your eyes, girl?"

"I don't believe we are in the business of offering free meals, sirs. Do you want me to speak to my boss?"

"You should know better, little goose! If you really want to collect, my pretty one, you'll be paid in kind, on this very table."

"Wham-bang, right between the legs!" one of the guards threw in.

"She doesn't get it. It's an honour to serve a Dome guard."

"An honour without price!" they chorused before laughing uproariously.

Nobody else laughed. Silence spread from one table to the next, conversations dying and gazes swivelling to take in the scene. Darrick straightened, sobering as he tightened his hand on the sword's grip. But there were five of them, and they weren't drunk enough to improve the odds. Before he could talk himself into it, the innkeeper burst from the kitchen, grabbed the serving girl by the shoulder, propelled her behind him and bowed before the officer.

"Forgive me, sirs, she didn't know. Trust me, we appreciate the honour you do us by gracing our establishment. May I offer you another pitcher of our best Montebello red?"

"Do so," the officer said. "But next time…" He didn't finish, so certain of his authority that he did not feel the need to bellow or threaten. Moments later, guests began to settle their account and leave. Like them, Darrick tipped generously, even though it wouldn't undo the girl's humiliation. She looked young. It was probably her first time working in such a place and she would learn. Yet, he hated thinking that she would grow to find official thuggishness perfectly normal.

◄ ►

The automobile rolled up to the entrance of St. Macaire's Palace a little after nine o'clock. Ministers, secretaries, clerks and petty clerks were already at work inside the wings overlooking the forecourt. The clickety-click of typewriters wafted through the windows thrown open to let in the springtime warmth. The main building rose between the two wings, housing the offices and apartments of the governor, as well as a connecting hall leading to another wing behind, used for state occasions, grand balls and official dinners.

The men guarding the entrance to the inner court stopped the vehicle. Half-burnt ethanol fumes emanated from the malfunctioning motor, thick enough to choke the guards who didn't keep their distance. The luxurious vehicle's only occupant was a liveried driver. When he was asked the purpose of his visit, he pointed to the coat of arms adorning the rear compartment's doors.

"I work for Lord Odrigo de Lorette. He asked me to come get his mother, Lady Claudette de Bergerville. She had an appointment with the Minister of the Registry."

"Very well, I'll check," the commanding officer said. "Meanwhile, please park that thing over here."

His airy gesture did not quite hide his fascination with the motor car. He went back inside to check the log. His underlings watched with undisguised interest as the driver manoeuvred the automobile by the windows of the guardroom. He set the parking brake and got out.

"If this is going to take long, can I go take a piss?"

A guard pointed him to the door leading to the basement. The others surrounded the parked vehicle, admiring the chrome inlays and the wood veneer. The ethanol fumes quickly dissipated, but they only got near enough to catch the sound of a faint ticking just before the car exploded.

◄ ►

St. Macaire's Basilica rose on the highest part of the island of Quebec. Its dome was the focal point of the governor's compound, a hodgepodge of buildings dating back to the Université Laval or to the first governor's efforts to link the most defensible ones with rough-hewn additions.

His successors had concentrated on the main entrance, adding guardrooms and sentry boxes, while lodging most of the guard company in a dormitory one floor above. When the high explosives hidden in every available nook of the automobile detonated, the blast shattered the nearest wall. The upper floors collapsed, burying the guardrooms and the people inside under the debris. The shock wave blew in the windows overlooking the courtyard, shooting glass shards and wood splinters into the offices. The sheer thickness of the outer wall saved it from toppling, but it was left in no shape to withstand an immediate assault.

Yet, once silence fell, quickly filled with the moans and crying of the wounded, no attack followed. The men set to clearing the debris did not stop to question the logic behind the bombing.

At the other end of the compound, Darrick heard the explosion and he muttered a quick prayer for Naoufal's safety. Had he been able to find shelter in a basement that was deep enough? Would he manage to join the rescuers, mix in, and escape?

The ironbearer easily imagined the destruction, the deaths, and the injuries he'd just caused. He was certain that criminals and thugs had died. He did not doubt that he had also killed innocents. But his dream of a better city counted for more.

He climbed the steps of the entrance to the basilica without stopping.

"Who goes there?" a guard asked, bursting out of his sentry box with a halberd held upright.

"Faucher de Limoilou!"

"Wh... what?"

Darrick whipped out his sword, pushed aside the halberd lowered too late and thrust forcefully into the chest of the man still trying to figure out which of the governor's sons he had in front of him.

Thanks to his father's procreative efforts, he had once been able to pass unnoticed as one son of many. Granger de Limoilou had complicated everybody's life by taking several wives and siring even more children. As he marched down the nave, Darrick shouted into the hollowness within what he'd sworn to tell his father.

Who am I? No, not the eldest assassinated by the second one. And, no, not the second one you executed under the windows of your office in Clarendon Castle, shot for all to see. And not the idiot you imprisoned for life in the asylum of Upper Beauport. And, no, not the fifth, the designated heir as long as he keeps his mouth shut. Or the sixth, born last year...

The nave was deserted. Weekdays, the faithful were scarce, especially if no mass was scheduled. Yet, sword in hand, Darrick almost wished for the irruption of a squad of the governor's guards. While most ironbearers carried a sword as a token of their rank and wealth, Darrick had learned to use his in France. And he wanted to face his enemies. To fight them.

The third one! I'm the third one, Father. Joseph Darrick Faucher de Limoilou. The banished one!

But there was nobody to hear and the echo of his footsteps was the only other sound under the vaulting. The diversion had worked. All the other guards had left the basilica to lend a hand to the rescue efforts.

A sudden rumble warned him to step aside and he gave way to a Compagnie Phénix-France dray pulled by four horses in a lather, steaming from the climb up the ramp laid over the stairs of the entrance. Standing at the front of the dray, Carolin tugged on the reins to hear Darrick's orders.

"Keep going. The doors of the dome are straight ahead. I'll meet you there." Darrick returned to the front of the basilica. Two of his men were disassembling the wooden ramp to turn it into a barricade that would allow them to defend the entrance. He found nothing in the sentry box, but he broke down the door of the guardroom and seized all the key rings.

At the far end of the nave, a pair of monumental doors separated it from the inside of the dome. The choir. The holy of holies. Normally, priests were the only ones to enter the inner sanctum. On feast days, the doors were opened halfway to let the faithful glimpse their bishop saying Mass before the altar holding the relics of St. Macaire.

Darrick's heart beat faster as he tried a dozen keys before finding the right one. The doors were solid steel, but so well hung that he needed only to push them with the flat of one hand to start them swinging on their hinges.

Followed by Carolin, he slipped inside, noting the extraordinary thickness of the walls. He looked up immediately to see the top of the cupola, about 100 metres up.

"Here we are," he whispered.

"At last."

His companion stared at the floor between them.

"So, everything is underneath," he said, almost disbelieving.

"Everything," Darrick confirmed. "The island's only nuclear reactor."

A well-kept secret. The power plant's construction dated back to the period just before the dark years, when physicists and engineers at Université Laval needed an experimental reactor to play with. Experimental in the sense that it did not use heavy water like most other Canadian reactors. Yet, designed for power levels that hinted at something more than a test-bed for new reactor designs.

Likewise, transforming the cooling tower into a cathedral choir could not have happened without an ulterior motive. In the short term, it probably owed a lot to the era's deep-seated mistrust of nuclear power, and the builders' lack of resources. They might have sought the material help of a revived Catholic church wishing to dedicate a basilica to the dead of the Dark Age.

Carolin had come across a forgotten trove of the university's archives about the project during his studies. A common friend had provided Darrick's mailing address in France, since the young man wanted to find out if the governor's family knew. Darrick didn't, but the more he thought about it, the more certain he became that his father was in on the secret.

Carolin hadn't been able to determine if the plant had ever served. The first governor could have used an additional source of electricity to make up for the deficiencies of the wind farms... but hiding the condensation plume of a running power plant would have been no easy task, unless it operated at night or during storms and foggy days.

"Let's get to work," Darrick said. "If we're lucky, we've got until the next changing of the guard. And maybe the next one if we manage to deal with the new shift."

Three women and 22 men were now inside the basilica. Half of the men, and all of the women, were students and friends of Carolin. They had never set foot inside a nuclear power plant, but Darrick had supplied them with every document he'd been able to get his hands on in France. He was also providing them with the enriched uranium of the Compagnie Phénix-France, in the form of rods locked inside wooden chests over four metres long... He hoped it would be enough to awaken the sleeping reactor.

The others had just volunteered to fight. Each of them had a reason for hating the governor, Granger de Limoilou, and each had chosen to trust his son. They had come armed for war – with old hunting guns, cutlasses, and sometimes with nothing more than knives or clubs.

Before he left to check on the basilica's defences, Darrick pulled Carolin aside.

"First impressions?"

"I won't promise anything until I've seen the crypt, but it's looking good. Everything is clean and well maintained. I've found where the access panels are cut into the floor and the grooves are practically dust-free. I even spotted some traces of oil near the base of the altar, still wet, as if somebody lubricated gears or something mechanical not so long ago. And look at the air vents up there. Not one is actually blocked by the hanging tapestries."

"I'll leave you the keys. Do you need anything else?"

"Luck. According to specs, the reactor needed 50 tonnes of enriched uranium to work as designed. We only have five."

"But you told me there was probably still some fuel left."

"We'll soon find out if I was right."

Darrick mastered the urge to strangle him on the spot. He didn't feel like joking.

Uranium's radioactivity did not last forever. After more than a century, it would have gone down by a lot… And that wasn't all. In an operating reactor, the fuel was replaced gradually, as it became poisoned with reaction products. Darrick had brought new fuel bundles to replace some of the old ones – if Carolin managed to identify the ones most in need of replacement.

"If there's nothing else, we're screwed."

"Then again, maybe I'll just be able to restart the reactor with a tenth of the required supply. With a huge helping of luck."

"We will have all the luck we need," Darrick spat. "Because it's our turn to have some."

Darrick toured the basilica, the mere tip of a gigantic underground edifice. Beneath the nave's floor, turbines and generators slept. The huge cylindrical dome combined the roles of a cooling tower and a containment enclosure for the reactor core below the altar. For his men, the basilica would be harder to defend than for the governor's guards. Besides the main entrance, several doors led to the main compound. Darrick assigned two men to watch each way in. The rest would guard the main doors. He wondered again if he should have recruited a few more sympathizers, but a small army tramping across the island would have been too conspicuous.

The hours went by uneventfully, as if the basilica had been utterly forgotten by the governor's men. Carolin and his team burrowed into the building's depths. Darrick only went down once below the altar. The pumps and conduits were clean enough to keep him hoping. In spite of its age, the plant might still be operational.

"Well?" Darrick asked.

"It's been used before," Carolin said, stopping to catch his breath. He was covered in sweat. Every person there had lent a hand to move the fuel rods. Hard work, even with the hoists uncovered below the dome's floor.

"Recently?"

"No, not in a dozen years, at a guess, but everything is set up for a quick start. Part of the fuel is unusable, so we'll replace it."

"What about water?"

"There's a line to the rainwater tanks inside the compound. That's enough to last most of a day. After that, who knows?"

Finally, Darrick climbed to the plant's control room, letting Carolin know he could find him there. The room ran all the way around the top of the cooling tower, just below the lip of the cupola capping the massive concrete tube. It felt more like a hallway, but the monitors embedded into the inner wall were paper-thin and the wheeled stools were easily stowed out of the way.

Actual windows had been cut into the outer wall, offering an unsurpassed view of the island and its surroundings. They revealed an expanse of countryside that might have been the main justification for establishing the control room in such an exposed position. It was the island's tallest watchtower.

Alone in the narrow gallery, Darrick completed several circuits, reading the instructions posted beside each workstation. He kept an eye on the windows, trying to spot attackers. However, while the other end of the compound was crawling with men and women at work, tiny ants picking their way through the demolished palace wing, the basilica's vicinity was still quiet.

Darrick took out a spyglass to inspect the sea near Port-Sillery. Not a trace of the man called Ségole Portelance – the name still managed to make him smile. Too bad. The fishing would have been great.

Things only started happening by the early afternoon. Off Sillery, a whole flotilla made up of canoes and boats from all points of the compass – not just a single fishing dory – appeared.

The ironbearer's spyglass did not let him make out the features of the men aboard the small craft, but he assumed they were the tribals. Newfs and Hicanos who'd sworn fealty to Ségole – whose real name was Fraser – to attempt an unprecedented raid. They were going to land on the island of Quebec and make off with anything that wasn't nailed down. At the same time, a small armed company showed up in front of the basilica.

Darrick swore. The way he'd planned it, the tribal raid would have been his second diversion, forcing his father to split up his men and delay a full-out assault of the dome. However, the tribals had come too late. They hadn't even landed yet and it might take several minutes for the good people of Port-Sillery to realize they were under attack. Several more minutes would pass before the commander in front of the dome was alerted, during which time the defenders of the basilica's main entrance would be desperately outmatched.

Darrick was on the verge of heading down when a loud ringing shattered the tomb-like silence of the control room. He guessed it was a phone, found the handset, and answered.

"Carolin here. We've gotten the reactor going and the generators are spinning. It's about a third of nominal, but we're producing power."

"I didn't hear anything."

"The dome walls are massive. But don't try to come back through the choir. We've closed all the doors and flooded the entire ground floor. The pressurized water tubes are deployed and they will dump part of their heat into the pool. Very soon, it's going to be a death zone, but everybody on the island will know we have a working nuclear reactor here."

"Enemies are at the door."

"Yes! Not only guards, but musketeers! Our guys asked me to call to let you know they need you downstairs."

"No need. I'll settle things from here."

"What?"

Darrick hung up. Once more, he toured the control room, turning on each monitor in turn. At last, he settled down in front of the screen identified with the tag "Defence lasers." The next screen over was connected to surveillance cameras. Not by coincidence.

In one document sent to Darrick by Carolin, the listing of the reactor's equipment included lasers, unspecified. The young man hadn't paid any attention to one more item, but

Darrick had been willing to bet his life that these weren't simple weather lidars.

He began by testing the cameras. Their magnification was far superior to that of his spyglass.

His augmented gaze swept over the landscape. Though the sky was clouding over, the diffuse sunlight was more than sufficient for the dome's instruments. Darrick began with the land behind the basilica. He smiled when he spotted a handful of men trying to sneak up on a secondary entrance. The poor devils! They didn't know he now controlled all of the dome's machines.

Turning back to the master screen, he deployed the eight lasers positioned all around the dome, secreted inside decorative gargoyles according to the specs.

He identified the laser covering the back of the basilica, requested a targeting zoom, and centred the reticle on a man crouching behind some bushes. He squeezed the firing button. The foliage went up in flames, as well as the guard's uniform, and then the man's hair. The guard rolled on the ground, his mouth open as he uttered inaudible shrieks.

Darrick cried out, shocked. He hadn't expected the weapon to work so well or to wield such power.

He tried again, aiming at a wall close to another would-be attacker. The man jumped and retreated hastily, spurred on by the phenomenon's inexplicable origin. His flight encouraged the others to flee as well.

Darrick was plugging into the laser covering the front of the basilica when Carolin burst into the gallery, panting hard from the climb.

"What's going on?"

The screen showed the plaza before the steps to the entrance. Half a musketeer company was standing in full battle array, guns shouldered, at the foot of the stairs. Among them, Darrick recognized Réjean Lacombe, sitting in a wheelchair. A man was leaning over, for a consultation perhaps or to tell him something. An officer maybe, since the man was older, pot-bellied, and white-haired. Or maybe not, since the stranger wasn't wearing a uniform, but an exceedingly well-cut costume.

That face was familiar... Darrick turned to Carolin and pointed at the screen.

"That's him? That's my father?"

The student nodded.

Darrick fired before he'd even thought through what he was doing. He'd had 20 years to picture this very moment, and he'd exhausted all the possible pleasures he might draw from permutations of his revenge. All that was left was anger, and the urge to erase an error and start over again. It was simple, really. He'd waited too long not to do it.

The beam struck full in the chest and the man exploded more than he burned.

"I didn't recognize him," the ironbearer admitted, his voice hushed.

Twenty years gone... He didn't feel that much older, but the years had counted double for his father. And they hadn't counted at all for his mother, who had died at sea only a few days before the ship of exiles had sighted the French coast.

The governor's nearest companions recoiled and backed away, their hair singed by the heat of the beam. A few guards tried to come to the governor's aid, undoing their capes or uniform tops to throw on the charred body. Others rushed forth courageously, sword in hand, but Darrick swung the laser beam before the entire group, sweeping the entire plaza from left to right.

The intense heat would have discouraged the hardiest souls. The flagstones fissured, the weeds growing in the cracks turned into a scatter of ashes, and drops of molten rock rained outward wherever the beam tarried a few seconds too many.

The officers ordered their men back, retreating to the edge of the plaza. The musketeers lined up again, facing the basilica entrance.

Darrick gazed upon them with growing irritation. They were mad! Why were they so obstinate about staying there?

"Time to end it," the ironbearer whispered.

"No!"

Carolin's hand came down on Darrick's, pulling back the joystick. The laser carved a glowing furrow across the plaza, only a few feet from the closest guards. Without Carolin, most of them would have been mowed down.

"What have you done!" Darrick roared.

I should have strangled him.

"But I... I couldn't let you," Carolin stammered. "It's not what I wanted."

Below, guards and musketeers broke and ran in spite of the orders shouted by their officers.

"Come on, look!"

The ironbearer grabbed the student's arm and plugged into the surveillance cameras watching Sillery. The zoom allowed him to leap over the two kilometres between the basilica and the small streets of the seaside town. The tribals had landed. For a long while, Darrick admired the show with boundless delight. His father had been so proud of Quebec, the impregnable fortress, the last bastion of the civilization of yore. No revenge could have been sweeter.

Yes, Father, I called them, I coaxed them, I promised them the greatest raid of their miserable lives, the sack and pillage of the fabled riches of the island of Quebec. And they came, no doubt as unsure as young newlyweds, and just as unable to resist their lust.

"Where did they come from?" Carolin asked, appalled.

"Out West, of course."

They were far more numerous than expected. Fraser had played it very close to his chest indeed… The tribals had to know that Quebec's gunboats would keep them from fleeing toward the mouth of the St. Lawrence. They presumably planned on heading up the Appalachian rivers and following mountain trails back to their hideouts… But numbers didn't matter, not for a man who had all the dome's lasers to play with!

The cameras allowed Darrick to pick out scenes of carnage amid the ongoing sack of Port-Sillery. Bodies shot with a blunderbuss or a tribal bow littered the streets. Houses burned. A few tribals were already heading back to their boats with a first load of loot.

Others turned their back on the port to flood the streets of Upper Sillery. Darrick finally identified Fraser as the leader of a heavily armed band of Newfs.

"This fish is too big for you, old man!"

He selected his targets and triggered a volley at the first row of oncoming Newfs. Five times his finger squeezed the button and five times human torches burned.

But not the sixth and then the seventh time. He squeezed tighter, but the laser refused to fire. While the tribal ranks had wavered for a moment, Fraser called them back to him and they marched with new resolve. Were they now looking for the way to the dome?

Darrick tried to switch lasers, even though other angles were suboptimal. The first laser might have overheated, fallen victim to accumulated wear and tear, or broken down when it had tried to swing too fast...

He used the screen to change the number of the laser linked to the joystick and he selected the targeting function again. Fraser's face filled the screen and Darrick fired.

Once again, nothing happened.

A quick glance at the secondary monitors showed him the reactor was still generating more than enough power. He tried the other lasers. Not a single one still worked. He finally gave up, staring at the pillars of smoke rising from Sillery's streets. Somewhere, a chip in the control circuit of the lasers had failed. Obviously, most parts were long past their design life-time. He should have expected it. Yet, he had come so close...

"And now?"

Carolin's voice trembled, but it was shaking from anger, not astonishment as before. Darrick understood: the young man felt betrayed. Just as the ironbearer had been betrayed by his father.

"That was your plan? Killing all your enemies with the dome's lasers and then replacing your father as our ruler?"

"Why not? He killed my older brother."

"That's because your older brother had the son from his first marriage assassinated."

"I'm ridding you of a monster!"

"Did you really believe that the population would tolerate a new governor with a trigger-happy finger and an all-powerful weapon? Especially if he took power after killing his own father and dozens of guards? Most of these men have wives, families, kids. Do you actually think they won't hate you for it? That we won't fear what you might do? You've already made yourself into a new monster. Like father, like son!"

"But..."

He bit his tongue. He had been on the verge of confessing that he was behind the Newf attack, that he had expected to repulse it with the dome's lasers to show the population that he would be their protector.

Only one thing left to do.

"Believe what you want. As my father's heir, I'm leaving this reactor to the city of Quebec. So that you can dream of a better world."

The surveillance screens showed guards and musketeers heading for Sillery. News of the Newf landing had finally reached them.

Carolin did not keep him from leaving. His arms crossed, the student stood in front of the controls, ready to prevent Darrick from trying to use the lasers again. By force, if necessary. Not that the ironbearer still wanted to.

Once he made it back down, Darrick used a whistle to gather his men. He would join the Sillery men fighting the tribals, along with anybody willing. Whatever happened next, he doubted that he would ever see his brothers again.

As he walked down the nave, his gaze wandered over the statuary erected along the side aisles. Each statue illustrated a vice or sin, both the ancient ones and the modern variants proscribed by the Church during the dark years.

There was a naked man standing erect and holding his own genitals torn off at the root. The carver had rendered its stance with a disturbing attention to the gory details: the ragged edge of the torn flesh, the dangling edge ends of veins and ligaments, the improbably gaping wounds of the groin, and the first signs of unbearable pain dawning on the lustful masturbator's face.

Other statues condemned pollution and abortion, greed and jealousy.

Yet, Darrick now regretted bitterly the absence of one additional statue. After the dark years, though, nobody had thought it necessary to remind survivors of the dangers of the sin of pride.

KALOPSIA

E. Catherine Tobler

So, they had an elephant.

We had a roller coaster.

Didn't matter how they got they elephant, did it? Zoo is a fair distance from our Playland in 'Couver, but I don't know. You ride that elephant up they broken Trans-Canada Highway like a jaguar? You ease over to they rubble-shoulder should someone come up behind you on a camel? Camels outpace elephants mostly because they sleek, but come now. Those zoo walls fell with every other wall when they bombs come and it's just a wonder they elephant doesn't glow in they dark with they rest of us. Maybe him wandered up here. Don't tell me they went all down zoo-way to get he. To intimidate us?

I can see they elephant over there, over they ugly wall of slabbed pavement. They wall divides their territory from our territory, worse than they saltwater-flooded deep-deep between. I can't bear they water, much as I want they lake on they other side of they wall; they deep-deep swallowed Momma whole like fish with bug. Was easy to row over in a swan boat, around they bits of carnival trash still poked above they surface; less easy to knock that wall over. We had tried.

They elephant walks a never-ending path along they whole wall, ridden by sister.

Na'Talie who hoists a radio antenna and has lashed an umbrella to they saddle for a bit of shade even if they sun ain't come out in days and they ain't no radio. Thick clouds like it's going to storm, but all it does is humidify. One hooked tusk of ivory protrudes from they left side of they face – they elephant, not Na'Talie – and I seen it used with great effect. Not that Na'Talie don't have tusks. They just inside where they surprise more. My sister like that.

"Lady."

"Tssst!"

Waved Robert silent, but could hear he as him scrambled up they coaster lifthill toward me. Didn't have to look to picture he, all elbows and knees and gawk despite being four decades old. Long black hair, longer black beard, eyes always hid behind goggles that had you looking at your own reflection. Was something to scold he and see my angry face shining right back at in they round lenses, dreadlock crown bobbing.

"*Lady.*"

"Tssst!"

Robert had they grace to drop to he belly when him reach they top of they hilled track; him wriggled to my side fishlike, peeking toward Na'Talie and they elephant. Wasn't so much new news to be had up here, as it was finding a calm in things as they ever had been. They had they fresh water and we wanted it. I wouldn't have hollered over someone bringing me that elephant, either.

When I looked at Robert, was my own face looking at me in they lenses. Him grinned through they grime that covered he, breathing a little hard from they climb up here, but he held him tongue until I nodded to tell he could finally talk.

Wasn't no express need for he to be quiet, but I sure did enjoy watching he squirm like a worm on my hook.

"Lady, there is a new boy come," he said, and this surprised they way they elephant had first surprised because they hadn't been no new people in a long while. No one wandering up from they south to see if things fared better near they harbour, no one looking for lost loved ones or lost hated ones; no babies born to my people, neither. No babies in far too long and this worried me more than some little.

"Boy say his name is Beth."

"You sure that boy ain't confused?"

After they bombs, most people weren't right in one way or another. You could list they all down – people more angry, more aggressive, more outright stupid or cautious or hungry or lame or fierce or flighty or what*ever* – but mostly everyone was broken. Was a matter of figuring each out, how they pieces had been broke and pressed back together, like they wall that kept us from they fresh water. That was how we knew how to use people, how to use they broken to our advantage.

"Probably confused. I mean… you know."

I watched my crown of hair bob in they lenses. Didn't care what they boy's name was. Other things mattered. Having another body meant another mouth to feed and water, but it also meant another body for they next assault on they wall. "He bring tribute?"

"Yes, Maj."

My eyes went to slits at that title and Robert's grin widened. Made for a curious look on he, wearing my angry eyes in him lenses and he happy mouth on him face. Didn't like being called majesty or anything, because it was those kinds of people who got they world in this mess as it was.

"Aight."

Robert scampered back down they way him come. I followed down they slanty lifthill, no longer holding they handrail chain. First time, I clung to that old metal like I was near death. Now, was no matter. Death was close all they while. Chain didn't change that. My feet knew they way and if not, I deserved to be rubble on they ground.

They track glided into they station, where a train of four cars still did sit. In they station is where they made they boy kneel to wait, all this time on he bony knees on they old wood floor. Jen was waiting with he, grinning like her had caught something remarkable indeed. They sticks that skewered her hair today was red like blood. I didn't see what her was grinny about until they boy looked up, until they shadow from he body lifted and I saw they goods cradled in he arms. Green sweater came open to reveal three yellow ducks. Three.

They rubber, staring at me with they black-and-white painted-on eyes. One was missing its beak, but they others looked whole, if dirty. I looked at they boy and him at me and him didn't flinch at my stare and that's how I knew him was to stay and be a part of these people. He didn't say nothing, only waited like him knew they protocols. Maybe him did; people sure did talk once upon a time, and that was how they knew about they ducks.

In they first days when they ash was still falling every day, we was less picky about they who joined us. They was lines of people looking for food and shelter and we took all from they start on account of me shooting they other 20 people who thought they would claim they coaster first. Didn't matter none, because this place needed consecration and blood is only second-powerful to water.

From these lines of people we took everyone who met they standard proposed by they sign that still hung today. YOU MUST BE THIS TALL TO RIDE. And that pointing finger never moving from its indicated height. We found this was not as sure a method as should have been. Some people who tall are not so smart. Some people who tall are not so skilled. We weeded again, outcasting they who did not serve our purposes. They was shut from they coaster's metal embrace; they was shut from family dinner and family stories.

Now it was a puzzle to join they family. Bring me a duck, I said, and prove you know this place and its secrets. Back in They Day, they ducks was everywhere, bobbing in they water tanks for they peoples to win for a handful of coins, floating all night unmolested because people wanted they, but wouldn't steal they. Bring me a duck, I said, and here were three and something more.

From they curl of they sweater closest to Beth's waist was a bundle of three things more. These were long cylinders with fuses on they ends. He lift these and give they to me, while keeping they ducks. Dynamite was a thing almost more precious than ducks. Surely could help bring that wall down and get us inside to they fresh water.

Didn't nobody make such offers without wanting something of they own. I knew this, a lesson learned as sure as they difference between people they sign chose and people who found they ducks. I handed they dynamite to Robert and reached for they ducks. Beth placed them into my palms.

"We possess an understanding now," I said. "You come into my house offering rare ducky tributes and they get you food and shelter. But these weapons, you know what we mean do."

Beth nodded he head. Him face was dark with filth and more than a little unshaved, but he eyes were truthful. "Maj, you mean to blow that wall and take their water and I want you to take it."

"Is that right?" I drew they ducks against my bosom.

"'S been so long," Beth said, and he voice went thick with want. "Ain't done a thing in forever. Finding those ducks was like finding *something*. Hunting, finding, bringing. Didn't matter what they were, when I heard, I had to do it. Got myself out and did a thing. And now… here. Want to do more."

Oldest story. People needing something to do with they hands. Didn't matter that they world lay in rubble and had changed beyond all we had been born into.

Left Beth where he crouched and left they station, too, moving under they metal scaffold of they coaster, into they centre where we had built a city all our own. They centremost part of they tracks, where they did loop together and make it seem like they cars could jump from one to another, had been all boarded up, into a vast container where I added they three newest ducks. They fell amid their brethren, they painted eyes looking at me with expectation. Maybe they too needed something done with they time.

Our plan was not complicated, even if they water complicated what we could do; could not lay they fuses we wanted to, being on account of they harbour blown all inward and slantways. They space where they carnival had once spread was under a good 30 metres of water in most places; some places, they rides still poked up: a tented roof, a flagpole, but even they great whirly ride which flung they peoples in chairs had been swallowed by they harbour waters. Only Jen had ever dared swim in they deep-deep, looking for what could be found. Her found a duck down there, her did. Said they was cartons of them, but I never could go, not with Momma lurking.

We loaded they coaster with care. They cars had been lightened, they lapbars and wheels removed, doors soldered shut to make each car float more than it rightly should. We lined each car with plastic tarps and packed they with explosives. Beth's dynamite was wrapped up tight and wedged into they front car. Over all this plastic-wrapped death, we layered in ducks. They painted-on eyes regarded me with eagerness. They was ready to fly, these ducks! Everything needed a purpose, hadn't Momma always said? Her had not, but it seemed sound.

I had never been out across they deep-deep, but made to go now because my people needed a leader. Needed to see I could do more than stand atop they coaster and holler threats toward Na'Talie and her lake people. One time, they made they home within they coaster's skeleton same as we; but one time, they also leave they metal bones for something better. Didn't get too far, not when they ground collapsed and sucked they down – when they harbour waters flooded in and ate they up. Oh, Momma, why did you leave your own living girls?

They swan boats took us into they deep-deep. Once they had only gone in circles, but now they was as free as they ducks about to be. We paddled with lengths of broken coaster track, they swans pulling they coaster cars across they dark waters. They whole of Na'Talie's lake was circled by that patched pavement wall, they deep-deep licking up against it in they night.

All around us was they deep-deep. They metal in they waters rose like shark fins and in they waning moonlight seemed to move ever so slight. First time I saw it, I pulled back from they boat edge and leaned into Robert, Robert who grinned he grin and curled me closer. Elbow to they ribs sent him sliding back to he side of they swan, my face hovering in he lenses.

From they waters, I thought I heard a sound like they coaster cars had come loose, but they had not. All around us, a long lapping sound, like they deep-deep had a tongue and was tasting our full length. We rowed on, pulling our barge of death and ducks and was breathing hard when we reached they wall. They lanterns ringing they top of they wall were not lit and this should have been a clue to me, but I could smell they fresh water beyond they wall, and it smelled like they home I had before they coaster took me in and made me her own.

Jen and Beth headed east and my boat headed north, we each taking half they coaster cars with us; we would ring they wall with our explosives and rig them to blow when we was home. But things never go they way one thinks. For a heart-beat, I thought it was just my dreadlocks bouncing in Robert's lenses with him taking a longer look at me than him should. But him was seeing something beyond me, over they curve of my shoulder. They curve turned into a tusk they longer I looked at it in they lens, they tusk of Na'Talie's damned ele-phant. My eyes went wide then and Robert, him shove me down into they boat, lifting up he oar as a weapon.

Thing of it is, you only ever see one elephant, you think that all they have. One elephant making endless patrols around they rubble wall. What you don't see is they has two more, they tusks made up to look all they same. And when you pick yourself up from they boat bottom, and stare at they three elephants, Na'Talie looking as fierce as they day she did when she left, showing off she tusks, you scream. I screamed loud enough to wake Momma from death, but her did not come to see she girls fight.

They three elephants swam through they dark water, one straight into Jen's boat, another straight into mine. And this swan boat, it had been a hard-working craft, but wasn't made to take no elephant head across its bow. They boat splintered, spilling me and Robert into they deep-deep.

Was strange, that water. So quiet and calm beneath they choppy surface. I could see they elephant legs paddling my way, looking almost serene as it came for me. That head dipped under they water, beady eyes narrowing, trunk expelling bubbled breath. Blind in they froth, I swore I could feel Momma's bony hand around my ankle. Wasn't nothing but a weed, self told self, but that weed gave me a tug and wanted to see me drown.

Elephant was on me, trunk wrapping my arm, and I heard Na'Talie screaming in her warrior voice that no one would take she wall, she elephants, she *land*. Felt like my lungs would burst, then thought they did, because they entire world exploded. Was blown straight out of they deep-deep and flying, as I watched in wonder fire blossoming against they night, bringing they wall down. And Jen and Beth, they airborne! Beth shrieked with laughter, burning sticks clutched in him hands.

Everywhere was fire and raining deep-deep and flying rubble wall and, oh Momma, they *ducks*. They ducks blew up with everything else Jen had set on fire; one explosion led to another, and another, and it was forever I was watching they ducks vomit into they sky on clouds of fire. When I fell back into they deep-deep, was a hard slap to my entire body. Then, it rained ducks, and ducks, and when I could at last see again, was my own angry face shining right back in they round lenses, dreadlock crown bobbing.

We swam to they first steady thing: an elephant surrounded by bobbing, yellow ducks. We climbed on that broad back and swam they elephant round and round. Swam to they gates blown off they wall and crawled off, and watched Na'Talie flounder in they deep-deep. Her didn't want to be with Momma no more than I did. Made Robert stay and hollered at that elephant till he let me sit again and swim he toward Na'Talie and haul she on board. Her stare at me like death. If death was crying and hugging and saying oh near lost you like Momma in they deep-deep.

And when I thought that was all? They coaster blew sky high. Wood and metal whizzed through they air like rockets, smashing into they deep-deep, shooting one lens straight out of Robert's goggles. And ducks. All they that we hadn't packed up, oh Momma, they rained down on us like constant tribute.

When they all settled, it was a strange quiet crept over us. They deep-deep lapped its tongue against our legs crossways over they elephant as him swam to Robert. We all climbed out on they narrow shore, Jen and Beth shivering on a slab of pavement. Was like none of us knew what to do, so Na'Talie hauled she people and she elephants from they waters and looked at me. Looked at me like life and possibility and then her bent and picked up a duck.

And placed it in my hands like tribute.

WHITE NOISE

Geoff Gander

George? It's Amanda. How are you holding out? Good. No one else is picking up anymore. Is your radio on? Satellite? That's good – more stations that way. No, don't go to your car; too exposed. Stay away from the windows, too.

What's that? Yeah, it's been three days now, I think. I had to switch half a dozen times last night. People at the stations are getting sloppy, or they're... well, you've seen the news feeds. I think they either don't know and they're covering it up, or they do know and they don't want us to panic. I mean, sunspots, electromagnetic disturbance, and then finally a terrorist attack? Whatever. One of the last things I read on the boards before they went dead was that regular talking doesn't have the right mix of sounds, pitch, or whatever, to block them.

No... no TV news here, either. Just reruns, with that scrolling message to stay indoors and keep a radio going until further notice.

Still haven't seen any of the neighbours. I read on the Net this weird post about how people who hear the noise get "empty," or turned into monsters or something. Anyhow, we've got enough food for a week so hopefully it'll all be—

George? George? You still there? Oh thank God. You went dead for a moment and I thought – Your station got cut off? I heard somewhere that all it takes is a minute of silence before you can hear it.

Yeah, Mom hasn't contacted me, either. I called her apartment and the super's office – nothing. I mean, maybe she's found a safe place. She doesn't have a car, so she couldn't have gone far.

Shit, station's dead!

Me again. I'm okay, I'm okay… yeah, I know I told Dad I'd rather die than listen to Garth Brooks, but I wasn't being choosy. Seriously, George, that was close. It took me almost a minute to find a new station, and I started hearing it. No, it wasn't like the static you get on the radio or TV. There was a pattern to it, but it didn't repeat or anything. Like a strange language? Maybe, but I haven't seen any little green men running around.

Ken? He's really stressed out. His folks haven't answered his calls and every time we lose a station he gets really high-strung. He says he's heard the noise after only a few seconds but I think it's just – huh, really? Maybe he is more sensitive, then. I sent him down to the pantry to bring up some more cans just before I called you. He should be done by now.

Oh, I hear him coming up the stairs. I'll pass him the phone when he gets here. He'd like to talk to another dude, I'm sure.

Hey, Ken, George's on the line. Do you want to talk to him for a bit?

Ken?

No, he's not usually so quiet. Hold on a sec, George. I'll be right back.

EDITED HANSARD 116

Miriam Oudin

55th PARLIAMENT, 1st SESSION
EDITED HANSARD • NUMBER 116
Tuesday, May 18, 2027

Speaker: The Honourable Katherine Elk Hoof

The House met at 10 a.m.

Prayers

ROUTINE PROCEEDINGS

Support for Families of the Lost Act

Mr. Felix Tall Bear (Batoche—One Arrow, NDP)
moved for leave to introduce C-61, <u>Support for Families of the Lost</u>.
He said: Madam Speaker, I am very proud to introduce a bill concerning financial support for the immediate families of those lost in the recent tragedies. Though we have all for good reason been concerned with addressing the continuing crisis itself, it is my hope that my colleagues turn their thoughts for

a moment to the families left behind, particularly in my home province of Saskatchewan and her neighbouring province of Alberta, though I know that the ripple effects have spread to all Canadians, including many of my colleagues in this room.

(Motion deemed adopted, bill read the first time and printed.)

Petitions

Wall Surrounding the Black Zone

Ms. Evelyn Carew (Cardigan, CPC):
Madam Speaker, I would like to present a petition signed by 37 people from Prince Edward Island.

The petitioners are calling for a promise from the government to build a wall around the black zone.

Goods from Alberta and Saskatchewan

Mr. Loïc Coulombe (Wendake—Loretteville, Lib.):
Madam Speaker, I have in front of me a petition from a number of my constituents who are asking the government to put a moratorium on distributing fruits, vegetables, and meats from Alberta and Saskatchewan to elsewhere in the country.

The fact is, we don't know whether there is contamination of some sort, whether there might be something in the soil or water that could damage plant or animal life that it comes into contact with. My constituents are concerned that there might be carcinogens or other health risks. The temporary lag in business is a small price to pay for certainty that the foods we feed our families are safe.

GOVERNMENT ORDERS

Pursual of Absent Persons Act

Bill S-2—Time Allocation Motion

Hon. Harshad Ram (Leader of the Government in the House of Commons, CPC)
moved:
That, in relation to Bill S-2, An Act respecting the so-called "Absent," which is to say those who have not returned from the Athabascan oil sands since the troubles there began, not more than five further hours shall be allotted to the consideration of the third reading stage of the bill.

The Speaker:
Under Standing Order 67.1, there will now be a 30-minute question period.

Mr. Vasily Sénéchal (Leader of the Opposition, Lib.):
Madam Speaker, I would like to express my grave disappointment at the Conservative party's attempt to shut down conversation about this very important issue. I don't think there is anyone in this chamber who does not want our fellow Canadians to return safely from the black zone. But ramming a piece of ill-thought legislation through the House is not in anyone's best interest. Nor is sending more soldiers and police to their deaths. It is critical that we consult with experts: disaster recovery consultants, geologists, xenobiologists, xenobotanists, communications specialists. My colleague would do well to remember that we can watch streaming video from

Mars but we can't see anything that's happening in Alberta north of 54. Sending more personnel into the black zone is literally more dangerous than sending them to another planet, and for some reason the Conservative party seems unwilling to spend more than five hours talking about that.

Hon. Nurul Huda Abidi (Newmarket—Aurora—King, CPC)

Madam Speaker, the hon. member is deeply mistaken about this party's motivations in bringing forward a time allocation motion. By preventing further speechifying in the House, this government can finally move ahead and act to save the lives of our fellow Canadians, including the civilians who made their homes in Fort McMurray and the frontline workers from the energy companies who first disappeared, the police who sought to extract them, the EMTs and other first responders, and the armed forces personnel who we have since lost contact with. We want all of them to come home. They cannot come home unless we stop talking about this bill and enact it. Calling a bunch of university professors and asking for their opinions on something that none of them have dealt with before is a complete waste of time. Xenowhateverologists are no better equipped to deal with this than we are. We all pray that our fellow Canadians are still alive, and if they are alive, they need our help and forward action, they don't need us sitting around making phone calls to academics.

Ms. Helen Waterfall (Ermineskin—Hobbema, GP):

Madam Speaker, I find it ironic that the hon. members are so sure that they know what's best for my province when neither of them, so far as I am aware, have been west of Etobicoke so far this decade. Have you done a flyover and seen the churn that's currently consuming Athabasca? Have you felt that satanic mud pull on your boots even in the supposedly safest parts of central Alberta? Have you?

The Speaker:
Order. I would remind the hon. members to address the chair and not to speak directly to their colleagues.

Mr. Vasily Sénéchal:
Madam Speaker, with all due respect, the member opposite has no better idea of what's good for her riding than any of us do, since, like all of us, she can't see it, she can't visit it, she doesn't know what is happening in it, nobody can even agree on its boundaries since they're all under several metres of pulsing sludge. No doubt everybody appreciated that photo op the member did in a hazmat suit standing by the big Do Not Enter sign. That looked very good, very heroic. But is that really research? There hasn't been a flyover in at least two months, at least not since March when we lost radio contact with seven jets, only five of which, I am sorry to remind you, Madam Speaker, returned home. I don't doubt that what the member saw on that flyover was very disturbing, but disturbing images glimpsed through the window of an airplane 10 weeks ago is not enough to base a policy on. If we wish to make informed decisions about what is to be done in the black zone, we need more than dramatic pictures. There needs to be discussion, both here on the floor and with expert committees set up for the purpose. I will not support a law whose only possible outcome is the needless death of more of our armed forces personnel and first responders.

Some Hon. Members:
Oh, oh!

The Speaker:
Order, please. There are seven minutes left for questions and I need to be able to hear the members speak.

Hon. Nurul Huda Abidi:
Madam Speaker, I believe it is an insult to our military and to our first responders to restrict them from doing what they are trained to do. Frankly I am surprised that the other parties would rather talk on the phone with professors than send help to the black zone.

Some Hon. Members:
Oh, oh!

The Speaker:
Order, I must insist. The hon. member from Newmarket—Aurora—King has the floor.

Hon. Nurul Huda Abidi:
I have spoken to the Alberta teams and, Madam Speaker, they are champing at the bit, they want to go help. They don't want us to be sitting around the House talking any more than we do. I received a letter from Diego Cordon, the chief of police in Red Deer, and we had a great conversation on the phone. There isn't enough time left for me to read his letter to you, but I just want you to know that brave people like him are eager to go and help, and I am frustrated that the parties opposite are slowing that process down.

STATEMENTS BY MEMBERS

Displaced Persons

Ms. Kisi Armah-Cohen (Edmonton—Holyrood, GP):
Madam Speaker, I would like to congratulate the generous and good-hearted members of my riding for volunteering their time and money, and even in some cases opening their homes, to the displaced populations of Lac La Biche, Cold Lake, Meadow Lake, Bonnyville, and surrounding areas.

My colleagues elsewhere in Alberta and Saskatchewan, particularly the members from Edmonton—Strathcona and Wetaskiwin who have worked so tirelessly on the Black Flood Emergency Committee, have been nothing less than champions, setting up dozens of reception centres across southern Alberta, and organizing hundreds of thousands of dollars worth of donations from well-wishers across Canada. The member from Wetaskiwin and I don't agree on very much politically, but credit where credit is due, he has the best interests of displaced Canadians at heart, as we all do I'm sure.

However, Madam Speaker, there is still much work to be done. Housing and feeding nearly 20,000 people who have been evacuated from their homes is no small task, especially when the families in my own riding are feeling their own worry, feeling their own stress about the advancing churn.

I know that these troubles may feel very far away to my colleagues in Eastern Canada, and of course unlike other natural disasters, this one cannot be photographed, which makes it hard to even imagine. But I would like everyone in this

House to understand, Madam Speaker, that this is a Canadian problem, not an Alberta problem, not a Saskatchewan problem. The zone has already crossed one provincial boundary and is fast approaching a territorial boundary: natural disasters do not care where we draw lines on the map, and in a crisis like this, neither should we.

Black Zone Containment

Ms. Grace Martin (Assiniboia, NDP):
Madam Speaker, in the five months since the troubles began, the damage has spread nearly 40,000 square kilometres, according to research that was being conducted at the University of Alberta before the brownouts made it impossible to proceed. Clearly containment is a priority, and we must consider effective strategies before it is too late. With all due respect to the member from Cardigan and the constituents who signed the petition there, a wall is not good enough, since by all reports the churn bubbles out of cracks in the ground and does not simply flow across the surface.

I have been in dialogue with experts in Florida, where the porous ground makes flood containment very difficult and where levees cannot prevent, for instance, a grassy park from flooding from below. I spoke to a team of scientists at the University of South Florida in Tampa, who have been doing some excellent research on containment of water floods. We are not dealing with water, to be sure, but I still believe that their work can help us make sure the damage does not spread even further than it has.

ORAL QUESTIONS

Travel Abroad

Mr. Vasily Sénéchal (Leader of the Opposition, Lib.):
Madam Speaker, I wish the prime minister were here to hear the remarks I've prepared today, because I think it is important that she hear them and respond to them here in the House and not by way of a prerecorded video call three days later. Frankly I think it is quite embarrassing that she is neglecting her duty to the House and to the country by taking business trips overseas at the taxpayers' expense, instead of comforting grieving families and creating solutions to the problems the rest of us are dealing with here at home. At the same time I am not surprised, since it is very typical for the ruling party to spend more time wooing West African oil barons than showing sympathy to its own citizens.

Hon. Stella Ip (Minister of International Trade, CPC):
Madam Speaker, as usual the member opposite has twisted the prime minister's motives in order to make her sound like some kind of monster. I think it is important that the record be set straight. The prime minister is travelling to other oil-rich countries because we need to strengthen our economic and political relationships with them in these troubled times. I wonder if the other parties have noticed that the sources of oil we have here at home are under threat. The price of oil hasn't risen this steeply since the OPEC crises of the 1970s. I wonder if the members here today thought about where their next tank of gas is coming from as they drove their cars here today.

Ms. Kisi Armah-Cohen (Edmonton—Holyrood, GP):
Madam Speaker, some of us didn't drive our cars here because we are committed to public transit and sustainable ways of living, and I might suggest that had the members of the Conservative party thought more carefully about environmental sustainability, instead of thinking about how to dig as deep a hole in the tar sands as it was possible to dig, we might not be in this mess in the first place.

The Speaker:
Order. The member for Edmonton—Holyrood still has the floor. I realize these are controversial issues but I remind members to watch their language in the House.

Ms. Kisi Armah-Cohen:
Madam Speaker, setting my previous comments aside for the moment, I have a different question. Clearly it would be reprehensible if the prime minister were simply wheeling and dealing with the president of Nigeria and wining and dining the King of Dubai and whatnot, rather than facing the crisis situation here in Canada. But I am wondering if the hon. members opposite would be willing to address rumours that their leader has arranged her meetings with the leadership of these countries for other, not-strictly-business-related reasons.

Hon. Stella Ip:
Madam Speaker, if the member is making an accusation I suggest that she come out and say it.

Some hon. members:
Oh, oh!

The Speaker:
Order. Let the member answer.

Ms. Kisi Armah-Cohen:
Madam Speaker, I make no accusation. I had simply assumed that the minister has opened even a single newspaper or magazine or website within the past week and would therefore know what I am talking about. Given her important position in the cabinet, I had not considered the possibility that she is not keeping up with current events. Well then, I suppose I must be the bearer of bad news. *The Toronto Mail* published an exposé yesterday morning which reported that other oil-producing countries are beginning to experience a churn similar to ours, but that they are for the moment keeping it successfully under wraps. Though I disagree with almost all of this government's policies and almost all of the actions and priorities of the current prime minister, I would actually be relieved to hear that she is attending summits about environmental issues rather than simply trying to bargain for better prices for oil on the open market.

Hon. Stella Ip:
Madam Speaker, I do, as it happens, read newspapers. It had simply not occurred to me that the member from Edmonton—Holyrood would be citing the *Mail*'s absurd story, which is backed up by no evidence whatsoever and which is an embarrassment to journalism. There is no black mud eating Nigeria.

The Speaker:
Order. Many members are rising for questions and it is important for as many as possible to be heard. Now the member for Yukon has the floor.

Mr. Stanley Joseph (Yukon, NDP):
Madam Speaker, I know that none of us would base accusations—

Ms. Kisi Armah-Cohen:
It was not an accusation.

Mr. Stanley Joseph:
Fine, none of us would knowingly bring information into the House that is not supported by evidence. But what would suitable evidence look like, given that the black zone can't be photographed? Even the cameras on the ISS can't penetrate the smog cover, and obviously the ISS has its own problems right now anyway. On top of that, contrary to what the Conservative party wants the public to believe, we don't know what the risks are in sending more vehicles into the zone. My party is not confident that it is safe to do so, and we find it repulsive that the Conservatives want to legislate them into advancing just for the sake of glamour shots of "sending in the tanks." That approach hasn't served us very well so far.

My point, Madam Speaker, is that if Nigeria or Dubai or other countries are experiencing similar natural disasters, I imagine they are also encountering similar problems in documenting those disasters, whether or not they are actively trying to cover something up. I would prefer to assume good faith on the part of those governments, but of course that would be easier if the prime minister were honest about her motives in meeting with them.

Hon. Stella Ip:
Madam Speaker, I wish everyone wouldn't speak as if it is a perfectly normal assumption that there is churn anywhere but Alberta and Saskatchewan. From what I understand, the type of bituminous sands we have here are unique to Canada, and maybe I think Kazakhstan or somewhere over there, so oil fields in other parts of the world don't have the same chemical makeup or underlying structure that would lead to this unique set of problems. I would like the members to stop coming up with conspiracy theories, and instead focus on the work the government is doing to make sure we all still have access to fuel and plastic, and the lifestyle to which we as Canadians are accustomed.

Scientific Expertise

Mr. Kwang-Hee Park (Cornwall—Akwesasne, Lib.)
Madam Speaker, if the Conservatives were willing to discuss this with a panel of experts who have spent their whole lives learning about geology and geography, as the leader of my party mentioned earlier, then we might well find an answer to the question of what's causing the churn and how to stop it without needing to turn to, as the minister calls them, conspiracy theories.

Hon. Cedric Vilandré (Minister of Foreign Affairs, CPC)
Madam Speaker, the opposition keeps moving the goalposts. First they are angry with the prime minister for advocating on behalf of Canadians in Africa and the Middle East. Now they are inventing imaginary disaster scenarios for those other countries and complaining that the prime minister is not calling up every university in North America looking for solutions to these made-up problems, which are suddenly more important than the churn that has killed, wounded, or displaced so many of our fellow citizens here at home. If this is what the opposition wants to hear so badly, then very well, I'll say it for their benefit: our prime minister is not solving imaginary made-up problems in Nigeria or sitting on the phone with some intellectual who wrote a dissertation on Belgian fossils. Instead she is making sure that our oil supply is uninterrupted and that Canada continues to deal with her business partners growthfully and with integrity. I hope that confession makes the parties across the way happy over there.

GOVERNMENT ORDERS

Message from the Senate

The Speaker (Hon. Katherine Elk Hoof):
I have the honour to inform the House that a message has been received from the Senate informing this House that the Senate has passed the following public bill to which the concurrence of this House is desired: Bill S-9, An Act to amend the Cancer Screening Act.

Gasoline Rationing Act

The House resumed from May 9 consideration of the motion that Bill C-11, An Act to amend the Canada Transportation Act (Gasoline Rationing), be read the third time and passed.

The Speaker (Hon. Katherine Elk Hoof):
The motion to adjourn the House is now deemed to have been adopted. Accordingly, this House stands adjourned until tomorrow at 10 a.m., pursuant to an order made on Monday, April 26, 2027 and Standing Order 24(1).

(The House adjourned at 3:44 p.m.)

THE BODY POLITIC

John Jantunen

The body appeared in the first week of August. It was already hot that morning even though it was too early for anyone else to be about, except for maybe the boy who brought the paper. The paperboy, yes, the very reason I was out before the sun had had a chance to colour the sky in reds and orange. I wanted to stop him, yes, to catch him, so that I could have a word with him about the state that my dailies were in when they arrived. More and more they looked, well – and this was the odd thing – they looked like someone had already read them. Or really, if I wanted to get to the crux of the matter, they looked like a lot of people had read them. With their curling edges and their torn pages, their smudged ink and smears of brown that could have been coffee but could just as easily have been something else, they looked, in fact, like they'd been passed from one end of a city bus to the other with each person in between taking what they needed and discarding the rest on the seat beside them, or on the floor, where they would sit until the driver, at the end of his shift, tired and too grumpy to take any care about it, would come along and gather them up, which would go a long way to explaining why sometimes the pages were out of order, like I'd found with yesterday's paper, pages out of order and one page out of order and in the wrong section.

So I was up early waiting for the boy to arrive and when he did?

—Be nice, dear.

That was my wife, the eternal her to my him, and it was good advice, excellent advice, just the kind of advice that I'd always relied on her for. She had sound judgment, if nothing else (and that's not to say that she had nothing else; she had all the regular charms of the opposite sex; had all the smells, all the curves and all the softness that made my fingers dance too lightly when we were lying together, making her laugh and tell me to be more firm, always more firm). And it was her judgement, since I'd retired, that I'd retreated into, telling myself, for a start, that it was easier that way. Easier because I no longer had anywhere to hide; no more job, no more quick nips on the way home, no more ways of pretending I was listening while my mind was on other things. Now my mind was always on one thing and one thing only. But what was it? The house? No, not that. It wasn't something as tangible as that, though I wished that it was as tangible as an old farmhouse at the end of a lane that was dirt when we moved in but was now paved right up to the driveway, the last on the road, the last, if anyone wanted to know, in the town itself, its back to a ravine and a wall of cedar hedges surrounding its front so that it was possible to believe that we were the only ones left. And if it weren't for the odd phone call, and the even odder visit from our son, it'd be almost impossible to believe there was anyone else, but he hadn't visited for... How long was it? Last Christmas? I'd have to ask her, she'd know. Right after I talked to the paperboy I'd ask her, ask her, I'd ask her?

First we'd have eggs and toast and we'd drink that stuff that came out of a bottle and didn't taste like coffee but which I was supposed to pretend did. Then I'd ask her?

—Damn it, where's that paperboy?

I hadn't meant to say it out loud but there she was behind me, holding the paper. Its edges were curled up and I could see a rip on the first page, a rip right through the lead article, an intolerable rip that had no place severing the head of the prime minister, a man who, granted, I hadn't voted for, but a man who still didn't deserve his head flapping off to one side, his body clenched tightly against her fingers. Her nails yellowing, flecks of red dotting the surface, dotting the surface like, like, dotting the surface?

—I already got it. He came while you were in the bathroom.

—You saw him?

—Well no, I didn't see him.

—Then how do you know?

—I heard it hit the door. And here it is. Now why don't you come in. I've made eggs.

But I wasn't listening. I was striding, most definitely striding, I could feel it through the soles of my slippers, I was striding through the door and down the steps, striding toward where the hedge broke at the end of the walkway, toward the road that still smelled like dirt except on rainy days when it smelled like what it was – crumbling blacktop – and my hands were swinging at my side, swinging like a man of 40, a man who had things to do, a man who didn't wear slippers all day and sometimes a bathrobe, a man who knew people and was known, a man who knew how to get things done, a man who, when I got to the road, would most definitely not be nice, not be a dear, I'd be a man who knew, who knew, I'd be a man who?

But before I broke past the hedge and confronted the road, confronted the very likely empty road with my anger and my venom, before I blasted the road for being empty, before I let that goddamn road have it good and square, before any of that I saw the body lying at the edge of the lawn. It was part-way concealed by the hedge as if, before it was a body, it'd tried to crawl under it, maybe to get out of the heat or to hide or maybe for no reason at all. Now though, with all that trying to get cool and trying to get out of sight and trying to do god-knows-what-else out of the way, it lay there, one leg and one hand resting beneath the hedge, being quite definitely a body. It was the smell that gave it away, that told me immediately that it was a body and not, say, a drunk passed out which would have made sense too since there were a lot of drunks these days (I'd read in the newspaper alarming statistics, alarming, and that was just the other morning while I was waiting for my breakfast on a day not unlike this). And being drunks they frequently passed out somewhere so why not in our yard, which was out of sight of the rest of town and might as well have been alone on the planet for all the visitors who made their way to the end of the lane, the asphalt pitted and bits of it strewn in the ditches so that it wasn't any better than the gravel it had replaced. No, I couldn't think of a better place for a drunk to pass out, except that it wasn't a drunk, it was a body, and one that was old, maybe three or four days if the way it smelled was any clue. The smell, or rather the stench – a clinging, cloying, sticking-to-the-hairs-in-my-nose stink – stopped me at five paces from it, all pretence of blasting the road spent in the odour that even now (has it been five days? six? I couldn't say) lingers, making me wipe and rub and dig about the inside of my nose with a pinkie hoping, somehow, to dislodge it so I could forget, even though now (seven days later? eight?) I'm way beyond forgetting and would be happy with just being able to smell the way I used to.

Not knowing what to do, I looked back at the house hoping she'd still be there, standing at the door, a reservoir of good advice, just waiting to splash a little my way, but the door was closed; closed against the bugs and the heat and (let's be honest, I told myself) the scene I was about to make had the body not intervened, had the body not brought me to my senses, had the body, the body, had the body?

—There's a body out there.

—Out where?

Standing in the kitchen now, facing her back, bent over the wood stove, making breakfast even though it was far too early to be eating, the question threw me, made me pause to consider, made me, all of a sudden, wonder if things were really as bad as all that.

Out where?

What kind of a question was that? Did it strike at the core? I thought not but then maybe it did, maybe I was wrong, maybe bodies had a habit of turning up frequently enough, with enough regularity, that their location was the most important thing, trumped all other questions, questions like, like?

—Didn't you hear what I said? There's a goddamn body out there.

—No need to scream.

—There's a body?

—I heard you the first two times. Now sit down, your eggs are ready.

—But what about the body?

—I'm sure it will be fine.

—Fine, how can it be? I mean, it's?

—Yes, dear?

—It's a goddamn body and?

—Please keep your voice down.

—And it's on our front yard.

—So you said.

—Well, don't take my word for it. You can see for your goddamn self.

Setting my plate of eggs next to a large glass of water to wash them down since we were out of the other stuff – the pretend coffee – she touched my arm and smiled. I knew what that smile meant, and for a moment I felt foolish, like a child who wouldn't take no for an answer and ended up in his room because of it. But then the anger was back and I wouldn't sit down, I wouldn't, I wouldn't damn well?

—What are you doing?

—I'm calling the police. What am I doing?

The phone was in my hand and my fingers were pounding on the keys. After three pounds the phone was at my ear and I was listening between rings, to the dead air between the rings, listening between the rings?

—Something wrong, dear?

—The phone's dead.

—Probably a tree down on the line.

A tree down, sure, it all made sense. But still I stood with the phone to my ear, listening between the rings, waiting and listening, listening and waiting?

—Your eggs are getting cold.

—Blast it!

I slammed the receiver down with enough force to send a spike through my knuckles, a pain that felt like a nail driven into my fingers, sparing only the thumb, like the thumb was special, like the thumb had a plan, an idea, like the thumb was, the thumb was, like the thumb was?

And then I was back at the table staring at my plate.

—What the hell are these?

—Blueberries.

—Where's my toast?

—We're out of toast. Maybe tomorrow. Now eat.

Good advice, yes, excellent. I took a forkful of the scrambled-up eggs. They were dry, I could tell from the way they hung dully on my fork. Not a hint of glisten. Not a trace of shine. Would it kill her to add a little butter, I thought, and my eyes drifted to the fridge. The fridge, yes. There it was, most certainly a fridge, sitting where a fridge should sit, next to the stove and a little further on, the sink. Nothing but the floor in between to keep me from walking right over to it and getting myself some butter – a little glisten, a taste of shine – but still I sat, staring, the eggs growing cold on the plate in front of me, the smell of something dead in my nose. Something dead. A body. A dead body.

—When was the last time Chris visited?

—Chris?

—Our son, damn it. The boy.

A momentary waver. A quiver to her hand. So, I was getting somewhere. After long last. Here it was. I was on the verge of it now.

—I don't?

—Was it a week ago?

—It's hard?

—A month?

—I?

—Was it Christmas, for Christ's sake? Was that when he came? Damn it, woman, speak!

—Yes. It was Christmas.

—And now the first week of August. Shameful, it's shameful.

With new resolve I pitched my fork into the yellow cloud of eggs. I crammed them into my mouth, thinking about toast and coffee, and bacon, and not looking at the fridge, most definitely not looking?

—Where are you going?

For she was going somewhere, was at the back door, her hand turning, turning, her hand on the knob, turning?

—I'm going to feed the chickens.

I couldn't think of anything to say to that so I harrumphed, harrumphed hard, with no regard for the eggs mashing against my teeth so that little bits flew out. There was one on my sleeve so I flicked at it. It made the most unbelievable sound as it hit the floor – a clattering – so out of place for a fleck of eggs, not at all like an egg should sound, especially a fleck so small, and then it occurred to me that it must have been the door and not the egg at all. Which made sense. Sure, in a world such as this?

At the window over the sink: The plate was in my hand, worried maybe about something in the sink so it clung to my fingers, trying to act all casual so my hand wouldn't notice it still hanging there, the same way my hand was trying to avoid my eyes because my eyes were onto something, on the verge, distinctly and definitely on the verge of the thing. And my hands wanted no part of it, my hands had enough to worry about. My hands were already thinking about the paper sitting on the table. Thumbing through it, thumbing, yes thumbing, all the way through, a test of their mettle and merit, a true test of their moxie, and me along for the?

—They burnt down the Parliament Building. The prime minister set the first torch, it says. He said we're on our own now. Say, what happened to you?

She was at the sink. Dirt covered in dirt. Hands, I could see, like they'd been dipped in it, her hair wild like straw, and a smell, something familiar, a smell I couldn't place but even now (nine, 10 days later) I can't get rid of. Most definitely the smell of something, of something, the smell of... something.

D-DAY

T.S. Bazelli

Seven days after D-Day

That's what we've taken to calling it: D-Day, the day every-body disappeared. One minute cars zipped past the bus stop, the next, they just stopped. Oh, they're still there, parked in the middle of the road. It's like their drivers cut the engines and just walked away. Only no one ever came back, and it all happened in the time it took to glance at my watch and back up again.

It's eerie walking around Vancouver these days. No women in tight yoga pants walking small yappy dogs, no kids running around the yard at the high school down Cambie Street, no early morning joggers.

But you should see the house. It hasn't been this full since the last time the grandkids came over for Christmas. There were five of us waiting at the bus stop on D-Day, and for some reason, whatever took the rest, just passed us by.

They're all staying at our house until we figure out what's going on. It made sense to invite them over, since we lived the closest, and I know you'd have done the same.

You'd be proud! I've been feeding our guests, and cleaning up around the house so that everything's in good order for when you come back. I know you will. It all happened so suddenly that it stands to reason things will go back to normal just as fast. We've even got a board up in the living room with bets on how long it will take, and you know I'm a gambling man.

It's been all right so far. There's a middle-aged couple from the Island, the Snows; a young kid, Ying; and this quiet banker, Tom.

We've been trying to get in touch with everyone's families but the phones just ring and ring. I drove Ying and Tom over to their houses but their families are gone too. No one's answering emails. For now, it seems safer if we stick together, just in case.

Eight days after D-Day

Something's wrong with the Internet. Whatever's happened must be global or else Vancouver's been cut off from the rest of the world. Ying's some kind of engineering whiz from UBC and she's been scouring the Net for days. Everything's still working fine, but all that social media, you know, those YouTubes and Twitters, and Facebooks, no one's posted anything for days. Ying says that's bad.

What if we're the only ones left?

Two weeks after D-Day

No matter how hard we try to figure out what's happened, we can't come up with anything. There's no way to prove who's right one way or the other. Did we miss the end of days? Did aliens just decide we weren't worth taking? Did some crazy science experiment go wrong? It's a great big mystery that's way beyond me, and maybe all of us.

The pantry's looking a bit thin now and the Snows want to prepare for the worst. They say we've got to focus on living. How long will the power last? How long will the phone lines stay open? How long until the sewers back up?

The Snows keep looking to me for answers. You'd laugh. I know I'm no spry young thing but I haven't been around long enough to know how to live without electricity. I say Ying's our best shot. She's been printing off manuals written by a bunch of twentysomethings interested in doing things the hard way. Hipsters, she calls them? DIYers? I can't get the jargon right. It looks like the future is the year 1900.

The kid's got some really good ideas (You'd like her).

Tom's an odd one. He doesn't seem interested in anything but passing the time reading through our book collection. Mostly he reads the Bible. I suppose sometimes we need to do whatever makes life more bearable.

None of this makes any sense. Why did we get left behind? Where did you go?

I imagine you coming home and having a good laugh about it over tea, your eyes wide, the way they get when you've got a good joke to share. I hope you're having an adventure, love.

Twenty-two days after D-Day

We've resorted to thievery! I suppose no one will blame us for trying to survive. Most of the fresh produce in the stores is starting to rot, and there are flies everywhere. Soon all the stores will be stinking and crawling with maggots.

We've filled up the house with supplies from the hardware store and the nearest supermarkets. There's so much to do to become self-sufficient, and it's all a little overwhelming. I'm not sure I can get a hang of it, but the Snows have been a great help. They're excited about all the construction. I think they're secretly a couple of environmentalists, which is handy. Judy Snow knows a few things about herbal remedies and growing edible plants. Bob Snow did a lot of camping and fishing in his youth. They're both trying to teach me all this now. I wouldn't know how to start a fire from scratch if I had to, but I suppose this old dog's got to learn some new tricks. Matches I can manage.

You'd laugh at me, learning new things every day. I think my face may be permanently frozen into a look of puzzlement. Ying finds me funny and started calling me Grandpa. Sweet, horrible kid. She spends most of her time trying to establish communications, glued to a computer sending out signals to anyone else who's left, but I'd hate for her to find out we really are the only ones.

All of us give Tom a wide berth. I worry about him. He speaks only when we ask him direct questions. What a world of pain he must be living in… He won't talk about his family or who he's lost. He always shies away when he hears us laughing and joking, but living requires a sense of humour, doesn't it?

I remain an eternal optimist. Ying's bet already got crossed off the board, but my wager is still on the table, and I may just win this one.

Twenty-seven days after D-Day

Tom started spouting the Book of Revelation at us. *And the sea gave up the dead which were in it; and death and hell delivered up the dead which were in them: and they were judged every man according to their works.* You know, all the doom and gloom parts. He's convinced we've been left behind on the earth for our sins. All I know is that if this is the end of days, it really isn't that bad. The worst part is not knowing what happened to you. I wonder and I worry more than I admit aloud.

Bob and Judy came back from one of their hardware store raids with a different sort of tool. I didn't want to take it. I have no idea how to fire a gun. Just having the things around are trouble, if you ask me.

"Just in case, Mr. Kagawa," Judy said.

But I took it and hid it behind the pot rack in the kitchen. I hope I'll never have to think about it again.

Thirty-five days after D-Day

We haven't seen any planes, or moving cars, or smoke. No one has answered any of our calls or signals. We've driven past the border and back again, but it's all just the same. It looks like everyone just vanished.

Weariness hit us all hard this week. The other day I caught Ying crying. "I'm never going to get married. I have no family left. No friends." All I could do was pass her tissues. We're all missing people. No one suffers any less than the other. In a way, I suppose that makes it easier for me, missing you. We stay busy, and I fall asleep every night exhausted, worried about the rest more than myself. I've lived a long life. I've had you. I count my blessings instead.

Tom thinks I'm a fool and that may be so.

Forty days after D-Day

Tom broke. He just broke. He came at me while I pulled weeds in the garden, Bible in one hand and kitchen cleaver in the other.

"God has spoken to me. He has called me to clean this earth of its last unbelievers," Tom said.

I clutched my dull, muddy spade tight. So small compared to the cleaver in his hand. And I remembered you at the kitchen table, two summers ago, cleaving up that roast pig to serve at our granddaughter's fifth birthday party. The thought of that almost made my mouth water. What was I thinking?

"So, you're God's hired mop, eh?" I asked. Tom wasn't impressed by my terrible joke. "I don't remember that from Sunday school. I bet if we didn't believe in God before, I'm sure we all do now, because how else could this have happened?"

Honestly, it was just talk. My hands shook so badly that I dropped my spade. Life did not flash before my eyes, but I could almost smell that roast pork.

"Just my luck to be stuck with two fucking Indians, a Chink and a Jap. Getting rid of you must be my ticket to heaven."

Who talks like that anymore, really? It didn't even make sense. If China was out of contact, so it stood to reason that a good few billion non-Christians made it to heaven if it really was the end of days. But, Tom wasn't right in the head. It made sense to him, and that was all he needed.

"Get away from Mr. Kagawa right now, Tom," Ying said.

I didn't realize she was standing there till then, with her hand on the trigger of one of the Snows guns.

"Or I'll shoot, and you're going nowhere but in the dirt. Now go away, and don't ever come back around here."

Cool as a cucumber that one. I owe her my life. I told her she looked convincing, and asked her where she learned to shoot.

"Video games, of course." She smiled.

Kids these days.

Three months after D-Day

The Snows secured a small boat and are going to go back to Campbell River to see if anyone's still there. They want to go home before the weather gets bad and I don't blame them. I joked that they wanted to get away before paying up on their bet, and I wished them luck. We all know they won't win this one.

Ying avoided saying goodbye. She spends most of her time in the office now, has a bunch of scavenged computers hooked up to the generator. I couldn't tell you what she's doing. Still looking, I guess.

I don't want to think about how quiet it will be without the Snows. I've never minded the quiet but this is something else, isn't it? Sometimes I think I hear your voice and I feel a little bit less lonely.

Five months after D-Day

You can hear the city falling apart. All the windows in those glass towers? They're starting to crack from the cold. The electricity's gone out in most areas, thanks to a windstorm a few weeks ago. Some lights on timers sometimes still go on and off, but they're not going to last – two people can't keep a city going.

Ying's taken over a giant house a few blocks away, all to herself. She says that she wouldn't have been able to afford a house that big no matter how much she saved in her life. The rooms aren't full of furniture but what looks to me like junk. Cell phones, computers, laptops, tablets, all the cables you can think of. She's always tinkering away on something.

She checks on me once a week and we have Sunday dinner together. She worries about me, she says. She worries about me? Can you imagine, it should be the other way around! I worry about the quiet, mostly. She's got no one for company but an old fart like me. I know you think I'm a ball of laughs, but you always did have odd taste.

But the house is warm, thanks to the generator and the solar piping the Snows helped install on the roof before they left. I sometimes boil water for an extra-hot bath. Mostly I cook on the grill these days, or eat out of cans. With everyone gone, there are more than enough cans to last a lifetime even if I never cooked again.

When it's quiet like this and I'm all alone in the house, I like to pretend you're at work, and the kids are young again and away at school. Sometimes I want to stay there in those moments and linger.

Ten months after D-Day

Happy birthday, love. Of course I wouldn't forget. This year I'd hoped to take you on a cruise because I know how much you always wanted to travel the world. I'm sorry that I kept telling you that we couldn't afford it, because of the kids and all. I'm sorry I had such a hard time keeping a job when we were just starting out. I would have loved to travel the world with you. Just my luck, this would be the year. I hid the brochures in the garage so you wouldn't find them. I was going to book the tickets for your birthday.

Instead, I invited Ying over and we ate the biggest cake you could imagine. It tasted like shit, because you know I can't bake but, damn, I tried. We put a candle on it, and sung you "Happy birthday" and everything. I miss you.

One year after D-Day

I caught Tom lurking around the house the other day. He seems right out of his mind. I didn't want to show it but I was terrified, shaking. I grabbed that gun in the kitchen, stuck a steak knife in my belt, just to look a little more intimidating, and walked out onto the front porch. I pointed my gun straight at him and told him to scram.

He shouted at me, rambled about fallen angels, but he left. I'm still shaking now.

Oh love, you might be proud of me, but God, do I wish you could hold me close and whisper that into my ear. Sometimes this house of ours, when I'm by myself, is too big, and too empty, and I can't handle it. It's not like me to be this serious. Sometimes I worry I'll end up just like Tom.

Two years after D-Day

Nature sure is something else. I've seen wolves and deer in the city! Mostly they leave me alone, though I am more cautious about where I throw my trash. Every day I go for a walk in Queen Elizabeth Park and feed the ducks with some crumbs. The waterfall no longer falls unless there's been a good rain and the observatory's crumbled in places. Sometimes I think I see the coloured birds that escaped, flying around town, in little flashes of orange and red. The ornamental gardens are overgrown now, but I rather like them that way. It looks wild, beautiful in a way that can't be created artificially.

Flowers still grow, and sometimes I pick some and put them in your room.

I've gotten used to the quiet now. I've stopped looking out the window to check whether or not the world has gone back to normal, but I still miss you terribly.

Three years after D-Day

Judy and Bob Snow came calling, right out of the blue! They brought some fresh crab and smoked salmon. We had a feast in our kitchen. Thank goodness the generator's still up and going. We didn't have a care in the world while they were here. They're doing great those two. The salmon are back, they say. Campbell River's gone wild like it used to be, but that's the way of things. They never met anyone else, but it sounds like they've built their own little paradise.

They've got the right attitude, in my opinion. You take what you get, and do your best with it. My god, that salmon was amazing. I can't remember the last time I had fresh food. They built a cabin, and have gone back to the ways their grandparents lived. Judy's pregnant too, wouldn't you know? It's amazing. They thought they were too old, but there you go. Sometimes miracles do happen, even in the strangest of times.

They invited me and Ying to come live with them. They say an old man shouldn't be living on his own like this, but you know me. I can't leave this place, just in case you come back and look for me. I know if you came back you would come straight here. And I know you would, if it were possible.

Ying doesn't want to leave her *"batcave"* (that's what she calls it). I tried to convince Ying to go with them, but she's as stubborn as you are. She babbled something about reestablishing a digital order. I have no idea what she's going on about. Should I be worried?

The Snows were disappointed. Maybe one day they'll understand, but I'm old. Sooner or later, one way or another, I'll leave this place that you and I made our home. Until then, I take comfort in the memories we made in this city. Everything reminds me of you, and when I'm here, I can almost believe you are too.

Day... I don't know.

I've done something terrible. Ying told me that she saw Tom around, so I went and checked out her place. The poor kid was so terrified she nailed up boards on the windows, and installed extra locks on the doors.

Tom smashed the generator in the yard, but Ying said she could fix it so she wasn't worried. She was more worried about Tom, and I don't blame her. I told her I'd look for him.

I put on my heaviest coat, because of the winter chill, and put the gun in my pocket. I tried not to think about it while I walked. (You know me, I'd be likely to shoot my own foot off by accident.) I also loaded up a bag with a few supplies.

As I'd suspected, there were signs that Tom was hiding out in the nearest church, Holy Name, just a little bit farther down Cambie Street. I found sleeping bags and pillows piled up in a nest near the altar, all lit up prettily by the stained-glass windows, but Tom was nowhere to be seen.

I dumped rat poison in the fountain of holy water, and all over his food supplies. I hope that God forgives me. If I've been damned, it's too late anyway. Maybe this is why I have been left behind. Maybe there *is* a defect in my soul. Maybe *He* knew I'd commit murder, and therefore wasn't worthy. But I can't afford to think like that or I'll end up just like Tom. I can't. I won't.

You want to know the truth? I don't feel bad about it, just relieved.

Five years after D-Day

Ying and I haven't seen Tom again. I'm afraid to go back to the church, only to find him there rotting as evidence of my sins.

I still go to the house from time to time, but my knees, in the winter, they don't work so well anymore, love. The house has a great view, but climbing those stairs is something that's harder and harder to do. I've found a lovely little rancher by the seaside and Ying helped me set it up. I know you would love it.

This is hard for me to write, after all these years. Ying still comes by from time to time to check on me. She seems to be doing all right, just gone a little feral like the rest of us. I haven't seen the Snows in a while. I hope they're doing okay, and that their baby is growing up plump and happy.

Some days I hope I'll disappear too, and maybe I'll end up wherever you are.

But when you do come back, love, I know you will find these words I've left you in our house. Meet me on English Bay, near that old apartment we lived in before we had kids, where you came to meet me that one sunny day, when I bent down on my knees to ask you to marry me. When I close my eyes I can almost see you there.

Just like then, I'll be there at 12 noon, waiting. It's a date. I'm still sure I'll win that bet.

MATTHEW, WAITING

A.C. Wise

He watches the Annes down by the shore. He hasn't sorted the latest batch yet, hasn't determined whether *she* is among them, the one he's been waiting for. At the moment, they're all Anne, because they all have the potential to be. An eternal optimist, he is.

Laughter drifts to him on a salt breeze. The Annes dart into the surf, holding their skirts up, but getting their hems wet nonetheless. Their bare feet turn red with the sand and they plunge their hands into the waves, as if anything good to eat remains since the Change. They won't find anything. Not that they really try. Not like the Dianas, who are off gathering lupins by the armful. At least parts of the lupin are edible, and might help them survive another year. The Annes are all full of hope, when they stop to think, which these ones rarely do. Mostly the Annes splash each other and laugh. Mostly they push each other into the surf, one pretending to be indignant, one pretending to scold, one pretending to drown.

It's all a game with the Annes, it always is, but not enough of a game. Not yet. The right level of imagination hasn't yet been displayed, and he hasn't yet found The One. *She* hasn't returned, but one day, she will.

He sighs. Soon, it will be time to call the Annes home. Gather them back to the house where they will all do the best they can, cooking what greens and weeds the Dianas have scavenged, adding it to whatever the Gilberts have managed to hunt. They'll light candles – they have those still – and when they run out, they'll burn driftwood, filling the house with the scent of old salt and the faint odour of ruin, washed in on the tide.

From the dunes and the long grasses gone wild above the red sand he waves. "Time to come home now, girls, I guess."

He doesn't wait to see if they'll follow, but trudges back toward the house. His breath is shorter these days. It's harder to wade through the long grass no one tends. He doesn't need to call the Dianas or the Gilberts; he trusts them to find their way back. Besides – they don't matter as much anyway.

It's the Annes. Always the Annes.

When he finds her, *the* Anne, the right Anne, he can rest.

She'll come again. He knows she will. She always has before.

The orphanage called it a mistake, but he knows. She was meant to be in his life. She saved him before, and she will again. Even though this time the story has turned out wrong. He's lived longer than he should. He remembers too much.

(*Hold on. It's okay, hold on, we'll get you help. It's... Of course there are still ambulances, there have to be. What do you think we pay taxes for? Just... just hold on. Not for me. That little girl needs us. What will she do if you go?*)

He climbs the stairs, his old bones aching. How did he ever manage to live this long? Salt breeze is in his veins, red soil replacing his blood. It leaves him stiff. Every day it's harder.

His heart is bad the doctors say. Or said, before everything Changed. And now? He hasn't seen a doctor in years. He hasn't seen anyone but the Gilberts and the Dianas and the Annes. The occasional Miss Stacy, doing her best to hold onto the knowledge of the old world. Sometimes a Josie, trying to turn every situation to her advantage. And every now and then an Allan, alone or in pairs, preaching the word of the lost God and declaring the difference between Now and Then to be God's judgment for the world's sins.

He doesn't believe a word, not from any of them. The only important thing is finding her, his Anne.

Below, in the kitchen and the parlour, in the much abused rooms never meant to be a functional holdout against the end of the world, he hears a riot of movement and voices. Annes and Dianas and Gilberts colliding, bickering about the best way to cook the day's salvage on the tiny stove meant for tourist-show, not every day work.

Everything they cook on it now smells of the rotten tide anyway. Or the mouldering furniture salvaged from neighbouring houses, fallen to ruin while they mysteriously remain. Or the trees, gone sickly, gone dark and wrong and riddled with beetles and worms, but still good enough for burning when nothing else remains.

He fingers The Book, one of only a few remaining copies. The rest have disappeared, lost to age, or perhaps resentful Annes setting out on their own, taking a remnant of his heart as a souvenir. Or perhaps it's the Dianas, ever practical, burning them for fuel. He's certain he's seen words in the ashes, fragments holy enough to weep over, to gather in time-gnarled hands and press to his wrinkled cheeks.

This copy is foxed, the pages worn and water-stained. Mould has begun to creep in, and there are chunks of text missing. He fills the gaps with memory. For instance: Marilla was always the practical one, the sensible one. Why did she have to leave him? He was never supposed to outlive her. What will he do without her?

(*Hang on. You have to hang on. Just a little longer. And of course he knew she wasn't really his sister, but it was easier when he had to keep her talking, trying to keep her awake just a little bit longer, waiting for the ambulance that wouldn't come. It was easier, fighting the Sickness, to tell her shared stories of a childhood that never was.* Remember when…? *And when he ran out of those stories: when his imagination failed, there were stories any and every book he could call to mind. He told them over and over again. As long as he could. Until the memories ran out. Until his voice grew hoarse. Until the words were too thick with tears.*)

He runs his thumb over the pages, taking comfort in the rustle of ivory turning to old bone. It doesn't matter that they're not all there. The important ones are – the ice cream, the raspberry cordial, the Lady of Shallot, the puffed sleeves. And most importantly, Anne holding him in her arms as he dies.

This is what he's been waiting for. This is what he needs. It's been a long road, and he wants to lie down, but can't. Not until he sees her again.

(*I never wanted a boy. I only wanted you from the first day. Don't ever change. I love my little girl. I'm so proud of my little girl.*)

His throat hurts. It's hard to breathe. He wipes his eyes and turns from The Book, from the window, where he can see the last of the Annes and the Dianas and the Gilberts coming home.

He makes his way slowly down the stairs. The kitchen is crowded. Now, instead of raucous noise, he sees only a fullness he is fond of, something that makes him feel less alone. He watches, unobtrusive, as the tumble of boys and girls move about the space – all elbows, all feet – crashing into each other when they don't mean to and whenever they can. He pays particular attention to the Annes. For all he knows, one of them could be *her*.

"Cordelia?" he whispers, whenever one passes close, a whirlwind, orbiting him briefly for half a turn before spinning away again.

None of them answer. The first test failed. He leaves out a dress with puffy sleeves most nights, but none of them gravitate toward it. He watches for the way they do or do not braid their hair.

"Are you okay?" A hand touches his arm.

He looks up, realizing he's leaning against the wall, sliding down it really, while his breath wheezes. He wipes his eyes – they are rheumy these days, always weepy whether he's sad or not.

"Fine." He straightens, trying to see the young woman in front of him. Is she a Diana or an Anne?

"Are you sure? Maybe you better sit down." She pulls a chair for him. In a moment, she brings him tea.

It tastes like salt. Who knows how it was brewed. He doesn't ask, only wraps his fingers around the cup, breathes and swallows deep.

She continues to watch him, concerned, chewing her bottom lip. She's quieter than most. Is that right? Sometimes the memories get muddled and some days he can't remember what Anne – *his* Anne – should be.

Amidst the bustle of the kitchen, the flurry of who knows what cooking on the overworked stove in the too-small space, she pulls up another chair beside him and takes his hand. Her fingers squeeze his. They are cold. Or perhaps it is his skin that is cold, the chill transferred to her. She glances around, looking to see whether the others are listening, then whispers conspiratorially to him – her words the only thing he can hear in the din despite their hush.

"You know, I can almost remember the world before the Change," she says. "I can't imagine what it must have been like for you, the things you've seen."

She squeezes his fingers again, flicker-bright. And oh, his heart aches.

"I can almost remember my parents. Cindy and Marlene Bransford. Maybe you knew them?" She pauses a beat, eyes full of hope. He can only swallow around the thickness in his throat. Only shake his head, overwhelmed by... Overwhelmed.

"No, I didn't think so. Anyway, it doesn't matter. I just wanted to say thank you." She grips his hand hard now, and he can't bear to look up to see that she's sincere. "Thank you. I wouldn't have had a home if you hadn't taken me in."

He doesn't feel her leave, whirl away in a new orbit, swept away by a fresh tide. When he looks up again, he can't find her. She's fallen into the mass of Dianas and Annes and Gilberts, and to him they all look the same.

Shouldn't he recognize her? Shouldn't he know her any-where, no matter what her face or name? They're kindred spirits after all. Why has she waited so long to take him home?

(*The little girl struggles to breathe. Her freckles are so dark against her skin, which has gone so pale, her red hair bright as fire in the sun. He cradles her head, trying to hold it up, as if holding her head above the tide. It killed them, but not by drowning. In slow, insidious ways, and there's nothing he can do to stop it. He's only a simple farmer, here on vacation. Now he's trapped, the bridge collapsed under the weight of evacuees – or bombed by the military some say. There are no ferries running from the island to the mainland, not anymore. Private boats all gone already or scuttled, trying to contain a thing that can't be contained. There's nowhere to go.*

The supplies promised, the medical helicopters come to resupply struggling hospitals or evacuate survivors, he knows they'll never come. But he can't tell her this, the girl dying in his arms. She can't be more than 16. And she reminds him of someone he knew once, a daughter or a niece, he can't remember, won't remember, because they're gone and it hurts too much. He can't think of anything to say to the girl, anything to comfort her as she gasps for breath, as her lungs collapse, as her body goes into shock, fighting against the sickness in its blood. So he says the first thing that comes to mind, a story he used to read to his niece or his daughter, the girl he can't bear to remember, when she was a child: Ms. Rachel Lynde lived just where the Avonlea main road dipped down into a little hollow, fringed with alders and ladies' eardrops and traversed by a brook that had its source away back in the woods of the old Cuthbert place…)

One of the Gilberts brings him something to drink. It is like the tea, but thicker, and smells far worse.

"It's for your joints," the Gilbert says. "So they'll hurt less. You shouldn't push yourself so hard, walking to the shore every day. You know there are enough of us to take care of the food and there hasn't been a raid in months. You've done so much for us, let us take care of you."

He drinks the tea in silence, drawing what warmth he can from the cup. He always seems to be cold these days. Wasn't it always summer on the island before the Change? Or perhaps it's only the summers he remembers – sun bright in the lupins and on the waves, and Anne toddling on chubby legs, holding Marilla's hand and laughing as the water drew near her toes.

No. He knows the memory is wrong, confused. Anne wasn't a toddler when he first met her. She didn't have dark hair like the girl he almost remembers, dark hair like the woman holding her hand and smiling back over her shoulder at him. It must be another story, one someone else told. He never lived that life. Never.

He squeezes his eyes closed. Maybe the Gilbert touches his shoulder and says something else before walking away. He doesn't hear. There are low voices, a murmured conversation. He is the subject. They are worried about him. If he keeps his eyes closed, maybe they'll think he's asleep and leave him alone.

It's not for them, not anymore. At first he stayed for them, the Annes, the Dianas, even the Gilberts. Someone had to take care of them, someone who remembered enough of the way things were Before to get them somewhere safe, keep them fed, keep them warm. Now it's only *her* he's waiting for, so he can sleep.

The voices move off, grow a bit louder. They're telling stories now. Not the stories he remembers, not the stories from the old days. They're stories of the future; they're so full of hope it breaks his heart. They all start, "When things get better I'll..."

He drifts off to the murmur of those voices, the fanciful tales of impossible future. So like his Anne, he thinks. Head always full of dreams. Don't ever change.

He wakes in the silent kitchen by the cold fire. They've forgotten to stoke it again, now it's only ash. It takes him three tries to push out of his chair, his old bones complaining the whole way. His fingers tremble and slip on the poker only meant for decoration. He stirs the ashes, but nothing. There's no spark.

A scouting trip to gather more wood; the very thought of it sends a spike of pain through his lower back. His pulse thumps double time. How long does he stand that way, hand pressed to his back before one of the Gilberts – the same Gilbert? – comes through the door with an armload of firewood? He can smell the rot even from here, the dark, mossy scent. The wood is bug-riddled, but it will still burn.

"Let me take care of that." The Gilbert takes the poker from his hand, urges him back into a chair. The fire is going soon enough and, soon after that, the kitchen fills with Dianas and Annes again.

By listening to the swirl of talk throughout the room, he learns two of the Annes left during the night. Not Annes then, something else he doesn't have a name for. He doesn't see the Anne that spoke to him yesterday, the one who was kind. She must have been one of the two who left, or maybe she was never here and he only imagined her.

There are only two Annes left now, and they are both quiet this morning, subdued with their heads bowed, speaking in low whispers. Perhaps they are thinking about running away, too. He watches them. Their features are drawn, pale. There are bruise-coloured shadows under their eyes. They're afraid.

His bones settle and creak. He wills the joints to loosen. *Come on, old bones*, he thinks, *just one more trip. I need you.*

While the Annes and Gilberts and Dianas are busy, not paying him any mind, he slips out. The sun is bright and the air is fresh. It stirs the long grasses that try to tangle around his legs and for a moment he can almost pretend it's Before, and nothing has Changed.

There's a long, straight piece of wood beside the door, smoothed by time and his hands. It looks almost clean; he's saved it and kept it this way, protected it. He takes it to lean on and it makes the walk a little easier. Once upon a time he would have done this in a cart. He had a good horse, didn't he? Running to and fro to the station where the Gilberts and Dianas and Annes washed up. He gathered them in and brought them here, protected them. He even asked once, how they knew where to go so he would find them.

"Stories," an Anne told him. "You're a legend."

On foot, it's much longer. He can barely see the road through the tall grass, because who is there to travel the road anymore and keep it smooth? But it's there, faint, a ghost of itself, and he walks it like a ghost – driving the stick in firm, buried in the red dust, using it as an anchor to pull himself along. It feels slow, unbearably slow, but he'll get there. He can't leave the Annes waiting. That would never do.

The sun is almost white in its brightness. He raises a hand to shield his eyes. Through his fingers, the road disappears to a vanishing point, a trick of the light and the red dust stirred up by the wind. Is that the station there already? Or is it a mirage? It wavers in the heat; he blinks stinging eyes, but it does nothing to clear his vision.

"Come on, old bones," he says aloud. "Just a little farther."

He ignores the ache in his joints as best he can. Ignores the erratic beating of his heart, the tightness in his chest. He ignores the sensation of falling, his knees striking the ground and the long grasses whispering over him, hushing against his cheeks and ears like voices telling an old tale. It's only an illusion, like the pain. He's still walking, and that is the station ahead of him.

And there, through the haze, he can just make out the girl sitting on the platform. She's clutching a battered case in both hands, straining her eyes to look either way. There's hope on her face, so much hope; it's fragile, almost-but-not-quite gone. She should know better than to give up on him. He always comes for her, like he's come for her again now. Her hair hangs in two red plaits, one on either side of her face, framing the pale skin and the freckles. Not the boy they asked for, but something better. A girl. His girl. His Anne.

He ignores the way his left arm tingles, the tiny pains shooting from wrist to shoulder. They're nothing. He ignores the scent of dust, thick and right next to his nose. He isn't lying down. The world isn't fading, crumbling, shrinking to a tunnel of grey surrounding the too-bright whiteness of the sun.

No, he's walking up to the station platform now, suddenly shy, his heart beating too hard only from excitement and barely contained joy. Then she catches sight of him, and he knows. Her smile – all that tentative, fragile hope, all the big, impossible love no one has ever given her a chance to show before, all the moments to come, the poetry and the slate broken over Gilbert's head, all of it. It's all there in her smile. And he knows. She's come home and he can rest. He's finally found her. His Anne.

JENNY OF THE LONG GAUGE

Michael Matheson

His heart hangs from the gallows where she left it. His skin and bones she took with her, and his name he traded away long ago. What's left of him hangs from the noose, swaying in the hot, dry wind, while his heart burns black in the beating desert sun.

The chinooks have become siroccos. They set the whole of the scaffold to creaking and his disembodied heart, tied in an oubliette bow, swings with it – traces a pendulum arc as a murder of crows descends on it with a furious beat of wings. Digging, tearing, snapping, biting, the crows feast and rise in a flurry, winging away still fighting over the last remnants of gore.

Their caws linger in the air long after they're gone, only gristle and half-cooked ropy trails hanging from the swinging gallows knot.

◀ ▶

His bones rattle in the lockbox hitched on the back of Jenny's cart and the iron-shod hooves of her pitch team clop muted on the dusty road. She lashes the Clydes and they quicken to a trot, braying in protest as she hurries them west toward Spiritwood, making her seasonal round.

A flash of black on brilliant blue catches her eye and she turns skyward, shielding her eyes against the sweltering sun with one long hand. High overhead a murder of crows wings its way north. She frowns; tightens her grip on the reins and slows up her team. They whinny, anxious to be on, while Jenny watches the murder fly. It blots out the burnished sun as its patchwork shadow shifts and writhes along the ground, keeping pace with the welter above.

With sun-browned hands, slender, fine-boned, callus-worn, she ties back wavy, black-bleached-nutmeg hair dark against the plains around her. Lets it waterfall over her shoulder as she turns in her seat to eye the lockbox on the wagon bed. "You got something to say?" The box shakes fiercely, though the wagon bed is still. "Didn't think so." She straightens, the box rattling on as Jenny lashes the reins. Her titan blacks neigh and pull forward past stunted trees and withering scrub.

The string of broken black bodies littering the path behind her goes unnoticed; glutted crows cawing weakly as they fade away in the choking dust.

◀ ▶

Jenny pulls hard on the reins as the wagon comes to a ford in the river. Her stallions snort and shake their heads, hooves splashing into the edge of the shallow, pebbled water. The liquid runs cool on the hot metal of their shoes as they slow up and stop. Across the burbling stream, no more than a score wide, sprawls a Lowlands camp, covered wagons sending up streamers of pale smoke.

She leans back in her seat, considering, shifting into the shadow of a tall, skeletal tree with gnarled and greedy roots dug deep into the riverbed.

Eyes trained on the Lowlands camp and one hand on the reins, she reaches back into the wagon bed with the other. Roots among tossed blankets and tanned hides. Ignores the rattling box. Her fingers find the 12-gauge buried beneath a sprawl of coarse-haired hides. The metal of the long shotgun is cool against her palm as she draws it free and lays it across her lap.

She flicks the reins and her Clydes drag the cart through the splashing water, clomping hooves sending up small sprays and wagon wheels sluicing long waves into the air. The cart dips and rises again as it comes up the other side of the shallow bank. But the shotgun, clutched in long, lean fingers, never wavers as Jenny makes her way into the camp to pick up more wares before she heads into town.

◀ ▶

The Lowlanders stare up at Jenny with blank, filmy eyes near blind from the driving dust. The sirocco whips at their tangled hair; picks at nests of nits and other, smaller things hiding in coarse tresses – only the elders of the tribe allowed hair shorn close to the skull. They follow her as the cart rattles through the waste of the camp. Wild dogs lie dying, poked by children with sharp sticks; the ones already dead split open to roast on cook fires. The smell of burning flesh fills the air.

Jenny slows her team to a halt, horses snapping sharply at children who come too close, made reckless by hunger. The women paw at her cart, stroking the grain of the wood. Listening to the creak of the wagon as the wind rocks it.

The flap of a covered wagon folds back, held open by a grimy hand corrupt with age spots and withered flesh. The chieftain's face pokes out after it, eyes scrunched up against the sun, deep black irises swimming in a sea of off-colour white. He drops down from the wagon and rears up, a tall man over six feet, all gristle and burlap, wrapped in sagging flesh over strong, lank bones. "You got something to trade?" he rasps, voice ruined by too many years of drinking down the grit in the air; inclines one skeletal hand at the slow-cooking corpse of a wild dog. "We have meat."

Jenny rises and comes to her full height, a fence post of a woman: rail thin and pole tall. Her hair streams in the hot wind and her long gauge rests in the crook of her arm, barrel aimed casually down at the face of the Lowlands chief. "I have hides," she croaks through a parched throat and dry lips. Her eyes don't leave his face. Around her the women paw at her boots; coo softly at the feel of the supple leather.

The chieftain caws like a brassy crow, shooing the women away. They scatter to the winds, dragging stupefied children after them. In their wake he turns again to Jenny. "Show me."

She keeps her gun trained on the Lowlander as she dismounts and circuits to the back of the wagon bed. He shadows her, feet kicking up a sea of dust, as Jenny leans in and pulls out several coarse-haired blankets.

He grumbles in disinterest. "What else?" Jenny tosses the blankets aside. Uncovers a hoary, suntanned hide. He glances at her out the corner of one eye. "How long dead?"

Jenny shrugs, pulls a contemplative face. "Couple weeks? Crows didn't get him."

He nods. Looks over the rest of her wares. "I'll take the hide. What else you got?" He leans forward to snatch up the skin and paw at the jumbled contents of her wagon.

She gives him a sly grin. "Got his bones."

He looks up at her with newfound respect. "Fresh?"

"Same as the hide." She smiles, yellowing teeth looking a little whiter than true in the harsh light.

"Mmm," he grumbles. Juts his chin at the cart. Impatient.

Jenny grins wider. Grunts as she pulls the concealed lockbox from under the coarse blankets and throws back the simple catch. The box opens with a creak and the bones within rattle feverishly, straining to be heard as the lid cracks wide.

He shakes his head. Glares down at the jumble of bleached bits bathed in their own light. "Won't take the bones. Still got life in them."

"They're dead," she says, as the dry bones rattle.

"Gallows stink is still on them."

"You don't want them? Fine." She slams the lid of the lockbox down. Heads back to the seat of her wagon, calling back over her shoulder, "Plenty of medicine men who'll take them in Spiritwood."

"I'll still take the skin," the Lowlander calls after her as she settles in. "You want dog for it?"

"Gold."

"*Gold.*" He spits in disgust. Looks away. "Always trinkets with you people."

Jenny stares down at him from her perch, shotgun resting on her arm. Her horses knead the ground, restless.

The Lowlander chieftain looks up into Jenny's eyes, appraising her. After a time he lowers his head. "Gold."

"Good," grins Jenny. Catches up the reins and whips her team on. "I'll be at the other end of the wheat fields. Bring it by tomorrow." Her twin blacks canter off, raising a man-high trail of dust in their wake.

The chieftain stares after her, squinting against the chalky silt. An old woman comes to stand beside him. Paws at the skin. He hands it to her without taking his eyes off Jenny. The Lowlander woman coughs as she wraps the skin around her shoulders and rubs it to her skin.

Grumbling, the chieftain stalks off to his covered wagon. Doesn't look back as the woman wearing the bought skin breaks out in a slow sweat. She hacks up something fierce and slumps to the ground, dry heaving, teeth rattling loose in her skull.

◄ ►

The wagon cuts through a high swath of blackened wheat, the stunted crop long ago gone wild, carefully trained borders overrun generations back: now a small lake of stalk and chaff. Jenny uncocks her shotgun and slides it into the wagon bed without looking back. Around her the stalks bend as the wagon tramples them, springing back in the cart's wake.

On the other side of the wheat field she pulls up the reins, her team snuffling loudly and shaking their manes. She leaps down from the cart and pats the side of the older stallion's head. The Clydesdale nuzzles up to her, rearing his head several times against her chest, and snorts. The other Clyde brays and lowers his head to bite at scrub grass growing beyond the ragged borders of the wheat.

Jenny runs her palm down the panting stallion's sharp-boned cheek as she rounds the wagon to fetch the feedbags. She watches the encampment, a haze of slow smoke and huddled wagons far in the distance and down a stretch of hill, as she pulls out the heavy leather sacks and secures them over her team's muzzles. They chew noisily, tearing at what passes for feed – hard maize and scrub root. Jenny pats the flank of the younger stallion out of long habit as she clambers back into the wagon seat to wait.

◀ ▶

They come in the night, the rustling of the wheat giving them away. Jenny has been waiting for them since the sun went down. She lies in the back of the wagon, the long gauge in her hands, one eye closed, the other looking down the cylindrical length of the barrel balanced flat atop the lockbox.

Her finger rests lightly on the trigger, hammer already down. Beneath her the lockbox shudders as the bones rattle. "Shut up," she rasps, and takes aim. Squeezes her trigger finger back and the explosion of the 12-gauge rips open the night, the thick slug slamming out of the hot barrel in a burst of light and powdery fire. A Lowlander falls apart wetly as the slug rips through his chest and knocks him back through the air. The others come at her fast and she drops them one by one, one eye shut tight as she fires, reloading cartridges two at a time and firing off shots in pairs. The muzzle of the gauge is red-hot and smoking when she finally stops shooting. Steam hisses off the slowly cooling metal.

The echoes of the shots fade into the darkness as she rises and gently hoists herself over the lip of the wagon, shotgun still in hand. She lands in a crouch by the side of the wagon. Waits for the telltale rustle of more Lowland men moving through the stunted wheat.

When Jenny deems it's been silent long enough she straightens, and without taking her eyes off the wheat field reaches into the back of the wagon to retrieve her flensing knife. Rail-thin legs covering long strides, she moves into the field.

◄ ►

Her cart loaded down with new hides still curing in the burning sun, Jenny pulls into the outskirts of Spiritwood: the town still rebuilding after the Big Dry in what had once been the heart of lake country. Shanties at its edges give way to larger establishments in the city proper. Cattlemen drive their slave stock through unpaved streets – harrying filthy, heat-sick stragglers on with a crack of the lash – past whorehouses and saloons fighting for space with gambling dens and dingy hotels: all the elements of a booming frontier town – except there's nothing left beyond Spiritwood's westward edge but the dust bowls of the Barrens.

Jenny cranes her neck to admire new-cut boardwalks. The planking is sound wood – a rarity in the scorched expanse of the desert burn, the forests of the North denuded centuries back.

A lawman tips his hat to her. Jenny notes the polished, virgin shine of his sidearm. Notes, too, the blight lesions sluicing along his forearms in clear runnels, poking out from under rolled-up sleeves. The sores haven't begun to weep yet, but it's only a matter of time. Jenny makes a mental note to move on quickly. The marshal watches her, not sure what to make of her; shudders as he sees the contents of her wagon.

Her Clydes halt on their own in front of a saloon and Jenny vaults down from the wagon before it settles, eager to be out of Spiritwood's board-stiff closeness. Eager to be out on the plains again. She leads her team to the trough, the wagon dragging behind. The water is caked with silt, but clean beneath the scum, and her stallions drink greedily, heads bent low. She strokes their sweat-flecked hides as she moves past them to the wagon bed, pulls the collapsible metal cover over the split wood and peeling paint, and digs deep in the pocket of her pants for the key. Retrieves the flensing knife from the wagon bed with her other hand and tucks it away in her hide jacket before locking up.

Jenny pulls a pair of leather gloves from the back pocket of her pants as she heads up the stairs. Slips them on and pulls them tight; not wanting to touch anything in a town where the blight has made itself at home. Takes a deep breath before she opens the swing doors and heads into the noisy, grimy saloon.

The first thing that catches her eye isn't the bar itself, or the patrons, mostly grizzled veterans and whores; it's the impressionist mural adorning one full wall of the interior: an iceberg floating in choppy seas. The rendering an imagined one with no subject available for reference since the polar melt. The painted blue is as cooling as the ice itself would be and Jenny leans her face toward a phantom arctic wind, drinking in the genetic memory of the cold.

"Something, ain't it?" The bartender flashes a broken smile at her, hands working the counter with a dirty rag.

Jenny startles at a white face behind the bar. Then comes up to lean on the wood with her elbows. There's plenty of room, though the tables are occupied well enough. "How long you had it?"

"Since my grandfather opened the doors, back when Spiritwood was just starting over: all of two streets and a rail-yard."

Jenny frowns at the boldfaced lie: the mural's new, and the saloon's belonged to the Chamakese family since George came down from Pelican Lake Reserve with his sons a couple of decades back and built it. She looks around pointedly. "I don't see many medicine men 'round."

The bartender rubbernecks awkwardly as his patrons raise their heads at Jenny's words; leans in to whisper, "They ain't welcome round here no more. Local marshal and his boys run what few of 'em were left out on a rail few months back." He answers Jenny's confused stare with: "New law passed in the territories. We don't have to treat 'em like people no more."

Jenny spits on the floor, thinking about George. About his sons. About herself. "Well how in the hell am I supposed to make a living now?" She slams one hand down on the counter, startling the bartender; shoves a finger in his face. "I ain't gonna end up like one of them doxies down by the depot."

He opens his mouth to answer but looks up past Jenny, eyes widening, and slips off down the bar to "attend" to other patrons.

Jenny glances over her shoulder as a tall shadow falls across her; turns to stare up at the men caging her in a semi-circle. "I think you'd make a right good doxy," leers the head man, big grey cow's eyes sizing her up. Both he and the two men who flank him are ham-fisted bruisers, built like trees and just as broad. Jenny knows their kind, the remnants of their eugenically bred lines still working the mines back East; she's put down more than a few of them in her time. She's not sure what men like this are doing so far west but there's always work on the frontier for big men who don't think too much. "What's the matter, whore, you didn't hear me?" the ringleader barks, shoving her back.

His hand flies into the air before any of them realize she's drawn the knife. His eyes widen as she cuts open his throat, hot blood spraying where she was standing a moment ago. She's already moving in among the other two bruisers, opening up bellies. They goggle stupidly at their own spilling intestines, trying to hold them in, before they topple, gurgling.

By the time the lawman makes his way in the bartender is crouched down behind the bar, whimpering, and the patrons are all carefully minding their own business. Jenny stands farther down the bar, finishing an abandoned drink. The lawman takes in the bodies on the floor, the crowd nursing their drinks in dead quiet, and lonely Jenny down the other end of the bar. She cradles the remnant of the alcohol in her glass like a dying lover. She can feel his frown from across the room as he steps over the dead men, leaving a trail of bloody footprints.

"You gonna run me out on a rail too?" she says as he sidles up next to her. She downs the alcohol in her glass in a single slug.

The marshal settles in beside her. Leans on the polished wood and folds his hands together on the bar. "Could hold you till a judge comes through." Jenny snorts, unimpressed. "But I get the feeling you don't like being tied down to one place too long. And, truth be told, I'd rather have you gone. So I tell you what: you leave town before the sun goes down—"

he pauses, Jenny casting a sidelong eye in his direction, "and we'll say you were never here."

"What about them?" asks Jenny, nodding at the bodies.

"Ma'am," he smiles, "world's dying by slow inches, I got a town full of people holding tooth and nail to what they got while the blight cuts 'em down, and a territory full of men waiting on Spiritwood to fail so they can wipe it off the map and start over. Three dead men from out East don't make a world of difference to me. One lone medicine woman, neither." He straightens, waiting for Jenny to leave.

She slams her glass down and slides it back toward the bar rail. "Ain't got no reason to stick around this shithole anyway." She stretches out the kinks in her shoulders, pushes off the bar, and shoulders past the sheriff. Knocks him a step back to make a point. He makes no move to stop her. Just settles back against the bar and reaches for a half-full bottle as the saloon doors swing uneven in Jenny's wake.

◀ ▶

Twenty kilometres north of Spiritwood, Jenny stands knee-deep in dirt and mud, digging a hole. The spade, acquired on her way out of the city limits, is a parting gift from an unsuspecting prospector. She wipes the back of one gloved hand across her sweating brow – even in the dead of night the heat oppressive – and shifts another load of dirt. The moon hangs low and silvered in the sky and somewhere off in the distance a coyote howls as she bends down to dig one final furrow out of the cracked earth.

Panting, she tosses the spade to the ground and clambers out of the hole to grab the lockbox from the back of her wagon. Carries the lead-lined crate over to the hole, balances it on one knee so she can unlatch it, and upends it. The skeleton of the hanged man dumps out into the hole, and Jenny spreads the mess around with one foot while the bones rattle – still caught in the grip of the radioactive blight that was killing him long before he was hanged.

Then Jenny goes back for the rest of her wares. Dumps hard-won skins into the hole by the armload. And when the cart is empty and she's finished covering over the hole she pats the earth down and jams the shovel in at the head of the impromptu grave as a marker. Lays one arm atop the other over the rough wood and rests her weary chin on the back of her hands, breathing slow.

She glances north to the lands of her own people, the Nakota. Considering. But there's no life to be had there, not anymore. That land is being winnowed; history repeating itself in cruel turn as treaties are revoked – those that still stand – and her people are driven farther and farther north; a new Trail of Tears already begun. With each territory law there's less land for any of the First Nations; day by day the men of the East hem in the West. And Jenny will not be caged.

She turns tired eyes, dirt-rimmed, closer north to the cattle yards and mills of Leoville, next stop on her seasonal round, some dozen kilometres distant. No point heading that way now. She glances back east. Dismisses the idea quick as it comes. Rubs at her sore neck before looking west, to the Barrens: a desert of salted, broken earth stretching out beyond the matchstick-dry grass of the plains, far as the eye can see. There's open territory out West; out past the Barrens; over the mountains; bordering the risen sea. Or so they say.

No one's ever come back to tell the truth of it. 'Course, that don't prove a thing: even if there is something past the Barrens – some fabled strip of land that ain't swimming in sand and choking dust – who'd want to come back from that to *this*?

Bones aching, long arms swinging at her sides, Jenny clambers up into her wagon, takes the reins and snaps them down with a lash that echoes against the baked scrubland beneath her stallions' hooves. And heads West.

At her back the sirocco stirs, drives her on and washes over Jenny's dust-caked skin to scour the ruined earth. High above, a murder follows; black wings beating against a black sky. And in her wake, nameless bones rattle beneath the earth, dry as the land in which they rest.

The wind sweeps away all trace she was ever there.

SNOW ANGELS

A.M. Dellamonica

Lindy was elbow-deep in window glass when the tech started giving her hell about her Winkles.

"You haven't been dusting." He ran a rag over their faces. They were on a stretcher beside Lindy's varnishing table: a boy, a girl, a something. Not kin, from their looks: the girl had Southeast Asian features and the boy was a mixed-race cherub with honey curls. "This one's got cobwebs. You gotta take better care."

"Who's taking care of me?" Lindy had been fusing scavenged windshield shards, filtering out the surviving smartcrystals and printing a self-charging pane which drew power from the weak northern sun beyond her window.

"Red here's got an elevated heart rate." The tech meant the devil child, the one in the cheap Halloween costume.

"Take it for analysis." Lindy didn't move. She had to stay still when she had a shard in progress. Glass was glass. It scratched; it sliced.

She'd tried to wiggle out of storage duty but the prime minister had been firm: no special favours for family.

"You must've done something."

Lindy wondered, briefly, why most of her fellow Jitterbugs were such assholes. Then she tuned him out; the glass was charged. She upgraded it to a touchscreen, growing a long, heavy pane, then loading up text from her latest interview as she lowered it to the floor.

Terese Bianchi's story:

Last Year was the spring I turned nine, the spring Mama brought my Nonna home to die. It was intense, and weirdly private. We kept to ourselves; we weren't watching the news.

I heard at school about the airplane full of people with persistent sleep syndrome; heard about the beer garden in Frankfurt. When our music teacher became a Winkle it was still so rare that someone went to his house, to check.

The Tuesday when the American president went down, they closed school early. I went home thinking today, for this, I'd find the news on. But our house was dead. Lights out, the air steamy from the dishwasher and the clothes dryer.

Mama was zonked in the rocker chair, holding Nonna's hand. They're in Storage now, together. Neither looks a day older.

By the time the tech gave up on trying to make her care about her trio of living tchotchkes, Lindy had loaded photographs of Terese onto the window with her testimony. This was one of two lancet panes slated to go outside the Prince of Wales Heritage Centre. It had to be perfect.

Her modem was running hot.

She lowered her bit rate, cooling the modem before making final tweaks to the pane's historiated initial. Big "T" for Terese, with a faux-medieval image of a uniformed schoolgirl. Last, she set the glass to fossilize, permafixing the images and text.

"Something burning?"

A middle-aged Sikh man was hovering in Lindy's doorway. Her afternoon appointment.

"It's my modem." She raised her left hand, showing the burned palm, ring of red where skin met the umbilicus of her modem. Coiling the umbilicus around her wrist, she made a bracelet of it, fib-op loops that hid a multitude of sins. "Are you Abrik Singh?"

"Nice to meet you." He helped Lindy lift the new pane, examining the images of Terese, girl and woman, and the status bar flickering below them. Eighty percent finished.

They set it on the table near the kids. Once the crystals were set, Lindy would polish the pane and seal it in several layers of weatherproof varnish.

"You burn like that every time?" He reached for her.

Lindy skipped back out of reach. "Don't."

"Oh, that's right—" He raised his hands, embarrassed.

Missy had made points a few elections back off being "close" to a rape survivor, before Last Year. Everyone knew she had a half-crazy sister who didn't like to be touched. She might as well have branded VICTIM onto Lindy's forehead.

But the public exposure was what bought her the modem she was, even now, burning to a crisp.

"You just surprised me," Lindy said, offering him one of the portable mics she kept lying around. The whole studio was wired for sound, but her subjects didn't know that.

Singh smoothed his moustache, left side first, in what looked like a habitual gesture. "What happened with the guy? He go to jail?"

"Yeah, but not for assaulting me. He went down in prison."

Leaving Abrik to fit her past into his personal theory of *Why me, why not her?*, Lindy took up another mic:

"People say the Naptime phenomenon began in Frankfurt, on Groundhog Day. Four weeks earlier, though, a passenger jet from Vancouver arrived at Lester B. Pearson Airport in Toronto with everyone aboard, but for the captain and co-pilot, deep in something like a coma.

"Abrik Singh was a marketing manager for Molson Breweries. He was aboard flight WS700. Abrik, what's your story?"

He toyed with the mic: "I was online during take-off."

Lindy offered an encouraging smile. "Online... working?"

"Reports, spreadsheets. The usual bull. I was concentrating hard because of the girl sleeping next to me. Woman, I mean. It was supposedly hot in Toronto. Remember what it was like, being hot?"

Lindy nodded. She missed summer heat almost as much as she missed antianxiety meds.

"She was in a skimpy white sundress, and slumped... whenever I glanced right, I was staring down her neckline."

"You try to wake her?"

"Nudged her. Even said 'hey.' She had that look, like a three-year-old after a bender." Abrik gestured at Lindy's three charges – boy, girl, polyester-skinned Lucifer.

"I decided if I kept working, it'd be okay. She wouldn't come around and find me checking out her boobs."

"Sounds like a polite thing to do."

"Three hours into the flight, we hit turbulence. I snapped out of it. The pilot was saying, 'Sit down, strap in.' I looked around. Nobody'd brought our pretzels. I was the only person awake on the whole plane."

"Were you frightened?"

"No, not really." He frowned. "I didn't think 'Oh my God, we've been gassed.'"

"Or 'Holy shit, I better do something?'"

"I thought: 'I've been at this for *hours*.'"

Lindy nodded. The unconcern that accompanied Last Year, Jitterbugs quietly coping as Winkles dozed off by the hundreds, was one of the unexplained mysteries of the Napocalypse.

"I darkened my display specs and kicked my shoes off. Next thing I knew, it was nine weeks later and I was being sliced out of a fantastic dream by this gigantic machete-wielding lunatic. Leopold Drummer."

"*The* Leopold Drummer?"

"The hacker giant, in the flesh, I swear. He'd decided the way to kiss people awake was to cut out their cybernetic modems." Abrik rolled up his sleeve, revealing a wrist-to-elbow scar, worm-white on his dark skin. "Put this on my shard, okay?"

◄ ►

After Singh had gone, Lindy hit Repurposing, a subterranean parkade where they disassembled used-up cars, stripping out the working parts before adding the husks to the walls Missy was building to keep wolves out of the city.

"Any glazier's modems?"

A bored-looking mechanic shook his head – she asked every single time – before pointing out the latest corpses. Lindy began busting out their windows and mirrors, gathering material for Abrik's shard.

Exertion and noise, the act of destruction, calmed her. She had filled an old blue recycling bin with glittering, fractured pieces when Paula Stern showed up.

"I got a complaint you're neglecting your kids."

"Don't fucking call them that."

Paula had been a teacher in Wetaskiwin. She'd come into the studio a few times, but refused to bare her soul for Lindy's project.

"You eaten?"

"Don't remember."

Paula handed Lindy a sandwich – caribou and sprouts on bannock. "I have to issue you a warning."

"Grab a bin. You'll save me a trip."

"Sure." Donning a pair of heavy gloves, Paula began shovelling glass shards.

Lindy bit into the sandwich, which was surprisingly fresh. The sprouts hadn't had time to collapse to wet threads. "You're in a good mood."

"Just got laid," Paula said. "Mike Chang."

"Tractor guy?" Mike had been instrumental in salvaging farm equipment from across the Prairies, keeping the grain and rapeseed farmers in oil and working machinery until they transitioned back to horse-drawn plows.

"Your Missy's gonna make him Minister of Finance. He's feeling full of himself. I am feeling full of him, too."

"Congratulations." Would that make it easier to get Mike into her chair? The prime minister might be prevailed upon to insist.

Right. More like, Oh, Lindy, you and your oral history. Isn't it time we moved on?

"You old enough to remember we used to call that a hook-up?" Paula asked.

"Mike's sowing wild oats," Lindy said, and got a blank look.

It was her delivery; nobody laughed at her, except when she wasn't joking.

They climbed out of the parkade into twilight and a fresh inch of snow, huffing steam as they toiled along, hauling glass. They stopped at a park bench to catch their breath. Lindy thumbed one of her portable mics when Paula wasn't looking.

"Hooking up," she said. "You said once your students were the ones who coined the term Napocalypse."

"Cute, huh? Better than the Winkling. Or the Big Sleep-over."

"Cute," Lindy echoed.

"Branding the end of the fucking world instead of…"

"Of what?" By chance they'd stopped in front of one of Lindy's bigger displays, neo-Gothic testimonials from a dozen Napocalypse survivors. She was tired of the medieval look, but this was the concept she'd pitched the Arts Council for her oral history of Last Year. Unless she wanted to end up in a canning factory or going on the caribou hunt, she was stuck with it.

Stuck until her modem burned out, anyway.

"If we'd acted sooner and Tweeted less, there'd be more of us left," Paula said.

"Acted how? People tried waking the Winkles. What was the success rate. One percent?" Lindy rolled the glass umbilicus off her wrist, revealing words, tattooed amid a hash of razor scars: LET ME SLEEP, GODDAMMIT. "You got one of these too, right?"

After a second, Paula responded by exposing her wrist.

"WAKE ME IF YOU CAN, KILL ME IF YOU CAN'T," Lindy read aloud, for the mic. "Why?"

"I had nightmares. The idea of sleeping indefinitely terri-fied me."

"Wow. So, how did they kiss you awake?"

"Acupuncture. Five hundred needles."

"Were you? Having nightmares?"

Tears spilled down Paula's face. "I was outdoors, in a meadow. It was the colour of a lawn but felt like mink, or how I imagined mink… buttercup-strewn mink.

"My body felt strong, vibrant. There wasn't an ache, a twinge of fatigue. Remember being a kid? Never hurting?"

Lindy was suddenly conscious of the sand in her joints. "Not really."

"My mind, too. Alert, untroubled. I relived a few of my best memories: cuddling a puppy, dancing with my husband at a disco in New Haven. I went back to toddlerhood and listened to things my parents said to each other, stuff I'd heard them say when I was preverbal. Mama had a wicked sense of humour – I never knew that."

"Parenting wore it out of her," Lindy couldn't help saying, but Paula wasn't listening.

"Later, I got to putting together a galaxy. Deciding where every star would go, drawing orbital paths. I licked a black hole and it tasted like limes.

"Then they poke-poke-poked me out of it, because of my tatts. Is it any wonder so many Sleeping Beauties turn on our so-called princes?"

◀ ▶

Paula handed her a foil-wrapped ball of rice and cooked meat when they reached the studio, but refused to schlep the glass up the three flights of stairs. Lindy hauled the bins herself, making two trips.

The second time, she found someone reading the kids' monitors.

Yellowknife wasn't so small that everyone knew everyone, though sometimes it felt that way. Before Last Year, the town had 20,000 people; now, since Missy had decided to collapse the surviving Canadian population into the North, it was bursting with 100,000 Jitterbugs and Beauties, plus 500,000 Winkles in storage.

At first it didn't click. He was just a guy. Tall – super tall – Caucasian and weathered, with grey eyes, he wore salvaged antique jeans that fit him well.

Lindy had a fleeting thought of Paula, hooking up. Was it national get lucky day? *Maybe he's here to laugh at my sowing oats joke. Gimme a plow, big guy?*

Then she saw the hashmarks branded into his forearms: 15 on the left for 15 dead cougars, nine on the right for bears killed on Winkle retrieval missions...

Matt Cardinal.

Shit!

"Sorry," he said. "Your door was open."

I bet that smile opens a lot of legs.

Lindy swallowed. He didn't seem to know who she was. "What do you want?"

"Twentieth anniversary of Last Year, innit?" he said. "Don't you want a testimonial from the Post-nap's answer to Shakespeare?"

He's up to something. Her stomach flipped.

Licking her lips, she scooped up a mic and said: "Matthew Cardinal was in the Edmonton Institution, serving a five-year sentence for armed robbery. After Last Year, he joined the Rocky Mountain retrieval team—"

"Retrieved these three, as it happens," he murmured.

Lindy fought the urge to step between him and the stretcher of kids. Where did that impulse come from? "Matt is Poet Laureate of Canada."

She gestured at the comfy chair. "Sit down. Tell us all about your Napocalypse."

Instead of sitting, he walked to her. Lindy backed up; he came until she was against a wall and they were inches apart.

Testing: Would she scream? Fight? Tell him to back off?

As if she'd ever had that much backbone. Twenty years melted away. Her eyes bugged; she could smell fear rolling off herself.

He picked the mic, ever so gently, out of her grip. "Guys at the penitentiary started nodding off in February, right after Frankfurt. Corrections sent the first three to hospital. Then they reallocated cells, shelving Winkles in their cots. They kept us Jitterbugs in another section.

"It might've been a relief. An unconscious prison population is less work. But they were losing guards too. Some guy goes home, eats his beef and beans, kisses the kids goodnight and sits down to watch the game. Nods off. Next day, nothing's getting him out of that chair. Right?"

She forced herself to answer: "He's just gone, yeah."

"We had 80 prisoners down and a skeleton crew watching the rest when this team of strung-out geeks shows up with defibrillators, scalpels, caffeine enemas, for fuck's sake. They play around with prince charming the guys. Pris-oners, right? Who cares?

"Soon they'd killed a fellow in for a short stretch. Evan. Drunk driver, I think. Threw a sheet over him, wheeled the body down the hall, kept going.

"Then they got lucky. Three guys in a row they woke up. One they got with a defibrillator. Stopped his heart. Three. Two. One. Clear! *Badoom, badoom.* He surfaces, screaming. Cry after cry, like a gut-wrenched horse.

"Thing was, there weren't enough guards anymore. Thing was, we weren't lambs in a pen. And the guys they woke weren't petty vehicular homicides.

"They didn't just piss and moan, those Sleeping Beauties, they didn't cry about happy dreams or paradise lost. Sam Gees, the screamer, tried cutting his own head off. While those poor misguided ghouls were trying to restrain *him*, the other two tore apart everything they could reach.

"They had long arms."

I hate this spoken-word crap, Lindy thought.

"Riot built, like a tsunami. Soon we had a dozen dead science nerds, the remaining guards' guns, the keys to the whole lock-up. We scattered, like kids fleeing a haunted house."

With that, Matt thumbed the mic off. "Howzat?"

Lindy fought to keep her voice steady. "I've collected similar stories from your fellow inmates."

"Oh, you bored? This a rerun for you?"

He *definitely* didn't know who she was.

She'd assumed one of the other prisoners had taken Matt's identity, to hide a more serious crime. But this guy hadn't seen Matt's drawings, hadn't heard his obsessive stalker blah blah: "My girl Lindy, when we get married, Lindy and me, the babies we'll have…"

Never mind she'd been 16 and he'd been nearly 30. Never mind that they'd met once, at a party.

Matt Cardinal had been even crazier than Lindy herself. This guy didn't know that, so he couldn't have been in lock-up.

"I got a million stories, you don't like that one."

She tried to smile. "Sure you do. Bear fights and Winkle retrieval."

"Worst was Hinton, near Jasper. Nine hundred Winkles stored in a barricaded mall. Cougars got in. I'll write you a poem about it."

Don't, she tried to say, but the words froze in her throat. The man calling himself Matt Cardinal slid out of the room like a slick of dark oil.

Lindy collapsed to the floor, hands over ears, shaking. *Now what, who is he, gotta run, what's he want, can't someone just come along and take care of this, of me...*

When the hand touched her face, she shrieked and hurled herself backward, banging her head on the wall.

It was Satan.

◄ ►

"Prime minister's office."

"I gotta talk to my sister."

"Hi, Lindy. I'll see if she's free."

Missy's window was mounted at Town Hall.

Melissa Hertz is prime minister of Canada.

I was visiting my teenaged sister at work – her first real job was printing windows at our dad's auto shop in Etobicoke – when a car drove itself in. It had an appointment to get its AC fixed. The owner had gone down in the back seat, and the summer heat killed her. It was... Lindy, you freaked out, remember?

While we waited for the police, I checked the news. A tenth of the city was comatose. There was a heat wave on. Thousands of Winkles might bake.

The electrical grid hadn't yet fallen apart, and the Internet was mostly working. People believed it would stop, we'd ride it out. But I've always been a pessimist.

That much was true.

"Lindy?" The assistant was back. "Could you email her?"

"Tell her it's a fucking emergency."

"Is it about your modem?"

Missy wanted the modem to die; she wanted Lindy on a work crew. Regulated mealtimes, laundered uniforms, barracks and a daily shower. That was her idea of taking care of little sis.

She imagined telling the assistant that Missy's precious Poet Laureate was the guy who'd stalked, drugged, and fucked her, all those years ago when Missy was off at college. The guy wanted to play identity thief; why not give him *all* of Matt's illustrious past? "No, not the modem."

"Hold on."

I put out the word. Bring cars. Bring evacuees.

We loaded Winkles five and six to a vehicle, packing supplies in the trunks. Canned food, blankets, batteries. We'd lay children across the laps of the seated, strapped-in adults.

There were so many.

I wanted to hook up trucks to pull bigger loads, but Lindy convinced me they'd crash and block the road.

We programmed routes to autopumps, to rechargers, and we sent the cars north, where it was cold, so the Winkles wouldn't fry. Port Saint John, Thunder Bay, Yellowknife – anywhere you could reach by road.

Within a week, people started going to bed in their vehicles. Deliberately, I mean. They'd set an alarm: if it didn't wake them, the car would automatically upload the route and head north.

I may have sent that first car up to the Arctic, but the Uplift wouldn't have worked if not for thousands of hardworking, dedicated Canadians who pulled together as the crisis worsened, keeping the roads open, the Internet functional, the fuel pumping—

"Lindy? You okay?" Melissa's voice, in the here and now, drowned out her remembrance of Missy's testimonial.

"I got a Beauty on my hands."

"What did you do?"

"Excuse me?"

"Were you varnishing? StatsCan says one in 600 Winkles are awakened by smells. Solvents—"

"StatsCan? Which is what – some guy with a calculator implant and three college stats courses?"

"I'm not having this argument with you again. Was it varnish?"

"Right. I routinely force the kiddies to sniff glue as they take up shelf space in my studio."

"Call Health Canada."

"You know what they'll tell me. I broke it, I bought it. Missy, can't you take care of me here?"

"I can't give you special favours."

Stretching, uncomfortable silence. Missy knew that Lindy's studio was bugged. She wouldn't say anything to damage her approval rating.

"Please?" She couldn't quash the whine in her voice.

Missy said: "If you join a work crew—"

"I *have* a job."

"Uh-huh. The first night – do you know this? – after some-one's awake, they're at risk of self-harm and harm to others."

"We're talking about a four-year-old."

"A child probably doesn't seem dangerous—"

"Fine, I'll hide the knives."

"If the solvents in your studio are that strong, they're prob-ably not doing you any good."

"Fuck! I wasn't varnishing."

"What is it, anyway?"

The devil had been sucking on most of one fist. Now it announced: "I'm a girl."

"That's great, sweetheart," the speakerphone enthused. "Do you know your name?"

"Zazu, Queen of the Snow Angels."

"That's not your name," Lindy said.

Through the speaker, a chuckle. "Important safety tip, sis. Unlike you, kids like to eat regularly."

"We are hungry," Zazu agreed, as if she were 50 and por-ing over a menu, someplace pricey.

"Too bad." Lindy said: "Missy, while I've got you, my modem—"

"You're in the salvage queue."

"It's getting dire."

"Rules are rules."

"I'm listed as a project of cultural significance."

"You know what I think," Missy said. "The oral history shards encourage morbid thinking."

"You mean I'm morbid."

"Dwelling on a past we can't have back—"

"What do you call keeping old government departments alive? StatsCan?"

"I call it crisis management. Democracy in action."

Her sister's tone made suspicion bloom. "Are you blocking my modem request?"

"I have no influence over the salvage queue."

"You are, aren't you?"

A click. The royal audience was over.

"Bitchbitchbitch!" Lindy screamed at the phone.

Zazu had homed in on a file cabinet at the back of the studio. She dug up a box of mac and cheez.

"I was saving that," Lindy snarled, but her mouth watered.

"Cook it."

She snatched the box, fighting an urge to clout the kid – and a wave of shame. "Fine. But we're only making half."

"You have weiners?"

"No." Cooking meant finding her hotplate and saucepan, then begging a couple pats of fake butter off the physiotherapist next door. Zazu waited, in her devil costume, in the hallway.

"Cutest thing I ever seen," Glenda – the physio – cooed.

"She's yours if you want her."

"You're so funny!"

Lindy sighed. "Wasn't joking."

"What woke her? The varnish?"

"No."

"Mac and cheez?" Glenda licked her lips. "The real deal?"

"Come have some," Zazu said.

Lindy shot the kid a dirty look, but what could she do? They had to have the margarine. *Mi studio es su casa,* she agreed weakly.

"Do you have weiners?" Zazu added.

"Pelee might. Sort of." Glenda all but skipped down the hall to consult with the former veterinarian.

Dinner for five. Now we are *making the whole box.*

It turned out living at the edge of starvation tended to shrink your appetite, so that last box of prefab pasta went a surprisingly long way. And Lindy must have forgotten what real weiners tasted like, because the sealmeat-and-gut abominations that passed for them nowadays were delicious.

Glenda, who'd always acted as though Lindy had a *smell* or something, made an appointment to come in when she saw the latest shards. She'd driven a bus full of Winkled biologists to Yellowknife from Galveston, Texas.

What had she seen in America, as the world ended?

Pelee, the veterinarian, went through the motions of examining Zazu. "Was it a smell woke you, honey?"

"Lindy wasn't varnishing."

"I'm not sure the city has a lot of kids' clothes. You'll have to scrounge. There'll be an extra food ration."

"I want Berry Loops," Zazu said immediately.

I want antidepressants and a hot tub, Lindy thought, though she'd loved Berry Loops.

"I don't think anyone's got breakfast cereal anymore, honey," Glenda said.

"Your majesty," Zazu corrected.

Pelee cocked an eyebrow.

"She's queen of the snow angels," Lindy explained.

After they were gone, Zazu went rooting amid Lindy's pile of stuff again, coming up with a broken-toothed comb. "Can I brush your hair?"

"You want to brush me?"

Zazu nodded.

"I guess." Why argue? The kid would take a few swipes and give up. But Zazu pulled out all the knots, working patiently and painlessly, until she could fluff Lindy with her little spit-slimed hands.

"Want me to do you?" Lindy offered reluctantly. Her head felt remarkably good.

Zazu shook her head. She climbed back onto the stretcher with the two Winkles and stuck her fist in her mouth, falling asleep.

Maybe she'll go down again, Lindy thought, dozing in the comfy chair. A belly full of carbs and protein made it easier both to find sleep and to stay there.

She woke late, and didn't think of Zazu until she found the saucepan sitting out, half-full of day-glo leftovers.

More leftovers than she remembered.

She scooped up a clump with her fingers, licking them clean, savouring the intense over-salted old-worldy goodness as she turned her gaze to the gurney.

The kid was gone.

◄ ►

This was a chance. A truly unfit caregiver would go about her day. Someone would find Zazu soon enough, and there'd be a hue and cry.

Oh, did she leave? I was varnishing.

Someone must be dying to adopt an urchin.

Lindy absolutely wasn't going to do the thing where you freaked out and went begging people to help find your lost lamb.

Wolves slip through the wall all the time, three people got eaten last winter...

She won't have got out of the building.

Be negligent for an hour, and then free for a lifetime.

"Fuck," she said. "Who'm I kidding?"

She grabbed her keys and ran out into the dim light of dawn. A wet, wheel-torn expanse of snow greeted her. Small footie prints, tinted red with leaked dye, led around the side of the building. There they met up with enormous tracks.

"Zazu!" She sprinted to the corner, and saw faux Matt Cardinal with the girl astride his shoulders.

"Hey!" she shrieked. Heads turned and Matt stopped.

Zazu had a waxy cellophane cereal bag containing coloured lumps that might once have been Berry Loops, along with half a box of powdered milk and a steel bowl from Lindy's studio.

Matt offered up his lazy panty-peeler smile. "You lose someone?"

Huffing, Lindy closed the distance between them. "Put her down."

"Kid's walking around in her sock feet."

"Then bring her to the stairwell."

"I need snow," Zazu said. She waved a steel bowl at Lindy.

"Your Maj," Matt said. "Dunno what you're planning, but snow here is fulla husky shit and biodiesel."

"Go there." Zazu pointed at the nearest tree, a big pine, laden with snow.

Surrendering, Lindy took the steel bowl. "Here?"

"Hold it up."

She had barely begun to lift when a clump of pristine snow dropped from above. The bowl filled. The rest slid into her collar and over her body, neck to ankles; an icy shock that left her feeling as though she'd been scrubbed.

The branch waved, freed from the burden of the snow's weight. She smelled pine oil.

"Cute trick," Matt said.

"Can we go in now?" Lindy pleaded.

"Go!" Zazu kicked her wet heels and they retraced the pink smudged prints. Matt had to duck low to get her in the door. Polyester devil horns scraped the doorframe, *szzt, szzt,* sending sprinkles of fabric paint swirling.

"Down you go, your Maj." He set her on the concrete steps.

Grabbing Lindy's hand, she began to pull her upstairs. "Breakfast time."

"Matt has things to do."

"Matt," Zazu repeated, tone neutral.

He was climbing along behind them.

"Who gave you the cereal?" Lindy asked.

"Lady. Vivian."

"Vivian Wu?"

"She said it would rot my mouth." Zazu bared her teeth, which were punky with orange macaroni and bits of seal.

"You should brush those," Lindy said.

"I will if you will."

Matt chortled. "She's got a point."

"Vivian didn't know your Aunty Depressin."

"Huh?" Lindy could've sworn that part of her inner monologue yesterday had been, you know, inner.

"Need meds?" Matt lit up. "I can help with that."

What would it take to get rid of this guy? He came up to the third floor, sticking like glue as Zazu trotted to Lindy's studio, watching as she sprinkled a teaspoon of her powdered milk onto the bowl full of snow.

She flopped on the floor, sticking her legs up. "My feet are wet."

Lindy pulled her out of the bottom half of the devil costume and swabbed at the little toes with a varnishing rag. "I have water, you know."

The kid stuck her thumb in her mouth and mumbled something that sounded like "Bleepul, bekka?"

"Thanks," Matt replied. "I had breakfast."

Kid clothes. What was she going to do for kid clothes? Lindy grabbed up a couple of her cleaner T-shirts, went over to the varnishing table and started stripping the girl and boy. Socks, underwear, shirts. No shoes—

Matt let out a string of profanity, undertone.

"What?"

Zazu's bowl of snow had melted, faster than it should have. The white flecks of dried milk were spreading within it, swirling chalky bits of colour. And the smell—

"Cereal?" Zazu rolled to her feet.

"Fuck." Lindy said. "Kid, I think you just turned meltwater to milk."

Zazu peered into the bowl, looking puzzled. "Weird stuff."

"It's cream." Lindy touched the fluid: it was ice cold.

"Part the cream, kid," Matt said. "Like the Red Fucking Sea."

"I know that story!" Zazu made the Moses gesture, a reverse clap, arms straight. Cream sloshed out of the bowl and onto the floor. "Sorry."

"It'll dry," Lindy said. Matt gave her a faintly disgusted look, plucked one of the T-shirts out of her hand, and started wiping.

Lindy took a sip of what remained in the bowl. Homo milk, fresh, with just the right mix of fat. She hadn't tasted anything so pure and sinfully delicious in 20 years.

Part it. What made Matt suggest that?

"Get spoons," Zazu ordered. She sprinkled a few Berry Loops into the bowl. Lindy meant to stare at them, but immediately blinked. Like that, the bowl was full of crunchy pink and blue loops.

Momma, don't let her eat so much sugar! She remembered Missy, at 11. Already a tyrant.

Matt went to the hotplate, returning with three spoons. He wiped them on the same shirt he'd used on the floor. "Don't you wash anything?"

"I'm clinically depressed."

"Clinically lazy."

"I see why you get along with my sister."

"No fighting." The kid dug in, crunching. "Lindy, eat."

What the hell. She took a spoonful, and the sugary goodness damn near blew her mind. She'd forgotten how she'd loved preprocessed food. *Cereal, pasta. All we need to complete the trip down memory lane is...*

Zazu spoke to Matt. "Can you find peanut butter and jelly for lunch?"

Lindy's skin rose up in gooseflesh.

"Anna loaf of Wonderbread while I'm at it." Matt grinned. "That shit lasts forever."

"You said you could get Aunty Depressin."

"I know a guy with a hoard of Paxil and Xanax."

Hey, little girl, want some candy? "Zazu, I don't need the pills." *The eff am I saying what if he can get it, just a little Paxil to soften the edges...*

"Anyway, Matt should—"

"Rumour has it you've been asking about a glazier's modem," Matt said.

Lindy ran dry, mid-sentence. The only thing she could hear was Zazu, crunching her cereal.

Modem modem modem modem, need a modem, Matt's got a modem?

She got another modem, things stayed the same. She wouldn't have to fight Missy and her work assignment. Things wouldn't go from awful to even worse.

"Um. Would you excuse us?"

Matt gave her a half nod, "I'll hit the men's."

When he was gone, she said: "Kid. Zazu. Matt's not – I don't think we should trust him."

"Trust who?"

"This loaves and fishes shit, you can't pull that in front of other people. You know where that kind of thing ends up?"

Crunch, crunch, crunch. Uncomprehending baby deer eyes.

"You said you knew the Moses story... " Did people tell little kids about Jesus on the cross? She had a sudden vision of the girl, nailed to a wall, crowned with icicles.

"Don't you want peanut butter?"

"Zazu, what woke you up?"

"I was done sleeping."

"Do you read minds?"

"I'm too little to read."

Shouldn't a superpowered four-year-old be supersmart?

"No." Zazu scoffed.

She sighed. "People will freak. There's nobody like you, kid."

"Is too." She held up her hand, curling the smallest two fingers under, showing three.

The words made her skin crawl. "There are others? Beauties waking up without acupuncture or caffeine enemas—"

"Acca punch her."

"Do they read minds too?"

"What's enema?"

"If there are others, where are they?"

Zazu stuck her nose in the cereal bowl, like a horse in a feedbag. Words echoed out of a slurp. "At Leepold's."

"Leopold? As in Drummer? He's missing, he's on the Mountie's most wanted list—"

"Is not missing." That childish scorn again.

Identity thief. Lindy lunged across the room and hit her speakerphone: "Give me Missy."

"What are you doing?" That was Matt, back from his piss and looming over her, close.

"The kid," she said, breathless. "Matt, we have to tell Missy—"

"Tell Missy what? The Second Coming has a thing for pre-Napocalypse instant foods?"

"Zazu says—"

"You really want to have another pointless convo with Big Sister?"

"No, but… " He was crowding her; she could barely draw breath.

She gestured at the windows on her varnishing table. All the testimonials. So many versions of "We let it happen. If only we'd done something. We waited until it was too late…"

That's why Missy was prime minister, right? Because she'd acted. Got people off their asses. Filled the cars with unconscious refugees, nagged people to staff fuel stations.

"If Winkles are waking, we have to tell."

"We fucking do not."

"She reads minds, Matt."

"And you can't handle her, I know."

"I couldn't keep a cat alive."

"I'm tagge care offoo," Zazu said, around a mouthful of loops. *I'm taking care of you.*

Lindy's hand went to her detangled, shining hair. Her skin felt clean where the snow had run down her dress. Longing rushed through her: all she'd wanted, for so long, was to be mothered.

"You're not giving her to a politician," Matt said. "But I'll take her off your hands, if you want."

Oh.

When she'd first seen him, he was looking over the kids' monitors.

Out in the snow, earlier. He'd have walked away with her.

She managed to say, "No."

Matt's enormous hand shot out, catching her jaw. "You want that modem, Lindy, or no?"

She did. She wanted the modem and the antidepressants and she wanted to hold out in her studio until Missy lost an election and all her influence. She wanted peanut butter and tuna fish and ibuprofen and her own Mommy. He wasn't wrong. What could she do for a child?

He saw it. Saw through her.

Zazu belched, dropped to her butt and began pulling her footies back on. "Let's find that jelly, okay?"

"Sure, kid." Matt smiled. "Say goodbye."

"To who?" Zazu climbed up. "Zip your coat, Lindy."

"Lindy's staying," Matt said.

"No!"

"I'll bring her the modem later."

"Like I believe that," Lindy said. She didn't meet his eyes; she'd have backed down for sure.

"Suit yourself." He reached for Zazu, but Lindy slid between them, taking the girl's hand.

They walked out to the edge of Yellowknife, the inner wall, where food supplies and scavenged treasures were kept in old container cars. The cache was guarded by a guy calling himself Customs Canada, but Matt tossed him a paper-wrapped package, and he waved them by.

We can't trust Matt, Lindy tried thinking at Zazu, but if the kid heard her, she didn't react.

Striding past several empty, open containers, Matt opened the first closed car. It smelled of dust and yeast.

"Come on," he said, stepping inside.

This is not good. If he's really the Hacker Giant... but a modem! And I can't do the kid thing.

Zazu followed him into darkness and cobwebs, without apparent fear. The container was loaded with stuff scavenged from groceries: canned goods and snacks, things nobody got around to eating. Ghosts of the old food industry.

"Here's your jelly," Matt said, producing a jar. "There ain't gonna be any peanut butter, but—" He fished around, coming up with a foil-sealed plastic jug filled with unsalted peanuts. "Dee Eye Why. Do it yourself."

"They look pretty dry," Lindy said.

"I got canola oil. Anything else you want, kid?"

Zazu turned a circle, then pointed her plastic pitchfork at a battered box of dead saltines.

"Great," Lindy said heartily. "Say thank you."

"Thank you, Leepold."

Matt's smile curdled.

Faking cheer, Lindy said: "Let's get back, eh?"

"Canola," Matt said. "In my truck. DIY peanut butter."

They trooped out, thanked the guard, walked farther. Lindy wanted to run for it, but Matt lifted Zazu to his shoulders again. All she could do was drift along beside them.

Finally, she asked: "What'd you trade the guard?"

"Flash disk. Old top 40 hits."

Matt's truck was a reconditioned police SUV, battered and fortified, with spikes welded to its bumpers.

"Into the back, monkey," he said, opening the rear door. Zazu began to climb in.

"Wait," Lindy began, and that was when he spun and plowed her in the mouth.

She dropped into the snow – *I was right, I was right!* – as he lifted Zazu's butt into the truck and shut it behind her.

"Go back to town," he said. Behind him, in the car window, the girl was glowering.

Lindy wiped her throbbing face, shaking the blood off into the snow. Before Matt could drive off, she bolted for the truck, jumping into the passenger seat. Her heart was hammering.

She thought he'd drag her out and abandon her. Instead he laughed, starting the engine and heading between the containers, deep into a maze of stripped cars, stacked three and four deep.

"So," she quavered. "Leopold Drummer?"

"You knew before she said. How?"

She swallowed blood. "I knew the real Matt."

"Huh."

"Rumour was that your sleeping app was what started the Napocalypse."

"There were lotsa rumours."

"It makes sense. They sent you to the Institution to experiment on Winkle prisoners." She remembered news footage, pictures of a pale man, corpulent, with long golden hair and thick glasses. "You lost weight."

"End-of-the-world diet. Biggest trend of Last Year."

"Got your eyes lasered?"

"Fixed the astigmatism, changed the colour."

"What do you want with Zazu?"

"It *was* the app. Delta Wave."

"She's too young for a modem."

"I know. It jumped the firewall into people without tech."

"How?"

"Dunno."

"The app was around for years."

"We'd posted an upgrade, for people on vacation. It was supposed to put you under, way under, into a healing sleep. You'd wake when you were fully rested."

"Zero out your sleep debt," Lindy said, remembering advertisements. "Your stupid app gave me migraines."

"Jitterbugs," he said. "We can't relax."

Was it as simple as that?

"But now – what? She wakes up for no good reason—"

"I was *done*," Zazu repeated.

"Yeah, done," Matt snorted. "They achieve some crazy state of enlightenment, who knows what the fuck. Performing miracles cobbled out of bits and pieces of myths and Bible stories. For fun, as far as I can tell. Just to make themselves friggin' happy."

He sounded offended by the mere idea.

"Do they explain what's going on? No chance." He snaked the truck through a narrow lane, banging through a stack of tractor tires. It was a fake, a curtain made of hanging rubber pieces. They thudded on the truck roof, like fists.

Beyond the curtain were trailers: temporary school class-rooms, a water recycler, a generator.

"Home sweet home," Matt said.

Lindy checked the rearview. Zazu was eating saltines out of her battered red box.

Can you get out of there, kid?

Zazu shook her head. "Did you make the peanut butter?"

Do as you're told, she thought, trying to flavour the thought with her sister's bossiest voice. *Get that door open right now, young lady, and run to town.*

"I want peanut butter!"

No miraculous escape, no fucking peanut butter!

Matt yanked Lindy out of the truck. The cop car came with cuffs – he locked her hands behind her back.

"Go," he said, nudging her toward the trailers.

She went, slow as she dared, and then froze beside an old iron bathtub. It was filled with ice: entombed within was a 10-year-old boy, blue of skin, with a carved willow flute.

"Hoof it," Matt said. "This ain't the zoo."

She stumbled into the classroom. It was laid out like an ambulance, or hospital room, with a cot on either side. A Winkle was laid out on the left, a teenaged boy in a Vancouver Canucks jersey. His eyes were pinned open and his teeth were digging into a bit. His upper skull was shaved and open; a laptop umbilicus vanished into his brain.

He had ice skates on, black skates with black wings growing from the ankles.

Lindy retched, and Matt turned her away, so she couldn't heave colourful cereal onto the boy's open cranium.

"He's perfectly okay," he said.

"Okay? It's not sterile in here," she managed, when she could breathe again.

"Yet he's alive," he said. "You could still take the modem, Lindy, and walk back into town."

"I'll fuck you," Lindy said breathlessly.

"What?"

"Let Zazu go."

He made a dismissive noise. "Way too late to go pretending you give a shit."

"I—" Part of her agreed; what was she doing?

"I miraculous scaped." Zazu stood at the trailer entrance, with her little hood pulled off her head – her hair was a shaggy black mane – and snow on her feet. She had a cracker in one hand and her faded plastic pitchfork in the other. "Whajja do to Jason?"

I told you to run, Lindy thought. She tried to boot Matt in the crotch.

It didn't work: he'd probably felt her getting ready before she'd formed the thought. Dodging her knee, he grabbed her throat. "No horsing around near the equipment, girls."

Lindy went wireless.

Configuring her glass umbilicus into slivers, Lindy arrowed a thin, snaking line into Matt's wrist, digging into his skin.

The grip on her throat eased, enough to yell. "Run, kid!"

Zazu had her hand in her mouth, sucking and watching.

She pushed through the wrist, a bright narrow icicle of glass, and arced it toward his face.

Matt shoved Lindy away. She dropped to the trailer floor, near the door, near the kid. A sticky tendril of hot smartglass stretched like a loose clothesline between her palm and his wrist.

"Loafs and fishes," Zazu said. "You got all you need."

It was true: Lindy could feel the trailer windows bending inward, disassembling. Outside, the SUV's windshield and mirrors were coming too. She drew all the smartglass in the automorgue toward her. The strings of glass thickened, forming a web between her and Matt.

He put his head down, charging, an enraged-bull bellow.

Zazu patted her, consolingly, on the back. The throbbing in Lindy's face subsided.

She jacked up her bit rate, crying out as the modem began to melt against the edge of the handcuffs, spreading the burn through her much-abused wrist. The glass fused, melting together in a wall, safety glass, half an inch, one, two.

Behind her, Zazu was moving, climbing up onto the cot.

"We gotta know," Matt bellowed. "Why are they waking? How fast will it happen?"

Lindy lumped up window glass around him, trying to block out the sound.

Zazu had, by now, pulled the other kid's monitors off, dropping them on the floor carelessly, along with little chunks of wire and brain. She pulled on the hinge of skull, mushing it down like someone forcing a suitcase shut.

"Arise, Jason."

Matt laughed, a brittle noise, muffled by increasingly thick glass. He snatched up a wrench and began pounding it against the makeshift wall.

"We should go," Lindy said. "He'll break out eventually."

"Can we take Jason?"

And do what? Feed him Berry Loops?

"Cereal's for breakfast."

"Stupid me." Lindy shook her head. "I can't get Jason into Matt's truck, not like this."

Zazu shook her head. Then she went outside.

"You have to stop walking around barefoot in the snow!" Lindy yelled.

"You're not the boss of me!"

Follow? Or stay? She was afraid to take her eyes off Matt. His lips moved, soundless threat. She could make out the words "… gonna suffer…"

Zazu came back a second later with the peanuts and canola. "Make the peanut butter."

"I'm a little tied up here," Lindy said.

Zazu climbed into her lap, peering into her eyes. After a second, the right handcuff slipped off.

"Kid," she said, "I ain't fit to be your mother."

Zazu dug her little fingers into Lindy's palm, drawing out the umbilicus and scorched pieces of the modem, tracing the line where the overheated cuffs had scorched her wrist, examining the old self-inflicted scars and the tattoo: LET ME SLEEP, GODDAMMIT. She kissed the wrist, and the ache from the burns faded. "Just make the peanut butter."

"Okay," Lindy said. There was a bowl on the counter that smelled clean; pouring the peanuts inside, she took a small Pyrex flask and began crushing them to powder.

"Here's the oil."

Lindy mixed, a drop at a time, into the peanut powder, until the texture seemed right. Solemnly, Zazu flecked the salt off one of her crackers into the mix.

They dipped a finger each.

"See?" Zazu said.

"Just right," Lindy agreed.

"Hey, Jason's up."

The hockey player's skull had knitted itself together. He sat, giving Lindy a beatific smile.

He probably has a wicked yen for Pizza Pops, Lindy thought.

"Yuck," Jason said. Then, to Matt, who was still pounding on the safety glass, he said: "You must be so tired."

Matt let out a belch of laughter. He sat on the floor. His eyes rolled up in his head and he began to snore.

"Huh," Lindy said. "I have no capacity for happiness, but he can go down, just like that?"

"Leopold understood less than he thought." The boy fluffed the black wings on his skates. They stretched, flexed.

Owl wings, Lindy thought.

He reclaimed his toque and rolled it over the incision on his skull. Wings sprouted from the wool. His stick, she saw, was a caduceus.

He leaned down to consider Zazu, then tugged on her sad, wet footies. They tore away above the knee, leaving little black-hooved feet. He tousled her hair, revealing horns.

"I'm going to go cut that Krishna kid out of the bathtub." He took up his stick, and clomped out. A second later she heard wood chopping at ice.

Zazu was looking, regretfully, at Matt. "He said Wonderbread."

"We need to refine your palate, kid. Bannock's actually better. Some things are."

"So we go home now?"

"I don't think taking a devil baby back into Yellowknife is necessarily a good idea. And my sister…"

She hesitated. If the Winkles were coming around, everything was going to change. Getting a new modem, coasting on – it wouldn't work out any longer.

"Missy never helps," Zazu said. "Let me."

"Do what?"

"Everything."

"You're awfully small to be taking on my problems."

Zazu raised a sticky, peanut-butter hand. There was a pink antidepressant in the middle of her palm. "Look. From the truck."

Lindy bit her lips.

"Are you…"

"What?"

Are you evil? Lindy thought, before she could help herself.

"Grrr," Zazu said, play-acting the Halloween devil. "I'm scary."

"You're four."

"Goin' on five."

If she was evil, did it matter? Nobody else was stepping up to offer.

"Okay," she said, and felt bone-deep relief.

"Okay, *your Majesty.*"

"Don't push your luck."

Zazu smiled, showing off her food-crusted teeth, and pressed her plastic pitchfork against Lindy's chest. "Let's find bannock."

Lindy nodded. "Hide the horns."

Zazu rolled the hood over her head and clasped the dangling handcuff on Lindy's left wrist, tugging. After a second, Lindy followed her out into the snow.

"Ready or not, here we come," Zazu said, and they began the trudge through the automorgue, trusting the tire tracks to lead them through the maze of cars, past the wolves to the capital.

KEEPER OF THE OASIS

Steve Stanton

The sand sifts between his stubby fingers as Riza digs, and the harder he pushes it aside, the faster it drifts back to void his work. His life has been like this from the first days of record: on his knees cursing the dusty ground and praying for relief from famine. He has been the official keeper of the oasis since his grandfather planted a palm tree on the day of his birth and consecrated the ground to him, the male heir of a proud tradition stretching back to the early days of restoration. The dry lakebed of the Algonquin Basin stretches around him in all directions, a desert left behind when the trees were razed by solar flares from Sungod and the Great Lakes boiled away. In the days of civilization, this hallowed spot contained one-fifth of the world's fresh water in the largest group of lakes on Earth, but now the oasis has dwindled to a toxic trickle along with the fate of mankind.

The gritty dust sparkles metallic in the blazing sunlight, forged in furnaces of stellar fire billions of years ago, spread across the galaxy and blown by prevailing wind to collect in Riza's quiet, terrestrial garden. The sand seems alive as it swirls around his busy hands, each molecule a miracle of complexity, each atom indestructible and eternal, destined to be carried by the breeze forever. Riza is nothing in comparison, a pilgrim on a sad sojourn to nowhere, his body but a fragile pattern of electromagnetism in a hostile universe, his consciousness a transient aberration. Why had he expected more? Why had he expected life and posterity?

The stench of dung assails Riza anew from a paper bag beside him filled with chicken bones and human excrement. He needs a hole deep enough to keep the desert jackals from digging up his garbage and spreading it round the ancestral tenement, but shallow enough for tree roots to find sustenance when the drought ends and seeds can flourish.

"Hurry up, Riza," his wife yells from a grated window in the house. "Emil's caravan has passed the outer gate." Inside the bleached mud-block walls, candles burn at midday to freshen the air and the dry toilet is clean for company. His wife is bustling with nervous anxiety, hiding fresh anguish behind a coarse burqa of activity, holding to tremulous faith in the aftermath of horror. The house has been swept clean of sin, and their souls whitewashed with sacred observance.

Riza squints under glaring sun at a sad trio of approaching camels stooped with weariness and thirst. The oasis has been sour with precipitate minerals for years, and shallow wells barren throughout the Algonquin Basin. Denuded palm trees stand like paintbrushes against the cloudless sky, their hoary trunks tapered to scant tufts of green hope against a cruel azure sky. He recognizes Emil from a distance, a man of haughty stance and regal stature, his white turban an unearned crown. Emil wears an ornate cassock in public show of dignity as he searches for his errant wife who disgraced the marital nest in blasphemy to Sungod.

Emil dismounts his camel and ties it to a post at the centre of the oasis where the mud has been baked to a fissured mosaic. He tethers the other two camels and slides bulky packs onto the ground – a tent in one and all his worldly belongings in the other, probably little more than a sleeping mat and change of clothes, perhaps a flask of water and tin of dried jackal meat. He works with slow and deliberate care in the searing heat, inspecting the camels for problems or parasites, patting their heads and combing their shaggy coats with his fingers. The dromedaries are the last of the domesticated mammals on Earth, saved from extinction by syrupy urine, dry feces and water traps in their nostrils, able to travel for weeks without drinking yet provide daily milk rich in fat, protein, vitamins and iron – more than enough to keep a nomad alive in the desert. Methodically, Emil raises each camel hoof in turn, looking for damage or defect, then drapes a feedbag around the neck of each animal. His murmuring voice drifts across the compound like a soothing melody – a man with great respect for life and the creatures in his care, a survivor and custodian of a sacred future.

Working against time now and harsh circumstance, Riza renews his effort to carve a trench in the dust, scooping with both palms between his knees and holding back sand behind gnarly legs. He pushes his bag of dung into the ditch, and the ground drifts in to cover his offering like a lady closing her loins. A funeral dirge echoes in his mind, a sad song of surrender to silence, and a scent of smoke stings his eyes from a distant fire. Veins of coal continue to blaze in the hellish wastelands to the south where perpetual underground fires smoulder and burn. No plant or animal survives in the devastation beyond the oasis, and only a vestige of life hangs on in northern pockets. Even the ants and roaches have died off – creatures that once made up the majority of terrestrial animal

biomass. Riza scans the distant horizon for any sign of movement, a rare bird or scrub of tumbleweed, but the Algonquin
Basin is dead and forlorn. Perhaps there are fish deep below
the boiling surface of the oceans, hiding in cool caverns of
darkness. Perhaps there is hope.

A vision of loveliness appears to Riza as he rises pain-
fully to his feet – a ghost in a red bridal sari embroidered with
gold and decorated with prayer coins, his only child on her
wedding day. Riza sobs with agony at the sight of her veiled
face, but vivid eyes smile at him with a remembrance of
youth. "Why do you weep over this arid dust?"

Riza ducks wet cheeks away from the ghost, but her presence lingers in majesty, a pleasant shadow from incessant
heat. He had welcomed the young bride home just days ago,
distraught but alive, crushed in spirit and trembling with
distress. Her husband had beaten her in holy ordinance for
refusing to conceive, for shutting her womb to any future in
this terrible place. Riza had cringed with misery as he
inspected the caning wounds on her back, righteous punish-
ments from Sungod, angry purple bruises festooned with
crimson welts, scars that would never heal in this world or the
next. Emil should never have taken her to the northern coast
for their honeymoon, squandering her dowry for a few days at
a remnant outpost on the salt beaches beside caustic waters.
He should never have given her the taste of sweetmeats and
pastries, nor graced her with fragrant oils and scented pillows.
How could she come back to the desert and live without longing in a land without rainbows? How could she raise babies to
return them to waterless ground?

Riza remembers her skin glowing with promise on that
glorious wedding day, her nubile breasts pushing upward with

the promise of fertility, and a red umbrella held ceremoni-
ously over her head in blessing. Consolation shone from a
golden sky as she performed the traditional wedding dance to
tambourine and mandolin and shrill birdlike cries from a clap-
ping crowd of attendants. The bone trumpet heralded her
consecration at sunset, a sound reserved for royalty in the
olden days, and the stars that evening glowed like jewels in an
infinite expanse of heaven. Her betrothed Emil was
Anishinabek by tribal right from the territory of the first fossils, a man austere of wit but a capable worker who feared
Sungod and enjoyed the privilege of obedience. What better
place for a virgin to find home and refuge?

Riza looks past the ghost to see her husband finally turn
his attention from the care and feeding of his camels to hoist
a packsack and begin walking toward the house. He does not
hate Emil even now. The man easily could have resorted to
bondage and rape in the absence of moral civility, he could
have taken what he needed without conscience like the hood-
lum vagabonds of yore who died out in vileness and misery.
Emil is a handsome breeder and will find a healthy suitor to
share his spawn. Riza dreads to see the man's righteous face
crumple into a mask of grief, his innocence forever sullied.
Emil will wail and rip his cassock in grand spectacle at the terrible news. He will suffer for weeks in exile in his desert tent,
walking to ground for a word of prophecy from Sungod,
plumbing the depths of doom and ruin. But with the gathering curative of time and reflection he will shrug off his weight
of guilt to the wisdom of holy law while the fallow ground
cries out unheard.

All men hold a crystal core in the centre of their being,
invincible and invisible, a private asylum packed solid with

sorrow and sheltered from probing eyes of introspection. Emil will hide his wife away in a frozen catacomb of pain and force a balm of forgetfulness upon his mind. Riza knows the place and has packed his crystal core with untold tales of dismay, year after decade, heartbreak upon tragedy. The horror of life has condensed into a hard and brilliant diamond in his soul, for he has seen too much for one man to comprehend: children ravaged by starvation and women maimed by violence and disease. He awaits his final settlement with Sungod, a goddess of consuming fire who barbecued all flesh on Earth in a moment of cosmic indifference two centuries ago – snakes and frogs, sheep and goats, all the children of men. Riza steels his gaze now and hardens his strong shoulder for the benefit of others, but he cherishes his right to die and holds it tight for the day of reconciliation. Death is his only heritage, and who will speak of his legacy?

"I wanted the best for you," Riza says to the girl in the red sari. She had fled to him for final sanctuary, to spill her blood under his roof while he slept. He could have done more to save her, his firstborn and only child. He could have stayed awake all night and cradled her with comfort in his spindly arms. "I must be a failure." A pall of despair drags on his neck, a shroud of responsibility he has carried all his life and finally understands. A single stroke from a knife can steal away destiny, and one barren generation can obliterate the memory of mankind.

"Tell my story," she says behind her veil, "that I might gain recompense for my suffering." Her gaze is intense with insight, and her eyes linger like beacons of promise as the ghost fades to a mirage of shimmering noonday heat and leaves only heartache behind.

Riza bows his head in duty, pitiful servant to her passing vision of glory. He vows to write the last narrative for a lost civilization, spill his harboured burden of truth for an audience unseen. By the consummate power of the word, the keeper of the oasis will bring justification to the elders and heritage to the unborn, he will summon hope for the hopeless and conjure a future for his desolate homeland, and his daughter will lie nearby to him always, close enough underfoot that tree roots can find purchase when the rains return and the cisterns fill with life. Someday soon the heavens must break their ponderous silence and Sungod will weep with shame.

One man can plant his crystal core in the dust, and another will water the seed in season. This much can be accomplished in a single lifetime, and only this much is required from Riza as he brushes the sand from his knees and turns from his garden of earth to greet Emil for the final time.

MANITOU-WAPOW

GMB Chomichuk

(with Curtis Janzen and Thomas Turner)

From a letter to the Crown from the Hudson's Bay Company representative at Fort Albany, 1836.

It is almost laughable now, the idea that we had entered into a treaty and that we, litigious and bold, had believed the Invaders would hold to their end. They only wanted a small piece of a great whole, we told ourselves. Who could truly own the Earth? It was a time when it did seem that any could lay claim in the vast land. Indeed that proved true. Only a few could keep it.

Journal of Colonel West, Selkirk: 1840.

When those first few cylinders fell, when those first few arrived, we looked to them as we had the French. Foreign and strange, in competition for this, the New World, conquered and claimed by the ingenuity of the British Empire. That the Colonial wanted their share was as foolish to the Crown as the French claim or the claim of the noble savage or the strange tall creatures that roamed the smoke-black hills on three legs. Each had their sovereignty. Ours was to make the world England.

Account of the Red River Rebellion, recounted to Peter Black by an Anishinabe man who has never been identified. 1848.
"This story is traded in nights without sleep. They had come long ago and soaked the mountains in a smoke like a dying fire that stung the eyes and makes one sick. We did not venture there. They did not venture far. Three-legs had taken the home of the thunderbirds in a spirit war long ago. The mountains and land beyond belonged to the tall beasts on three legs with the spirit eye. One does not go to war with spirits. Soon our lands were being taken by the people from across the water. The English and the French, then all the others. We had no place to move to, and so, like mother wolves, we fought."

Diary of Alexander Ross: Lower Fort Garry: Spring 1845.
Today I abandon the cottage for the fort. I prefer my home for its place outside the walls. But the children need me I think, or perhaps I need them. A reason for hope. With Eden Colvile dead and his staff fled, it falls to those who are able to do what we can. What else is life for, then? I've not travelled across the ocean, braved the trap lines and long nights of the forest winter to die asleep, alone in my cabin, killed by cowards for my coat and rifle. Those that mean to stay need those willing to endure, if not to lead them, then to lead by example.

Diary of Alexander Ross: Lower Fort Garry: January 1845.
What was left of the Council of Assiniboia has gathered here in a pile of stones that is more of a storage depot filled with pelts and sundry items than a garrison. It seems that the defence of this bend in Red River falls to us. It is strange to

me how quickly our own riflemen had thrown open the gates to the Muskegon. Once we called these people by different names. We would judge them separate and make their women our country wives. Now we embrace them as we are, natives to this world, facing an invader that sees us not as tribes or monarchies, not parliaments, nor assemblies nor confederacies, but as commodities. Word has come from Foss, the Invaders mean to enslave us. We are all one people now.

Diary of Alexander Ross: Lower Fort Garry: February 1845.

Lady Simpson's piano has lifted the spirit of this terrible place. I think sometimes of the journey it took to reach here unscathed. I see in the faces of the people here who have never seen a piano the awe of the machine that makes music for them at the hands of Dr. Cowan. William learned to play in medical school in Glasgow and is a skilled hand at the keys. It was the first piano in Rupert's Land, they say. Which may be true. Fitting, maybe, that the first may be the last to be played. We have found the music to be a simple but effective comfort in the long dark nights. If those that carried it here by ship, York boat, and canoe, had known the value to these few here in the dark, they would have brought 100 more without thought to the burden. What strength may come from a song. What comfort from a tune that stays in your whistle. Perhaps it is the forgotten purpose of music. To keep the monsters at bay during long nights.

Diary of Alexander Ross: Lower Fort Garry: February 1845.

I think it was Lady Simpson's piano that brought the creatures from inside their strange conveyances. For we know now that the three-legged beasts that glare fire are machines, not creatures. They are clockwork crab shells with bits of science crammed inside. Like steam engines without steam, with legs rather than wheels. How do I know? I have seen their riders. I have seen the flesh of the horror that prey on us. They came here. By God and country they came here, and I saw them, touched them.

John Ballenden thinks it was the fault of a young blacksmith's apprentice. Baptiste Kennedy had bought a scrap of tripod shell from a trader. The man said he had found it past the rapids near Mackenzie Rock. He had thought to heat it as to ascertain if it was in fact a sort of metal as was a topic of debate. Day and night outside the wall, at the forge, he heated and struck at the thing. In the morning on the following day, thick snow across the prairie grass and our breath in the air, we saw the monument to our horror. A tripod standing motionless across the river.

I tried my best to calm the people. We had all heard of them. Some had seen them at a distance, all had met someone who had. It was part of life here. But even as I said it, I knew. This was not an animal as some predicted. I felt what the Indians called its spirit eye, looking deeply at us. A cold intellect. I felt a sort of envy in it, though I cannot say why.

When the ray reached out and set the blacksmith's shop alight it set up our powder store too and the calamity threw the stones of our wall into a tumbled heap. More of those cursed beams stabbed into the fort. From the Men's House I could see the barracks burst into flames which roared to hungry life. Men charged from within, fire across their limbs and backs. The old man from the Sixth Regiment believed that powder was the target. A reduction in our defences before the rest occurred.

Which was to say that all who tried to venture out, to forage, to hunt, to go for water or flee for their lives, were burned down to ash out there in the open ground beyond our fort. They had laid us to siege, though for what purpose then, none could say.

I think now I understand what they waited for. It was six days later, when we were huddled and fearful in the mess hall, that Dr. Cowan thought to strike a tune on that piano. He played and, by God, he lifted us up to sing. He played a long piece full of joy and wit and mirth. We went to sleep that night with the lightest of hearts and a hope we had not known. That night they came.

We had slept together in the Big House as was now the custom. Watchful of each other. John Black had a cough which kept him up. Maybe that's why they took him. To quiet the night, because we never saw him again.

First it was the spirit eye that came. I had been awakened by it. Suspended there on its long stock. It moved along as if in water, suspended in the air. A strange serpent with a lantern for a head. It had a pale red glow. When it withdrew, they came. Three of them. Of course, three. Rounded bodies with great dark eyes and curved beaks. They moved along, lifted by corded tendrils in great bunches, eight on each side which connected to the body, anchored to the side of their mouths. There seemed a great endeavour to be had in each motion. A strain to lift up and move forward.

Some others woke and, with voices caught and terror full, we shook the others awake.

The creatures heaved themselves along slowly and made their way to the piano. One watched us closely and we knew fear and silence. The other two set to examine the musical instrument with some interest. Maybe it was the magic of the thing. To them it was our strange object of worship and it brought us strength when the keys were pushed. To them it must have been very alien indeed.

I must have been trembling fiercely for Miss McLeod reached to take my hands and pulled them to her bosom. That simple act awoke in me a sort of madness for life. I would have it out. I would survive. I would not hide in the dark from monsters. I stood suddenly and found I was not alone. Mary, Captain Foss' country wife, too had stood. She had in hand a knife, from the kitchen I think. We were at them then. Not in any unison or coordinate action. We simply entered the fray. For my part I am ashamed to set down that my fists and fury were nothing on the cold flesh I pounded. I gave everything and those tendrils laid me to the floor. While the beak snapped and took a slice of my leg, the grey cords as thick as my arms beat me down. The Muskegon woman, though, struck another beneath the eye and the knife opened a wound that sent her blow up to the wrist into the creature. The writhing explosion of motion and hot terror tore the room asunder and the creature's death throes sent those 16 tendrils flailing. Then the rifles took the rest. Out of their skyward wagons these hateful things died as men do, with blood and pain and screams.

We shook with hate and fear and many were sick with it. But it was Dr. Cowan that saw the mark on the creatures and knew it for what it was. There on the bare grey skin he saw it. He rolled his shirt and showed us one to match it. An inoculation scar. He was obsessed with it and talked of nothing else. While others cheered our victory and set about to burn the horrid creatures, he took me aside and told me a secret I cannot set here. But it gave me hope. He bade I write a letter, setting down what I had seen and have a volunteer take it to Montreal. Graham Turner, bless him, vowed to do just that when we two, the Doctor and I, told him what we knew.

Excerpt from letter of Alexander Ross of Lower Fort Garry to the Reverend William R. Seaver of Montreal, June 1846.

Dr. Cowan is dead now, a tragic casualty of events. But as he was sure and made me promise to get word to you, so I entreat you to make some use of this information that was bought at so costly a price.

Diary of Alexander Ross: Lower Fort Garry: September 1846.

It is bad here. Many colonials have joined with the Invaders. Once they fought us to shake off tyranny. Now they embrace it to destroy their own people. As people lose their lands and loves, so too their allegiances now suffer.

Yet the world I fear is at war with these creatures. The red weed has stopped up the rivers and closed the trails. It gets thicker and taller each day. Our oxen have eaten the red weed and died of it. Now none will eat any food that has come from soil mingled with those tangled roots. We must work tirelessly to keep our wells clear of it too, it seems to seek water not to draw from but to trap it. A strange plant that wishes the landscape was a barren desert. Those who lay still near the red weed, to rest or sleep sometimes, grow tangled in it after only an hour's time, as if it seeks them out and grows toward them.

In the thickest areas of the red weed, great stocks as tall as pine trees grow with pods like tulip bulbs the size of ox carts atop them. The Colonials that have *turned* have begun

a sort of harvest of pods for their new masters. They hew
them down and sheer away the bulbs' husks with axes to
expose a pulpy fruit. Our Muskegon scouts have observed
that the Colonials then bring the harvested fruit into the
smokelands where the braves do not dare to travel. I have
arranged a troop of volunteers to seek answers beyond the
scorched boundaries of the Invaders' territory.

We have begun a careful collection of munitions from
allies and scavengers. Few heavy guns, but many small arms
and kegs of powder. A Hudson's Bay Company man has come
into the fold and secured a large number of supplies meant
for the garrison at Two Rivers. Word is they are gone now,
reduced to a cinder. Somehow, for some reason, the creatures
have not returned here.

Diary of Alexander Ross: Lower Fort Garry: October 1846.

Fort Riley is in flames. A handful of survivors have made
the journey across 700 miles to bring news that the tripods
roam the Americas far and wide. I once envied the American
cavalrymen and their fleet horses. But a scarred man from the
south told me of a detachment of American cavalry moving to
reinforce Pembina that were caught out in the open. Men and
horses lit like candles and charging, burning, across the fields.
To die smouldering and screaming from the fearsome Martian
ray.

*Decoded Letter. November 19, 1846: Sent from Alexander Ross
of Lower Fort Garry to _____ of Montreal.*

Your people have made it here. They are safe. But they
have told me their appointed duty and I see now that you, sir,
must be mad. Either by hunger or grief or drink. But you are

surely mad. Bless you. By the time you read this your plan will already be concluded. In victory or failure.

The red weed chokes the river nearly to death. We huddle in this, the first stone fort built in Rupert's Land, and wonder if it is not better to dig a place to live beneath the earth. For surely no hope remains for those that live above it. One man jokes and laughs in the grip of fear that we could build a new world of men underground. Tunnel our way to a safe land. The others took to his ideas as jests. But some feel he believes it. A madman is no good to me.

Diary of Alexander Ross: Lower Fort Garry: January 1847.

I understand now why the things leave us be. We live in the looming shadow of a dead machine. It stands vigilant there day and night and for a year we struck on ways to tip it over. Thank God no such invention equal to the task occurred to us.

The machine provides for us a sort of camouflage from the other machines that stalk the land with increasing frequency. Perhaps they are territorial? Once they see another here, with the trapped human slaves at its feet, they move on. Perhaps they are fearful of it. Maybe the ghosts of their dead ward them off. I cannot judge now.

Letter from Alexander Ross: Lower Fort Garry: February 1847 to W.R. Seaver of the Montreal Resistance.

As you thought, the black smoke is a protective screen. Your plan to send a small group in quickly with no thought to attack has succeeded. They have returned with a device. None of your men are fit to travel after the deed you bade them perform. Sick with symptoms of the black smoke that

hangs over the territory of Assiniboia. I fear I must concur
with our doctor and medicine men: your brave men will not
last out the moon.

With this note are three volumes of the work of Edward
Anthony Jenner whom your own man called the father of
immunology. I don't claim to understand what you are working at. But as always I remain one willing to get what needs
accomplishing settled to the last.

Should these pages reach you, then they are carried by my
servant still. You can trust this man. He is a loyalist and a
humanist. You can verify his identity with the phrase I spoke
to you on the deck of the *Countess of Darlington* on our crossing of the Atlantic. He has been running missives for me since
the river garrison at Fort William fell. He has with him the
device your men procured. I understand a little of what I am
told. The device bears closer scrutiny. May God be with you
in your endeavour. Please do so with all haste.

Diary of Alexander Ross: Lower Fort Garry: April 1847.

We found a great pit and in it were, I think, the great
majority of the Muskegon who had lived anywhere within 100
miles of the fort. They had been drained to husks. I am sick
with the sight of it. Yet I am also sick with guilt. I was glad
they were not my people. The thought rose in me unbidden
and I was ashamed of it. How hot must a fire be to re-forge a
man? I cannot bear the thought.

Diary of Alexander Ross: Lower Fort Garry: June 1847.

You are right to have me inspect the device. It appears to
be a type of inoculator. I believe the Invaders have set a curative against earthly illness. Perhaps that is why they attacked

the hospitals and quarantines first. When first I saw the tripod over the triage tent of Fort William, I feared they simply had no mercy. But I see now a terrible design. I have spoken to Dr. Trent who himself witnessed a similar attack and spoke to two others who did as well.

The Muskegon here arranged a meeting with their elders. A tripod took many captives in the early days. But they added that they took only those who had encountered us. When "the white sickness" had laid many of their fellows low. They say Three Legs get stronger with each battle. They say that each sickness is a battle. Just as we saw our illnesses sweep the ranks of the noble savages, so too I think these creatures observed and learned.

Diary of Alexander Ross: Lower Fort Garry: December 1, 1847.

We have it. There is the weakness. They fear our coughs and ills more than our cannonades. That is why they waited so long and took so many native lives first. We had infected these poor people with our ills and these horrid creatures used that to build immunity.

I have sent our man back to you with more devices. My people have not been idle in the interim. They have gathered tales of the Martian. Two accounts I am certain have the ring of truth. The Martian flesh, marred just as your Doctor saw. Bearing the scars of inoculation.

From the ledger of Alexander Ross: Lower Fort Garry: Summer 1848.

A portion of the Sixth Regiment, along with artillery and engineering detachments consisting of 17 officers and 364 non-commissioned officers and men accompanied by 17

women and 19 children left Ireland for Fort Garry via Hudson
Bay. The tripods caught them in shallow water. Fourteen people made it to us. Three soldiers, seven women, four children.
Less than 100 members of the Royal Canadian Rifles are with
us, plus the Muskegon and the Métis men who say they will
fight.

Diary of Alexander Ross: Lower Fort Garry: Summer 1848.

The majority of men and women are set to work under the
Colonial whips. Turncoat lackeys of the Invaders. I would
shoot them but I need the shot. These men have traded our
freedom for their salvation. The red weed has taken to the
forests and begun to choke them as they do our rivers and
farms. But the prairie grass resists. The Muskegon tell me it is
because there are too many types. Too many seeds. They say
the red weed needs time to study its prey. That the weed is like
those who brought it, like the tick that hangs on deer and dog
and people if we are not vigilant. The shaman says the weed
and the Martians will drain our strength slowly.

Netley Creek still gives us rice aplenty; the red weed does
not seem to spread there. None can say why. Cuthbert Grant
tells me from his sickbed that it is because we need it. He says
the earth itself is trying to aide us as best she may.

Diary of Alexander Ross: Lower Fort Garry: Fall 1848.

I have received a letter from Seaver in Montreal.

The small area of Lachine has become their whole
Canada. The alien conveyances run the length of the city
proper. From there to Mount Royal is reduced to a charcoal
cimitière. Even as I write this they could be gone. Ashes. Or
worse.

Last entry of the diary of Alexander Ross: Lower Fort Garry: Fall 1848

The fort is preparing for what may prove our final act. For months now we have been digging beneath the walls under the leadership of a madman. Every gun taken, every bullet scrounged, will be hurled at the Invaders to draw them here. We will fight them to the last.

But a final stand is not our plan but our means. First we will lay our trap. And then they will come.

Jesuits have helped us prepare a final offering. Every sick man and woman in Rupert's Land we have brought here. Every malady and illness we can move has been brought here. The physicians and thinkers in Montreal will put their theories to the test. A reversal of the infernal technologies and theories that have made these creatures at home here. By right the earth is ours. Men do not die in vain, I am certain now. We have won our right to this world by a thousand poxes, by a hundred thousand bloody fluxes. The Invaders think they can adapt a population at a time. They think they can bleed up and inoculate a few at a time. No. We have 100 volunteers. I myself have been administered 19 injections.

The children are leaving with the Muskegon that have promised to take them into the great wide lands where the tripods do not yet stride. Where, if we are lucky or right or favoured by God, they shall outlive these horrid things by simple virtue of being born human and of the earth.

Our last group is moving off now. I can see them going from my place at the wall. When they are gone our engineer will knock loose the final strut and down our three-legged watchdog will fall. We will be open for conquest again. Our din shall give cover to those who leave.

They are already calling this place by its new name. They say it is the narrow place were the Great Spirit stood. They call this place Manitou-Wapow in Muskegon and *M nani-doobaa* in Anishinabe, both meaning the straits of Manitou, the Great Spirit.

They laugh at how I say it: Mani-toba. No longer an invader but a liberator. Today I live and die in Manitoba.

SAYING GOODBYE

Michael S. Pack

November 3

I think I'm the last person on the islands.

I took the boat across the channel yesterday, hoping to see Lloyd. I had some carrots for trade, but I found his house in Sandspit empty. When I took a look around town, I found Lloyd at the base of some steps. It didn't seem right that an old piece of shoe leather like Lloyd would die from a fall, but we don't choose how we go. By the state of his body, I'd guess that happened a week ago, maybe two. He won't need my carrots.

He was the last man living on Moresby. A family used to migrate around the west coast of the island, but I haven't heard from them in years. The storms took them, one of the winter storms when Arctic winds scream over the strait howling like the big bad wolf doing his best to blow out the moon. Not a time to be on the water.

I buried Lloyd on the hill behind his house so the grave overlooks the Pacific. He came from the Prairies, but he lived for wind and waves. He told me once that the first time he'd seen the ocean he'd fallen more in love than he had with any of his three wives. Back before, he'd sailed in the merchant marine. Even after he retired, he worked the halibut boats.

After the world fell apart, he never stopped sailing his boat across the strait to the mainland. Weeks would pass, then he'd show up at my cabin with his discovered treasures. He taught me what I know about boats. I'll never make a proper seaman, but I know my way around.

I think he'd like where I buried him. I hope so.

I scavenged a bit. Lloyd had a collection of comic books. I'd read them over the years, but I don't mind reading them again. In his cellar I found some jarred food. I took those where the seals looked good; left the rest. Pickles. Salmonberry jam. Peaches. Hell if I know where Lloyd found peaches. He used to have a pair of binoculars, but I couldn't find them. Maybe he traded them to a survivor on the mainland for the peaches.

I took Lloyd's boat, the *Hannah Marie*, from the dock and trailed mine behind on a line. With the *Hannah Marie* I could sail clear around the island. Or follow Lloyd's path and head to the mainland. It would be hard sailing, going alone like that, but I've thought about it.

December 4

I managed to get the old generator running for a bit. I listened to the ham radio, the one I traded for from the brothers. I don't have a set-up to transmit much but I can pick voices out of the air. I used to chat with this guy down near Port Hardy. He promised that he'd bring his wife up to visit. He never made the trip. That was years back. I've talked to a few others over the years. A woman used to sing on the radio sometimes. Never knew where from, but she sounded American. Maybe Alaska or Seattle. She wouldn't answer, but I liked her singing. I haven't heard her in a long while.

Lately, I haven't heard much but static. Tonight, I heard someone talking. I think she spoke Japanese. She sounded alone. Far off and alone. I tried to talk back, but I doubt she got the signal. If she did, she probably didn't understand anything I said. Maybe she heard me. Maybe she heard my voice speaking on the radio and knew she wasn't alone in the world. Not completely. Not yet.

December 16

Wish I had a beer. It's been seven years since my last six-pack.

December 24

I cut down a little pine and brought it into my house. I cranked up the genny to try the lights, but too many of the bulbs have burnt out on the string. I thought about looking through my neighbours' homes to see if any of them left a string of tree lights, but it felt wrong to steal Christmas ornaments, even if they won't ever come back for them.

I found a DVD in town last week. I wrapped it up in some paper and tape. Tomorrow morning I'll find out what Santa left me.

December 25

Ran the genny long enough to watch the gold medal hockey match from the 2010 Olympics. Canada against the

U.S. When Canada scored the winning goal in overtime, I stood up and cheered. I'd done that before, watching from a pub in Prince George, but that was a long time ago. It made for a good day.

Santa knew just what I wanted.

January 2

The Japanese woman was crying on the radio. I tried to transmit a message to her. Don't think she heard me. Are we the last two people on earth? Here on opposite sides of the Pacific, where we can't even see each other. Can't be sure anyone even hears us. She went off the air at about 3 a.m. I stayed up the rest of the night. Listening to the silence.

January 15

The chill of the storm cuts through the walls. The winds have died down, but freezing rain keeps falling. I'll have to check for damage tomorrow, and hope the roof isn't too slick from ice.

Nights like this put me in mind of *that night*. The night when the last evacuation teams went door to door, all over the islands. Last call, last ferry to the mainland. Get out now or forever hold your peace. They had nothing to offer me. They promised an all-expense-paid vacation to some cramped refugee camp down south, but I'd come to Haida Gwaii to get away from people. Besides, Gloria stayed. They wouldn't let her take her dogs, and she wouldn't leave them.

The ferry sailed with the wind howling and the chop on the ocean dangerous and angry. Desperation led people to make bad decisions. Later, Lloyd found wreckage floating in the strait. The currents spared our beach most of the debris. I've always been thankful for that. I had good friends on that ferry.

The boats had come before, but they wouldn't come again. The last stubborn holdouts clung to the island like we clung to life. We couldn't let go, not until life let go of us. Over the years it did, and we slipped away, one by one.

After the storms, Lloyd would've taken us over to the mainland if we'd wanted, I suppose. Never asked; he never offered. I don't know if that was a good decision or a bad one. You stop second-guessing, but you keep living with the consequences.

January 22

Cold rain has kept me indoors for days. I ended up flipping through Grandpa's old photo album. He had a lot of pictures of his only child, my mother.

Time moves slower here on the island. In my Grandpa's days, back in the time before, the worries of the mainland would melt away from my mother's face when we'd visit. All that stress would rush back into her as soon as we stepped on the ferry to cross the strait to Prince Rupert, but for those precious days on the islands, the clock would stand still. A child wants to always speed it up, and it took until I grew up to understand why the islands drew my mother back. It was the only place she could rest. She liked the Interior well enough, and I know she loved my father. Still, the islands called her home.

She never said why she ran away in the first place.

February 3

Snow dusts the ground. Growing up in the Interior, I wouldn't have even called it a proper snow. Winter doesn't come as hard to Haida Gwaii as it does to some places. If I pull my toque down over my ears and fasten my coat across my chest, I can't even feel the cold.

Not that I'd turn down a nice hot cup of cocoa right about now.

With marshmallows. Yeah, that would be nice.

February 17

I looked for silence until I found it.

March 11

I took a hike up to Spirit Lake and had a picnic. It was a nice spring morning with just a hint of winter still on the breeze. I come up here every spring. I think about Gloria. I picked wildflowers as I hiked the trail. I left them for her. She's buried not far from the lake.

I've dug too many graves.

March 20

My Grandpa taught me to carve argillite. He shaped the soft, black stone to honour the traditions of the Haida of Skidegate. The masters carved beautiful pieces, and Grandpa wanted me to remember the way of his people. My people too, but I didn't think of it that way, not then. I grew up on the mainland, far into the Interior. I considered trips to Haida

Gwaii an imposition on my time. When my mother insisted I go, I resented the ferry ride. I complained loud and long about the lack of fast food, the limited connection to the precious Internet, the lousy television reception.

Now, I'm happy to hear a Japanese woman's voice on the radio. Now, I'm glad to be on the island. Away from the mainland where it all went to hell.

I found a nice piece of argillite and began carving it. I think I'll make it a dog. Not a very traditional design, but I've had dogs on my mind.

March 23

I met her at the university. We ended up paired up for some project. She studied chemistry with a minor in not going to class. I wanted to be a socials teacher, which made more sense at the time than it does now. A professor once joked to me that history is the art of never saying goodbye. That sounds like a bad joke, but I laughed.

Gloria and I hit it off. At spring break, I brought her to the islands. She fell in love with the place. I fell in love with her. I have a picture of her from that trip. She's posing with the carved totem bear just north of town. She has this smile on her face that I will never forget.

April 3

For three days, I've listened to the radio all night. She's gone, I'm convinced of it. I wonder what happened to her. Did time just catch up? Did she lose power? Did she take a bad fall, like Lloyd? Or did she make up her mind to end it, like

Gloria had? I suppose I'll never know. I'll keep the radio on again tonight. I have enough fuel for a few more nights.

I don't think I'll hear anything. It makes me feel alone. Somewhere, out there in the dark, there must be places with people still. Places where the lights come on at night. How long since I saw the last airplane overhead? Five years? Six.

Longer since the last boat went by the islands.

April 7

I woke this morning and for the briefest instant I forgot. Almost, I could smell the whiff of coffee brewing in the kitchen. Almost, I could hear Gloria's bare feet in the hall. Almost, I could imagine the door opening; she would slip into bed beside me. Almost, I could feel the touch of her hand on my arm. How sweet it would have been.

I closed my eyes, and when I opened them I saw nothing but an empty room. I lay still for a very long time, wishing I could go back to sleep. Wishing that I could find that dream again.

April 9

I have no more reason to keep this diary than I have to keep trying to broadcast my voice out to an empty world. I continue to write, and to speak, for the same reason that some people talk to graves.

I don't expect an answer. I don't expect an audience. I don't know if I'm talking to myself or to God or to the world that was. Or the world that might one day be. To no one. I have words. I have to say them.

After a time, my own voice sounds odd when I speak. I'm a stranger to myself.

April 10

I listened to the radio for a bit this morning. I gave up after an hour or so.

Down near the old ferry terminal, I watched seals playing on the rocks. They didn't seem to mind me. Once, the terminal had been the island's lifeline. Everything came through there. Food, mail, even friends. I remember happy days when the ferry would come in to dock, and the late evenings for the overnight trip to the mainland.

We thought someone would come back to the terminal. A rescue mission. UN peacekeepers. Somebody. Anybody. A ferry would arrive with news that all of it had been a mistake. No danger. All okay. No panic. The world will keep turning, the cars will keep running, and the planes will keep flying.

I left the terminal to the seals. It's their place now more than it is mine.

April 12

I've run out of fuel for the generator. I sat for a while, staring at the dead radio. For over a week I've listened to static while straining to hear a human voice in the crackles. Willing someone to speak to me. No one did. Now, I hear nothing but silence. I think I will never hear a human voice again.

We all have regrets.

April 15

Once I do some repairs on the *Hannah Marie* to get her in proper shape, I plan to sail up the east coast of the island to see if there's any fuel still left near Masset.

April 17

I finished the carving of the dog. This morning I hiked back up to Spirit Lake to say my goodbyes. The last goodbyes. I've said them before, but I always thought I'd go back. Now, I suspect I'll never hike up to the lake again.

In the most important way, I've been alone since she left. More than the evacuations, her decision drove it home. The end. Humanity had a good run. Some folks said it was the end of the world. Nonsense. The world didn't end when a comet took out the dinosaurs. It didn't end with the Ice Age. It won't end now. The world keeps going. People on the other hand... not so much.

When she realized that, Gloria took her dogs and went up the trail. We still got news then from the radio. People still passed messages along. We'd hear stories about how someone had begun rebuilding in Vancouver. No, over on the Island, near Victoria. Or no, down in the States, near Seattle. The Americans had found a cure. Or the Chinese. Someone. None of it was true, but we liked to believe. I think the desire to believe pushed Gloria over the edge. She could have faced the end. She just couldn't cope with the constant rollercoaster of hope.

She took her dogs with her. That part haunts me. She took her dogs, but she left me. I promised myself that I wouldn't hold it against her.

April 18

I've begun sailing north up the east coast of the island. I remember making the trip on a fishing boat with my grandpa when I was eight or nine. I complained halfway there and halfway back, but I remember listening to Grandpa. He'd let me complain, "air it all out," he'd say, and then he'd go back to telling me about halibut fishing or hunting for deer.

He'd point out the totem poles that spotted the coast. "Our memory," he would say. He'd talk some in the old language. He didn't speak but a very little of it; I never learned even that much. I wish now that I'd paid more attention and kept the old ways alive for one more lifetime. Maybe that seems pointless, at the end of all things, but it isn't. If I remembered all the things he tried to teach me, that would have meaning. Even if they die with me. Because they might die with me. I could say I was like my grandpa, the keeper of a proud tradition. I can't. I don't remember his traditions, his ways, or his people.

I remember him, though. In the end, when it all came crashing down, I came back to his place. Maybe that's enough.

"If one voice knows the song, the whole world knows the song," Grandpa told me. I told him to put a video on the Internet. I didn't understand.

April 20

Still sailing, rounded the cape on the north edge of Graham Island this morning.

A long time ago, I read that when the first peoples came across the land bridge, the islands of Haida Gwaii were one of the first places they made permanent villages. I don't know if that's a fact or just a might have been.

I suppose it makes sense these islands would be the first stop for those migrations back in the old, old days. My ancestors, those on my mother's side at least, would have come down across the great glaciers of Alaska, or else in boats around the icy waters. Here were the islands, waiting for them, a place to fish and hunt dwarf caribou. That's something else the island does: it shrinks things. The deer around Masset don't grow much larger than dogs. The world closes in, surrounded on all sides by water. For me, the world shrank until only I remained.

Odd what settles on the mind, isn't it?

So, the place where my ancestors first set up camp, all those thousands of years ago, and now it will be the place the last of my line survives. I can fool myself and think that some made it off the islands in the early days. I can pretend the refugee camps survived. I know better. I'm the last. The Haida Gwaii islands will see the last leave just as they saw the first arrive. I wonder if they'll miss me when I'm gone.

I'll make it to Masset in the morning.

April 21

I saw a pod of grey whales off to the north. Their kind has no reason to miss humanity.

April 22

I've found less than I'd hoped. A few gallons of fuel that might have enough kick to run my genny. Some food that hasn't turned, but not much. I hit up the old hospital, but found nothing. The Haida brothers, Tommy and Christopher, had cleared out the pharmacy years back. I know; I traded a good hunting knife to them for antibiotics. I found a roll of duct tape, hidden behind a rusty filing cabinet like treasure. I took it and felt almost guilty.

Tommy died three years back. I think three years. You lose track of time after a while. I know it was summer and the brothers had gone out fishing. Tommy ripped his hand open on a line, and infection set in overnight. They tried all kinds of medicine, but none of it worked. I heard from Chris less and less after that. Last time I saw him, he was in Port Clements, scrounging around for motor oil. I don't remember how Lloyd had talked me into that trip, but I remember the wild look in Chris's eyes. Feral. Broken. Never saw him again. Later, Lloyd said he was gone. I didn't ask how he knew. I didn't want to know.

April 24

I sailed back a ways, anchored the *Hannah Marie* near Tow Hill, and rowed to the beach. The abutment runs out into the ocean. It looks north. My grandpa told me that if you had a good set of binoculars you could see Alaska. He was pulling my leg, I'm sure of it. Still, you can't beat the view. Up on the side of the hill, I could still hear the waves crashing below while salt foam sprayed around the rocks at the base.

The old timers used to call these islands "the place where two worlds meet." I understand about that place. I left my father's world for my mother's. I watched one world die. I watched another world be born. In a thousand thousand years, maybe another people will come and find this place. They will set foot on these islands and tell legends about those who went before.

In the cold winds above me, a raven flies. I watch him for a while before making my way back down to the beach. I wonder what will remain when I am gone. Impermanent as fading memory. Flowers on a grave. Footprints on stone. Above me, the raven warbles. Perhaps he tells his own legends. Perhaps he remembers.

I have begun to think about those voices that no longer call out on the radio. About saying goodbye. Lloyd once swore that the *Hannah Marie* would make it across the Pacific. I hoisted the Maple Leaf on the flagpole and I set sail for the west. If nothing else, the rocking of the boat will help me find my dreams.

OF THE DYING LIGHT

Arun Jiwa

Zara walked through the suburbs as the sun disappeared behind the empty shells of houses. She glanced at the street-lights as she passed. The light bulbs were all removed. She paused at an intersection, adjusting her pack. Sid walked ahead huddled in his jacket. She had entered the city on the highway north from Calgary, and had yet to see a single person.

Zara didn't notice the seasons anymore – it always felt like the shortest day in winter – but the trees sensed the change. Fallen leaves in shades of golden fire crackled under her feet. In her last visit to Edmonton, birds had been in the trees, but they had faded away like everything else.

It felt like the neighbourhood was holding its breath. The trees were stripped of their lower branches and others were cut down. Zara couldn't afford the delay, but the hoarding of light meant that people still lived here, and their desperation meant they would trade.

Zara walked up to the parking lot, startling a group of kids. They ran by in unsettlingly bright clothes, pointing.

A girl stopped to look. Zara knew that look. How gangs and civilians alike sized up an outsider. Zara carried candles and lanterns in her backpack – slow burners – solar cells sewn into her jacket, and her shotgun was visible as well. The girl appraised Zara a moment longer before running off.

Zara looked at the row of empty houses; a night out of the cold and away from the shadows. But not tonight. The parking lot would attract the crowd she needed.

The kids had retreated to a gas station at the corner of the lot, watching her. Zara got the sign out of her pack and propped it against a lamppost. Sid sat on the curb, watching them. Since the accident, he rarely spoke, rarely slept. Some part of him had never come back from the shadows after that night. Ever since the accident he had walked north, and Zara followed him.

She would eventually follow him to the end of the world. He knew where the darkness lived, and he would lead her to it. She'd stayed with him through dark hours on the lightless roads north from Calgary, the days fading as they travelled north – even the light had abandoned this place.

She sat down with Sid. "Game," he said.

The kids were playing Shadows. The largest group were the shadows, who had to turn the other players into shadows. Ordinary people were the second group – always outnumbered by the shadows. The last player, the light carrier, had to burn as many shadows as possible. Once burned, the shadows wouldn't come back.

Zara watched a girl dispatch the shadows, wielding her white stone and stick. The game ended when the shadows turned all of the people or when the light carrier burned all the shadows. In the game, the shadows never won.

A drum sounded from near the gas station and the kids disbanded toward the houses. The sun had nearly set when Zara's customers began to arrive. Normally they traded light bulbs, solar panels, car batteries, lamp oil, or tallow candles. Slow burners and fast burners. Tonight was different.

Zara traded for as much food as she could carry. Edmonton was the last surviving city in Northern Canada with food to spare, and there would be hungry nights on the path ahead.

After trading a sack of harvest apples for his wards, one of her customers introduced himself as the mayor. "Not the mayor of Edmonton," he added. "Only of this neighbourhood. I wanted to thank you for stopping by and looking out for us."

There were only two other light carriers in Western Canada. One patrolled through B.C., the other worked in the rural areas in southern Alberta. They stayed away from the northern communities, which meant this group probably hadn't seen a light carrier in a year. She nodded.

He stood a moment longer, fidgeting with his cap. "I know you've other places to be, but if you're looking to settle down I could make you a reasonable offer." He stared at the ward Zara had traded to him. Her symbols were carved into the branch, and she had tied the light-infused glass shards to one end.

"Even if it's only for a week or a month. You could educate us, and help us build a stronger defence." He glanced at Sid. "We take care of our children."

In another life, she and Sid would have lived here, helping them. But her son walked a different path, toward the eternal night, and till her eyes failed, Zara would follow him. "I'm sorry," she said. "I can't afford the time."

The man nodded, put his hat on, and rejoined the waiting group.

Another customer who visited her that night was pregnant. Zara gave her a ward for her unborn child, to protect it from the shadows. She turned away the woman's payment.

The light-carrier's trade was criminal, she often thought; the people who came to her paid with hope and only got false reassurance.

She carved the wards into pieces of wood and added pieces of glass that would glow at night to deter the shadows. But the wards felt too fragile and her heart broke at seeing the hope of these families. They might not see another year.

She couldn't make wards as quickly as she used to; her eyes were failing and the charms lacked potency. She busied herself for the night ahead, marking the tarmac with her symbols and wards, estimating space needed for the rituals, positioning candles before darkness reclaimed its territory.

Shortly after Zara finished, a grandmother arrived with her grandson. Zara equipped both of them with wards. The child didn't question the need for the wards and the protection, but the grandmother looked at her ward, turning it over. "Don't worry, Mother," Zara told her. "When you go, the shadows will leave you in peace."

"Shadow" wasn't the right name for the creatures, but that was where they hid. They crawled into the empty space left by the soul exiting the body, stopping death, and reclaiming the once-human for the night.

The workers from the fields returned home in groups, carrying lanterns tied to poles. A girl and her mother visited Zara at last light. The girl waited while her mother bought wards from Zara.

When her mother was finished, the girl showed Zara a calendar. "The days have been getting shorter," she said. "We've been tracking the shadows, and it seems like they're getting stronger, coming out earlier every night. We've told the council and they've promised to build up stores and defences."

"We?" asked Zara.

"Me and the other kids," said the girl. "Our parents are too busy, working in the fields, trying to meet their quotas, and they don't have time to do this. So we do it instead and compare notes."

"How old are you?"

"Eleven," replied the girl.

Sid was 11. Zara looked back at him. He hadn't moved from his position on the curb, his attention fixed on a line of ants marching across the concrete.

"Be vigilant," Zara said to her. "It'll save your life one day. Be vigilant, and protect your family. They're all you have at the end of the world." The girl nodded and put the calendar away.

"What are they, really? We're taught to be afraid, but none of the adults really know why." The girl's mother had already started walking away and stopped to call the girl.

Zara wished she could tell her that the shadows could be defeated and life would be set right. But she couldn't tell her about the greater horror that lived in the North, where it was always night, and humans hadn't been able to keep their homes. She couldn't encourage their hope, but if Zara didn't survive this trip, people like her would need to hold back the shadows.

Zara took the jar with the shadow from her backpack. "This is what I hunt," she said. "They only have shape in the absence of strong light." The shadow thrashed in the bottle.

"Is it alive? Is this what the shadows are made of?" The girl touched her finger to the jar. The shadow slammed the side of the jar.

The girl flinched, but didn't step back. "Where are they from?"

Zara waved to the girl's mother, telling her it was ok. "They're from the North. Somewhere beyond Fort McMurray. But they're all over the world now. Back in the early days, before the War, before all this, someone summoned a being that shouldn't have ever been on Earth. They're parasites. They live inside us."

"What will you do when you find it?"

Zara took out her lighter and flicked it on. The shadow in the jar writhed when the light touched the jar.

"Burn it."

◀ ▶

Zara wrapped herself in her jacket and waited. Few people would come now, unwilling to risk being outside after sunset. The lights in the nearby houses turned on, flickering like stars.

Evening's last light had faded, turning to the hour when the world shifted from hope and the warmth of the sun to the lightless shadow-space that Zara haunted.

A woman approached Zara, lantern blazing against the darkness.

"Shadows won't surface for another hour," Zara said. "You're early."

"I've brought food," the woman said. "You must be hungry." The light deepened the lines on her face, hiding her in shadows.

Her lantern joined the light cast by Zara's candles. Zara relaxed as soon as the woman passed the wards. She glanced back to the curb. Sid sat in the darkness, watching them.

"Hello there," the woman said to Sid.

"You came alone?" Zara asked.

The woman nodded.

"Put out your light," Zara said.

◀ ▶

Mira had brought soup and bread. She supervised the community farm operation, and her monthly grain allowance made the bread possible. She'd brought additional provisions as payment, which Zara, ignoring her hunger, packed away.

The soup and bread stirred up memories of her old life: a house in the suburbs on fall days like this one, before the shadows, before everything fell apart. Zara fed Sid and made minimal conversation with Mira, so they shared the uncomfortable silence together. Mira told her what she required and took out another parcel.

Zara unwrapped a corner of it and slipped it back.

"I saw your son," said Mira. "And you travel a lot. I thought this would help on the long nights."

"Thanks," she said, and watched Mira relax slightly.

"He doesn't come every night," she said. "Maybe once a month."

Zara poured the remaining soup into a jar and wrapped the last slice of bread. She carefully placed both of them into her bag.

"Has he attempted to communicate?" asked Zara.

"No," said Mira. She fiddled with the handle of her lantern. "I see him sometimes, if I look out our window. I intend to talk to him. It's just that if the kids see him, I'm afraid they'll go out after him, and…"

"You're right," Zara said. She unpacked three thick candles. She had carved wards for summoning on them.

Mira looked out into the darkness. "Miguel died in the early days. He was up at Fort Mac, working on the rigs when they attacked."

Zara took out the lighter and lit the candles. Zara remembered the War. Sid had been an infant. In the chaos, Zara had learned to channel the gift the light carrier had passed on to her.

"The last thing I remember saying to him was that I wished we'd never met. I should've stopped him."

Zara had starved in the early years. She watched as the shadows took the weak and dying, the young and old. Protecting Sid and feeding him were the first lessons she learned when they attacked.

"Will he be able to understand after all this time? Will he know that I'm sorry?"

Zara looked up at the stars. By the time their light reached anyone close enough to see, the star was already dying, swallowed by the darkness.

"Pay attention," Zara said. "When you see your husband, talk to him, but don't give him anything. Don't let him touch you, don't touch him in return. And don't cross the wards."

Mira nodded and looked out at the street.

The shadows had begun to gather, but none of them would be visible yet to Mira.

Zara placed three candles in front of her and Mira. The lights from the houses dimmed to pinpricks as the shadows arrived.

◀ ▶

They came soundlessly, as a wave of darkness and cold that swept away colour and shadows cast by the feeble lights surrounding them. To Zara, they appeared as forms. Children, their bodies forever at the moment of death, and their parents walked alongside them. All the colour of their clothes had been washed out, their faces clear of expression.

Mira stood in front of Zara at the edge of the circle, holding a candle. She would only see the formless darkness until her fears made the shadows coalesce into something real.

The smell of sulphur that accompanied the shadows pervaded their circle, and a sudden chill cut through Zara's jacket. Sid sat with his back to the empty storefront. He had seen this too many times. Zara checked her pockets again to ensure that the empty jar was there and ready. She had wound rags tightly around her hands in preparation for the worst.

"Call him," Zara said.

"Miguel," she called. "Miguel, it's me, Mira. There's something I need to tell you."

Zara had chalked a set of wards in a circle around herself, Mira, and Sid. Another warded circle was drawn in front of this area for the shadow. Zara took off her jacket and wrapped it around Sid. The dress she wore underneath had hundreds of wards sewn into the fabric. At this hour, they glowed softly with an inner pulse of light.

A shadow drifted over and stood in front of Mira.

"Wait a moment," said Zara. "Lift the candle to your height, and you'll see him."

Mira gasped. "Miguel, is that really you?" She began crying. "I'm sorry. I'm sorry that I didn't stop you." Miguel wore the overalls and hardhat from the day he died. Mira wept and spoke gently to the night.

Zara looked away. These moments cut too close to her own life for comfort. Seeing them, Zara remembered Kirk and the day he had returned, turning on her and Sid. She didn't want to offer this option to people, but it was the only way they could exorcise their past.

Mira screamed, breaking Zara from her thoughts. Miguel's shadow had drawn Mira into an embrace, smothering her. She had stepped across the warded line, Zara's candle at her feet and its flame put out. The shadow dragged her farther away from the wards. Miguel's shadow laughed. It was a high and empty laugh that dragged across Zara's heart.

Zara fumbled with her lighter, running after Mira. She clicked it but the flame didn't catch.

As soon as she stepped out of the warded area, shadows surrounded her. Her dress glowed, weakening the shadows, but it wasn't enough. They enveloped her, till she could only see the blackness. Her throat constricted, the pressure on her chest restricting all movement. It was like this the first time. The first time she had fought back. The shadows had taken away all of the light, but they couldn't take everything. Not Sid. She clicked the lighter again. This time the light flared.

The shadows released their grip at the momentary flash and leapt back. Zara touched the lighter to the symbols on the pavement. The symbols ignited, flaring against the shadows that surrounded them. Zara's dress glowed, drawing in the light from the fire. The flare subsided momentarily, and she stood.

Another shadow leapt at her and pushed her back onto the pavement. It opened its mouth, a black abyss drawing in her life. It bent down to Zara, to pull her life through its throat. She thrust the lighter in its face and tried to flick it on.

Sid stepped up to the warded circle, watching her struggle with the shadow.

"Stay inside," she screamed. "Stay inside, Sid!" The lighter flashed again, and Zara stuck her hand down the shadow's throat. The burst of light ignited inside the shadow, and the creature dissolved.

Another shadow flew at her, but before Zara could react, it disintegrated. Sid stood over her, holding one of the candles. He looked at her. "Go," he said. "She needs you. I'll be all right."

Mira writhed on the pavement nearby, tendrils of shadows forcing themselves down her throat.

Zara ran to her, pushing through the shadows. The light on her dress faltered. She touched the lighter to the rags wrapped around her right hand, and the blue flame ignited them.

Zara touched her flaming hand to Mira's chest. The shadow's tendrils writhed and scattered, falling off Mira's twitching body. Zara removed the lid of the jar and held it to Mira's face. She moved her flaming hand over the body, causing Mira to convulse violently. Zara straddled Mira to keep her from shifting and waited for the shadow to leave her body. It dribbled out through her nose and mouth: a thick tarry mass that Zara collected in the jar.

Behind her, Sid set more of the symbols aflame, clearing the shadows. They scattered away, a few of them writhing in the remnants of flame.

Zara dragged Mira's unconscious body back into the circle, and chalked new wards around them, smaller than the circle she had drawn before. Sid sat down, withdrawing into his thoughts again. Zara offered him some water, and she ate an apple while they waited for the first light of morning.

◀ ▶

Mira spent the rest of the night in shock, looking out into the night for any sign of the shadows. But they didn't come back, and, soon after, the fire on the pavement burned down.

At dawn, Zara wrapped up the bottle that contained Miguel's shadow and handed it over to Mira. Mira's hands trembled as she took it.

"The glass won't break," Zara said to her. "But you should keep the rag wrapped around the bottle, just in case. Your neighbours may be superstitious, and it's better if you don't give them a reason to suspect you."

Mira nodded. "Thank you."

"It was unfortunate that your meeting had to end as it did," said Zara.

"But it didn't," said Mira. "I've lived for too long with the guilt, and whatever that was, it wasn't Miguel."

"Bury the bottle in your yard at the full moon," said Zara.

Mira hugged her. "I don't know where you're going," she said, "but be safe."

Sid stirred in his sleep, leaning against the backpack.

Mira looked at him. "They grow up too soon," she said

"Sometimes they never grow up at all," Zara replied.

◀ ▶

Zara walked north, away from Edmonton, to the place where the light was scarce, where unnameable shadows haunted the night roads.

As Zara walked, waiting for the sun to set, she felt that the shadows had already won. They had grown till they swallowed the whole world. There were too many of them. More than she could ever protect Sid from. Every day the sun delayed its arrival, and the shadows inevitably gained another hour of their lives.

Sid stood on the shoulder of the highway, watching the sun set. She sat down near him.

The blindness was coming to her, had been coming since she had received the gift, and the dying light that reached her reminded her that it would soon be eternal night.

"I've got some dinner," she said. He sat and opened his mouth while she fed him the cold soup and bread. He finished and lay his head down on her lap. She held her lighter in one hand and with the other gently stroked his head.

In a few hours they would walk north again, to find and face the nameless demon that had spread shadows throughout the world. For now she sat with her son.

@SHALESTATE

David Huebert

Warm, very warm. And wet, very wet. The Great Unpredictable Nonwinter left us very warm and very wet. But we survived. The forests flourished, and we survived. The redwoods grew tall in the North, and we survived. The bears died off – first white, then gold, then black – and we survived. The bats bred and bred and bred, darkening the skies and filling every night with their abominable wailing. The enemies of @shalestate came and went. They built great #Econations and shunned oil and electricity and worshipped the ancient texts of the heretic Kyoto, but they perished in the end. And we survived.

It rained for 100,000 years, and we survived.

We survived because of the Great Technological Know-How, and the ComfyBunker. But now there is no more Technology. No more Know-How. There is no more Bottled Sunlight. There are few acceptable pairings left. The Endless Bacteriafree Fountain has dried up. The Mentholsuits have all but lost their soothing chill. The water is stagnant and full of diseased bat blood and we have no way to filter it. The mushrooms are tainted, due to lack of clean water. They weaken the stomach, and not everyone can digest them. Three Followers died last year, two the year before that. None of them older than 50. Soon there will be no more surviving, not in this place.

Yesterday the Programmer received a long-awaited message from the Server. DataHQ has ordered the 54 remaining Followers of @shalestate to leave the ComfyBunker and head north, across the Plains of Benevolence. Some people grumble and complain, saying John is too young. But JohnJaneHalMother insists that he is strong enough for the journey. He will have to be; there is no arguing with DataHQ.

Our task is to find new Technology, and we are eager to go. The Followers have been preparing for the Magnificent Ambulation for decades now. The Grandmother often reads us the story while we huddle, huddle around the coolness of the Mentholpit at night. It was prophesied in the Wayback by the First Programmer, the soothsayer Suckleborg. He had two brains and could breathe underwater. It is all written on the Walls of the Faithbook. We will crawl out of the Comfy-Bunker, emerging in the ruins of the ancient metropolis, Vanity City. We will travel past the Neverending N-Bridge Pipeline and onwards, into the Enormous Aquaforests of the North. There will be no more CritterFarm, no more Endless Bacteriafree Fountain, no more sleeping beside the Menthol-cove with Rose, nestling and covering her ears against the screams and flaps of the bats.

The night before we leave, the Programmer gives a speech. He reminds us that there are only 10 Gestating Followers remaining, only 10 of us offering the Window of Conception. He looks at me as he says this, prodding with his beady pink eyes. I shiver and squeeze Rose's soft little hand. The Programmer tells us, though of course we already know, that there are 19 Germinating Followers who must share the Gestating Followers. We must maximize Population Yield. The

Glorious Rotating Monogamy Programme is more vital, now, than ever.

◀ ▶

We climb and climb and climb. It is tiresome, tiresome. The Apprentices lead the way, followed by the Apothecary, the Grandmother, and then the rest of us. The Apprentices carry the largest packs, bearing most of the weight of the Followers. The Father Fathers carry smaller packs, because they must carry the Mother Mother. The rest of the Followers take what they can. Gestating Followers with small children carry no extra weight. Our task is to look after our children, ensure they make the journey. I am worried for Rose.

Sometimes the Apothecary and the Grandmother walk arm in arm, and I know he is helping her along and she is telling him stories. He loves her stories. It is nice to watch them together. Sometimes the Grandmother makes me think of my own mother. Maybe she too would have had grey hair and lined cheeks if she'd made it to that age. I wonder if my mother would have liked the Apothecary, would have walked with him and told him stories.

The body feels heavy, heavy. Rose is panting, panting, and coughing, coughing. The higher we climb, the warmer and wetter it gets. So warm and so wet. The air is heavy, heavy, and thick, thick. The Programmer tells us it will be at least three days before we get out of the ComfyBunker and arrive on the Plains of Benevolence. And once we are there, he does not know what to expect.

None of us know. But the Apothecary has faith. He is hopeful. I see him watching Rose and me. Watching, watching. But he watches in a good way, a warm way. Not the way the Programmer watches. The Programmer only watches Rose, watches her and watches her, never speaking. When he sees her looking back, he smiles and nods slowly, bringing his chin to his neck. What a strange way to treat a child.

The Programmer has translucent skin. It glows softly in the dark, revealing a mesh of sinew and vein. In the Wayback several Followers had this happen; it is chronicled on the Walls of the Faithbook. When it first happened, it was decreed that no Follower should glow like the cave insect, and that if anyone was found to shine in the night they should have to suffer Reintegration. But no one threatens the Programmer. There are others like him, after all. I have seen the Apothecary's toes glowing in the middle of the night. I have seen a neon, yellowish shadow behind Rose's kidney flesh. I have seen the Mother Mother's sunken eyes, shimmering red behind her eyelids as she sleeps.

I would like to make the Programmer stop watching Rose, but I fear him. When it is my turn to lie with him, he is cold and faraway. He does not look into my face or touch me gently like the other Germinating Followers. At times he seems very frustrated, and at other times he stares at a wall and moves fast, fast inside me. I have the feeling that he is trying to imagine that I am not me. That I am Rose.

We eat a lunch of dried mushrooms and smoked bat. The mushrooms are delicious and the bat is chewy. The meat hurts the jaw, but it nourishes us. We could never have survived without the bats. In the Wayback, when the bats first began to darken the skies, they caused great fear. After the Mass Extinction Event, at the beginning of the Great Unpredictable Nonwinter, the bats began to breed and breed. The Faithbook says that the Ancients had predicted a different kind of Mass Extinction Event. They were not ready for the wet and the warmth and the flooding. But the bats were ready. They learned to swim and they multiplied, and at times they seemed to be speaking to each other. And the Faithbook decreed that we should eat the bats, that they would carry us through the Great Unpredictable Nonwinter. They are plentiful, and the weak ones are easy to hunt.

After lunch the thighs are burning, burning as we resume the climb. The Father Fathers are carrying the Mother Mother just ahead of us on her makeshift stretcher. There are four Father Fathers – one red-haired, three brown-haired. All of them waddle strangely, as if they were trying to imagine that they still had their seedbags between their legs. Rose used to make fun of their walk, but I warned her that the Father Fathers oversee the birthing process and are the most revered members of our community. They were very kind to me when Rose was born. Once in a while the Mother Mother releases some gas. The gas is pungent, like the smell of a stagnant pool. I feel revulsion until I recall the smells from when I was the Mother Mother, carrying Rose. I smile and pat Rose's head.

Halfway through the afternoon, Rose gets very tired. I have to pick her up and carry her for a stretch because I cannot stand to listen to her panting anymore. Her eyelids flick shut and her head jerks and I see that she is trying not to fall asleep in my arms.

I feel a hand on my shoulder, and hope it is the Apothecary. But I turn around and look into the horrible, pink eyes of the Programmer. "RoseMother," he says, "you are not strong enough. I will take the child."

"Thank you," I say. "Perhaps I can manage a little longer." I turn away and march forward, holding Rose close. Up ahead, I see that the Apothecary has turned back to watch. Beside him, the Grandmother marches along. She carries over 60 years, more than any other Follower. And yet she is so strong, never fading from the climb. The Grandmother gives me hope.

◄ ►

For dinner we have my favourite, boiled salamander. The meat is fleshy and the taste is not too bad. Rose loves watching the salamanders in the CritterFarm, loves feeding them their daily guano. So she does not enjoy this meal. She cries and I have to go get her some more smoked bat. After eating the bat, she cries again. She drinks all of her water and most of mine and I want to ask for more but we can't appear weak. Rose has not urinated all day.

The Apothecary starts a small fire. There are some matches and SustainaLogs left over from the Technological Know-How, but not many. We sit around the fire and the Grandmother reads to us from the Faithbook. She tells us about the Plains of Benevolence, how they were flooded when we descended into the ComfyBunker but now they will be full of surface life. There will be fruit and meat and drinkable water everywhere we turn. It will be like the Aquaforests of the North, without the gigantic carnivorous moose.

The entire time the Grandmother speaks, she is stroking the Mother Mother's bulbous belly. She strokes calmly, calmly, and I feel the warmth of the future in the gesture. The Mother Mother sucks on a sweet stick, part of the hoard left over from the Technological Know-How. I watch her sucking on the sweet stick and I remember the flavour of it from when I was the Mother Mother. It was a strange flavour, a sweetness that burned. I did not particularly like it and yet I always wanted more. I also remember how the Grandmother used to stroke my belly when Rose was growing inside me. Her touch was sweet and warm, like a dose of Bottled Sunlight. Even as the Grandmother strokes the Mother Mother, the Programmer watches Rose. Watching, watching, a nasty twitch in his nose. Rose keeps her eyes on the ground, drawing shapes in the earth with a stick.

We fall asleep, as always, to the sound of the bats. They are nattering, nattering, and flapping all around us. We sleep in the open air because there is nowhere good to set up the tents. In the middle of the night there is a loud shriek, followed by a hushed voice. I know it is the Mother Mother and the Father Fathers. She is worried about the Future, about what might become of a helpless child on the Plains of Benevolence. We are all worried.

For breakfast we have blindfish and dried mushrooms. The Apothecary eats with Rose and me. He impersonates the Programmer's voice and Rose laughs and laughs. But then the Programmer looks over and she seems afraid. Before he leaves, the Apothecary slips me his water ration. I give Rose the extra water and she drinks it all in a gulp. Right away she needs to pee, and I know that some of the water was wasted.

We climb and climb and climb, thighs burning, burning. We pass several stagnant pools. They are stinky, and full of guano. We also pass two large ponds and we can see some blindfish swimming through them. The Apothecary suggests that we stop here and catch more fish for our journey. The

Programmer says no, but the Apothecary insists and the rest of the Followers agree.

The Programmer walks over to the Mother Mother, whispers in her ear. She whispers back, and the Programmer announces that we will stop and rest while the Apothecary catches more fish for the journey. The Mother Mother is pale, pale. Her belly is large, perhaps too large. We are all wondering what she might be carrying in there. I am sorry for her. It would have been better to wait until the child came, but we could not wait any longer.

Up here, it is very warm and very wet. Almost unbearable. I am desperately thirsty. The Apothecary rolls up the legs of his Mentholsuit and wades into the pool. He sets his net and waits for the blindfish to swim between his legs. I rest with my back against the cave wall, watching the Apothecary. The top of his Mentholsuit is pulled down, giving him greater flexibility. His torso is bare, except for the string of the sacred First Aid Kit he keeps around his neck. He stands still, arms poised, eyes flickering as he watches the swirling fish. I feel the moisture of the earth through the thin fabric of the Mentholsuit. Rose sits between my legs, resting her head on my chest. "Mother," she says, "what is it like, to be dry?"

I chuckle. "I don't know, my little salamander."

"Salamander?" she says, laughing as she looks up at me.

"Yes." I make a face and crawl my fingers up her arm. "Little Sally Salamander."

Rose laughs, her eyes going wet. Then she starts to cough. I rub her back but she does not stop. She keeps coughing, coughing, her face turning red. A few of the Followers look at us, whispering to one another. Soon the Programmer comes over, handing Rose some water. She takes it and drinks. After a few sips she regains control of her breathing. The Programmer leans toward me. "RoseMother," he says, "she is weak and so are you. I will take her from here."

"No, please. I can manage."

The Programmer sighs and walks away, toward the Mother Mother. From where he stands with his feet in the pool, the Apothecary watches, watches.

◀ ▶

The next morning there are two Followers dead: KateMother and a two-year-old child, Rufus. Rufus had been sick since the day he was born, but KateMother's death is a shock. We bury them and sprinkle mushrooms in their grave. The Composer leads us in a song and then we climb, climb. Rose does not laugh the whole day. She does not cough or urinate. She does not complain. She climbs, climbs, when she can, and the rest of the time I carry her. The Programmer watches Rose, and the Apothecary watches the Programmer. With every step the world gets warmer and wetter. So wet and so warm. But the cave seems brighter now, and there are fewer bats. We are eating blindfish and dried mushrooms for lunch when Rose asks me again. "Mother, what is it like, to be dry?"

I do not call her "Sally Salamander." I look at the Apothecary and remember the feel of his chin hair on my neck. "It is like fire," I say. "Fire that doesn't burn."

That night, the Apothecary comes to me as I sleep. He sneaks up behind, stroking my hair, whispering for me to stay quiet. He has brought two full rations of water, and one of the Mother Mother's sweet sticks, for Rose.

"But it is not our turn," I say. "The Programmer's offering still swims inside me."

The Apothecary puts a thumb on my lips. "No one will know. It's harder to keep track here." Beside us, Rose begins to stir. "I will leave before the rising hour."

He moves closer and I wriggle around him, breathing the leathery hum of his flesh. I peel off my Mentholsuit and climb on top, keeping my head low, low. As always, our bodies come together amidst the flapping of bats. Rose wakes and looks at me and I motion for her to be quiet. The Apothecary, still inside me, smiles at Rose and hands her the sweet stick. He whispers, telling her that everything will be all right. Rose rolls over, turning her eyes away from us, and puts the sweet stick in her mouth.

◀   ▶

I awake to grunts and shouts. The Father Fathers encircle me. Two of them grab my arms and the other reaches into a sack and begins to tie my wrists together. The Programmer is stooping over Rose, picking the sweet stick up from the earth. The Apothecary is on his knees behind the Father Fathers, his hands bound. The Mother Mother is watching, watching, rubbing her belly and squinting. She looks like she is in pain.

There is an abrupt trial, led by the Programmer. The Mother Mother is very quiet. She keeps sneaking furtive glances in my direction. The Grandmother grows heated, waving her arms in the air, but the Programmer keeps shaking his head. The Father Fathers nod solemnly and the Grandmother storms away.

The Programmer announces the final decision: the crime is Violation of the Glorious Rotating Monogamy Programme and the sentence is Reintegration. The pale Apprentice cries out, asking whether we can afford the sacrifice. "We are dying," he pleads. "There are only nine Gestating Followers left. To reintegrate RoseMother is to contaminate our Lifewater at the source."

The Programmer assures everyone that it will be all right. He says the Server has declared that we will survive as long as we abide the Glorious Rotating Monogamy Programme. The Followers grunt and nod. The Apothecary does not resist as the Programmer takes the First Aid Kit from his neck. He looks into the distance, his eyes poised, as when he hunts the blindfish.

The Father Fathers dig two holes in the earth, side by side. At least they are side by side. They lay us down in the holes and pick up their shovels. The Programmer looms behind them, with Rose at his side. He has his hand on her shoulder and I can see his index finger running back and forth along her collarbone. She is tense, tense, biting her soft little lip.

The first shovelful of dirt falls over me, thudding, thudding, on my chest. A few grains scatter across my face. I look at Rose. Her mouth is moving and there is fear in her eyes. I want to hold her in our little tent in the Mentholcove, listening to her breath as she settles into sleep. I want to see her feeding the salamanders, her eyes bright as the creatures curl their tails and flick their tongues. I want to listen to her laughing as she runs through the mushroom forest, looking over to make sure I am watching, her eyes sparking with love and glee.

Another shovelful hits me, this one falling across my thighs. For a moment, I think about calling out. I could accuse the Programmer of glowing like the cave insect. But who among us has not become like the cave insect?

My eyes fall on the Mother Mother and I imagine the Future that will emerge from her womb. I see it as a magnificent creature with red, red eyes and the wings of a bat. I see it taking flight across the sky above the Plains of Benevolence, hovering, hovering, among the things they call clouds. I see it trailing a mane of golden hair and laughing as it scoops Rose up and takes her in its arms. I see them laughing together, flying far into the North. They will find Technology. They will find Know-How. They will cross the Neverending Pipeline and ride together on the backs of the gigantic carnivorous moose. They will be glorious, glorious, and free, free.

I feel the Apothecary looking at me and I glance over and nod. I am not sure what my eyes say but I want them to say that everything is all right. We are here, together, in the damp, damp earth. Together, together. I look at Rose, but a clump of dirt falls across my eyes.

CITY NOISE

Morgan M. Page

Two cans of beans and an eggplant, a big one like you used to get at a supermarket before everything went for-real organic. Pretty good haul from a half hour with this client, and he was sweet, too. It's enough to eat for a couple of days. And a Rolex – doesn't work but looks like the day it was made. Sarah puts them into her satchel, stained and patched a hundred times over, different colour leathers, holding together all these years later.

She gets onto her bike; it's dinged up pretty bad and starting to rust, practically ready for the scrap heap, and she heads away from the condo. The building's mostly intact, has almost all of its windows, just a few missing here and there like knocked-out teeth. She heads up Bay Street, across Wellesley, and rides around Queen's Park, not through it. It's still daylight out, but the park's not a good place any time of day. The long-since burned-out shell of parliament quietly looms over it in the south, and she's always glad to get some distance between her bike and that wretched place.

When she gets in, past two sets of doors, five sets of locks, down the long dark hall in the basement filled with debris that hides the door to their little apartment from possible burglars, she finds Johnny on the floor again. Must've been another bad day. Sarah puts down her satchel near the door carefully, so she doesn't mush the eggplant, and sits on the floor next to him.

"Hey, baby," she says in her client voice. Stops herself, readjusts. Regular voice: "What's going on? You okay?"

He doesn't move. Doesn't make a sound. Doesn't take a breath for a good long while, and then exhales slowly and says plainly, "It's just loud again today." Johnny sits up, and he's got that look on his face that used to just break her heart. But you can only get your heart broke so much until you're numb to it. "Maybe we should move to the country. Get away from all the city noise."

"Yeah, maybe some day." Sarah stands up then. Their little daily drama, his dreams of fleeing the city. "But there's no work out there. Not for me."

◀ ▶

It didn't change too much for Sarah after The Crash. Sure, it was better before with the Internet and video games and her dates gave her cash she could spend however she wanted, but, when you already live on the fringe of society, it doesn't make a big difference when society just stops functioning. So now she trades favours for canned food and "fresh" produce.

But, really, the only thing she misses. The thing that keeps her up at night. The thing that dominates her thoughts any time she passes a mirror. The only thing she can think about when she thinks about the future. Hormones. Now, she's pretty lucky because before The Crash, Sarah got her bits nipped and tucked permanently, so it's not like she has to worry about her damned body flooding her with testosterone each and every passing day. Not enough to make her hair fall out. But she misses the little blue estrogen pills that made her breasts perky and her skin so much softer.

Right when it was all going down, five years ago, her first thought: Get to a fucking pharmacy, bitch. The looting had already begun, but, luckily, no one was really on the lookout for estrogen pills. Each pharmacy was cleared out of every kind of pain medication, and most of the important antibiotics and medications, but without fail, there they'd be. Bottles of estrogen. Estrace the synthetic, and Premarin the natural made from pregnant mare urine. She briefly considered trying to raise a horse, but couldn't quite put together how that would lead her to a wellspring of estrogen without, like, having to drink glasses of horse piss – and she knew enough about science to think that probably wouldn't be terribly effective.

But those sources long since dried up. She's not the only transsexual in town, and there are, of course, post-menopausal women and all the little drug dealers who think they can charge a ransom for any pill they find.

But without hormones her body betrays her, as it's done her whole damn life. She's tired all the time, and maybe someday her bones will become brittle and snap, or cancer might eat her up. And she's got to keep her girlish figure for clients and sweet, broken Johnny, which is what brings her to Jetta's loft near the Distillery.

Sarah parks her bike, locks it to a pipe, and goes up the three flights of dark stairs to Jetta's. Outside the door, one of Jetta's boyfriends, all muscle, shaved head, stands watch with a couple of candles going. He looks Sarah up and down, and she rolls her eyes because he's seen her a dozen times before. When he moves aside, she slides the stupid-heavy metal door open.

Inside it's all twinkling lights, candles and oil lamps everywhere because the sun's starting to set. Racks of clothes line the apartment, and at the other end is a well-stocked kitchen with just about every stainless steel kitchen gadget you could imagine, and tiny Jetta back there chopping carrots.

"Mija!" she calls out, turning to see Sarah come in. "How are you, mami?"

"I'm good, honey. I'm good," Sarah smiles. Sure, she's Jetta's client, but she always makes her feel like this is home.

"I'm making carrot tonight! A big carrot for all my boys!" Jetta finishes chopping and puts it aside. "You want to stay for soup?"

"No, I'm good. Really." Because everything comes at a price and you only want to owe Jetta so much. "You got time to give me a little booster shot in my boy pockets?"

It takes her a few minutes to set up over by the medical exam table stolen from some hospital. First, Jetta sterilizes the needles. Now, Sarah is not stupid. She knows that you aren't ever really going to get those needles sterile. But there isn't much choice. Then Jetta goes off to another corner of her loft, opens a great big safe – another item lifted from elsewhere – and comes back with a plastic bottle. There's a picture of a smiling woman and the most beautiful ass you've ever seen in the world, with the words "SILICONA – COLOMBIA" in a circle around the picture.

When Jetta's ready, Sarah pulls down her skirt and her dirty tights, lies down on the exam table, and lets the woman do her work. Jetta pumps the silicone into her hips, five needles on each side. She leaves the needles in, each one atop a big round bubble of silicone, until she's finished with both sides. Then she takes out the needles, says, "You know this

gonna hurt," and starts rubbing. Sure, the tearing flesh feeling
of the silicone going in is bad, but it's nothing compared to the
rubbing Jetta calls her "special massage." She pushes the silicone around, forms it into the perfect hips. She injects some
more into Sarah's boy pockets, the little dimples on the sides
of each butt cheek that are supposedly a dead giveaway of ass
masculinity.

Silicone is forever. Mostly. "You gonna lose some, maybe
half by next week," Jetta says, as she dabs superglue over the
injection holes and covers them in Hello Kitty Band-Aids.
The silicone absorbs a bit into the body, but most of it will
stay. Hopefully.

All the girls have heard horror stories about silicone gone
bad. The body can reject it, or it can move and disfigure you.
But at least Jetta's face is reassuring. Her cheeks are round,
her lips are plump – all in a slightly unnerving but exquisitely
beautiful way. She's more than just a woman, she's an artistic
representation of femininity. Or one kind of femininity, anyway. She could be any age – 27, 43, 52 – it's impossible to tell
with such flawless skin. Clearly, she had work done before
The Crash. Professional work. Maybe in Guadalajara, Bang-
kok, Rio. Quality work.

Sarah's so sore, she tries not to cry as she leans over and
reaches into her satchel, pulls out the Rolex. Jetta snaps it up
and looks it over, gets a look on her face like Ursula in *The
Little Mermaid*. "Mm, this is good. My boys love it. Next time
you get something good, you come back here and we'll top
you up. Make those breasts of yours really pop!"

◄ ►

When she opens her eyes, slowly, sleepy, he's not beside her. Runs a hand over the warm spot where her Johnny should be, and then she frowns and rolls over. Just a small shaft of clear moonlight coming in through the tiny grimy basement window, slicing through the dark room and hitting the edge of the bed. Her eyes adjust, and no Johnny. She catches the tension in her eyebrows as she's squinting through the darkness, doesn't need more lines, more reasons to get pumped. Relax.

Sarah gets out of bed, wobbles, rights herself, and makes her way carefully to the doorframe. One hand on the wall, she walks down the short hallway. First door, the bathroom. No Johnny. Farther down, she reaches the living room.

At first she can't make out anything. Then a little whisper. She takes a step forward, so quiet, so careful, listens close for that little whisper. And there it is again. And then a little movement, enough that she can start to make out the edges of someone in the dark corner of the room. Her Johnny.

The only words she can make out, words spoken like terrible secrets, words meant to stay secret from her, are "I can't."

"Johnny." Silence. Stillness. "Johnny, come back to bed, honey. Please." Nothing for a few seconds.

He stands up and crosses the room, moonlight hitting just the lower parts of his legs as he sulks back over to her. "I'm sorry," he says. Means it, too. Takes her hand and leads her to the bedroom. "It's just so loud. It's too loud in here, I couldn't sleep." Dead silence.

"I know, honey," she says, climbing into bed. "But there's nothing there. There's no one there." She almost catches herself, but it's too late. The words have already fallen out of her mouth. He stops, won't get into bed.

"You think I'm crazy?" Johnny says, the hurt thick in his voice. "I can hear them. I'm not crazy. Su Ling could hear them! You said you believed her."

"Can we not have this fight? Can we not right now?"

"Do you think I'm crazy?"

"I didn't say that. It's just, you know, trauma. Like it was hard on everyone, when it all went down, and we all process it different, you know?"

"That's just a nice way of saying crazy."

"Johnny, I'm sorry." She reaches out for his hand in the darkness, squeezes it. "You're not crazy. I just don't know what to believe." She pulls his hand, gently, pulls him back to bed. Sarah puts her head down on his chest and runs her finger across the long, thin line of scar tissue under his pec. "I'm sorry. I love you."

For a while, they lie there in silence, neither of them asleep and both know it. "We need to get out of here. It's better in the country, like Su Ling always said. We need to get away from the city."

◀ ▶

It started about a year after The Crash. After everything stopped working, after the fighting, after the looting, after so much death. First, the rich fled the city. No use staying, they'd just be a target for gangs of thieves and looters. Sarah heard there were rich families holed up in farms way out in the middle of nowhere, up near Algonquin Park or somewhere like that.

With no government, no one came to collect the bodies. The remaining city folk started to bury them, mostly to make things hygienic. But there were too many, and digging's a lot of work. People made huge pyres. Sure, it stank up the place with the scent of charred flesh for a while, but that was quickly overpowered by the rotting garbage smells. Life after The Crash was smelly. And that's when Johnny, Su Ling and, Sarah was certain, many others began to hear it.

Johnny had been with her since before The Crash. They'd met at some sweaty queer dance party in the West End, around the time they'd both started transitioning. They'd stuck together as the whole damn world fell apart around them. He was strong and funny and sneaky then, a great looter early on. Until the pyres had burned away the last of the dead. They'd both seen friends and neighbours and so many legions of unknowns go up in flames.

He got a funny look on his face one day, looked around like someone had called his name. They were in an alley, had just looted a stockpile of canned food Johnny had found in the basement of some building. He thought they'd been caught, grabbed Sarah's hand tight and ran.

Soon after, Johnny told her. "It's like chatter. I don't know, I can't describe it. I think it's an ear infection." And so, Sarah saved up a bunch of stuff from tricks to barter for some medicated eardrops. No change. He tried to push it out of his mind.

Two streets over in the Annex, their old friend Su Ling was living in the attic of an old Victorian with whatever girlfriend of the week she had at the time. They used to go over for dinner sometimes, pool their food together and have a feast. Well, a meal.

One night over something that was almost borscht, Su Ling said she was leaving. "It's time. It's just death here."

"But what's out there? You gonna farm or some butch shit?" Johnny laughed.

"I've never even been out of the city since The Crash," Sarah said, picking at a beet with her fork. "What's even out there?"

"I have to. It's not right here—" Su Ling tried to explain.

Her girlfriend cut in, "She thinks she's going psychic. She hears—"

"Marla!" Su Ling snapped. "I just. I hear this, like, talking in my ears. It's worse in some parts of the city. It's like city noise. I gotta get out of here, and get some fresh air. It'll be quiet in the country."

A full minute passed before Johnny opened his mouth and let it spill out that he heard it, too. But there was no relief in sharing, all it did was unnerve the four of them further.

Su Ling left a week later with her pretty girlfriend in tow.

◀ ▶

Derrick is usually easy. He is quick, relatively clean, and polite. Skinny, white hipster boy with manners, a seemingly unending supply of canned food, and the faintest hint of a paunch coming in as he hovers around 30. He gives her four cans of beans and a mason jar of moonshine for the date when she gets to the collective house.

Sarah's pulling her best post-apocalyptic Amy Winehouse – hair up in a messy bouffant, floral print retro dress that's damn near mint condition, except for the small tear in the seam just under her armpit that she really needs to fix up before it rips further, and beat-up burgundy cowboy boots.

The date goes quickly. Rub, tug, blow, repeat, and it's over. She gets up and goes over to the gold-framed mirror on the wall of his room, one long crack down the middle of it, cutting her face in two.

"You ever been outside?" she asks, fixing her hair in the mirror's reflection.

"Like out of the city?" he says, still lying there in the afterglow.

"Yeah, some place rural. The country or something."

"My buddy and I went out to this farm in, like, Aurora," he says. "It was a pretty sweet set-up, but it's way too much work. The city's harder, I guess, but you don't have to get up at dawn here and work in the sun. My back!" He laughs, and she can see him through the mirror, rubbing his stomach.

"You're just a city boy at heart, huh?"

"Not cut out for working. I'm the first to admit I'm a trust-fund baby." His voice darkens only a little. "Or I was. Anyway, I like the city better. Make some booze to trade, and I can get up whenever I want."

◄ ►

The roof of their building is covered in gravel and plastic bins full of abandoned attempts at rooftop gardening. Neither of them have green thumbs, no natural inclination to keep things alive except each other, so it's all dead and dried out, growing weeds instead of tomatoes. Johnny passes Sarah the mason jar, wipes the booze from his mouth with his other hand.

She takes a sip of the bitter drink and watches the patch of sunset light slowly moving across his brown skin. Johnny's dirty white tank top is off, tucked into the waist of his jeans, and he's leaning against the raised ledge, resting his head on folded arms. In that moment Sarah can see beyond the drama, the craziness, the pain, and all the wretched process-ing to the beautiful boy she took home one night, so many years ago. *This forever*, she thinks. And she drinks more of her trick's moonshine.

"All right," she says, and coughs for a second. "All right, I'm in. We can try it."

"Try what?" Johnny asks, letting one arm droop down over the ledge.

"Let's leave the city. Let's go outside. I'm in. I'm with you."

Johnny turns to her and, slowly, a big smile spreads across his face. She can't remember the last time she's seen his eyes so bright and alive. They kiss and laugh. He runs his fingers through her hair, presses his forehead against hers.

"It's going to be so great!" he says, beaming at her. "We'll get fresh food! We'll grow things or pick berries or something! We can go anywhere. Anywhere! No more worrying about get-ting mugged or burglars or anything. I'll get a bow and arrows and we can hunt for our food."

"No more tricks," she chimes in.

"No more tricks! And it'll be so quiet out there."

They stay up there, future-dreaming together until it starts to get too cold and too dark out, and they have to retreat to their basement hideout.

◀ ▶

The darkness is complete. Without streetlights, the head-lights of passing cars, the tiny glow of digital alarm clocks, and the reassurance of a smartphone lighting up periodically to let you know who's liked something on Instagram, it is total. And on a cloudy night, there isn't even the light of the moon and stars. So, when Sarah opens her eyes there is no meaningful difference besides the feeling of air on her exposed eyes.

The dark used to terrify her, even into her young adulthood, even before it became so thick after The Crash. Now, just a mild sense of unease creeps through her body. It's just the night. And she puts one arm around the warm body beside hers, around her Johnny, the muscles on his body feeling as tightly coiled as ever.

She makes a list in her head as she waits to fall back asleep. They've spent two weeks pulling it all together – the tins of food and bottles of water from her eight regulars, a compass and sleeping bag Johnny bartered some books for, and the not too beat-up backpacks Jetta gave her as a going-away present at her last pumping session.

Beneath her arm, Johnny's chest rises and falls. She can't see it, but she can feel it.

This city has been everything to her. This city gave her life, an escape from the terrors of small-town queerdom. Access to doctors who took her seriously, or seriously enough that she could get what she needed. A chance at something like happiness. Shelter through the whole ordeal of The Crash, and enough work to keep her alive and well. And this beautiful boy under her arm.

And for him, for his madness or his gift, however you want to frame it, but for him regardless, she will give up this city.

Tomorrow, they leave.

BROWN WAVE

Christine Ottoni

The dark stink of brownwater rises up off the river. It settles around the buildings at the edge of the lake. Light glows in the east, hanging low beyond the clouds in the sky.

The slumtop smells the river first. The concrete lodging towers sit at the edge of town where there is a bend in the river. The stink hits the windows and fills the empty halls. It presses up against doors, pries at cracks in the walls.

Richard and Eli live on the top floor in a corner room. Richard sits on their bed and rests his hand on his brother's sleeping shoulder.

Brownwater is muck today, Richard says. Eli opens his eyes.

C'mon, Richard says. Breakfast and school.

They have always lived in the slumtop. Or at least since Eli was very young. He can't remember being anywhere else. Eli sits up in bed, stretches his arms over his head and yawns. He looks out the window toward the factory where Richard works. The great black building is farther down the river at the opposite end of town. Smokestacks reach up into the mist.

Richard puts on his blue jumpsuit and rubber boots. A pot of beans is cooking on the stovetop, rattling, uneven on the element. Steam rises into the damp air. Eli is hungry.

He kicks off the thin blanket and moves to the foot of the bed, reaching for the chest of clothes. The floor is too cold for sockless feet. Eli stays on the bed while he gets dressed. A pair of pants and a sweatshirt. He puts on thick socks and tucks his pants into them. He swings his feet onto the floor.

They eat quickly and take their backpacks down from the row of hooks by the door. Richard helps the boy into his slip jacket and boots. He locks the room and they leave the slum-top. Eli runs ahead down the open concrete stairwell, the slap of his boots echoing to the floors below. Outside, the grey mist falls around them. Richard pulls Eli's hood tight over his head. When the hood slips back, the wet air stings at his eyes. Eli tucks his face down into his collar. They walk.

The school is at the centre of town. Eli and Richard follow the main road and pass by the ground houses. They have high concrete walls and gravel lawns sprayed with bright green paint. The kids from the ground houses walk to school on their own. Their slip jackets shine blue and yellow, slick with wet. Richard straightens his back and leads Eli by the hand.

At school, kids run across the compound out of the rain. They duck into the class buildings, metal cubicles arranged by form across the pavement.

Bye, Eli, Richard says.

Bye, Richard, Eli says. He hikes his backpack up higher on his shoulders and heads toward his class with the others. Eli is the only one in his class building who lives in the slum-top. He sits at the front of the class by Miss Riley's desk. The other kids leave him alone, mostly.

Once, at lunch, a girl named Violet gave him some of her chocolate milk.

You've never had it? she said.

Eli shook his head.

She pushed the little plastic package toward him and he took a sip. It was too rich. The dark brown liquid coated his throat and tongue. It left his mouth thick.

Everyone says your parents died in the flood, Violet said. She took a gulp of the chocolate milk. She smiled at the boy.

In the class building the students sit at their desks, face the front of the room. Miss Riley pulls a stack of coloured paper out of the supply closet. Usually, the students are allowed one piece each a week. They use the paper right down to the little strips. But today Miss Riley puts all the coloured paper on her desk and then turns to the chalkboard. She draws a shape, a long oval with a triangle on top and two bits splitting on the end.

This is a fish, she says. Today we are going to make fish cut-outs. She is smiling at the class but Eli thinks she is sad. Her voice is soft.

She chooses a red piece of paper and makes her cut-out with one long swipe of the scissors. The excess paper curls to the floor. She helps the students make their fish, as many as they want, and they tape them up on the classroom windows. The grey light from outside bleeds through the colours, lighting them up.

After school, Richard is waiting for Eli. He holds his hand out for the boy and Eli takes it. They walk back together through the mist to the slumtop.

The rain turns hot that night. Steam rises off puddles on the streets below. Richard tells Eli to stay away from the window; it never closes all the way tight. Little drops bounce and fizz onto the sill, slip onto the floor of their room.

Eli tells Richard about the fish and the paper and how Miss Riley seemed sad all day.

So it's called fish? Richard says. He likes to hear about school. They are sitting on the floor, across from each other over the chest. They are eating zip-packet beans and carrots. Richard got them at the factory for his lunch ration. He always brings food home for Eli. He tears away the airtight plastic and scoops the food into the pot so he can heat it up. They eat from tin mugs.

I liked Miss Riley when I was little, Richard says.

Eli uses his hand to swipe the last bit of beans from his mug. He licks his fingers.

In the morning it's raining harder. Richard drops Eli off at school and heads to the factory. The rain beats down, fierce pellets against his hunched shoulders.

The compound is quiet, empty. Eli doesn't see any other kids. They must be inside the class buildings already, out of the rain. Eli crosses the compound to his class. The door is locked. The lights are off. He can see the fish cut-outs still taped up to the windows. Miss Riley should be there at the front of the room.

Eli walks home, back up to the slumtop. He peels off his slip jacket and rain boots, leaving them to dry by the door. He sits at the window, waiting for Richard to come home, watching the little white houses below. He can see grown-ups packing up their cars, piling boxes and bags into the trunks and on top of the roofs. He wonders where they are going.

When Richard gets home it is dark outside. The clouds are thick over the town. He looks worried.

No kids at school, Richard says.

I came home, Eli says.

At night they wake up to the sound of the flood horn. They can hear the water coming. The surge roars in between the bellows of the horn. They sit up under the window and see the wave come, crushing over the ground houses. The water is like chocolate. Heavy, deep and brown.

The horn stops. It is quiet. Eli pushes himself against Richard's side.

We'll stay here, Richard says. He gets up from the window and checks the lock. He pushes the chest in front of the door.

They stay awake in the slumtop until the clouds turn grey with light again. Richard tells Eli to stay back, away from the window. They sit in the damp room, drinking hot water from mugs while Richard crouches, one hand on the windowsill, staring at the town.

Eli lies on the bed. He sleeps and dreams of the brown wave. He sees Violet, clawing through mud water. She smiles and chocolate milk runs down her nose, drips from the corner of her mouth.

Eli wakes up and he can hear people shouting outside. Loud pops and broken glass. Richard sits at the window.

It's okay, he tells Eli.

They wait in the slumtop. One night, when Richard is asleep, Eli looks out the window. But all the lights in the houses are off and he can't see if the water is still there.

Will the water stay below? Eli asks Richard in the morning.

No, no, Richard says. It'll wash out.

Richard tries to be careful with the zip packets. He counts them, sets aside what they are allowed to have each day, but it's not enough. Eli can see Richard is not eating. His hands shake as he passes mugs of food to the boy.

We gotta leave, Richard says.

Where'll we go? Eli says.

High ground.

They put all of their things into the backpacks. Sweaters, socks and mugs. They put on their slip jackets and boots and Richard pushes the chest away from the door. He steps out into the hall, holds his arm in front of Eli.

If I say Go, Richard says, you gotta come right back here and lock this door. Be quiet and hide under the bed. Okay?

Okay, Eli says.

They move through the slumtop. Every door is open and the rooms are empty. The wind groans in the halls.

At the bottom they cross through the ground houses. All the windows are broken, the green pebbled lawns washed away. Pools of still blackwater have formed around the houses.

Where is everyone? Eli asks.

Hold my hand, Richard says.

Eli thinks of the flood horn, what happens if it bellows while they are on the ground.

They pass a house. There is a figure lying on its side in the entranceway. Eli stops to look, his hand pulling on Richard's.

It's a man. His upper body is inside the house, his legs are hanging out onto the front stoop. Black pants cling to his legs like dead skin slipping from bone. His feet are bare, the soles wrinkled and blue.

Don't look, Richard says. He pulls on the boy's hand. Keep walking.

They head up the north road. Eli can see trees, dark pine tops, rising past the edge of the last houses. This is the farthest he has ever been from the slumtop. Mud sucks at his boots with each step.

The road slopes upwards in a hill and they struggle to get their footing on the washed-out ground. Pine trees line the road, bent and broken, dripping damp. Eli and Richard step over branches stripped off the trees by wind and water.

The ground levels off. Ahead they can see the mud road twisting forward into the forest. Eli pauses at the top of the hill.

Richard puts his hand on Eli's shoulder.

Keep walking, he says.

Eli's boots are heavy; clumps of earth cake on top of his feet, weighing him down. They walk again, making slow time, lifting their legs high to avoid puddles and sticks. Eli's legs ache from the effort.

I'm hungry, he says.

We can't stop, Richard says.

Eli takes a step over a puddle but loses his footing and slides into the blackwater. His leg sinks in up to his knee, his boot fills with water. He struggles.

Richard! he cries. Two strong hands are under his armpits, lifting him up. He is free. The air is cool around his foot.

The blackwater puddle lies flat. His boot is lost, devoured.

Richard helps Eli pull off his sock and roll his pant leg up to avoid the wet. He takes off his backpack and straps it frontwards over his chest. He lifts the boy up onto his back. Eli remembers when he was little and Richard would piggy-back him across town. Richard used to be so big. But Eli feels his limbs are longer now. His legs dangle awkwardly at Richard's hips. He wonders if he will ever be as big as Richard.

Richard walks and Eli closes his eyes. He dreams of the great, brown wave. He wants to reach his hands toward it, run it through his fingers, slipping warm past his hands. He wants to know how the brownwater feels.

He wakes up. It's raining again. His other boot is gone, slipped off and lost somewhere along the road.

They stop to rest and Eli gets down from Richard's back. He balances on his bare foot, holding onto Richard for support. He pulls off his other sock, puts it in his pocket and settles his foot into the mud.

Richard and the boy squat under a tree. They are on the edge of the dead woods. Nothing grows there, Richard told Eli once. It's all old growth, cracking and falling over. Spiked branches reach high over their heads, doing little to shelter them from the rain.

Richard bends down and laces his hands together, stitching his fingers up in a tight cup. He dips his hands into the blackwater and scoops it up. The puddle ripples softly. He lifts his hands to his mouth and then the boy's. It tastes like rotting wood.

Eli is tired, his feet are cold. The grey glow is low in the west. Richard stands and looks into the woods. It is dark, a tangle of sticks and trunks.

We should find a place for tonight, he says.

Eli stands. His feet are numb beneath him. He stamps them, trying to work feeling back into his toes.

We gotta try, Richard says. He leads Eli off the road into the trees.

They move under branches. Every dead tree has been bent by wind and water. Eli struggles to keep up with Richard. His back keeps disappearing behind black tree trunks, rocks slick blue with moss. Eli trips on roots, wet fingers coming out of the ground, reaching for him. He scrambles away.

They pick their way through the trees until they come across a clearing. There is a rusted car frame and a trail leading off farther into the woods. A small building, just a hut, sits down the trail. They can see it through the sparse trees.

Richard crosses the clearing to the car. He searches the inside, checking under the rotting seats. He opens the trunk and waves Eli over.

Here, he says.

Eli joins Richard and looks into the car. There are a couple of zip packets. Beans and beets.

Richard looks up at the hut, then back at Eli.

Stay and guard the food, he says. I'm going to look quick.

Eli is scared. He reaches for his brother. But Richard squats down and puts his hands on the boy's shoulders.

Eli, Richard says, we need more food. You see? I'll be right back.

Eli stares at Richard, he tries not to cry.

Wait here, Richard says. He gets up and walks down the path toward the hut. Eli is alone in the clearing. He thinks of the wave. He wonders if it came this far. Wonders if this place was drowned out in brownwater like the ground houses. Eli scrambles onto the hood of the car, his muddy feet sliding on the metal. He wants to get a better view through the trees but Richard has gone inside, into the dark.

Eli shivers and pulls his slip jacket tighter around him. He is alone. It is quiet, like it was in the ground houses. He thinks of the man in the doorway. He doesn't want to be alone.

There is a great silence, stretching long, upwards into the sky over the clearing. There are no sounds of children or cars or grown-ups. No steam-wail of a factory smokestack or roar as the river surges around the great bend by the slumtop. Eli watches the trees.

There is a movement. Richard is walking back down the path, carrying something small in his hands. He crosses the clearing and smiles at the boy. He sets a pair of shoes down on the hood of the car. They are grey rubber.

You can wear these, Richard says. And there's food over there. We'll stay for tonight.

Eli puts the shoes on. They are too big. He jumps off the hood of the car onto the ground and looks down at his feet, the hollow shoe-space around his ankles. His feet will move around in them, but they will be fine. Maybe he will grow into them.

Richard starts walking toward the path. He turns to Eli and calls out to him.

The boy takes a step in his new shoes and follows his brother across the clearing.

RUPTURES

Jamie Mason

for Syd Ward

This is how we live now. The sector of the city that's still cohesive is under martial law; the event horizon where the pavement disintegrates and drops into oblivion is heavily guarded. You can get within a mile or two of the misty, yawning canyon of the Abyss but the army has cordoned off the rest. They're enforcing a strict curfew on everyone except us.

Because there aren't enough police and soldiers to guard all the ruptures that are appearing these days they're using rent-a-cops like me. I have a new partner named David, a high-school graduate whose primary relationship seems to be with his cell phone. He's so entranced by its screen that he barely notices anything else – our uniform dress code, shift start times or when the aperture we're guarding opens and closes. He's grown up with ruptures so he's not the least bit scared of them.

Have you put a note in the duty log? I ask.

David ignores me, focusing on his keypad as he taps out a text message. He hits the SEND button, then sits blinking at the screen for a full half-minute to underscore my triviality.

You're not the boss o' me, he grumbles. He takes up the binder on the ground beside his camp chair, opens it and scribbles a notation anyway. I stifle a smile and cross the deserted street to the barricades.

The rupture pulses and mutters as if breathing. It's larger than it was when we started our shift – almost as big as the one that swallowed city hall last week – a huge, yawning electrostatically charged mouth mumbling its hymns to the Abyss. Magnetic spray arcs the maw of the quantum destabilization as it emits a low, disturbing hum. A police cordon extends for two blocks in every direction and all the buildings have been evacuated.

I check my watch. Lunchtime. Whistling quietly, I step back toward our guard post. There have been only a dozen or so fatalities attributed to this rupture. No big deal, considering. With any luck, it should close before that number climbs too high. That's part of what I'm getting paid to ensure. Because this is how we live now.

◀ ▶

Know how we learned that time has buoyancy? McLaughlin sucked his cigarette to ash, then butted the remains in the dashboard ashtray. Monkeys. Back when we had control over the ruptures we usedta send monkeys through. But they'd only be there for a short while because time is an ocean and living organisms are ping-pong balls that can submerge only so deep for so long before they pop back out. That's buoyancy.

I checked my cell phone – a nervous habit I had whenever we were on ops. No new texts.

Then one day they opened a rupture to AD 1215 and sent a monkey through. Little rascal came back holding a banana.

Now where the fuck do you get a banana in 1215? Beats me. But if anyone could find out, it'd be a monkey. And he sure did!

I knew the story. But listening to McLaughlin tell it was part of the pleasure. Older than me and a font of wisdom, Mac taught me most of what I knew about rupture chasing.

Notification came 10 minutes later. The rupture was due to materialize 15 miles southwest of our current position. We moved out. I drove while Mac kept an eye on the Chronoflux Quotient. It's climbing, he muttered. I steered down a dirt road, squinting ahead through the darkness. Apparently, ground zero for our rupture was the middle of a farmer's fallow hayfield. So we parked by a fence and walked.

Can you believe the new evidence handling instructions? Mac lit a fresh cigarette off the stub of his old one. Christ on a cracker! We have to record our recoveries on four separate documents now. Un-fucking-believable.

It's a redundancy measure. (I disguised my weariness at having to explain – yet again – the newer, more streamlined corporate approach to rupture chasing.) They want to be able to cross-check the evidence and make sure we're not boosting any before it gets logged for storage.

Where the hell do they put it all? Mac's peeved tone persisted through the abrupt subject change. There must be... fuck. Millions of items! Hey. He tapped his wrist display. It's coming on, amigo.

We lingered by the edge of the field as the singularity rippled into existence. Two thieves emerged – both young, one a Native kid wearing a black windbreaker, the other in a ball cap and white sneakers. I went after the Native kid but she beat me to the fence. I fumed, watching her disappear into the trees before turning and hiking back to help Mac take charge of Ball-cap.

Looks like silverware. Mac shook a pillowcase, producing a metallic rattle. Pure stuff and good for smelting down.

Nice catch. I smiled. Why don't you take that back to the car and log it? I'll finish up here.

Mac hesitated for a moment, trying to catch my eye as I patted down the suspect. Mac needed to ask why I wanted to stay behind. But I pretended to be preoccupied long enough that he eventually gave up and marched to the car. I heard him pop the trunk. Then his silhouette appeared in a shaft of light from our laptop.

Ball-cap was terrified. I rifled his pockets and came up with a pack of Mokri cigarettes, the swastika tax label visible. What's this? I demanded. I fished an SS notebook and a fist-ful of medals, including an Iron Cross with oak leaves and swords from his other pocket.

I'll keep these, I muttered, stowing the lot. A little some-thing for the souvenir hunters. And not a word to the old man down there or I'll sneak into cells and kill you. I twisted his arm and added: I can make it look like an accident.

◀ ▶

Hey.

I poke David. On the brink of voicing a complaint, he stops short and looks up from his cell phone at the rupture.

It's growing.

◀ ▶

I tried to be clean. I really did. But like they say: things change.

Mac had nothing to do with corrupting me, but he brought me along until I was one of the most competent chasers in our district. Pretty soon I was up for senior investigator, but they passed me over for promotion. Our new boss – a pencil pusher who was intimidated by competence – handed the job to his pet bitch, a crotch-snuffling suck-ass he hired a year before who jumped at the boss's every little whim. Me? I had 15 years in. For a while I was angry enough to kill. Then I chilled out.

Loyalty? I figured that went both ways. So I intercepted the next sealed skid of evidence I saw, tore the shrink wrap, grabbed an item that had already been cataloged and would never see the light of day again, and stuffed it into my back-pack. And continued, every chance I got.

Disposing of stolen evidence was even simpler than boosting it. Items recovered from ruptures sold for top dollar – and fast. An original Van Gogh, for instance – a previously un-known work, and so new I could smell the paint drying as I photographed it – was the sort of thing I could retire on. I received 100 bids within a minute of posting it online.

Loyalty? Fuck that. I used to believe in loyalty. Until I started believing in every man for himself.

◀ ▶

Between us, Mac and I made 85 arrests that last year we chased together – a record for the district.

Time was, he said as we drove back to HQ after the silver-ware bust, they used to send us in there after them. He

paused to listen to the radio bulletin about the U.S. president's visit to Toronto.

Imagine working security for that zoo? I asked.

No fucking way. Mac shivered. I'd rather be ducking back
into ruptures. You know the higher-ups stopped us when they
figured we might do something stupid in there? Not that they
give a shit about our health and safety! No, they were worried
we were dumb enough to go back in time and screw up history.

The shit-rats haven't managed to change history yet, I
pointed out.

They're never there long enough! Mac tapped my shoulder for emphasis. Besides, they're too lame-brained.

I pondered this for a minute. You'd have to, like, step
through a rupture right up next to Hitler – with a gun already
pointed at his head! – to make that kind of difference. And
what are the chances of that?

Even 15 seconds wouldn't be long enough. Mac cracked
a window to stream out smoke as he referenced the longest
rupture on record. Buoyancy is time's self-defence mecha-
nism. Whenever there's a breach between one point and
another, buoyancy attacks the intruder and drives him out,
like antibodies fighting a virus. If time is the immune system,
then ruptures are like wounds on the skin.

Lesions in time! I intoned. Thus creating a form of theft
unique in the annals of crime.

Fuck anuses. Mac rubbed his face. I'm tired and need a
fucking drink.

◀ ▶

David drowses beside me as I examine the pulsing rupture, now grown to the size of a locomotive.

Back when Mac and I worked together, the government was struggling to contain what it had unleashed. Stolen item recovery was deemed essential to halt the spread of the "cross-dimensional contamination" (their term). Sure, crippling the black marketeers was part of it, but the powers that be actually thought stopping the spread of items leaking in from the past might help them control the rupture problem.

It didn't.

As I sit here now in this camp chair, my shadow thrown onto the cold cement by a nearby streetlamp, I watch the semi-sentient thing groan and rotate and flex in the night air of the deserted street. Thinking back, I reflect on how naïve we were, how little we understood.

Three a.m. I take up the duty log and make a note.

Mac's been dead two years now.

◄ ►

There was always a ton of paperwork after a chase: statements for local police and RCMP, Canadian and UN military affidavits, reports to Crown Counsel, plus XyTech's own online report. I spent four hours processing Ball-cap and left the office at 2 a.m. with four hours overtime. Mac was long gone. I signed out at the reception desk, then pulled up the cover on my hoodie against the rain. As I crossed the street, a stretch limo appeared and blocked me at the edge of the parking lot.

The door opened and the Native girl in the dark windbreaker I'd chased earlier that night stepped out and waved a pistol: get in.

I hesitated briefly before clambering in beside the fattest man I've ever seen wedged inside an automobile. Bloated from the mahogany scalp of his shaved head to the toes of his high black patent leather shoes, he gripped an oily cigar between the fleshy first fingers of his left hand. When he gestured for me to sit with his right, I noted the clutch of gold rings almost lost between rolls of brown flab encasing his knuckles.

Take a seat, he croaked. His accent was rural black from the Deep South. Jessie will ride in front with the driver, who doesn't mind the company. My name's Janus. You will help me with a project. The compensation for this will be substantial for you. The penalty for refusing will be massive. Think about it.

Janus hit a button on his BlackBerry. The limo glided forward and the fat man resumed delivery of his rap in a rapid, asthmatic wheeze.

You predict them. We predict them too. The ruptures. And like you, we can tell where and when they lead to. But our equipment is more sophisticated. Surprised? Don't be. Corporations in the States have been doing R&D for years, financed by powerful criminal organizations like the one I represent.

Which is—?

None of your concern. Tomorrow at 1946 hours Pacific Standard a rupture in time will open at the corner of Canada Avenue and Second Street in Duncan. You will go through and deliver a package, then you will reemerge. For this task we will pay you $25,000 Canadian. No questions asked. Do we have a deal?

Sure.

Janus hit his BlackBerry again. The limo abruptly stopped and the girl called Jessie held open the rear door for me.

We will be in touch with the package and half the money. The rest is yours on completion. Tell anybody about this and you die. Understand?

Yeah.

Good night, then.

◀ ▶

Ya know the first ruptures were silent? Mac pushed a fresh cigarette into the side of his mouth. And they were smaller, too. This was back when the military first started generating 'em. The ones nowadays are bigger – much bigger. And they make that weird low humming sound. First ones didn't do that. They just looked like... You know how paper looks when you tear it? It looked like that. Just little rips in the air right in front of you that would glow for a minute or two before they'd close up. Well!

His lighter clinked.

They're much bigger now. Hey. I wonder if that's why they built the Destabilizer out west, hey? Because there's lots of room out here in B.C. and they figured the ruptures might get bigger.

My cell phone wheeped. Notification: 25 minutes to the rupture in Duncan. We were parked in a lay-by in Cobble Hill. I drew a deep breath and released it as quietly as I could. Nerves: time to put the plan into action. I slid the car into gear and pulled onto the highway.

So Mac... you said you used to go inside the ruptures...

Yeah. Why?

What, ah, what was it like?

I felt his attention settle on me as I navigated the curve by what was once the golf course. A series of wildcat rupture openings closed it a few years before, back when the phenomenon was new and people assumed they were natural. This was before we had the statistics and the technology to predict them – long before the military 'fessed up.

Why? Mac's repeated question dropped heavily into the silence.

Just curious. I shrugged. Janus's package – a small black box the size of a candy bar – weighted down my jacket pocket. We coasted downhill past the turn-off to Maple Bay and made for the bridge. I kept my cool. It wasn't until we'd crossed the river and begun hunting for downtown parking that Mac spoke.

I remember feeling this weird tingle. He frowned. You pass into the rupture and everything darkens, like it's suddenly twilight. And I figured that's because the past happened before the sun rose the day of the rupture. Like the night is smoke – he held up his cigarette and cracked the window – streaming backward to touch the past. The noises are softer – everything inside a rupture is always less intense, like when the volume or contrast knobs are turned down on the TV. You're brighter and louder and more conspicuous than anything else there. You clearly see and feel everything that's going on until it starts to darken and fade, then there's a rushing in your ears and you pop back out into the present. But a piece of you is gone.

Like how? I turned into the public lot by the train station.

It's – hmm. Hard to say, really. It's like… Here's what it's like! Mac sat forward and tapped my knee. The president, the guy visiting Toronto right now? Remember when he got elected? His hair was blond. Seen it lately?

It's all grey. I stepped out and locked the car. It's always like that. Yank presidents always leave office with a head full of grey hair.

That's because they leave part of themselves behind. When they clock out from their shift in the Oval Office, a piece of them is gone. It's like that with ruptures.

I considered this. Per SOPs for a rupture in an urban area, the cops had evacuated and cordoned off a two-block radius. The constable manning the barriers at the corner of Canada Avenue and Second Street snorted at our IDs.

Rent-a-cops, he muttered. Government should be handling this!

You mean, like, obtaining approval from nine different subcommittees before approaching a rupture? I smirked. Sounds like a winner!

We were halfway up the block before the cop hurled a response at our backs. His words melted into the murmuring throb of the aperture pulsing in the middle of the intersection.

You know what I always think of when I see one of those things? Mac paused, hands in his pockets, head tilted to examine the anomaly.

I cringed because I knew the answer.

It looks like a woman's—

SHIT!

What?

I pointed: It's that kid from last night!

WHERE? Mac whirled, searching.

The Native kid who got away! She just ducked around the edge of that building!

I'll go! Mac moved double time in the direction I pointed. And the moment he turned the corner, I entered the rupture.

◄ ►

The destabilization's hum swarmed me, flooding my ears, my anus and heart, causing every inch of me to swell and fall into harmony with and vibrate in time with the tonal song. Meanwhile, I watched my leg extend an impossible distance into the void. I remember feeling as if I'd suddenly been turned to clay, squeezed, stretched and elongated. I couldn't breathe for an uncomfortably long moment, and there was this weird tingling in my scalp. The rushing in my ears rose like an ocean, only subsiding as my Play-Doh foot and ankle touched down to harden into a base against which my body could Doppler-shift back to its accustomed dimensions.

I blinked. I was in a big city, one with a familiar skyline, but was having one of those moments when you see something you recognize but can't name it. The sort of thing that happens frequently when you smoke dope or grow middle-aged. Your eyes dim, too, but the dim light here wasn't from bad eyesight. It was a slightly darker world.

Because it happened before the sun rose the day of the *rupture*...

I looked around. I was supposed to meet someone Janus promised I would recognize, but so far I was alone. This was the sort of street you'd expect to encounter a fair amount of traffic on at twilight – the rush-hour crowd heading home – but it was completely still. Until another rupture opened right in front of me.

I froze. If I turned my head and looked over my shoulder I could still see the one I'd stepped through pulsing its weird purplish orgasms of electrostatic light. Yet here was another one ripping its way into fiery existence in this previous moment in time. From...

An earlier time from mine? Or a later one?

I fought a wave of dizziness as the rupture stabilized into a shimmering corona. A shape appeared – a female moving, silhouetted in the flames. Then Jessie emerged, stepping down from the aperture into this When.

I blinked.

Hey, cuz. She grinned crookedly. Got a present for me?

I produced the small, black-wrapped, heavy package containing something obviously very important, and handed it over. Jessie slid it into her hoodie pocket with a smirk.

Be seeing you, cuz, she said, and stepped back into her rupture. A moment later it sealed up and disappeared. I stood staring for a full minute, wondering: how far into the future – or the past – did it lead? And what would have happened if I went in after her? When my brief visit in Jessie's reality was up, would I be pulled through two ruptures back to my own time, or only as far back as this When? Had someone figured out how to time travel by stepping through one rupture after another?

A sucking sensation gripped the back of my head. Again I was yanked and stretched – this time, backward. I re-coalesced in my own time, lying flat on my back in a street crowded with flashing sirens and thronged by emergency response personnel. Mac knelt over me, shaking my shoulder.

Hey, are you okay? I knew you were gonna try and enter one! Listen, did the blast affect you? They've set off another one of those rupture bombs. Same kind that killed the president. Buddy, you gotta get up. We got work to do!

◀ ▶

There were now too many ruptures for us to chase theft from every one. So XyTech handed me and Mac uniforms and told us to start guarding LTAs – long-term anomalies: ruptures that appeared and remained in place for hours or even days on end. It was boring work – rent-a-cop stuff. But we both had bills to pay.

When you were on shift you were expected to remain sober enough to answer call-outs to ruptures that appeared in your area. I'd get a call and saddle up with camp chairs and a cooler of food and drinks and meet Mac at a shopping mall or empty field or in the living room of someone's evacuated home – wherever the rupture materialized. We'd remain on-station, making notes in the duty log on the anomaly's behavior until relief arrived. Mostly, we just sat staring at them.

You might expect that with all these holes in time opening up that the past would start leaking into the present but it never did. Nor did we start leaking into the past. Instead, the LTAs just grew and linked up with one another. The throbbing sound deepened, and the purplish light brightened to an obscene corona around the largest apertures, now resembling suns in eclipse – great winking holes of negative light that swallowed vast sectors of our When – cars, streets, buildings – leaving behind not the past but… nothing.

The broken teeth of cement boulevards, the snapped wires of telephone wires and the skeletal steel girders of half-demolished buildings dangled out over the fog-ridden Abyss, straddling the event horizon at which everything just… stopped.

◀ ▶

I killed Janus the next time I saw him. But by then it was too late – the damage was already done. And besides, Jessie just took over and began handing out orders. Because she paid better than Janus ever did, I did two more rupture runs, returning each time to a darker and slightly more smoke-streaked, night-ridden version of the world. Whatever they were doing in the past was having profound effects on the present.

I encountered Janus once. He had apparently entered a rupture during his lifetime that let out into the same past which I, coincidentally, happened to be visiting. Although dead in my When, Janus remained stubbornly alive in our common yesterday.

What are you doing? I demanded when I saw him lumber through the aperture.

Earning a living, he wheezed. Prime minister says the ruptures represent Canada's next great economic opportunity and I'm gettin' my piece of the action!

How? I demanded. But I already knew. Janus had developed the means to harness the ruptures' massive energy for warfare, using me to transport the separate pieces of technology to his couriers for assembly at some predetermined point in the past. The next great opportunity for Canada, it seemed, involved blowing holes in reality large enough to swallow entire provinces. An environmental disaster to dwarf the Alberta tar sands – anything in service of the almighty dollar!

◄ ►

I never saw Janus again. After my last trip, I'd accrued enough savings to remain comfortable for the rest of my life. But guilt, and a weird desire to confess, tormented me.

The science fiction shows have time travel all wrong, I said. My voice, though hushed, carried easily through the deserted marble lobby of the Royal B.C. Museum where Mac and I sat watching a rupture mutter and twirl in the air by the elevators at 2 a.m.

Those shows don't convey how confusing it is! Because they take place in linear time – start at point A, end at point B. But inside the ruptures it's impossible to even think that way! The concepts of point A and point B become totally meaningless. It's like…

I searched for an analogy. And gave up when the one that came to mind – being blindfolded and spun around, then having the blindfold torn off – fell short. Mac seemed to relate to my boggled silence.

You're telling me! He fiddled with his new smartphone. At age 67, he was just entering the mobile age. Yeah, buoyancy makes sure we don't change the past. But just going there and coming back is mind-fuck enough.

Things – I mean, we're just not… It's something we're not meant to see! It's unnatural. And it's like your brain recognizes that and—

Look. Mac held up a hand and smiled. It's like going to war. Nobody understands what you experienced unless they were there, too. Seeing bodies blown apart? Seeing the insides of people? We were never meant to see that! The mind rebels.

I considered that my rupture trips were perhaps taking a toll on me. My bank account was fatter, true, but I was having trouble sleeping. And I'd lost weight because I could barely keep anything down. Not because I was sick – it was all mental. Now I knew why.

The whole experience of it! I collapsed in my camp chair. Jesus, Mac, it eats at you…

He nodded, fine-tuning the settings on his device – preoccupied, but still listening. Not like there are any support groups for this sort of thing yet, he muttered.

And then when you've stepped through and another rupture opens right in front of you, I said, and before I could stop myself, added: Or seeing someone you know who's dead. That—

I stopped short. What had I—? Paranoia flooded in.

Before I even finished piecing it together I craned my neck and looked away to avoid Mac's stare. Because I knew I had said too much. Mac knew I had stepped through more than just that one rupture, which meant I was probably on the take. Dirty. The trust between us, cultivated over years of working together, was now broken forever.

◀ ▶

Vancouver and Salt Spring are gone. Such a fucking drag. I was gonna visit this summer…

David mutters this news in the same nasal monotone he uses to complain about his girlfriend, his hourly wage, his personal disappointments, his godforsaken lot in life. An entire province gobbled up by the void and David contextualizes it in terms of the personal inconvenience to him.

The rupture we guard, now twice the height of the train station, fluctuates ominously, spitting purple fire in the pre-dawn gloom. I am mesmerized. How much of the world do you think has been swallowed? I whisper, gazing into its static depths.

It turns out that smartphones have an app for that. David calls up his and turns the screen to me. I see a narrow strip of the West Coast, including a chunk of Washington state and Vancouver Island, hovering between two bulbous intrusions of shadow. Encroaching fronts of—

Nothing.

Eventually we'll get gulped down, too. David shrugs. In another – he checks the display – 22 hours and seven minutes.

Doesn't that bother you?

Well, I— Hey, shut up, my girlfriend's texting.

I sigh and make a note in the logbook. David texts his girl-friend while I tidy up details in a report that will never be read – each of us reacting to the apocalypse according to our indi-vidual generation's signature dysfunction.

David stands and wanders off down a side street. A few moments later I hear the shrieking dub-step dong that is his ringtone and know he will be gone for the better part of an hour, chitty-chatting with his girl. I replace the logbook and stare into the restless vortex of our impending doom.

Inside the ruptures the concepts of point A and point B become totally meaningless…

Beginnings. Endings. Life. Death…

We were never meant to see that.

I wonder: if the ruptures lead into the past, and they swallow the whole world, why doesn't everyone just go into the past? Or is there not enough room back there? Or—?

The mind rebels.

I ponder the yawning Abyss menacing the western edge of Duncan. Now another one is pushing toward us across the strait from the mainland. A small strip on the inner coast of Vancouver Island is all that remains. The question is: whether it's better to join the yawning chasm or take one's chances?

I count to 10. Make a decision. Then sprint through the opening.

◄ ►

I've been expecting you.

Mac pushes a fresh cigarette into the side of his mouth. It's him all right, but a younger version – one from before we met. Mac, able to suspend aging and remain young forever by adroit navigation of sequenced ruptures.

We're not supposed to meet for another 30 years. Mac's lighter clinks. He takes a meditative drag. But I guess sometime after we do, you begin going in and out of ruptures, running errands for organized crime. The results are...

I know. The ruptures get worse. I wave a hand. And for some reason, they begin swallowing up everything. What I don't get is why instead of going into the past, everything just vanishes.

Ever heard of string theory? Mac asks.

I shake my head.

It's the idea that whenever reality comes to a fork in the road – choice A or B – the road splits and two different realities emerge, one where choice A was made and the other where choice B was made. Both realities coexist, travelling parallel but separate paths into the future. These strings are never supposed to meet. And never *did*. Until the military began experimenting with the Destabilizer.

The ruptures—?

Imagine reality as a series of threads aligned in a woven carpet. Mac holds up his hand, the fingers parallel to give a visual. Keep each straight and taut and the threads work together to create a durable weave. Our ruptures caused the threads to tangle and snarl, fraying the carpet. And the rupture bombs only made it worse. He waggled his fingers then clenched a fist. If that carpet represents the sum of all possible realities in the quantum multi-verse, then it's become threadbare and is falling apart.

Jesus, I whisper.

Now there's a traffic jam of different realities. Whenever one possible future collides with another, the result is destruction of both potential worlds. The Abyss is a garbage dump of extinguished reality strings.

I close my eyes.

What can we—?

Do? Nothing.

I actually laugh. After all our achievements in technology, culture and civilization?

Nothing. Mac flaps a hand. Erased as if they didn't exist.

But that's—

I pause, groping for words.

Insulting, I manage finally.

Mac laughs.

No, really! I am shaking with rage. Is this how we live now? After everything the human race has achieved! It just... *ends?* No bang, no whimper? Just a grand reminder of our

monumental insignificance! The whole of... *HISTORY!*
Juggernauting over a cliff? Into *nothing?* That's insane! Like
an author abandoning a story before finishing the final

RIVER ROAD

Amanda M. Taylor

My sister Jill tapped her handmade machete on the gunwale, a steady pattern of tat-tat-tat ratta-tat as she stared vacantly at the branches that passed. The waters of the Red River slapped the aluminium hull of our freight canoe as I scanned the trees through my binoculars in the predawn haze. Ice clung to the bare boughs of the elms and oaks, their trunks submerged in lapping, murky floodwaters.

"Stop it," I whispered, and the machete skirted into the leather sheath on her thigh.

The abandoned suburb came into view as we crested the break in the old dyke, and I darted the binoculars again: the cab of a rusted truck barely broke the lapping muddy waters; broken windows, shattered inward; houses and garages half-obliterated and charred by memories of what tore them down; overgrown lilacs with heavy buds, waiting for the waters to recede. There was only silence, which let my mind rouse their smell – it was only a month away, blooming in that holiday time before the mosquitos came.

"See anything, Kimiko?" Sandip asked me from where he sat in the stern, paddle a rudder in the weak current. He was ashen bark, skin not yet warmed by summer's kiss, but marked by acne. The neck of his crocheted sweater was rolled up high, turtleneck snug beneath his chin.

I shook my head and tucked a strand of my black hair back over my ear. It was too dark to tell what might be waiting for us – it had been too dark all night, but luck was on our side. It was the safe time of year to scavenge. Well, the only time we could.

The canoe turned under his direction and I hunkered down on the seat in the bow. Each silent breath brought a lasting fog, taken sluggishly by a passing breeze that tinkled the ice in the boughs.

"It's too cold," Sandip whispered.

"It's better this way," I said, and offered a reassuring smile. "They don't like the cold. They don't like the water either, that's why we're here."

"You'll do fine," Jill said, and gave his knee a squeeze. "I came last year and it was easy. Except for when I fell in, so don't do that."

"Right," he said, eyes darting to the trees he guided us through for cover. "In and out, right?"

"In and out. This is the easy part. Want to come back with us next week too?"

"We'll see," he said, but half-smiled when Jill squeezed his leg again. "It's a change of pace, that's for sure."

"That's why I like it," I said, and stood up again, binoculars forward as we closed in on the warehouse. The large building was half-submerged, like all the rest, blackened by mould, time, and aged violence. The side we approached had not been spared, with rusted, bent girders crumpled inward and a gaping hole of concrete blocks spilled into the waters, disappearing below the surface. There was a small knit scarf in a familiar pattern. "There, you see the marker?"

"Oh – yeah." The canoe angled toward the hole in the building.

My binoculars swept again, double-taking back to movement in the water. "Hold!"

Sandip and Jill shrunk down as I stood up, bringing the binoculars into focus on the bloated corpse in the water.

A pent breath escaped. "Just a horse. Don't worry – it's just a horse."

"What a waste," Sandip said, as he nibbled at the dried skin on his bottom lip. "They're hard to come by."

The canoe scraped into the submerged cinderblock and I stamped into the side to keep myself from pitching into the freezing water. I braced on the gunwale, binoculars swinging from the strap around my neck. "Warn me next time!"

"S-sorry!"

"He didn't mean to," Jill said, and scooted forward in the boat to grab a bent loop of rebar jutting from the broken wall. She hauled us into the shadow of the dilapidated building, the metal hull grating and echoing off the space. We climbed onto the landing where the knit scarf was, and I untied it as Jill checked out the stairs.

"They should be good," I whispered.

"Excuse me for being careful."

As she crept up to the second floor of the warehouse I looked across the mottled darkness. Here and there gaping holes let in the growing morning light, bright pockets that seemed to make the surrounding areas darker still. The sounds of water lapping echoed across it, but disappeared under the creak of the metal handrail of the half-intact stairwell.

"Okay, I think," she whispered.

I snagged my bow from the belly of the canoe and motioned for Sandip to go up. The hatchet in his hand trembled. We met Jill on the second floor, when there was a shrill sound and they dropped to the ground. Overhead, the beat of dark wings fluttered and scooted past, shadows fleeing toward the light.

"Jesus!" Jill hissed when Sandip grabbed her. "It's fine – it's fine, just bats, okay? They'll be gone now."

"Sorry... I'm fine, really," he whispered.

I edged past them, the echoes of the bat cries still clinging in the far corners. I searched the space, lit from a wide roof cave-in that had crushed most of the shelves into the floor below. "Come on. In and out, find anything useful – metal, plastic. No rot, okay? And watch your steps – I don't need to be fishing you out of the water downstairs. And I don't want to see you coming back for the lantern."

"How often is someone glad to see a hole in the roof, right?" Jill said and grinned at Sandip. She snagged his arm and pointed at a path that looked secure.

We branched off, and each slow step became a chorus of echoes, as heels tap-tap-tapped to test the aged flooring. The closer I got to the west wall, the stronger the wet wood-rot smell grew. Beneath it rose the clay-mud soak from the river, dripping staccatos that offset our heeled beats. Gyproc and particleboard crunched underfoot, laminate flooring showing grime and blackened mould.

I found a cache of saw blades, rarities that I stacked in my pack with care, and smaller bits like screws, sandpaper, and drill bits. They all went into the bag, and the same shuffle and scramble from Jill imitates those I'm making. Discarded, hardened glue, and rotten, cheap MDF – sorting the grain from the chaff. My mouth is in my shirt to evade the choking smell of mould by the time I find a box of bar clamps and a pipe-fitting wrench. No pipe. I wanted to bring it back to the farm, but maybe the toilet has seen its last. The crumple of flooring down into the water below redirects me back over my steps for safety. I can't make out what Jill and Sandip are saying, but she's laughing and the sound carries.

Back on the stair landing, I hushed them and scanned for movement in the dim light as my bag clanks into the belly of the canoe.

"Not much left," Jill whispered.

"We need everything we can carry from here. I want the scouts to find somewhere new before the water goes down." I scanned the brightening morning outside, lapping cold waters hugging the submerged trees. The clouds are evaporating overhead, burning off in the sun. The quiet glup of the riverwater is almost comforting. From our vantage I can see the sentry watchtowers deep in the city. Alien architecture, with jagged, rotating edifices lit with bright beacons that can even be seen from the farm. There are memories of them coupled with my childhood, shadows and sounds that cohere into feelings and a sucking pain in my heart.

Sandip and Jill chattered nearby, and I clambered up the stairs to find them.

"Fuck," Jill whispered, and she motions to me from across the floor beams. "Kimiko! You better see this!"

The beams and remnant floorboards creaked underfoot as I hurried toward them, and the pain in my chest warped into anxiety as I saw the body of the tracker lying between them. Its body looked stiff with rigor, skin glistening with slime and dead-pale. Its hulking girth and broad shoulders were slumped, untouched by decay. They never decayed, and my memories drew on the fall, those vice jaws on my grandfather's leg as he screamed for us to go, just go, and get out. Mom wouldn't let go of my arm – it bruised that night. The snarls followed the screams and muffled weeping into my own hands, hyperventilating to try and stop.

"I've never seen one up close before," Sandip said.

"It was dead, we didn't kill it – we're okay."

Jill was swaddled against mom's chest, screaming. She wouldn't remember. She never remembered.

"Kimi, hey – hey, are you okay?" Jill asked, as she took my shoulders and gave me a quick hug. She laughed a bit. "I'm fine, don't give me that look. It's already dead."

"Let's just get out of here. The sun's coming up."

"You got it," Jill said, and hoisted both her and Sandip's bag up over her shoulders, clanking the metal within.

"Damned beasts," Sandip said, and hoisted the spade he had in hand.

A half-cry escaped my lips as he brought the shovel down and severed the tracker's head, crushing its skull with a squelch and spew of black blood.

"What the hell did you do that for!" I started counting in my head.

"Shit!" Jill had his arm and dragged him back toward the stairs. "Shit!"

"They destroyed everything, I just needed... I just needed to do something back!" He almost tripped over an exposed I-beam, and jerked out of Jill's grasp. "What's the problem?"

I grabbed his shoulder and pushed him ahead of me, glancing back at the crushed skull of the tracker with a double take. Twenty seconds. Better to overestimate. "You just tipped them off to where we are. Were you not listening when Marc gave the lecture this morning? You crushed the implant in its fucking skull, and now we have two minutes to get the fuck out of here before its signal is heard!"

"What?" His face was slack, his feet moving under our efforts now. "But there was a set of pulleys—"

"Forget it," Jill said, her eyes averted from mine and a flush high on her cheeks. "We have to go!"

Forty seconds and we were on the stairs, our bags clanking into the belly of the freight canoe. My hands shook as I pressed oars into their hands. "Get in. I'll take the stern. Just get in, forget the rest!"

A cluster of shiny bits tumbled out of Sandip's bag as he climbed into the swaying boat. I gripped the stairwell, rusted flakes of paint digging into my fingers as I kept us from capsizing. Past a minute. We had to get out in the water.

"Kimi, I'm caught," Jill cried, and she jerked and ripped the long-sleeved jacket. She gasped and stared at the fabric left behind. It had been Mom's.

"I'll patch it, I promise, just get – now!"

The boat teetered as they grabbed their oars and I pushed off, muddy flood waters splashing as I steered us toward the dyke. Sandip muttered under his breath as they got their paddles in the water. The scant current was trying to pull us deeper into the suburb – toward where the main control tower was, downtown where the Golden Boy once stood. Dad didn't believe it, but when the ships arrived, he couldn't ignore it anymore. No one could ignore it. The statue was probably buried in the mud now, like we would be if we were caught in the city limits.

The oars cut deep, and I barked to keep us in time, pushing over the dyke to hide amongst the icy trees, fighting the current of the river all the way. One hundred and 19 seconds. The klaxon from the watchtower in the city rang across the water.

"Kimi?"

"Just keep paddling." I panted as we tried to keep pace. I checked over my shoulder again. Black specks in the sky, flies on the horizon that were gaining pace. The warehouse was out of sight, but our wake cut a clear line through the slow waters between the trees. My eyes darted. "Come on, back to the dyke."

"What?"

"Get your packs on," I said, water rippling behind my oar as the canoe jerked toward a cluster of oaks on the submerged ridge. I slowed us enough as we threw them on. "We've got to flip it, see the trees? We need to hide."

"Are you kidding? The water is barely above freezing!"

"You got us in this mess," I hissed at Sandip. "Don't argue when I'm getting us out of it. Come on!" I leapt over the edge, and almost lost my breath as the spring melt hit me. We'd be lucky if it were above freezing. "Keep a hold on the canoe – come on!"

Jill hesitated only a moment as our eyes met before she joined me in the chest-high water. Sandip just stood there, his eyes to the north.

"They might not kill us if they find us, we don't have any tech," Jill said, smiling despite the obvious chatter in her teeth as she tread. "Right?"

Sandip scrambled with his pack, and a circular saw emerged.

The fire in my belly bucked against the cold. "Throw it in the water, and then yourself. Get rid of that right now, if you value our lives!"

"We need it – my father, for the barn," he said, looking at the power tool.

"Don't be stupid! We don't have the power and we never will, now throw it in the water before I drown you with it! I won't be caught by the ludds with tech on hand!"

He twitched and dumped it over the edge, shouldering his bag again and stumbling into the water, tipping the canoe in the process. I could hear the buzz of the engines now, but grappled the canoe rather than satisfy my morbid curiosity. I didn't need to know how long until they were overhead, I had to breath, I had to get us in the trees, and I had to make sure Jill made it home safe. Mom's voice was in my head.

It was difficult to see beneath the canoe, our panicked breath and the slosh of water magnified against the aluminium hull. But those sounds were soon drowned out by the buzz and roar of the hovering patrol ships. I gripped the gunwale just beneath the surface, and held our cover in place. Their hands soon slapped to find purchase.

"Kimi, the water," Jill gasped, and I hushed her.

"I'm sorry," Sandip whispered, treading between us.

The hull of the canoe reverberated and magnified the sound of the engines, making it difficult to discern where the ships flew. I saw Jill close her eyes in the roar, my lips in a hard line above the water. Sandip's eyes were through the bottom of the canoe.

"Keep moving," I whispered, but it was drowned by the shuddering sound. Each kick of my legs welcomed the numbing cold up my legs, the water finding each crevice and bit of warmth as we tread.

Another screech followed as the ships buzzed by, moving toward what I could only gauge to be the direction of the warehouse. Marc's voice was a reminder to fight the cold. They'd investigate the tracker. We had time before they investigated further. But only a little. "We need to move. We need out."

"I can't feel my feet," Jill whispered, and spat out a mouthful of water.

"I know. Stay here." I sucked a breath of air and ducked under the water, feeling my way along the gunwale to emerge outside of the canoe. The beacon in the city watchtower swept across the sky, a hum at the base of my skull. It almost overrode the engine whine from the hovering ships, but they were there – to the north. My eyes darted, and I snorted river water. We were safe within the trees, the tinkle of ice in the branches almost serene by comparison. There was an apartment complex at the bottom of the dyke, not 100 metres upstream, beyond a trio of houses whose roofs were the only sign. The water lapped at the second-floor balconies.

Another breath and I was under the freezing water, before gasping for air in the tight space beneath the canoe, the sound made more desperate by our aluminium cover.

"Okay." I could hear Jill's teeth chattering. "I'm going to push us to an apartment nearby. We'll take refuge inside until nightfall."

"We'll follow," Jill said, her voice a cold shell. "Under the canoe."

I nodded and ducked back into the water before I could think. The cold permeated less now – it had already dug into my skin, a numbness that made my muscles loathe to respond. I kicked anyway and grabbed the canoe, pushing it in the current toward the apartments, my hiking boots growing heavier with each push of the frigid current. My satchel dragged too, a wide hand on the small of my back urging me to go under. There was no buzz, the spotlight was gone. This was our only chance. Our oars drifted alongside me, tied to the canoe but eager to escape.

I spat out a mouthful of water as I reached the balcony, and my arms trembled as I knocked on the canoe roof and hauled myself out. It was then the buzz echoed off the water and my head jerked – I couldn't see them anymore, I couldn't know.

"Get out now – they're coming."

"Help," Jill gasped through blue lips. I trembled and almost lost grip, my cold limbs atrophied. But she was up and over the rail, and Sandip found his way too. I tied a quick hitch in the canoe's rope, leaving it capsized but secured. We scrambled through the shattered patio doors and into the apartment, abandoning our bags with a wet "thuck," and kicking dust and dried leaves with each step and drip.

I led us into the second room, a slumped bed atop a metal frame prominent in the room. We ducked into the shadows beneath a high, long window as the buzz grew louder, vibrating through the concrete walls and shaking little puffs of dust into the air. Swallows' nests above the bed were white with mould and silent, the bed a mess of twigs and droppings. A pink plastic crib on the far side of the room had a lattice of cobwebs between the bars, and the far closet was half-open, shapeless shadows hinting at more within.

Jill squatted and wrapped her arms around her head, chattering with cold. She shrugged him off when Sandip tried to touch her, so I put my hand on her knees instead. The patrol went by again, sweeping lights followed by the pings of echo-location.

I was shaking too. Head against the wall to stay upright, I scanned the small room. How long would they stay? How diligent would their search be? The buzzing ships passed again, and I cringed down, the sound twisting in my gut and contributing to the tremble in my limbs.

"W-what do we do?" Jill whispered into her arms.

"We stay until tomorrow," I said.

"What?" Sandip snapped, and I glared at the volume. He was bluing too.

"I'll f-find blankets. We will. Our clothes n-need to dry. And we n-need them to go away." I got silence in reply, save for the last drips falling from our clothes and leaving a cloying, stuck cold. Time slowed with my blood it seemed, thoughts elusive moths flitting around the light of my mind. The only warmth. They were chattering. No – no, it was me.

They didn't follow when I got up and threw open the closet, sending a puff of air whose chill I regretted almost as much as the dust that swirled and stuck to my jacket. There were loose, faded shirts that crumpled when I moved the hanger, natural fibres disintegrated long ago and waiting for the end. Soft knit sweaters were hidden behind, clung with webs but whole. One grey, it looked handmade, and another with a dinosaur motif on the front. I kept them at arm's length from my soaked frame.

"Get up." It was a barren croak, and I had to lick my lips. "Get changed. Everything wet needs to c-come off."

I left the sweaters with Jill and crept out of the apartment. The drywall in the hallways was cracked and crumpling, black mould stippled in the corners and along the baseboards. There were signs of long-gone habitation: a clutch of rusted, penknife-jagged cans whose labels had faded into illegibility, and the blackened halo of a fire. It scuffed underfoot, blurred charcoal into wet lines that followed my trail to the next apartment. The buzz of the ships shook the building again, and I slunk against the wall to listen as they passed, shivering all the while.

The next apartment was locked, but another still had its doors off the hinges. A laminate countertop had collapsed under its own weight, crushing the waterlogged cabinets underneath. The small kitchen connected to an empty living room, into which the river waters lapped and reached for a dry bedroom. I pulled more clothing from a closet, puffs of decayed and moth-eaten fabric fluffing in the air with my motions.

My breathing was fast, quick, and quiet, the air stolen by the cold – a struggle to take each one back. I couldn't keep my limbs from shaking. Another scan – no blankets. Another apartment was gutted, the remnants of furniture and cabinetry visibly cannibalized, a half-burnt drawer showing their fate. I was at the end of the hall and walking on careful, frozen footsteps before I found a box which hid a pair of synthetic blankets sealed in clear zippered plastic. I took them and hurried back as the roving ships passed again, their lights lost in the growing daylight.

Their clothes were hung up, and Sandip turned with a start, clad in the dinosaur sweater and skin-soaked boxers. Jill was squatting beside the bed, the sweater pulled down to her ankles. I thrust the pants out, and turned to strip as I said, "Everything wet. T-take it off, you need to dry."

Gooseflesh met the cold air, and I closed my eyes, shuddering still as I let it dry. I pulled on a turtleneck as I heard Sandip's steps, and his eyes stayed down as I tugged on a skintight pair of jeans. They stuck on my hips, leaving the small paunch of my gut free. The last sounds of the hover-ships faded, the bleating calls of check and ping echoing through the otherwise silent city.

"All day?" Jill's mouth hid in the sweater.

"Yeah. Come here, we'll stick together." I motioned to Sandip.

He edged closer as I flapped the blankets, cream-coloured felt that caught my hangnails. "I didn't mean any harm."

"I know." I thrust one into his hands and propped up the bed on the end table to create a lee. I hunkered down and Jill snuck into the crook of my arm. "Can't change it now. I'll get us home."

He joined us and I strong-armed him in close as he flapped the second blanket over us.

"Let's stay quiet now. And rest if you can," I whispered, and squeezed one shoulder and then the other as we slumped beneath the musty mattress.

I could hear the slow drip of our clothes where they hung, a poignant pluck loud compared to the lapping river outside. Jill's breathing slowed from shuddered huffs into deeper, slow pulls. My arms were numb, from cold or their weight I don't know. It was warmer beside them, but my feet... Marc's chiding voice was there as he cupped my toes and blew heat against them, snow still on the mat by the door. Hushed whispers as the baby slept in a wood crib by an ember fire. The cattle were fed, their munching shuffles heard through the adjoining wall. Precious warm kisses.

I twitched with a start and opened my eyes, swallowing my fatigue as I strained to pull a tingling arm free. Sandip shifted. Fuck. Stay awake. The light was bright outside, the day blessedly free of any ship or drone or tracker. My eyelids drooped. What good would I be against them, anyway?

I woke again when the light was fading, to a sharp jab in my ribs.

"Good job on watch," Jill whispered. She was sitting up beside me, her legs still beneath the shared blanket.

I squinted at her before I saw that Sandip was still sleeping nearby. I tried to wiggle cold-stiff toes and sat up, sloughing the blanket onto him. "We should move. We can get back by dawn. Get him up, okay?"

"Our jackets and boots are still wet."

"We'll make do. We'll take the blankets." I stiffly rose, hobbled on cold feet.

"Should I search the building?"

"No!" The words snapped, and she looked down as Sandip sat up into the blanket. "No. We'll go home. Just let me go pee."

The canoe was waiting, flipped and ready with our wet packs when I was relieved and dressed. The waters were calm, the skies overcast. Jill was in the bow, wrapped in a blanket, and Sandip had the other in hand for me.

"I haven't seen any movement – or heard anything unusual. Not that I've been awake long," he said, and handed me my binoculars too.

"Sure you don't want this?" I waved the blanket.

"I think you need it," Sandip said, and held the canoe steady. "Here."

"Did she get you with her icy feet too? Just like when we were little…"

I sat midship and wrapped my lower body in the blanket. He hopped in and pushed us off as I took up a paddle with Jill. The river would guide us home – guide us to the safety of the ring dyke community, and the chickens in the farmyard – and Marc's waiting arms.

"Let's see if we can do this right?" Sandip murmured, and directed us out into the current and the waiting night.

LAST MAN STANDING

Frank Westcott

Disaster struck. One man left standing. No woman to speak of. He could *see*. If there was one. How would he procreate? *Could he*. If he could. Find a woman. And he had any juice left.

Food would be scarce. And there was no power to speak of. Candles. One windmill. Tilted. No cows. To speak of. He stammered even if no one was listening.

His mouth felt like a broken slot machine after the fire. No handle to open it. Lips sealed. He stammered anyway, inside his head even if there was no one to listen, if he spoke out loud, *if he could,* and his lips weren't sealed. In the silence. Around him. Gracefully. Or gracelessly. Whatever the case, if he spoke, if his lips magically opened. But he stammered in his thoughts, as if he spoke them and there was someone listening. Able to. But there wasn't. He heard. With the last scream of death from the barn.

They called the barn the dying place. Or the other way around. The dying place was the barn. You get things turned around when you are the second last man standing, or sitting, for that matter. I was the second last man standing. It was the way the cards were written, *dealt,* off the dealer, off the bottom of the deck, *his deck,* after he fell to the floor in the barn, and the cards scattered all over the place. His place. And the air. Around him. Like ice in the water of time that no longer existed. Because this was the future. *We were seeing.* Toronto. After the storm. The last storm. *We would see.* Witness. Or be alive for. There had been many. Predicted. All of the them. Except the last one. It came first. Thing. In. The. Monring. *Morning.*

My fingers slip on the keys now like the last man's speech inside his head. *You see.* I can *see* into the future. This future. His future. Toronto without a bus. Line. Or streetcar named desire, if that's what you wanted. Time had fallen out o the CN tower, re-named something else I can't remember. What. And the periods are slipping all over the place too on this machine. I wonder where the comma went. Oh… there it is … ,… Found one. How many commas on a typewriter, anyway. I can't remember. Memory's not too good after the storm. The second last one. That is why I am the second last man standing. Or sitting. For that matter. I can't remember if I said that already. All ready. All aboard. But I might have. And the conductor called from the train.

"Boarding all. All aboard. If you are boarding. Last man standing. No last man standing. No second man standing."

I am the second man standing. The last man can't see me. He is blind now. Temporarily, until he gets his speech back. Stammers. Now. Like a horse with hiccups. *Neigh-i-neigh* is what he sounds like with every word he thinks, and does not say, but thinks he does because he is stammering inside his head like he would if he could get his words out and his lips weren't sealed.

Time does that. Is like that. After a disaster. Train wreck. Bus wreck. Plane wreck. Any wreck. And this is a disaster.

"Last man standing," the conductor calls again. But the last man doesn't hear. He is listening to himself stammer, and wondering where the stammer came from.

"Must be the train," he mutters inside his head, stammering like always, now. Like now. Always. He'll never speak write or type right again. Disasters are like that. Having trouble with my own words now. Stammering inside my fingers that used to no... *know*... which word I meant and how to spell it direct from my brain. Disasters are like that. Too. The way he speaks. And the way he writes. *I write. Mixed that one up too.*

It's cold in here. I am going to turn up the heat. But I can't find the thermometer thing. I go into the kitchen where the thermostat used to be. But there is nothing there but the train station. Now. The house moved and became a train station that looks like a subway because it is under ground now. But the roof, a roof, came with it. Oddly. But this is the future. Toronto is gone. Buffalo slid over from texas where it went first. And there is no more TV reporting disasters. This is the last one even though I am the second last man standing waiting to the last man standing to stand alone.

He wants to procreate one last time, but doesn't realize there is no procreation to be had. All the test tubes are gone. "Why do they call test tubes test tubes?" I ask him. But he doesn't answer. Can't. His lips are sealed. Frustrated by time and space. Because they no longer exist. Only the future exists. The present is gone. Into the past. And the past never existed. Had to make room for the present going there. Time warp. Life warp. Some kind of warp this is I haven't got a name for yet. And probably won't if the last man standing becomes the last man standing, and I am gone.

That's how it works. You have to wait for it. And not get on the train even if the conductor calls you. All the people on the train are sitting. So there are only two of us standing. I am dis-integrating. Slowly. That's how it works and how they said it would work.

The last man goes into a field looking for a cow to drink from the windmill first. The water. He is thirsty. But doesn't know if the water is poisoned. Like everything else. That's how they do it. Did it. Poison. And the waters tilted with the windmills and exploded taking fingers and time and chicken with it. Fingers. And Tim Horton's. And Kentucky Fried. Even if Texas got here. And Buffalo slid over. Without wings. And remorse. Or hockey. And Buffalo Sabres. They've got a new team in Phoenix, I hear. Heard. Before the last TtV went out. That was supposed to be TV but the room shook with the shaking of the train leaving. The trembling . Of the after life those on the trai n entered. Are entering. Now. In the field of dreams they wish they had played on instead of this one. Build it and they will come. Well, somebody built heave n and that is where they are going. The ground is shaking. Trem-bling. More than ever. Now. And I see the last =man drinking from a cup. Sorry about that = sign. Don't know how it got there. These typewriters they left me are sucky. Half the keys don't work. And the half that do have other symbols on them. Slid over from the shaking. And the melt. In the ice. After the pisen, *poison*, left. And there was oly only the two of us stand-ing. Like that. I'll go dslower. To make less mistakes. The trembling plus having to use two typewriters to get all the let-ters I need is slow enough.

I gotta make this short. Keep it short. Only 800 words left. That's all they gave me. And I am done. Two thousand-ish, they said. So it is done. The last man is looking for that woman for a final procreation, but he doesn't know that the future doesn't know the difference between a man and a woman. The future has no procreation. There are only souls. Wasted. Or not. Used. Or not. Lost or not. Found or not. It doesn't matter. Everything is the future now so we can go on living. The past is gone. The present is the past. And if the present existed we'd all be dead. So we have to go on in the future. Never getting there.

Toronto laughs at us. The last man stammers. Collapses. And becomes the last man kneeling. I think he is praying. Or catholic. Or something. But he is only dying.

\I am disnintegrsting more. And the shaking is getting on me now. To me. The bus left before the train. And I wish I had taken it and not seen my future where I had to be the second last man standning. I walk over to the last man and check to see how many words I have left. I take both typewriters so I can get all the words in without with as few mistakes as possible. It is hard writing this way.

"Get up," I say to the last man standing, who is now kneeling, still, and blabbering about something he heard yesterday, but he doesn't know yesterday is gone and only the present now, and this is the future and he better get up because *he* has to be the last man standing.

I walk to the foyer where texas used to be for awhile and see Floriada inching closer. You'll have to translate. The typoes. One typwerwriter quit and now only one-winging it on one... and the last man stands so I can sit and follow my destiny into the future, which is now.

I have no regrets. Only a tilted windmill and father time complex. I wonder what the futre holds but I am not there yet.

The train rumbles out of the station and I follow it as best I can. With my heart. Because that is all I have left. My heart. It is undone. The last man standing gives up on procreating. His lips are sealed. And he still stammers in his head thinking he is speaking out loud, and he is embarrassed. Just like he used to be before his lips were sealed by the fire. It doesn't matter. He'll be dead soon, too. Death is like that. So are disasters. You are dead before you know it. And if the future wasn't all there was. Is. I couldn't write about it before it got here. But that's what futures are about. Isn't it. Aren't they. They the getting here.

The train follows me out of the station.

I wave good-bye to the last man.

He is looking for a semen cup to leave soeting *something* behind. But he already has 'cause the future is now, like I said. I board the plane, *train.*

"Ah… second man," the conductor says.

I see he is written in italics and wonder at the font. I didn't know this typewriter was a selectrix and had a ball font you could turn and get different script. My fingers have stopped moving. The future is written. Anyway.

Two hundred an d five words left. Not many to go. And the end is near. In sight. But it hasn't happened yet. Because it never will. It is the future. The end. That is the secret of living in the future. It never gets here. Ands if you want to live for eternity you just have to stay in the future. Forget the past. Even the present. Just remember the future. As you *see* it. Read it.

The last man standing is stammering inside his head to a cow he can't see and isn't there but he wishes it was so he could see it drink from the waters of the tilted windmill flowing in the stream of life and consiousness where cows drink from streams o f futre tenses and remedies for all that ails you as long as it isn't beer ale. That would be a laguer without a key. Lost my spell check with the typewriter reincarnation. Four words to go before there are only a few left and I wish this typewriter had a ribbon so I could see what it writes... but it does in the future... else how do you think you see it...

I re-read the beginning in the future like you reading it for the first time. Are you sitting? Or standing? Or neither. What is YOUR future?

I read,

Disaster struck. One man left standing. No woman to speak of. He could *see*. If there was one. How would he pro-create? *Could he.* If he could. Find a woman. And he had any juice left.

Food would be scarce. And there was no power to speak of. Candles. One windmill. Tilted. No cows. To speak of. He stammered even if no one was listening.

DOG FOR DINNER

dvsduncan

The dinner special was dog. Why should that night have been any different? The meat was popular, amongst those who were permitted to eat it, and was relatively plentiful, though not as plentiful as it had been a few years ago. The city packs had been heavily hunted and trapped. The surviving animals were wary and clever, more like ghosts than prey. Most of the meat came from the country now. That was fine with Joyce Collingwood because the country dogs tasted better.

Her cleaver came down with a solid thud. Good dog meat meant good stew. She looked around the market tent and then back at the ragged, red parts on her block. There were few potential customers at the moment but it was still early. Most of her trade was done after sunset, when the wind died and the fog rose. Then a blaze would be built in the centre of the tent to keep the damp out and a minstrel would fill the air with music. She hoped it would be the hurdy-gurdy man with the honey voice. He sang about the world before the Great Fire.

A burst of laughter attracted her attention. Guardsmen were pushing their way through the flap in the far wall, holding it open for their fellows and letting rough gusts through. Joyce quickly threw a cloth over the raw meat. No one wanted gritty stew. When the last guardsman was in, they stood as a mob to consider the stalls. One of the merchants quickly rearranged the flaps to keep the wind out.

"Hey, Joyce," one of the guardsmen called, as he separated from the group. His name was Otis, though whether that was his first or last name Joyce neither knew nor cared. He considered himself handsome. His uniform had been freshly laundered but it was already mottled with dust. "What's for dinner?"

"Dog," she said, without turning around.

"Again?"

"My customers like dog."

"I could be your customer too, if you'd only cooked something a Gaian could eat."

He was smiling. Broadly. She could feel it. There was no need to look up from her work. She asked, "Why not try the dog?"

"You trying to convert me?" he asked in return.

Joyce sighed and wiped at her cheek, spreading a broad smear of blood across it in the process. Then she looked up to meet his eyes. Two of his fellows had joined him, both large and well muscled. They all wore the same smug grin. She knew what they saw: a skinny teenager with a wild mop of red hair dressed in a stained apron and the coat of a Penitent.

"The trouble is that, by order of the Caretakers, it's illegal to prepare or eat meat," Otis said.

"Unless I have a dispensation," she told him. He knew that her paperwork was all in order but the coat and nails alone should have been enough for him.

"And why would you have a dispensation?" Otis asked, feigning ignorance. His backup chuckled.

Joyce shot a poisonous look at the pair behind Otis and then returned her full attention to the oaf directly in front of her. She glared and said nothing.

"Oh look," Otis continued, pointing at the three nails pinned through the left breast of her coat. His eyes grew wide as he asked, "Are you a Wrather?"

"A sister of the Convocation Penitent."

"Yes," Otis nodded sagely to the continued entertainment of his fellows. "A Penitent. Of course. But even with a dispensation you are only allowed to serve animals that died of natural causes. How did this dog die?"

"Blood loss." Joyce had had enough. She folded her arms across her chest and narrowed her eyes. The cleaver was still clenched in her left fist.

Otis looked at the bloody steel in mock horror and backed away, his hands held up as though he were pleading for his life. He crooned, "I am so sorry, Sister. My friends and I meant no offense. We'll be on our way. Gaia be with you."

With that said, the trio moved on, finding it difficult to walk in a straight line as they gave full vent to their amusement. Joyce watched them go before turning back to her butchery. She pulled the cloth off the meat and brought the cleaver down with a solid blow that severed a canine spine. Under her breath, she muttered, "Gaia go with you. I don't want the bitch around here."

She was not speaking entirely of the goddess. Joyce chanced a glance across the tent. The dowager had been watching the exchange. That was bad luck. Joyce went back to work. There was a lecture coming but let the old woman scold. The guardsmen were arrogant bastards. Someone had to stand up to them. Their job was to keep the peace in the name of the Caretakers, not to harass women trying to make a living by selling dog stew. Joyce finished hacking the corpse into manageable parts and exchanged her cleaver for a carving knife. The bones she threw into a stock pot while setting the meat aside for cubing. To the guardsmen, she was little more than that bleeding pile. Just meat. But her flesh was her own and would never be theirs. Let them eat dog if they dared. They would never taste her, despite the wishes of that crooked tyrant. Joyce looked again, a flicker of eyes to mark the old woman's progress.

The dowager could see how pretty Joyce might be with combed hair and a clean face, dressed in a clinging gown or not dressed at all. Youth and beauty brought a good price and there was a place for young and beautiful women in the dowager's pleasure house. Joyce wanted no part of that. This the dowager took as a betrayal.

Perhaps it was. Perhaps Joyce owed her body in return for all she had received, but she could not give it. The old woman might have named her, taken her in and raised her when no one else would, but it was too much to demand. Surely that demand was the greater betrayal. Or perhaps Joyce was no more than an animal raised for slaughter. That thought left her with a dull ache inside. She had felt safe if not loved. Now that was gone. Joining the Convocation of the Penitent had done little to ease her sorrow, but it did ensure that the dowager could never take her by force. The bishop and the deacons would guard her against that.

Joyce watched the old woman hobble along, making a slow progress from table to table, ancient eyes inspecting every detail. Stern. Fierce. Grey. Everyone bowed. Each

showed their regard. Even the guardsmen were respect-
ful. The dowager had the means to feed or frustrate their
vices.

She passed by Joyce with only a nod, unable to keep the
anger from her eyes but remaining silent. Joyce kept her own
eyes averted and, wishing no confrontation, made the briefest
acknowledgement possible. It was much the same as every
other day. Joyce would gulp down her panic and keep her face
stiff. The moment would pass.

A train rumbled and Joyce looked up, thankful for the dis-
traction. The tent hid the concrete beams overhead but she
knew they were up there and the station above that. She had
been found there and named for it. So far as she knew, she
had never been more than a few kilometres away from it.

She knew the towers, all clustered around the station, that
were principally billets for the guardsmen. She knew the burn
belt from Metrotown Enclave in the east to the industrial
areas around Pit One in the west. Best of all she knew
Central Farm, which had once been a park, where she went
to collect her herbs from the hedgerow and barter for vegetables. This was her little world. It kept her alive. That was more
than many achieved.

With the meat cubed, Joyce raked the charcoal and
placed the flesh on the steel plate that served as a cooking
surface. She added a few crushed herbs and some fat. It siz-
zled. While the meat seared, Joyce began preparing vegetables. It was early spring and the only root vegetables available
were those from last season. Joyce could not afford the best
of these. She picked up a turnip. The surface was wrinkled
and soft. She took care to remove the decaying portions without wasting any part of the healthy flesh beneath. She tasted

a small cube of this to be sure it had not been tainted and then chopped the remainder. Onions came next. She cursed to herself when several proved to be rotten at the centre. She salvaged what she could before moving on to the carrots, limp and spotted black, muttering at the state of them.

"Good afternoon, Sister."

The voice surprised her. Joyce had been entirely concerned with her preparations but now she looked up. Archdeacon Nathaniel was standing on the far side of her work table. He wore the same type of rough grey coat that wrapped her and the same pattern of nails glinted over his heart. He was a big man with a grizzled beard. Joyce flushed, hoping he had not heard her angry words.

"Peace be with you, Archdeacon," she said.

"And also with you," he returned. "Have you been well?"

"Yes, Archdeacon. I did not expect to see you today."

"I have just come from discussions with the bishop. He is concerned that you are alone in this place."

Joyce blinked in surprise, then said, "I didn't think the bishop even knew my name."

"He does," the archdeacon assured her. "We have often spoken about you."

"Yes, but I'm not alone. There are others. There are other brothers and sisters that work on the farm. We gather together and pray every morning before the wind. Many of them come here in the evening to eat the stew I sell."

"It is good to have the community of other Penitents, that is true, but this is not the same as having someone to hold and cherish you."

"Hold and cherish," the words rolled through her. "But I..."

"We know the dangers you face," the archdeacon told her. "And the dangers faced by the entire community. You are without a guide."

"That is true, but we know that we are not forgotten," she assured the archdeacon.

"Indeed, you are not," the archdeacon said. His usually grim visage was lit with a paternal smile. Joyce thought that this must be what it is like when the sun peeks through the clouds. "We have decided that you shall have permission to marry and we have a man that will make you a good husband."

Joyce felt suddenly numb. She did not know what to say but her look must have said enough. The archdeacon said, "There is no need to worry, Sister. He is a fine man. I have picked him for you myself. He will come to see you tomorrow evening but I wanted to tell you today so that you could prepare yourself."

"Prepare myself?"

The archdeacon made an oddly indefinite motion with his hand that seemed to take in all of her. "Perhaps if you combed your hair and washed your face. He will value your earnest faith but if you showed some of your other fine qualities..."

"I don't know what to say."

"Sister, you need only agree."

"I knew this day would come," she said, "but so soon? I don't need a husband."

"You need him more than you know and he needs a wife. He has been sent here as the local priest. He has no wife and it would be best if he married a local woman. You have courage and youth. You will make him a good wife. Please consider it. This marriage will be a great service to our cause and you may learn to love him."

"I will be here tomorrow night. I have to be. If he comes to the tent, I will speak to him," she assured the archdeacon.

"Excellent," he said, satisfied that she had agreed to that much. "I will return to Vancouver with the news but I would like to travel with a full stomach. When will the stew be ready?"

Joyce smiled as earnestly as she could and told him. When the archdeacon walked away with a promise to return for dinner, Joyce went back to her cooking but now her hands were guided only by long habit. Her mind was elsewhere. A husband. She did not want any man, not those that the dowager would force upon her nor some stern protector hard as the nails he wore. Life offered her little enough freedom. Necessity dictated most everything she did. What would she have if she had a husband?

Would he make her give up what she had? As the stew simmered and she made meat pies, Joyce tried to think it through. The archdeacon was a stern but fair man. He might have chosen well for her. Perhaps she should be glad of it. It was a hard world. To have the help and comfort of another was no small thing. Still, she should be the one to choose. The choice should not be made for her. But if she turned her suitor away, what would that mean? Would it drive her out of the Convocation and leave her truly alone? Perhaps the dowager would win after all. That was the most bitter thought of all.

Most people had little choice. Women had least of all, but Joyce had fought for her place in the world. Her little empire might be no more than a stew pot and a table, but at least she owed it to no one and she ruled it alone. Alone. For better or for worse.

All day and into the night her thoughts ran in circles. She did her business in silence and she did not hear the honey voice of the hurdy-gurdy man as he sang. By the time the lanterns were turned down and the last customers shuffled from the tent, there was more resignation than resolution in her. She hung her pot from a line outside the tent, ready to be scoured by the grit of the morning wind, and then went to bed. Her troubles would not be as easily worn away.

By this time tomorrow she might be betrothed.

That thought was a poor pillow and, as Joyce curled up on her bedroll beneath the table, sleep was elusive. Her mind conjured up images of her intended. He would be serious and unbending. She had met enough of the priests and the deacons to know the type. They were harsh and joyless men with hard eyes, stalwart protectors but exacting masters. He would uncover her every fault and chastise her for each. There in the dark, she began to enumerate her sins and shortcomings, the chief of which was pride.

By dawn, sleep seemed further away than ever and it was time for prayers. Joyce rose to prepare herself. She needed the water ration for cooking and so scrubbed with pulped leaves, hidden from view beneath the coverings of her table. Then she pulled her hair back and tied it in place. Her smock was only slightly stained. It would do for another day. She pulled it on and dragged the coat over it. Thus prepared, Joyce crawled out into public view and straightened to stretch the soreness from her back.

The tent was nearly deserted. The hemp panels hung limp and damp, tinted by a ruby light. There was the sound of dripping from somewhere and the sounds of people still abed all around. Quietly bundling lengths of course twine, sacks and a harvest knife took only a moment. These she placed in the market basket. Then she pulled on a pair of cracked and ill-fitting goggles, wrapped a scarf tightly across her nose and mouth, pulled a shawl over her head and prepared to depart for her morning errands. It all felt so ordinary. The goggles rode on her forehead for the moment, not yet necessary though ready for use, and as a final measure Joyce pulled on a pair of gloves. They were a good pair with only a few holes. They had been a gift from one of the other Penitents. Thus protected, she stepped through the tent flap into the wider world.

That world was made indistinct by the fog. The towers were no more than silhouettes and the sun was a red glow, but they led the way. Follow the shadows toward the dawn and then turn right at the main road. That road was called Boundary. A rusty sign told her that, though it gave no indication what boundary it might mark. Farther up she would cross Kingsway. She did not know which king. The Caretakers were the only rulers Joyce knew.

For much of the way the road was still reasonably good. Most of the old surface was gone but the holes were regularly filled with gravel and the invasive brambles kept down by the traffic. It was only a short walk, easy for a young woman even if she were carrying a burden, but that morning the weight on her shoulders was heavier than it had ever been. She stopped, held back a sob. All she wanted to do was return to her bedroll and cry herself to sleep.

That would not get her vegetables in or make the stew or banish her problems. That was not how she had lived. She would not live that way now.

Joyce raised her eyes toward the crest of the hill and began walking once more. She climbed to where Boundary and

Kingsway met on the high ground. The mist was thinning now. Only a breath of wind stirred the air. Joyce glanced to the east and gauged how much time she had before that wind rose in earnest. That was perhaps an hour away. She moved more quickly. She was nearly at the farm.

It was an orderly tangle of wind breaks, vegetation and dew traps. Stone hedges bordered most of it and divided the fields. At this time of morning there were only a few people about. These were the overseers considering the necessary tasks for the day. Most knew Joyce by name. She usually wound her way through the fields on the way to prayers, the route more direct than following the road, and that had been her intention this morning, but once in the fields she seemed to take root. She needed to pray but she realized quite suddenly that she did not want to go to the meeting. Perhaps they knew about her betrothal. There would be questions and congratulations and offers of help with the arrangements. There would be excitement and solemn declarations. She could not face any of that. What she most earnestly wanted was a time of solitude.

Removing the gloves, Joyce knelt with her knife in hand. Rosemary and parsley were growing from a cleft between two rocks. Sage grew a little farther on. Her blade cut cleanly through the stalks and sent the water drops falling like jewels. Perfume rose to scent the morning. She worked quickly, sorting the harvest as she went. This was a good spot. It had not been gleaned in some time, half-hidden as it was by a large bush. On any other day this would have been a perfect moment.

"Hello."

Joyce started. She had been lost in her work and the other had approached quietly. She looked up to find a man leaning over the wall. He was young and thin. Wisps of blond hair escaped from beneath his hat. A heavy scarf was wrapped around his neck, ready to cover his mouth and nose when the wind rose. His goggles were likewise around his neck, hanging loose by their straps. He had a pleasant face, strong but open. Three nails glinted on the left breast of his rough coat.

"I suppose it is too late for dawn service?" he asked.

Joyce looked at the sky, judging time by the colour in the east. "They will be doing the confessions now, so it would probably be done by the time you got there."

He nodded, then observed, "You didn't go."

"No," she admitted the obvious. "I will make my prayers privately."

"Sometimes I like to pray alone, too, but I had hoped to meet the people."

"You are new here?" Joyce asked, though it was unnecessary. She knew everyone in the local Convocation. When new members arrived, they were usually brought to the market tent to be introduced to Joyce and her stew. Those new arrivals were becoming more frequent. The community was growing.

"I am from the Prairies. My people ranched in the foothills."

Joyce had only a vague idea of where the Prairies might be. She knew that they were to the east across high mountains and that the journey was difficult and dangerous. She said as much.

"An uncle of mine works on the train. He arranged for me to travel with some cargo. They have had problems with the mountain men and are happy to have another man on board if he can fight."

"Can you fight?"

"All members of the Convocation must be warriors," he said rather too seriously.

Joyce giggled and then caught herself. Such frivolity was unbecoming. She said, "I'm sorry. I didn't mean to mock you."

"It's all right. That sounded like a boast but I did not mean it that way. I can fight when I have to. The mountain men raid us too and we have to defend what we have."

"Are you going to Vancouver?"

"I was in Vancouver for a year. Now I have come to stay with my cousin. She works on the farm here. Perhaps you know her, Sandra Clement?"

"Yes," Joyce said, and then a little silence settled between them before she thought to introduce herself. "My name is Joyce Collingwood, by the way. Yes. Just like the station. I was found there when I was a baby."

"Oh," the young man said. He seemed surprised but smiled and nodded as though he knew all about it, then looked at her thoughtfully before saying, "You are very pretty."

Joyce was shocked. The last person to tell her that had been the dowager. Instinctively Joyce pulled the scarf up to cover the lower half of her face. It had fallen away while she had been harvesting the herbs. The cloth hid her blush. Or so she hoped. "You shouldn't say such things."

"Truth shall fill the penitent mouth."

"And discretion council his tongue."

"I am sorry if I embarrassed you, but you *are* pretty."

"A man should not say things like that to a woman he meets in a field. If the deacon hears about it, he will be mad."

"And he will tell the priest."

"We have no priest of our own. Not yet." Joyce paused and her lip quivered a little. "There is one coming tonight."

"You don't sound happy about that. Surely you want to have a leader."

"Yes," she admitted, "but there is more to it. He is going to marry me."

That was the first time that Joyce had said it. Hearing it in her own voice was worse than thinking about it and she let out a little sob.

The young man looked concerned and asked, "But surely you are happy about having a husband."

"I don't know. I don't know him. I don't know anything about him. He's probably some old man with cold hands."

"Are warm hands important to you?" the young man asked.

Joyce looked at him in shock and then broke down entirely. Great sobs erupted. Her head dropped into her hands and she took shuddering breaths. All the weight of the world pressed down on her. She wished that everything would go away. It did not. An arm curled around her shoulder, warm and comforting. Joyce collapsed into the embrace without thinking, pushing against a strong chest as she let her tears flow. It was only when a nail scratched her ear that she realized what was happening.

"What are you doing?" Joyce shrieked as she tore herself free. She toppled forward, landed on her hands and knees, then scuttled away from her comforter like an enraged crab. "What if someone had seen us?"

The young man held up placating hands. "It would be all right."

"All right? I tell you I am getting married and you put your arms around me?"

"It really will be fine," he assured her. "We had chaperones. You see?"

Joyce looked in the direction indicated by the young man. She had been wrong about the time. The Penitents had finished their prayers and were returning to the fields. A group of them stood a short distance away, watching her and the young man. Joyce scrambled to her feet, grabbed her basket and fled. When she dared to look back, the young man had his back to her and was deep in conversation with several members of the Convocation who had seen their indiscretion.

Joyce had no idea how she could face any of them after this. She wanted to run back to the market tent and hide under her table but she needed supplies.

In the farthest part of the farm she cut the last of the necessary herbs and then bartered for vegetables. These cost too much but her heart was not in the bargaining. She was disgraced. Despair. Promiscuity. Ingratitude. There was no end to her sins. She could not even imagine the penance that would be laid on her.

With supplies in her basket, she crept homeward. Like a punishment, the wind began to rise in rough gusts, tearing the fog away from the land and raising the stinging grit. Joyce dropped her face behind a hunched shoulder for protection. The scarf was not enough. As she walked, her eyes were drawn to the vast area of the burn where the blackened rectangles were only now softening beneath brambles and the stunted twists of trees. Most of those ruins had been homes before the Fire. Divine wrath had consumed them. The survivors might dispute whether it had been God or Gaia but the truth of the devastation was plain for all to see. The old world had been punished for its evils. Those that did not repent their faults must continue to suffer. That was why Joyce was suffering.

The thought crushed her. She had done something to bring this all upon herself. She had tried so hard to be righteous but she had failed. She deserved the whipping wind. And she deserved whatever was to come. Tears and the flow from her nose soaked the scarf and made breathing difficult as Joyce struggled to carry her burden down the hill. The world, already murky through the dusty glass of the goggles, was now blurred by brimming eyes. Joyce tripped and dropped her basket as she tried to right herself. The food scattered. Turnips and potatoes began to roll downhill. The wind caught the lighter bunches of herbs and spread them across the slope.

Screaming and sobbing, Joyce dove after her precious provisions. Then he was there again. Losing his hat while scrambling after the herbs so that his yellow hair flew in the wind. He captured the errant bunches, returned them to her basket, and then joined the pursuit of the rolling tubers. Joyce wanted to shout at him until he went away but the words could not find their way past the grief. She could not stop him. She could not drive him off. All she could do was watch as he captured each wayward vegetable and stuffed it into his coat until all could be returned to the basket.

When they were done, he stood over her like a conquering hero all red-faced and expecting praise.

"I hate you," she spat. Suddenly she was angry. All the pain and the fear and the guilt were gone in one white-hot flash. She was not to blame. She had always tried to do the right thing. She was humble, austere and generous as the deacons had taught her. All this grief was the doing of others. It had been done to her and one of her tormentors stood before her now. She picked up a stone and warned, "Get away from me."

"It is okay," the young man said. He had retrieved his hat and was wringing it in his hands. "I spoke to the others and they understand."

"Understand what?" She threw the stone at him, missing by a good margin. She picked up two more. "Get away. You know how wrong that was. To hold me like that." She let a second stone fly. This one found its mark, striking the young man on the left arm. It stung. He put a hand to the wounded spot and straightened, suddenly looking much sterner.

"This is not proper behavior."

"Proper?" Joyce threw the other stone. "Proper?" She bent down and picked up additional ammunition. "I am a promised woman." Another stone flew. "I told you that." The next stone struck the middle of his chest. "And still you... you handled me." She knew the others must surely be watching this scene as well but all care had been burned away by the rage. It was at least satisfying to see the stiffness go out of the young man as he retreated before the stoning. Beaten, he stood aside in silence at a safe distance as Joyce recovered her basket and stormed down the hill. The tears were back but there was something triumphant about them now.

If she was to be married, then so be it, but she would not be crushed by it. To be the wife of the priest was to hold a position of respect. She would have influence in the Convocation. Then that blond satyr would learn his place.

Safely back in the tent and bent over her table, that thought propelled Joyce Collingwood through the afternoon. She scarcely heard the hubbub of the other merchants as her cleaver fell again and again like judgment, true and resolute.

Even the dowager passed unnoticed as Joyce poured all her energy into the production of another dog stew. She knew it was not right to dislike someone so. God was love even when he corrected his people in wrath. But she could not shake the feeling of his arm around her shoulder and the comforting pressure of his chest. It was not right for a man to embrace a woman like that unless they were joined by blood or vow. If the others had seen anything, they had seen that he had embraced her unasked. Then Joyce faltered. She had pressed herself into him, so very grateful to be held in a moment of despair. She had been complicit.

The realization struck her suddenly, the memory rising up without warning to extinguish her righteous fury. In that moment, the tent flap parted and a severe figure stepped through. Her heart sank.

There was no mistaking a priest of the Convocation Penitent. His bearing alone marked him, the iron collar and scourge of correction being mere confirmation. He took in the interior of the tent in a single, sweeping gaze before striding directly to where Joyce worked. This man was made of the same stuff as his collar and was as ancient as the hills. A lump formed in her throat as she watched him approach.

"You are Joyce Collingwood?" he asked, though it was not entirely a question. She was the only Penitent selling food in the tent and the only woman of her age in the local Convocation. He knew who she was.

"Yes," she managed.

"I have come to discuss the arrangements for the wedding."

Joyce could only lower her gaze and nod.

"Please, do not let me interrupt your work," he said. "I will tell you how it is to be. You will be honoured to know that the bishop himself will be conducting the service."

"Yes, Father," Joyce said. There was a slight quaver in her voice. She was slicing onions and doing it badly. She sniffed. Her eyes watered.

"There is no need to fear this, child."

Joyce looked up into the priest's face. She wanted to tell him that she was not afraid, that it was only the onions that made her cry, but that was not true and she could not lie. Not to him. Especially not to him. She managed a weak nod.

"It will be a happy marriage," he told her.

Joyce wanted to believe that with all her heart. No words could express how she felt.

"You think that because I am old, I have forgotten the ways of a young woman's heart. I have not. I know what is in yours. I know that you are afraid now but I also know that in the years to come you will find that this is a good match."

Joyce was finding it hard to breathe. Something had her by the throat and all she wanted to do was run. She kept her eyes on the work table, trying to think, but all thought and, indeed, all feeling seemed to have drained from her. All she managed was to mutter, "Water."

"What was that, child?" the old priest asked.

"I need to get water to make the stew."

"Ah. Perhaps I can help?"

"No," she said, more forcefully than she intended, and the priest raised an eyebrow. Joyce cowered slightly and amended her tone. "I meant that I am used to getting it myself, Father. It will only take me a few minutes."

"Of course, child."

Joyce lifted two buckets from the table and started toward the flap.

"Joyce," the priest said behind her.

She froze.

"You must call me Matthew. After all, we will soon be related by marriage."

Joyce swallowed, carefully pronounced, "Yes, Matthew."

It was difficult not to run out of the tent but she managed a steady pace. There was no thought to what would happen once she left. All that was important for the moment was reaching the open air.

Outside, night had fallen and the fog was thick once more. Out of habit, Joyce moved to the cisterns where the dew traps emptied. She stopped at the door, sagged, and looked hopelessly out into the night as though seeking an answer.

Instead, her eyes found guardsman Otis with his two friends following her out of the market tent. Their eyes locked for a moment. Something flickered across his face she could not identify and then he smiled his idiot smile.

"Hey, Joyce, I hear you're getting married. They say you're going to marry a priest. Is that the guy, that old fossil at your table?" Otis and his friends swaggered closer. They were bloated with laughter. "He looks stiff as a poker. Of course, it's good to have a stiff man. You know what I mean, Joyce?"

Otis was far too close now. He had always been at least the width of a table away from her. Now she could smell him. He seemed so much taller, so much stronger as he loomed out of the fog.

"Bet you like stiff men but you need a young one." His hand reached out for her shoulder.

It never touched her.

Something hissed out of the dark and struck the guardsman on the wrist. He yelped. The hand withdrew as he
turned to face his attacker. The young man with the blond
hair was standing there.

"You will not speak to a sister of the Convocation Penitent
in that fashion and you will certainly not touch her," he said,
and there was iron in his voice. The friendly face he had worn
that morning was gone.

"You know what you get for hitting a guardsman?" Otis
asked. His truncheon was out now.

The young man said nothing. Instead, he stared hard at
Otis while tapping something against the palm of his free
hand. It took Joyce a moment to realize what it was. Her eyes
widened and she looked up in search of a collar but he still
wore the scarf wrapped tight around his neck.

One of the other guardsmen, either brighter or better
informed than Otis, had noted the scourge as well. He
seemed to realize what it signified and now looked wary of
continuing the conflict. Otis had no such reservations.

"I am going to make you so sorry," he announced, and tried
to step forward only to be restrained by his more prudent
companion. Otis shook the hand off and demanded, "What?"

"Look what he's holding."

"I know what he's holding. He just hit me with it," Otis
snapped. "I'm going to shove that whip down his throat."

"He's a priest," the other guardsman croaked under his
breath. "We can't touch him."

"This bone rack? No way," Otis retorted. "Anyway, I don't
care. He hit me."

"We can't. You know that," the other insisted, and then
added in a hiss, "We have orders."

"Shit," Otis spat, and then looked squarely at his opponent. "Let me see it."

The blond man raised his chin and pulled the scarf down. In the dim light, iron glinted at his throat. Otis swore again, longer and more fluently, and then warned, "You watch your back, Wrather. People like you have accidents. You know what I mean? One night, you'll have an accident."

The young man said nothing back, neither did he move nor look away. Otis stood before him quaking in impotent fury, trying to contrive a graceful retreat. In the end, all he could do was spin on his heel and curse his friends into following him. Joyce watched in astonishment as they left, leaving her alone with her saviour.

"You idiot," she scolded him. "I have to live here. I have to see them every day."

"You will be protected," he assured her.

"Just because I am married to a priest?" The word stuck in her throat and she repeated it. "Priest."

"Yes, because you will be the wife of a priest. After the riots last year, none of the guardsmen and not even the Caretakers would dare touch you. Not you and not me. You saw that here tonight."

"You are a priest," Joyce said. She was shaking now.

"Yes." He stepped closer to her. She could feel the heat of his body and realized that he was breathing hard. He was all iron and fire. It seemed that he might reach for her, take her in his arms again. Abruptly, Joyce backed away two paces.

"Don't touch me."

The words hit him hard. His shoulders fell and the eyes with them. The iron was gone. The fire was out. He said, "I am sorry. I don't know if I can do this."

"Do what?"

"Any of it. Face them. Lead this Convocation. Marry you. I don't think I am worthy or strong enough. My uncle expects it, but I don't know if I can."

Joyce could not find her voice for a full minute after that. She could only stare at the young man. In the end she asked, "Marry me? You are going to marry me?"

"If you are willing. Didn't the archdeacon tell you that I was coming today? From what you said at the farm, I thought you knew all about it and had decided to accept."

"He said you would be coming tonight."

"I was anxious to see you," the young man admitted. "I came early. I was afraid you might be ugly but you were so beautiful and then you were crying and I felt so sorry about it. I just wanted to hold you and tell you it would be all right."

"And I hit you."

"Yes."

"I hit a priest."

"Yes. Please don't tell Uncle Matthew."

"Father Matthew?"

"Yes," the young man said, squaring his shoulders a little. "He came to make the wedding arrangements and see that everything was prepared properly for the bishop."

"Then when you put your arm around me," Joyce paused. "We were betrothed already."

"If you meant what you said about getting married, yes. It really was all right. The Convocation understands that. I spoke to them. It will be harder to explain you throwing stones at me."

"Why didn't you tell me who you were?"

"I was going to tell you in the garden but you ran away before I could. I was going to tell you on the hill but you wouldn't listen."

Joyce felt the blush rising in her cheeks. The young man smiled and shrugged.

"Please," he said, "never tell my uncle or the bishop about any of this."

"No," Joyce said. She was horrified that either should ever find out.

"I know I am a stranger to you and that we did not start off well. I hope we can start again. Maybe you can love me. At the very least, I hope that you will be content. We could make a life together and be happy if you will stop hitting me."

Joyce half-laughed at that, not certain what to say.

"The Convocation expects a priest to give strength to the people he leads. I will need someone to give me strength. My name is Father Daniel Whyte and this will be my parish, though I do not feel worthy of that honour. I feel alone. I think that you feel alone too. We can change that. I wouldn't deny that it is a hard life being married to a priest, but it has its rewards too. Will you share it with me?"

"I don't know."

"Perhaps we can talk about it more," the young man said. "But we better get back. Uncle Matthew will wonder what has happened to us."

"And I have a stew to finish."

"What kind?"

"Dog."

"I might just have some vegetables," he told her.

MAXIM FUJIYAMA AND OTHER PERSONS

Claude Lalumière

Over the percussive noise of the rain, Maxim hears male voices shouting and cursing. The sound comes from the direction of his home. He detours half a block so as to hide among a patch of trees that affords him a good view of the apartment complex's front door. Near the shore of False Creek, the downtown Vancouver neighbourhood where he currently lives, there are trees everywhere. Even more so now than before; even after only a little over a year of urban neglect, there are already signs of nature taking back the city.

Two middle-aged white men are trying to enter the building. But the old Chinese man who lives on the third floor is blocking the door. The Chinese man isn't talking loud enough for Maxim to make out his words over the distance and the rain. The message of his body language, however, is unambiguous: *you may not enter.*

The white men are wearing drab business suits that have seen better days. Their hair is long, their beards unkempt. They do not look dangerous, merely pathetic. Four metres away from the door, they continue to shout obscenities and threats at the building's de facto guardian. The Chinese man responds firmly, shaking his head.

The Chinese man takes a step forward. The two men in business suits take three steps back. They know they have lost, Maxim observes, but still they do not leave, nor do they cease their verbal abuse. The taller of the two men bends down to pick up a rock. He hurls it toward the front door. The throw is ineffectual; the rock lands half a metre short of the Chinese man, who again steps forward. The white men retreat twice that distance. Without saying a word, the Chinese man picks up the rock. He looks at the white men, flexing his forearm with the weight of the rock in his hand.

The men yell a few more threats and insults, but Maxim can hear the defeat in their voices. Finally, the shorter man tugs on his companion's jacket and the two are off, scowling back at the source of their defeat and humiliation. As the men leave, the rain tapers off.

This is not the first time Maxim has witnessed his neighbour – who is barely above 150 centimetres tall but powerfully built, his demeanour projecting a physical arrogance that seems unaffected by his diminutive height or his advanced age, which Maxim estimates at around 70 – chasing off people trying to enter the building. Once the white men are completely out of sight, Maxim emerges from his hiding spot. Careful to avoid the intimacy of eye contact, the Chinese man steps aside so that Maxim can enter.

As Maxim climbs the stairs to his apartment – a fully furnished tenth-storey luxury condo that showed no signs of ever having been inhabited before he claimed it – he recalls reading an article that discussed housing costs in Canada, back when there was such a thing as housing costs: Vancouverites, on average, spent 80 to 90 percent of their income on housing, compared to Torontonians, who spent 50 to 60 percent, and Montrealers, who spent 25 to 30 percent, which was the recommended ratio for sustainable living. If the so-called "invisible hand" of the market really worked, the article speculated, housing would not be so expensive in Vancouver; the city's vacancy rate for condos and apartments hovered in the 20 to 25 percent range, which should have brought prices down, but it didn't. Vancouver remained the most expensive city in which to live in Canada, regardless of how many housing units were left uninhabited, forcing people out to ever more distant suburbs. Most of the vacancies consisted of condos such as Maxim's. Near the once-bustling Granville Island, it offered a breathtaking view of the downtown cityscape across from the water of False Creek.

Maxim has now resided in this apartment building for a year. When he first arrived there were no live residents. Of the 25 units, only 12 had corpses in them. The first thing he did was start to drag the bodies, one by one, outside the building to leave for scavengers. But there were 23 corpses; after the fourth one, his stamina gave out. Then he hit on the notion of throwing them off their balconies, and that went much faster. He did all this in full daylight, to minimize personal risk, as he remembered reading that most predators and scavengers hunted at dawn or twilight.

Birds and insects converged on the splattered remains immediately, but that night Maxim observed coyotes feasting. The next morning there were heavy rains; by the time the weather calmed just before sunset, there was barely a trace of gore left.

A week later, three Latinas – aged, Maxim guessed, between 20 and 50 – moved in two floors beneath him, taking over the entire level. The following day, the Chinese man appropriated a unit for himself on the third floor. No one has settled in the building since, because the man always chases anyone new away. He never interferes or interacts with either the women on the eighth floor or with Maxim.

◀ ▶

Maxim Fujiyama lives in Vancouver, British Columbia, Canada, North America, Planet Earth, Solar System, Milky Way Galaxy. Maxim doesn't like people to make assumptions about shared knowledge when they express themselves, either verbally or in writing. Everything should be defined and contextualized carefully, so as to make sure there can be no misunderstandings. For example, there's another Vancouver 490 kilometres south of the one he lives in; the other Vancouver is in the state of Washington, in the United States of America. Aside from seeing it on maps, he knows nothing of that other Vancouver.

Two years ago, his hometown boasted a population of 700,000, with the Greater Vancouver metropolitan area comprised of more than 2.5 million inhabitants, the third-largest urban agglomeration in Canada. Now, without official statistics, Maxim is hesitant to make a precise guess. But, for one year now, he has been keeping tabs.

Two years ago, it would have been impossible to take note of every person encountered or observed in a single day, or even walking the length of a downtown block. There was too much activity going on at all times.

According to his observations, Maxim has identified 1,324 different people in Vancouver. At least 597 of these can be assumed to currently reside in the city, as he has recorded their presence throughout the past year at various intervals. Another 344, seen no more than three times and not more recently than 60 days ago, he lists as "transient or deceased." Another 104 were only observed for the first time in the past eight weeks, so their status is still "indeterminate." He counts 170 whom he observed regularly for the first few months but then disappeared; these are noted as "deceased or emigrated." Finally, he identified 109 corpses as "newly deceased," as he had previously counted them among the survivors spotted in Vancouver. He does not keep tabs on other corpses: those who died more than a year ago, such as those of his parents. There are too many to count, and they fall outside the scope of his survey.

He has not spoken to any of the survivors. And no one has tried to talk to him. The inhabitants of Vancouver seem content keeping to themselves, which suits Maxim. He only ventures from his base of operations to scavenge or observe and record the population of the city. There are also nonhuman animals in Vancouver; beyond the usual urban fauna of squirrels, cats, dogs, crows, pigeons, sparrows, and the like, Maxim has seen numerous foxes, rabbits, and coyotes and a handful of timber wolves, lynxes, cougars, and bears. He lacks the expertise to be able to distinguish individuals of most of these species, so he has not been keeping tabs on their population, although he does enjoy observing them.

Today, Maxim recognized four people already on his list of permanent residents, seven people from the pool of newcomers, and two individuals he has never seen before (the two men who tried to gain entry into his building).

Precision makes knowledge and communication possible. Maxim is a precise person.

◄ ►

Maxim is uneasy using the word "person." What does it mean? Who or what is a person? Can only humans be called persons? Are dogs persons, too? Cats? Parrots? Lions? Dolphins? Elephants? Mice? Iguanas? Octopuses? Sharks? Some say that chimpanzees and gorillas are persons and should be treated as such. Who or what defines the limits of personhood? If being human equals personhood, does that mean that chimps and gorillas are in some way human? For many years, humans were thought to be Cro-Magnons. Persons were Cro-Magnons; other animals, from primates to insects, were not. Fossils from other branches of not-quite-human hominids had been found, but all of these were thought to be extinct. Later DNA analysis told us that, no, they were not truly extinct, and, yes, they were human, too. They still live among and within modern humans – or at least what remains of the human population.

When the Cro-Magnons migrated out of Africa across Europe and Asia, they encountered these other humans – the Neanderthals, the Denisovans, and probably others whose DNA has yet to be located in the current human gene pool, such as the Red Deer Cave People, and others whose fossil record and DNA may as yet be undiscovered. To what degree did these different types of humans fight or cooperate? How much did they recognize each other as akin or distrust each other as alien? The details of those encounters are forever lost, but one thing is now certain: these different branches of early humans interbred. Were they all persons? Some modern humans are part Neanderthal, part Denisovan, part who-knows-what other species of early human. Are all modern humans equally persons, regardless of their genetic background?

Before, when Maxim still lived with his parents, when Vancouver was a populous metropolis, Maxim felt more alienation than kinship toward other humans, including his mother and father. He was keenly aware that humans were all different, as he felt similar to no one, not even to his parents. When he first read about the Neanderthal and Denisovan genes present in, respectively, European and Southeast Asian lineages, Maxim grew even more intensely aware of the differences that separated him genetically from everyone else.

Maxim's mother, Giselle Beaulieu, was a Francophone from the province of Quebec, more precisely from Longueuil, a suburb on the south shore of the Island of Montreal, across the St. Lawrence River. She moved to Vancouver to teach French at the Vancouver School Board. She never mastered the different "th" sounds and never quite grasped the role of emphasis in English pronunciation, but her vocabulary in both languages was extensive. Being of Caucasian European descent, her genes included Neanderthal DNA, thus so did Maxim's.

Tomoyuki Fujiyama, Maxim's father, was Japanese. He had come to Canada at age 17 to study biochemistry at the University of British Columbia and ended up staying to become a professor at that same institution. He spoke perfect CBC English and only slipped into Japanese when he drank too much alcohol, which he always did at parties. Sometimes, too much drink would cause him to forget how to express himself in anything but Japanese, although he still understood if people spoke to him in English or French. Under normal circumstances, his spoken French was inconsistent but serviceable. According to the latest findings in genetic anthropology, the Japanese, and most mainland Asians, like most sub-Saharan Africans, had never bred with either Neanderthals or Denisovans, so they are thought to be fully Cro-Magnon.

Maxim, however, doubts that the whole story is quite so simple. Geneticists have been able to identify surviving Neanderthal and Denisovan DNA strains only because they had located and identified the DNA of these other primates. There were likely other species of early humans, as yet unidentified, with whom the Cro-Magnons also interbred, both in their African homeland and as they spread across the globe.

Maxim believes that every ethnic group is genetically distinctive, the result of interbreeding between different species of early humans – several more varieties than merely Cro-Magnons, Neanderthals, and Denisovans. Beyond that, due to emigration patterns and further cross-breeding between racial and culture groups, every individual possesses a unique blend of Cro-Magnon, Neanderthal, Denisovan, and other hominid DNA. Every individual human is thus differently human compared to other individuals in the population.

Not better nor worse. Not superior nor inferior. But different. Essentially: alien.

If these different species of humans could interbreed, then the line separating species is thin, if it exists at all. Then, the line separating person from nonperson must also be thin, if it exists at all.

In the playground near a side entrance to Granville Island, there's a family of dogs who has taken up residence. The male is a brown Labrador and the female an uncut Rottweiler, with full ears and tail. They have had at least two litters. Each of their nine pups looks completely different from the other. The adult dogs guard their territory but are not overly aggressive. They allow some other animals passage through the playground and warn off others. Sometimes, they even invite humans among them, wagging their tails as the bipeds approach, and integrate them within their pack's play. Some humans they growl at, though, baring their teeth. Maxim presumes their senses make them keen observers, and he is convinced their evaluations are not arbitrary but carefully considered, although the adult male and female do not always come to the same conclusion. Contrary to Maxim's expectations, due to their breed and gender, the female Rottweiler tends to be more trusting and welcoming of visitors, while the male Labrador is more cautious. When Maxim first observed the pack, the female took the pups with her to scavenge for food while the male stayed behind to guard their home; after they came back, he would go scavenge on his own, leaving the rest of his pack home. Sometimes, he returned to find other animals – dogs, cats, humans, coyotes – with his family. After a few such occurrences, he switched roles with the female, rounding up the pups to go with him and growling at his mate to stay behind. Now, if he finds intruders with his mate when the pack returns from scavenging, he and his pups rush in barking and chase them away. When the female leaves to find food on her own, he corrals all the pups and makes them stay with him. He then stands guard vigilantly over his offspring and territory, not letting anyone approach, relaxing only once his mate is back with the pack.

Are these dogs not persons because they are not humans? Regardless of the answer, it would still be too logistically complicated for Maxim to include nonhumans in his survey. His criteria for inclusion and exclusion trouble him, though.

◄ ►

When Maxim became sick, his parents were still healthy. Maxim dimly remembers the early days of his illness – nothing beyond vague images of his parents nursing him. He remembers, too, that three days before he was affected all hospitals and clinics across British Columbia had been closed down "for reasons of national security and public safety." That had been 14 April. All schools and most government services across Canada had been shut down three days earlier than that, with the same uninformative and nondescript reason given. Starting on 3 April, people had been falling sick in Vancouver – and, according to what Maxim gleaned on the Internet, around the planet; making a link between the unexplained epidemic and governments' secretive security measures worldwide was unavoidable. Rumours flew all over the Web, but no official source gave any clear answers as to what was happening. At least, not before Maxim got sick, and there's been no way to get news since he recovered.

Maxim has no clue how long he was ill or how long he convalesced. By the time he fully regained awareness, his parents were no longer looking after him, and he had clearly not been tended to in quite some time.

He found his mother and father in their bed, both deceased, under the sheets as if asleep. From the smell and look of them, he assumed they'd been dead for several days. Not that he'd even been around a corpse before, but he couldn't imagine that only a few hours could result in such decomposition. Now that he was aware of it, he could no longer ignore the smell. He could not stay here.

Maxim, having been bedridden for an unspecified long time, was aware of his own filthy state. He forced himself to take a shower – a quick one; there was no hot water, and he shivered under the ice-cold blast. In the kitchen, where he hurried to pack supplies, he confirmed that there was no power. Nothing from the fridge was salvageable but there were plenty of canned goods, nuts, and crackers. Hunger assailed him suddenly, and he devoured an entire box of flax-seed crackers. He tossed the rest of what was still edible, along with several changes of clothes, into a large wheeled suitcase.

One last thing before he left the family condo behind for-ever: he tried turning on his tablet but it had no juice left. It was most likely a futile effort; already, Maxim suspected there would be neither Wi-Fi nor mobile connections available, but only dead air.

◀ ▶

The morning after the altercation with the two white men in business suits, Maxim finds the building guardian dead, sprawled on the floor inside near the main door. Maxim kneels to inspect the body. There is no blood and no obvious clue as to how the man died.

The three Latinas emerge from the stairwell and step into the lobby. Maxim hears their gasps. He turns his head toward them, his hand still resting against the old man's chest. For the first time since his departure from his parents' home, Maxim speaks. "I found him like this."

Maxim's voice breaks before he hits the end of the sentence. With no warning, he weeps – his bereavement at waking up orphaned in this fractured world finally breaking through. He tries to contain it, but he can't. His entire body shakes and sobs. He doesn't have the strength to get up or even to stay in kneeling position. He plops down, sitting on the floor; his will to do anything but give in to the tears flows away. The youngest of the women crouches down and hugs him to her.

◄ ►

Maxim is fluent in three languages: English, French, and Japanese. He does not need to understand Spanish to grasp that the women are arguing about him and that they are all three of them scared. Probably not scared of him, though, or they wouldn't have let the youngest one lead him into their floor of the building or leave him unsupervised as they argued among themselves.

Their living space is different from his. Maxim has not moved any of the furniture or in any way altered the neutral decor and layout. If Maxim were to vacate, he could do so immediately and there would scarcely be any evidence that he ever inhabited the condo. The women, on the other hand, have clearly made the space their own. Their place is bursting with colour and knick-knacks. No wall or surface is left blank. The effect is busy and alive but not cluttered. It feels like a home, in a way his own space does not.

The women have stopped talking, and the silence grows thicker with each passing second – until the oldest woman utters a terse sentence to the one who was kind to him, which is followed by another silence, this one volatile and pregnant with conflict. But it's short-lived. The youngest woman says one word in response to the eldest, then turns back toward Maxim.

To sit next to him on the couch, she has to displace a handful of large, colourful cushions. Maxim is holding on to another of these cushions, clutching it to his chest. It smells like flowers, and the aroma soothes him.

She puts a hand on his forearm: "I'm sorry. I want to take you with us, but…"

"Take me where?"

Her grip on him tightens. "I… We don't know yet, but it's not safe here. Not anymore. Anyway, you can't come. My aunt says family only. Will you be okay? Are you alone? Is there anyone left that you can…?"

Maxim looks at her hand on him as her words trail off. Then he looks at her carefully, and he notices that she's younger than he'd previously believed. She's no more than two or three years older than he is. Maxim is short at only 165 centimetres, but she's a few centimetres shorter, with long hair that looks well maintained, despite the lack of, well, just about everything. Looking straight into her big bright eyes, Maxim says: "My name is Maxim Fujiyama."

That makes her laugh, and Maxim knows that he has never seen anything so beautiful as this girl laughing.

"My name is Perla, Maxim," she says brightly, but then her face darkens. "You don't have anyone left, do you?"

Maxim's heart is beating so hard, it almost overwhelms her voice; the sound of her voice makes it beat even harder. He says, "I have you, Perla. You're my friend."

Perla looks away from him, takes her hand away, and wipes her face with her forearm. She turns her head back toward Maxim and shakes her head, her eyes moist. She leans in and brushes her lips against his ear as she whispers, "Yes, I am your friend, but I'm not a good friend." She lets her lips linger on his cheek for a split second before she gets up and says, in a loud, cold voice, "You have to go. Right now."

He then notices that the two older women are looming only a metre away, sternly glaring at him. He leaves without another word, without another glance at Perla. As he climbs the stairs up to his floor, he overhears the family of women yell at each other.

Maxim does not sleep that night. He sits on his balcony until sunrise, keeping an eye on the front door. No one comes in, but neither does he see the women leave. Have they changed their mind? No – before the dawn mist has fully lifted, just as he gets up to step inside, he spots the three of them exiting the building. Each of them is carrying a large rolling suitcase and a big handbag strapped around their shoulder. He watches them walk south; he stares at Perla, expecting her to look back at him. She never does, and soon the trio is out of his sight.

◄ ►

A sharp noise in the night awakens Maxim. Alert, he listens carefully, but all seems still.

Twenty days later, and there have been no further incidents in the building. Sleep comes less easily to him now. The feeling of loneliness that welled up in him in the aftermath of finding the Chinese man's dead body continues to overwhelm him when he lies down in bed at night, and, even once he does succeed in falling asleep, his slumber is much lighter than it was before. The slightest noise wakes him up, feeding a gnawing worry that Perla's family was right. Is it no longer safe to stay here? Is it safe anywhere anymore?

Routine affords Maxim some comfort and sense of security, so he continues to update his survey. He has witnessed no trace of his former neighbours in the last few weeks anywhere in the city, and he presumes they have migrated southward. Out of the 1,376 different people observed in Vancouver since he started his survey, he currently estimates an urban population of 602; another 340, provisionally listed as "transient or deceased," have been observed no more than three times in a short span and not more recently than 60 days ago; another 148 were only spotted for the first time in the past eight weeks, so their status is still "indeterminate"; the 170 "deceased or emigrated" whom he observed regularly for the first few months but then disappeared is so far a steady sum; finally, he has so far identified 116 corpses as "newly deceased" since his awakening.

As Maxim drowses back to sleep, another noise shocks him to full wakefulness. There's no mistaking the sound: a door being slammed. And now: the sounds of multiple people running, multiple hands pounding walls. There are people inside the building.

Maxim gets dressed quickly. He hesitates, pondering whether and if he should bring anything: his notes, some food, knives, extra clothes…

There's a loud bang at the door. Maxim freezes, unprepared, unsure what to do, unsure that there's anything he can do…

The door bursts open. A fetid stench fills the apartment. Maxim can barely see the outline of the intruder: of average height but uncommonly bulky.

Maxim bolts for the open door. Something sharp cuts his cheek. He yells from the pain, and at the same time the intruder crashes into something in the dark and stumbles onto the floor. Maxim escapes down the stairs. On most storeys he can hear people beyond the stairwell, in the condo units: objects being thrown around, the burst of things shattering on the floor, various bangs and crashes. It sounds like random destruction to Maxim's ears; why are these people doing this? Maxim makes it outside without further incident.

Standing on the moist, feral lawn – it rained earlier this evening – he touches the cheek where he was cut, and his hand comes back dripping. Now that his adrenaline rush has subsided, the pain in his cheek gets sharper. Outside, it's cool, only a few degrees above freezing, and Maxim is underdressed. He starts shivering. He tries to concentrate, to come to a decision, but he's getting dizzier, his mind cloudier. The wound on his cheek is still open, the blood loss weakening him.

He's barely conscious when the female Rottweiler from Granville Island comes up to him, barking.

And that's when Maxim succumbs to the night's ordeal and faints.

◄ ►

The dog's tongue leaves a trail of saliva on Maxim's lips as he emerges from unconsciousness. The Rottweiler is being gentle as she licks the wound on his cheek, but her aim is broad. One of the pups whimpers, so she stops tending to Maxim to see to her offspring; immediately, five of the other pups swarm him, sniffing him all over and licking his hands. They try to get to the wound, but by now he thinks it's best to leave it alone; he shields it with one of his hands, careful not to touch it as his fingers are filthy with mud and grime.

Judging from the state of his clothes and the aches and bruises his back is suffering from, the Rottweiler dragged him all the way here – across the grounds of his building, across the remains of the pedestrian path that lines the shore of the False Creek inlet, and across the small pedestrian bridge – to the playground on Granville Island.

The Labrador male stands guard near the mouth of the bridge. His body is rigid, alert. It's dawn; usually the dogs would go on a scavenging run. But they show no sign of budging, of wanting to leave the security of their home. Are they worried about the same group who invaded his building?

But there are many bridges that lead to Granville Island, many paths that lead into the playground they've made their home, and it's impossible for the dogs to guard them all and stay together at the same time.

The day goes by without further incident. At dusk, Maxim and the Rottweiler leave the playground together, in search of food.

Maxim considers investigating if his building is safe now, but he decides to steer clear of it.

◀ ▶

Maxim makes no special effort to keep up with or follow the dog, and soon they're no longer wandering together. He's grateful to her, and he knows where to find her if he wants to see her again, but for now he concentrates on finding lodging for the evening. He settles on a one-level rowhouse that's been completely trashed, but has plenty of bulky furniture, which makes it easy to barricade the doors and windows.

He sleeps deeply, through the night and well past sunrise. His slumber is haunted by vivid dreams: surrealistic montages of physical violence, sexual fantasies and fears, cannibalistic orgies, cities being run over by swarms of invading monsters.

◀ ▶

The three big scabs on Maxim's cheek indicate that his wound is healing well. It's still a little sensitive, but there doesn't seem to be any infection. He settles into his new home and his new routine, which is not that different from his old routine – scavenge for food, clothing, and supplies; explore the remains of the city – except that he has abandoned his survey, having lost his notes when he was forced out of his previous lodgings, and that now he makes a point of spending part of every day with the dog family in the Granville Island playground. The pups love to play with him, and he has developed a strong bond with the mother. The father, the Labrador, accepts him passively, neither encouraging nor discouraging his presence within the pack.

With increasing frequency, Maxim feels as if he is being followed. He vacillates between being worried about his safety and dismissing the sensation as paranoia.

When he returns home from today's visit with the dogs, he finds his door open. Warily, he goes in anyway. There's no one else in the house, but there's food left on his table: apples, berries, lettuce, other leafy greens he can't identify, and some dead fish – a better haul than he usually manages these days. He eats everything.

The next day, he again finds food on his table. And the next. And the next...

◄ ►

Maxim decides to stake out his old apartment building. It's easy enough for him to hide unseen among the trees and keep a vigilant watch on the front door. Although Maxim has abandoned his formal survey, to satisfy his curiosity he still observes and surreptitiously follows the people he encounters in the course of his daily wanderings, but no one has ever led him back here. Are the invaders still here? How many of them are there? Who are they?

The instant he sees the first one of them emerge from the building, Maxim realizes that he already knew, that there had been just enough light to dimly make out the one who had raided his former apartment. But it had been easier to pretend not to have seen, to pretend not to know.

Like most mammals, they come out at dusk. There are nine of them. Are there more who stay behind while the others go hunt and forage?

Mammals. Yes, they are mammals. They are primates. Perhaps they are even human. But are they persons? Are there more groups of them elsewhere in Vancouver?

They wear no clothes. They're furry, like monkeys or apes. But they walk fully erect on their hind legs, like humans. Some of them carry sticks, which they partially use as canes.

Their fingers end in sharp claw-like nails, the sight of which makes him touch the scabs on his cheek. None of them are very tall; in fact, Maxim, himself of less than average height, is taller than any of them. Their frames are broad and muscular, though. Their heads, feet, and hands all seem disproportionately large. Big. Maxim snickers silently to himself: *The Bigfoot people really do have big feet.* Maxim thinks that *Bigfoot* is a stupid name, though. *Sasquatch* is better, and that's what he'll call them.

The question reverberates in his mind: *Are they persons?*

Cro-Magnon DNA dominates the stew of primate genes that make up Maxim Fujiyama. He wonders how close or how far to his own genetic makeup these Sasquatches are. Maxim is convinced that, yes, they are human, but they are differently human than he is, more differently human, more alien than any human he has ever seen before.

There's a gust of wind, and the odour hits him; a stench similar to the one when his previous apartment was broken into. Maxim's senses become hyper-alert to his surroundings. He turns his head toward the source of the wind: there's a Sasquatch standing at an angle behind him, approximately a metre to his left.

Maxim yelps in surprise and fear. He runs away as fast as he can, but he's distracted and careless; he trips on a loose paving stone. He skids on his scabbed cheek, and it starts bleeding again. It's only a superficial scrape, but it stings sharply. He picks himself up, his heart beating furiously. He looks back. The Sasquatch has made no move to chase him. It's a female and particularly small. Their eyes meet, and she darts away, vanishing from Maxim's view before he can figure out in which direction she has fled.

◀ ▶

The next morning, the Rottweiler is waiting for Maxim outside his door. She accompanies him around the city. Since he
gave up on the survey, Maxim's explorations of the city have
been more playful, more random, more fun. Yet a part of him
feels restless and rudderless, as if he were waiting for something, some change. But he knows there is nothing to wait for.

Today, the Sasquatch makes no effort to hide herself. She
follows the two of them from a safe distance. Maxim sees her
on rooftops; across the street, crouched on the hood of
derelict automobiles; watching them from ahead, then running away as he and the dog approach.

The Rottweiler sees the Sasquatch, too. The dog tenses
every time she sees or smells her. Maxim pets her when he
notices her change in attitude; the Rottweiler never barks at
the Sasquatch, but occasionally she does emit a low grumble
that doesn't quite reach the level of a growl.

When Maxim returns home, the dog licks his hand then
trots away toward Granville Island. For the first time since the
bounty started, there's no food waiting for him inside. He
chides himself for not having made any effort to forage for
anything today. Today's expedition was longer than usual – the
presence of both the dog and the Sasquatch made it more
exciting – so now he's both hungry and too tired to go out and
find food.

There's a bang at the door, which reminds Maxim that he
hasn't yet barricaded the entrance for the night. Maxim sits
motionless, not sure what to do. Then, there's another bang.
Maxim gets up and opens the door a crack. Nothing happens. He opens it a bit wider and finds three apples and a

fish have been left for him on the ground. There are two rocks next to the threshold. He notices the corresponding dents on the door.

As he collects the food, he sees the Sasquatch approximately four metres away, staring at him. Again, when he catches her eye, she darts away.

◀ ▶

As Maxim play-wrestles with three of the pups, he wonders if he should give the dogs names. He has discovered that, because he has no name for any of them, he doesn't distinguish between the various puppies, even though none of them look the same and they all have different personalities. In his mind, they have remained "the pups" – a collective rather than a group of individuals. The parents are clearly individualized in his mind because he refers to them as "the Rottweiler and the Labrador," "the female and the male," or "the mother and the father" – all of which have taken on the weight of names. But he has so far resisted applying human names to his canine family.

His family. It's the first time he's consciously thought of the dogs this way. Soon the family will grow: the Rottweiler is pregnant again.

Maxim scrutinizes the shore to the south of Granville Island. Yes. She's there again. For the past five days, the Sasquatch girl has been watching Maxim play with the dogs. Since their initial encounter, Maxim has been observing her as much as she lets him. He has come to the conclusion that she's in her mid- or late teens, no more than a few years younger than himself.

Family, Maxim thinks again. Yes, he will give all the dogs names. And the new pups, too, after they're born.

Maxim gets up and walks toward the small pedestrian bridge. At first the pups follow him, but he motions them away and they start playing with each other. He turns back toward the shore. The Sasquatch is still there, carefully observing his interaction with the dogs.

He walks toward her – slowly, calmly, halting every few steps, gauging her reaction to his approach. He looks back toward the dogs. The Rottweiler and the Labrador are watching his every move, occasionally glancing at the Sasquatch. They're getting used to her, he thinks, so they don't bark or growl. They're waiting to see what Maxim will do.

Maxim crosses the bridge. The Sasquatch hasn't moved, as if she were waiting for him. They lock eyes. For once, she does not dart away. He steps within reach of her. He puts a hand to his chest and says, softly, "My name is Maxim Fujiyama."

He extends his other hand toward her, palm upward. She looks at it but doesn't move. Maxim stays still, his hand still offered. He closes his eyes.

He waits. Is she still here? He doesn't want to startle her, so he keeps his eyes closed. He waits.

When the moment of contact comes, it startles him, but he remains immobile.

Her palm is roughened with calluses. Her fingernails are hard and sharp. Exploring the skin of his forearm, she draws blood. Maxim's eyes pop open as she lets go of him. She's poised to run away, but she hesitates, closely observing Maxim. He smiles at her.

She changes postures and takes his hand, frowning at the fresh cut on his flesh. It's only a little scratch; still, he'll have to wash it to make sure it doesn't get infected. She kisses the wound; her mouth is surprisingly soft.

Maxim laughs. She laughs, too.

He reaches out and takes her hand in his. Their palms press tight against each other.

Together, they both laugh harder.

AUTHORS' BIOGRAPHIES

T.S. Bazelli writes software manuals by day and novels by night. When not at a computer, you can find her making a mess in the kitchen, building things, or travelling the world in search of stories. She currently lives in Vancouver. She blogs about writing and folklore at www.tsbazelli.com.

GMB Chomichuk is a writer, teacher, mixed media artist, graphic novelist and proud Winnipegger. He won the Manitoba Young Writers Award when he was 15. He won the Manitoba Book Award for Best Illustrated Book in 2011 for his graphic novel serial *The Imagination Manifesto*. He has been nominated for the Michael Van Rooy Award for Genre Fiction and nominated for Canada's Best Graphic Novel by the Canadian Science Fiction & Fantasy Association. He is the founder of Alchemical Press and is always on the lookout for literary oddities. He puts words and pictures together. Some people call that alchemy. He calls that comics. twitter.com/gmbchomichuk and his works-in-progress are at www.comicalchemy.blogspot.com.

A.M. Dellamonica has recently moved to Toronto after 22 years in Vancouver. She is a graduate of Clarion West and teaches writing through the UCLA Extension Writers' Program. Dellamonica's first novel, *Indigo Springs* (Tor, 2009), won the Sunburst Award for Canadian Literature of the Fantastic. Her most recent book is *Child of a Hidden Sea* (Tor, 2014). She is the author of over 30 short stories in a variety of genres: they can be found on Tor.com, Strange Horizons, Lightspeed and in numerous print magazines and anthologies. She is online at www.alyxdellamonica.com, facebook.com/AlyxDellamonica, instagram.com/alyxdel lamonica, twitter.com/alyxdellamonica and www.pinterest.com/ alyxdellamonica.

dvsduncan was born in Vancouver, and now lives in New Westminster, B.C. with his wife and a generously proportioned cat. He holds degrees in English and Landscape Architecture but it is life that has taught him the most. His stories are all true, though not factual. Make of that what you will. www.dvsduncan.com

Geoff Gander is part of the authors' group East Block Irregulars, and prior to taking up writing was heavily involved in the roleplaying community. His stories have appeared in *Heroes of Mars* (Metahuman Press, 2012), *AE SciFi* (2012) and *Imaginarium* (ChiZine Publications, 2013), he has twice contributed to the "retrogaming" *Advanced Adventures Line*, and his first novel was *The Tunnelers* (Solstice Publishing, 2011). He primarily writes horror, but is willing to give anything a whirl. When he isn't writing or toiling away in a cube farm, Geoff likes to read, watch British comedies, roleplay, and entertain his two boys. This story first appeared in *AE – The Canadian Science Fiction Review* (2013).

Orrin Grey is a writer, editor, amateur film scholar, and monster expert who was born on the night before Halloween. He's the author of *Never Bet the Devil & Other Warnings* (Evileye Books, 2012) and co-editor of *Fungi* (Innsmouth Free Press, 2012), an anthology of weird fungal fiction. When not hiding out in his red room, he's found at twitter.com/orringrey and www. orringrey.com.

David Huebert of Halifax is a PhD student at Western University. His poetry and fiction have appeared in journals such as *Grain, Event, Matrix, Vallum, Dalhousie Review*, and *Antigonish*

Review. A first book of poetry, *We Are No Longer the Smart Kids in Class*, will be published by Guernica Editions in the spring of 2015. "@shalestate" is an excerpt from a novel-in-progress. twitter.com/davidbhuebert

John Jantunen moved to Guysborough County, NS, in 1999 – to wait out the apocalypse. When it didn't happen he relocated to Guelph, Ontario, where he now lives with his wife and two children. He has written two dozen screenplays, 20 or so children's books and as many short stories. He is currently writing his fourth novel, a sci-fi/horror/romance called *A Many Splendour'd Thing*. His first, *fallingoverstandingstill*, is available through Vocamus Press (www.vocamus.net) and his second, *Cipher*, is forthcoming from ECW Press on October 1st, 2014.

H.N. Janzen has lived all over, from Beausejour, Manitoba, to Revelstoke, B.C., and is currently attending the University of British Columbia, Okanagan. A compulsive writer, Hilary has written some of her best pieces when she was supposed to be doing something more important. She works in a used bookstore and co-manages a live action roleplay based in Kelowna.

Arun Jiwa lives in Edmonton, Alberta, where he practices at making things up and writing them down. Arun is a graduate of the 2012 Viable Paradise SFF Workshop. He is currently working on his first novel. www.arunjiwa.com

Claude Lalumière is the author of the collections *Objects of Worship* (ChiZine Publications, 2009) and *Nocturnes and Other Nocturnes* (Infinity Plus, 2013) and of the mosaic novella *The Door to Lost Pages* (ChiZine Publications, 2011). He's the co-creator of the multimedia cryptomythology project *Lost Myths* (lostmyths.net), and he has edited 12 anthologies, the most recent of which is *Super Stories of Heroes & Villains* (Tachyon Publications 2013); he's currently working on his 13th, with David Nickle, *The Exile Book of New Canadian Noir* (Exile Editions, forthcoming in 2015). www.claudepages.info

Jamie Mason, author of *ECHO* (Drollerie Press, 2011), is a Canadian sci-fi/fantasy writer whose short stories have appeared in *On Spec, Abyss & Apex, AE: The Canadian Science Fiction Review* and Exile Editions' 2013 release *Dead North: Canadian Zombie Fiction*. www.jamiescribbles.com

Michael Matheson is a gender fluid Toronto writer, editor, anthologist, and book reviewer, as well as a managing editor (CZP eBooks) with ChiZine Publications, and a submissions editor with *Apex* magazine. As an anthologist, he is putting together three books for 2015: *Start a Revolution* (Exile Editions), *This Patchwork Flesh* (Exile Editions), and *The Humanity of Monsters* (ChiZine Publications). Michael's own work is published or forthcoming in *Ideomancer*, and the anthologies *Chilling Tales 2* (EDGE, 2013), *Dead North: Canadian Zombie Fiction* (Exile Editions, 2013), *Future Lovecraft* (Innsmouth Free Press, 2011), and *Masked Mosaic* (Tyche, 2013). www. michaelmatheson.word press.com, and twitter.com/fomcontest

Silvia Moreno-Garcia of Vancouver is a short story writer and editor and the operator of the micropress Innsmouth Free Press. Her short stories have appeared in *Imaginarium 2012: The Best Canadian Speculative Writing, The Book of Cthulhu, ELQ/Exile: The Literary Quarterly*, and *Shine: An Anthology of Optimistic*

Science Fiction. She is the author of *This Strange Way of Dying* (Exile Editions, 2013; shortlisted for a 2014 Sunburst Award) and the editor of *Dead North: Canadian Zombie Fiction* (Exile Editions, 2013) and *Future Lovecraft* (Innsmouth Free Press, 2011).

Christine Ottoni is an emerging writer and poet living in Toronto. Her work has appeared in Canadian journals, magazines and anthologies. She completed her undergraduate education at the University of Toronto, where she studied English Literature and Philosophy. She is currently working on her first collection of short stories at the Humber School for Writers. A lover of cheese, hummus and beer, Christine spends her free time snacking in Toronto's West End. Twitter.com/chrissiottoni.

Miriam Oudin is a teacher and avowed Hansard addict who has published academic articles about ancient economics and short stories that always end up being dystopian for some reason. Her study of marriage in computer games, "Leopards at the Wedding," will appear in the Mad Norwegian Press anthology *Chicks Dig Gaming* in the fall of 2014. Miriam spends most of her time discovering creative ways to die in roguelikes and writing double dactyls about TV shows.

Michael S. Pack fled the Deep Southern U.S. after an encounter with a particularly fierce mosquito swarm. He now resides in northern B.C. with his wife and a small herd of cats. Michael writes science fiction, fantasy, and other weird stories. He is currently working on an epic fantasy novel. His stories have appeared in various anthologies including *Metastasis* (WolfSinger Publications, 2012) and *Shapeshifters* (Fox Spirit Books, 2012). www.rivenlucidity.wordpress.com

Morgan M. Page is a writer, performance + video artist, activist, and Santera in Toronto. She is the winner of two 2013 SF MOTHA awards (New/Upcoming Artist of the Year and Group Exhibition of the Year), and her video work has screened across the world. Her first novel is due out from Topside Press in late 2014. www.Odofemi.com and twitter.com/morganmpage.

Steve Stanton works as an author and book reviewer. His science fiction stories have been published in 16 countries in a dozen languages, and his psipunk trilogy, *The Bloodlight Chronicles*, (ECW Press, *Reconciliation* 2010, *Retribution* 2011, *Redemption* 2012), will be followed by a new sci-fi novel, *Freenet* (ECW Press, 2015). www.stevestanton.ca

Amanda M. Taylor is a speculative fiction writer and research scientist born and raised in Winnipeg, Manitoba. She was an apprentice in the 2014 Sheldon Oberman Mentorship Program with the Manitoba Writer's Guild, and is currently pursuing a doctorate in soil science. This is her debut publication, and she is working on her first novel.

E. Catherine Tobler is a Sturgeon Award finalist and the senior editor at *Shimmer Magazine*. Among others, her fiction has appeared in *Clarkesworld*, *Lady Churchill's Rosebud Wristlet*, and *Beneath Ceaseless Skies*. Her first novel, *Rings of Anubis*, was published in 2014. www.ecatherine.com and twitter.com/ECthetwit

Jean-Louis Trudel was born in Toronto. He holds degrees in physics, astronomy, and the history and philosophy of science. Since 1994, he has authored (alone or in collaboration with Yves Meynard as Laurent McAllister) a trio of novels published in

France, four fiction collections, and 26 young adult books published in Canada. His short stories in French have appeared in magazines like *imagine...* and *Solaris*, and in various other venues. In English, his short fiction has been published in several Canadian and U.S. anthologies, but also in magazines like *ON SPEC*. When time allows, he also translates and reviews science fiction. This story, in its original French version, was published as "*Le dôme de saint Macaire*" in *Solaris* (2008). www.culturedes futurs.blogspot.ca

Frank Westcott lives in Alliston, Ontario. He has published prose, poetry, short stories and book-length non-fiction for both children and adults. In 2011, his short story "The Poet" was a co-winner of Exile's inaugural Carter V. Cooper Short Fiction Competition; the story appeared in the *CVC Short Fiction Anthology, Book One* (Exile Editions, 2011). Frank is also a singer, writes lyrics and composes music. In 1984, McMaster University selected him for their Alumni Gallery in recognition of his music and writing. www.frankwestcottpoet.com

A.C. Wise was born and raised in the land of poutine, and while she currently lives in the land of cheesesteaks, her passport is still firmly Canadian. Her work has appeared in publications such as *Clarkesworld, Lightspeed, Shimmer*, and anthologies including *Future Lovecraft* (Innsmouth Free Press, 2011), *Fungi* (Innsmouth Free Press, 2012), and *Imaginarium 2012: The Best Canadian Speculative Writing* (ChiZine Publications,), among others. In addition to her writing, she co-edits *Unlikely Story*. www.acwise.net and twitter.com/ac_wise

THAT DAMMED BEAVER

CANADIAN HUMOUR, LAUGHS AND GAFFS

SELECTED BY BRUCE MEYER

THE EXILE BOOK OF ANTHOLOGY SERIES · NUMBER FIFTEEN

Margaret Atwood, Austin Clarke, Leon Rooke, Priscila Uppal, Jonathan Goldstein, Paul Quarrington, Morley Callaghan, Jacques Ferron, Marsha Boulton, Joe Rosenblatt, Barry Callaghan, Linda Rogers, Steven Hayward, Andrew Borkowski, Helen Marshall, Gloria Sawai, David McFadden, Myna Wallin, Gail Prussky, Louise Maheux-Forcher, Shannon Bramer, James Dewar, Bob Armstrong, Jamie Feldman, Claire Dé, Christine Miscione, Larry Zolf, Anne Dandurand, Julie Roorda, Mark Paterson, Karen Lee White, Heather J. Wood, Marty Gervais, Matt Shaw, Alexandre Amprimoz, Darren Gluckman, Gustave Morin, and the country's greatest cartoonist, Aislin.